1

Long Ago and Far Away

PART I

1

I don't remember things like I used to. And since turning fifty, it's gotten worse. Names, in particular, give me trouble. People I knew, athletic figures, neighbors, relatives even. All are possible candidates for memory loss. Oftentimes, I'll remember the name eventually, but it's irritating when it doesn't just pop right into my mind. The same holds true for places, events, things I've done. Whether it's last week or last decade, I draw blanks, on occasion. This is why I want to get all this down while I can still remember it; while it is still relatively fresh in my mind.

It all started last winter. It was early Saturday morning, the Saturday after Christmas, in fact. It was about 2:00 AM, and my dog Hugo insisted it was time to get up. This was close to our usual "up-and-at-'em" time, so I was neither surprised nor upset at his request. As I rolled onto my back for those last few moments before arising, the room started to spin around. Or so it seemed. I had become quite dizzy, but wrote it off as what happens sometimes when you change directions too quickly. But as I swung my feet out of bed and started to walk to the kitchen, I realized that I was wrong. In truth, I couldn't walk at all, at least not without swaying from side to side. I staggered to the kitchen, flipped on the light switch, then uncertainly made my way back to the bedroom. Sitting on the edge of my bed, my mind was racing as to the possible reason for my problem. I finally settled on brain tumor, cancerous, of course. I could already envision the oncologist muttering, "I'm sorry, Mr. Jackson, but there's nothing we can do." Okay, so I actually didn't really believe that, but I was stumped, and a little frightened just the same.

After a few minutes, the dizziness had pretty much gone. Slowly, I stood up and tentatively started to walk. Better. I was able to walk and move around normally, without the dizziness and imbalance of only a few minutes earlier. Weeks later, my doctor would throw a multi-worded description of my condition at me, but I only caught the last word, vertigo. I almost felt proud. Jimmy Stewart and I had something in common.

My vertigo presented very little problem for me in the ensuing months. Only twice did I come under it's influence, and both times after I had been laying or sitting. Neither attack lasted long, and neither was as severe as the first one. For several months I had no problem, whatsoever. Spring slid into summer, my favorite time of the year. It was baseball season, the sport, maybe the one and only sport. The weather was sunny and warm, even in Sheboygan, Wisconsin. It was a great time for running, my one true avocation. Marathon time was near, and it was time to start training. Things were going well. It was August, and everything was about to change.

My thirteen miler went pretty well. It was the first Saturday in August, the official start of marathon training. I do my long runs early Saturday mornings to avoid the heat of the day. Fortunately, I have a four-legged alarm clock to assist me in my training by insuring that I do not oversleep. By 7:30 I had run the thirteen miler, taken Hugo for a walk, done my leg stretches, taken a bath, and had a cup of coffee at my breakfast/lunch/dinner counter. From there I proceeded to the couch for a serious post-run nap. This would be my routine for the next eight Saturdays.

Finney woke me from my nap at 10:30. Finney is my pet cockatiel. I named him after Jack Finney, the world's greatest author. Jack's most famous book, the time travel novel 'Time and Again' is an absolute classic. I must profess a weakness for, and a fascination with time travel. While I don't believe time travel is possible, I find the concept intriguing and endlessly profound.

Anyway, Finney (the bird) has a neat little trick whereby he lifts the small seed cup off the side of his cage and drops it to the bottom. He thinks that's pretty funny and is quite proud of himself afterward. It was the sound of the seed cup hitting the bottom of the cage that woke me. I slowly got off the couch, hobbled over to the refrigerator, and gulped down about ten ounces of soda. After a long run I'm usually quite sore and very thirsty, and today was no exception. I couldn't help thinking that there were eight more of these Saturday morning "routines" to go. The marathon was scheduled for the second Sunday of October, and, believe me, the training is worse than the race.

The next few hours passed uneventfully. I read the morning paper, had some lunch, and started to watch the Cub game on the tube. But I was restless. I don't get restless often, but, on this particular day, I just couldn't sit still. I changed clothes, put on some shoes, left the boys in charge, and headed out the door. Despite running thirteen miles earlier, I decided that what I needed was a nice long walk. What I got was something that defies not only description, but explanation, as well.

I headed north, crossing Indiana Avenue, down the big hill, toward Kiwanis Park. As the park came into view, the memories came flooding back. This had been happening more and more, as the technological age had deadened my senses. I passed the larger baseball diamond, crossed the street and sat down on the bleachers over-looking the main park complex.

The park has changed a great deal since I was a kid back in the '50's. The northern part of the park had been cornered by four little league/softball diamonds. I remembered playing my first little league game on the northwest diamond in 1963, and a playoff game later that summer on the northeast diamond. We lost both games, and I still remember them well. I remembered pitching against some of my classmates on the southeast diamond, and umpiring little league games on the southwest diamond many years later.

Only the northeast and southwest diamonds remain; the other two were seeded over several years ago.

Baseball isn't very big in Sheboygan, anymore. It wasn't always this way. Sheboygan was a big baseball town at one time. How and why it changed is beyond my knowledge and insight to discern. But it has changed, and I miss it.

I got off the bleachers, and started walking toward the north end of the park. North of the baseball area, the basketball court remains, as does the shelter house next to it. But the playground has changed immensely, and the football field and surrounding running track are gone. I kept walking the sidewalk, up the hill near where the tennis courts and horseshoe pits had been. It's a skateboard park now, and, I must admit, the area is used much more now than it had been. The enclosed skateboard area was crowded on this beautiful Saturday afternoon. Skateboards, roller-blades, small bikes, all zipped up and down the tubular configurations of the park.

I reached the top of the hill, and looked back down onto the park. For some of reason, I was reminded of the old existential paradox: it's not the same park anymore, and it never was. I had to move on. I knew where I wanted to go now, had probably known it from the start. It wasn't far now, six or eight blocks, maybe. Not far at all. It would take me years to get there.

6

The North Side Park. That's what it was called when it was built in 1924. It wouldn't get a formal, official name until 1946 when it would be dedicated as Sheboygan Memorial Athletic Park. When the American Legion purchased the park in the '50's, it would be re-named Legion Memorial Park. We simply called it Legion Park. It was a beautiful park, almost a stadium, really. It was the home for the local semi-pro baseball team for years. Al Simmons, Jimmie Foxx, and Mickey Cochrane played in the exhibition game there. So did Satchell Paige, years later. The Cincinnati Reds and Chicago Cubs played an entire exhibition game in the park in 1933. I know these things because a few years ago, I did some research on the park.

The Park is gone now. It was razed in 1978. A factory now stands on the spot. Only part of the left and center field walls remain. I had played American Legion ball there in the early '70's. I loved the park. All my buddies and teammates did. When the park was demolished, I went over there and took a couple of those great red bricks that had once been the right field wall and were still laying on the ground waiting to be hauled away. I couldn't help it; I wanted a souvenir.

Anyway, this is where I was headed. I don't know why. I just wanted to visit for a while. I get nostalgic once in awhile. Not as often as I used to, but sometimes, like that day, I can get lost in it. Maybe the technological age had finally gotten to me, not that I've ever really joined it. But, I needed to retreat. I would succeed more than I could have ever imagined.

Twin Whip used to be located on the northeast corner of 17th and Erie. I remembered it fondly as I crossed Erie Avenue, getting ever closer to my destination. It was an ice cream stand that served those great twist ice cream cones. It's long gone, of course, gone the way of the milkman and the neighborhood grocery store. And so many other slices of life that silently slid into history. I lost myself in the reverie of a by-gone age as I continued on toward the park, or at least to where the park had been.

That's when it hit me. The dizziness and the imbalance struck without warning. I could hardly stand. Had it not been for a nearby tree, which I held on to, I would have been down. Some sight that must have been, a grown man holding onto a small tree for dear life.

Needless to say, I was quite scared. The vertigo had never attacked while standing or walking. It had always infested while laying or sitting. This was altogether new, and frightening. After about a minute or so, the vertigo slowly began to subside. A couple minutes later I was feeling better; a little shaky, but better. I silently thanked the tree, and still shaken, resumed my quest. How did that happen? Why did it happen? What had triggered it, if anything? Is this something I would have to live with for the foreseeable future? My mind was awhirl with these confusing and frightening questions as I, slowly now, walked on. I turned left on Michigan Avenue, crossed the viaduct, and turned right on 18th Street, now only about two blocks from my destination. I had only taken maybe ten or fifteen steps along 18th Street, when I stopped dead. It felt like I was frozen to the spot. I started shaking again, just lightly now, but it had nothing to do with the vertigo. I made a conscious effort to breathe, feeling that if I didn't, I might not be able to breathe automatically. Gradually, I regained some semblance of composure, though that may be over-stating it a little. I was still too incredulous to be anywhere near totally composed.

The Michigan Avenue viaduct? What Michigan Avenue viaduct? It had been torn down years ago. And not replaced. How then, I asked myself not too calmly, could I have possibly crossed over it? Finally, after several minutes of cerebral meltdown, I was able to uproot myself and turn around. There it was all right, the Michigan Avenue viaduct. There, also, was the Vollrath Company office building, less than half the size it should be. There, also, was a black Packard parked in front of the Vollrath Company. It was right behind the dark green DeSoto. There, also, was a considerably narrower 18th Street, something I hadn't noticed until now. How could this be? Where was I? When was I? Near the main entrance to the Vollrath Company was a small bench, so I walked over, had a seat, and tried to get my bearings.

Nothing happened, at least not for a while. After a few minutes, I looked at my watch, possibly thinking it might help. It was 2:45 on a beautiful Saturday afternoon in August. I could only guess at the year. But it was time to stop guessing and start determining. Besides, I had a destination, one that suddenly became very concrete, indeed. I arose from the bench and continued on north. As I neared Superior Avenue, I could see it. I couldn't take my eyes off it, actually. It was beautiful. Different from the park of my day, of course, but beautiful, nonetheless. I slowly approached the huge wooden structure. Respectfully. Reverently, almost. I crossed the cinder parking lot, a lot capable of holding up to 300 cars, I remembered. Where 300 cars would be parked in this lot, I sure didn't know, unless they were parked vertically as well as horizontally. On this day, there were no cars parked in the lot. I was glad, for some reason. I guess that I just wasn't ready yet to meet someone of the era. Actually, in the fifteen minutes or so that I had been "here," I had yet to even see anyone. I refused to ponder the possible implications of this and walked over to the gate. It was open, and I walked in.

It was the North Side Park, all right, hardly the Legion Park that I remembered. On my right, as I entered the park, were a short stretch of wooden bleachers extending down the right field line. I cleared these bleachers and walked out toward the field. The grass was a little too long and uneven. The ground itself was dry and a little rocky. The base paths weren't evenly cut. The bases looked like square, stuffed pillows. It was beautiful.

I noticed all this as I slowly walked toward the pitcher's mound. It was a mound all right, several inches higher than in my time, with the dirt cutout area smaller in diameter. I stood on the scuffed-up mound and surveyed the park, mentally comparing it to the park I remembered. The similarities out-numbered the differences. The grandstand looked much the same, deep green paint dominating the view. There was no press box as yet, but the dugouts looked the same, with drinking fountains standing guard next to each one. The right field bleachers were the standard green as was the wooden outfield wall. The red brick that would comprise the outfield wall would not arrive until the late 1940's. The park dimensions were still the distinctive feature of the park. Legion Park was the only baseball park I knew where the power alleys were the deepest parts of the park. It was somehow gratifying to see that the park hadn't changed in that regard. If anything, the park looked a bit smaller than I remembered. Perhaps, when the new wall was built, the dimensions had been expanded a bit.

Gazing out from the pitcher's mound toward the outfield, I noticed a few other differences. There were no light posts, which in my time had been in the power alleys, technically, in play. Instead, three flagpoles stood in straightaway center field, neither of which currently held a flag. There was no scoreboard. It should be in front of the centerfield wall, but obviously was not yet erected. I laughed softly at this omission: why no scoreboard? Didn't they keep score in the early 1930's?

9

The early 1930's. I had it narrowed down, now. My visual tour of the park had done it. Like I said earlier, I know something about this park, more than most people probably. I have a fascination with baseball parks. A few years ago I joined the Society for American Baseball Research, SABR. Naturally, I gravitated to the Ballpark Committee. As a project for the committee, I researched and wrote a brief history of baseball parks in Sheboygan, concentrating on my beloved Legion Park. And while I don't remember everything, I remembered enough to narrow down my current time frame. As best I could tell, this was the early 1930's. So I knew when I was. I knew where I was. But what I didn't know was what to do next.

Finally, after a few more minutes, I walked off the pitcher's mound, and into the third base dugout. I had a seat on the wooden bench and contemplated my situation.

I had been on edge for the past half hour, the approximate time of my "visit" here. As fascinated as I was by my discovery and inspection of the park, I knew I didn't belong here. How did I get here? Why was I here? And more important, how do I get back? What if I was stuck here? Where could I go? How could I live? I had nothing except what was on my person. My keys, some loose change and maybe fifty dollars in my wallet. Those Federal Reserve notes would look mighty suspicious in 1930's America. I had no answers, and I was getting scared.

Actually, I did have one answer. I had pretty much traced back my arrival to my brief spell of vertigo on 17th Street. That seems to be where it all changed. Did I have to wait for another vertigo spell to get me back? That could take weeks, or months. What if it sent me to another period of time? And what was the point of all this? Was I here for a reason? Should I be looking for a sign of some kind? And where were all the people? I had seen some light vehicular traffic on my brief walk to the park, but I hadn't actually seen any people. There had to be people.

All these harrowing thoughts were swirling through my mind in a much less-orderly fashion than I have tried to present here. I had to move. I needed some answers. I resolved to get off my dugout bench and explore Sheboygan of the 1930's. I was ready to move. And then he entered.

This wasn't a caretaker or a policeman. He was much too well dressed to be so officious as to be threatening of my presence in the park. His movements were deliberate, even tentative as he made his way toward the infield. He'd look around occasionally as if trying to get his bearings. Then he stopped at first base and actually scratched his head in puzzlement. He hadn't seen me yet, perched in the corner

of my dugout. But it was only a matter of time until he did, so I hopped off my bench, walked up the three dugout steps, and strode over to meet him. I was going to have to talk to somebody from this time eventually, and this was as good a person as anyone to start with. How did people from the '30's talk? Did they have different vernacular? Different slang? Different values? Different mannerisms? I was about to find out, because I was now close enough to get a better look at him.

I recognized him immediately. They called him "The Beast." It wasn't a description of his appearance or demeanor. Rather, it was, supposedly, an incredibly accurate description of what he could do to a baseball when he connected with one of his mighty swings. He was dressed in a brown pinstriped suit, yellow shirt, brown and yellow tie, and black patent leather shoes. His brown hair was slicked back on his head, and in his hand was about the largest cigar I had ever seen. He saw me walking toward him, and he, in turn, started toward me. He took a long, slow puff on his cigar and slowly let out the smoke. By the time the last of the smoke had disappeared, we were next to each other. He stood about six feet tall and weighed maybe 180 pounds. I made a mental note to look it up if I ever got the chance. He extended his huge right hand.

"Hi there, partner. Say, this may sound awful funny, but could you tell me where the heck I am? I seem to have gotten turned around somewhere along the way."

I shook his hand. "You're Jimmie Foxx," was all I could stammer.

"Why, I sure am. How'd you know?"

The sincerely humble retort actually made me chuckle and greatly put me at ease. I don't know how often I've been in the presence of greatness, but I was certainly there now. This was Jimmie Foxx, alias "The Beast," alias "Double X," one of the greatest baseball players of all time. Hall of Famer. Lifetime average of .325. Career home run total of 534. A man who could hit a ball has hard and as far as anyone. And he was genuinely surprised to be recognized.

Yet, I had to remember when I was. This was the 1930's. There was no television. No ESPN Sports Center. No "Sports Illustrated." No Internet. No real way to see your favorite sports personalities except by actual attendance at the sporting event. Except for that, and an occasional picture in the newspaper, what other visual representation did someone like Foxx have?

He mercifully released my hand and waited intently for an answer to his query. I had recovered from my initial shock. This was Jimmie Foxx, and I was going to have an actual conversation with him. Remembering whom I was, where I was, and where I was from, I decided to proceed cautiously.

"Where do you think you are?"

"This should be St. Louis, but it sure ain't like any part of St. Louis that I know."

"St. Louis?"

"Sure, We had just whupped those Brownies again, and I was taking a little stroll back to the hotel. It ain't far, and I like to take a walk now and again. I stopped to look at this boffo suit in this store window, and the next thing I know, I'm outside this park. Heck, I know a baseball park when I see one, so naturally I came in. Come to think of it, this place looks a little familiar. Did I play here once?" With this last utterance, he took another long drag on his stogie and blew a big mouthful of smoke straight up in the air. Then he looked back down at me, waiting for my response.

"When you were looking at that suit," I ventured, "did you get a sudden headache or even feel a little dizzy?"

"Why yes, now that you mention it. I got frightfully dizzy for a minute there. I get that once in awhile since the accident. But I've never had anything like this happen."

"Accident?"

"Yeah, a few years back I had a car crash. Fell asleep at the wheel was what happened.   Lucky to survive it, doctor said. Since then, I get these dizzy spells sometimes."

The symmetry was obvious. But I still wasn't sure how much I should tell him, could tell him. Instead I decided to gamble.

"What is today's date?"

"Today's date? Why it's August the fourth."

"What year?" I was actually holding my breath.

"The year? Are you kidding me?" Seeing that I wasn't, he answered, "Why 1933, of course. Didn't you know that?" he asked warily.

"Of course, I did. I just wanted to make sure. It seems that something unusual has happened to both of us, and I'm at an absolute loss to explain it."

"Well, maybe you could try explaining it, because I don't understand any of it." Another long drag on the stogie. He closed his eyes this time as he exhaled the smoke upward. I got the impression that this was a man who was not going to be spooked by anything I told him. Still, I knew I couldn't tell him everything. A time traveler from another century was a tale even he could not readily accept. I finally knew how I had to proceed.

"This isn't St. Louis, I'm afraid. This is Sheboygan, Wisconsin, and this place is called the North Side Athletic Park. Somehow, we've both been shifted in space, you from St. Louis, me from Milwaukee. I don't know how this has happened, but it has something to do with that dizzy spell you had. I had one similar to yours, and like you, found myself outside this park. I'd been here maybe fifteen minutes when you walked in."

He didn't say anything for awhile, merely replacing a strange expression for the words that wouldn't come. I had thrown a nonsensical jumble at him, and even a talkative, out-going guy like Jimmie Foxx needed time to assimilate it.

"Is that how they're dressing in Milwaukee these days?"

I quickly checked my attire. I had never even considered that my clothing might give me away. It was OK. I was wearing a retired pair of running shoes, white ankle socks, dark blue shorts, a gray and black T-shirt, and a blue cap. Fortunately, I wasn't wearing one of my old race T-shirts, with the year boldly emblazoned on the front.

"It's the casual look. I'm just not a snazzy dresser like you, Jimmie." That not only appeased him but flattered him as well, because he puffed lovingly on his cigar and continued on.

"So you're telling me…say, I never caught your name."

"It's Don." I had no reason to lie about it.

"Hi there, Don. I'm Jimmie. Glad to meet you." With that he grabbed my hand again and pumped it vigorously, as if for the first time. I marveled again at his equanimity.

"Now where was I? Oh, yeah, you're saying that I got shifted from St. Louis to here, just like that. And all because I got a little dizzy? What for?"

He had me there. What was this all about? Were we supposed to meet someone here? See something? Or was there something deeper and more meaningful to this? Important questions, but this didn't seem to be the time to analyze the metaphysics of our situation. My silence must have answered his question, because he continued, "What do you think we should do now?" I had been in the park for about thirty minutes, Jimmie about half of that. It was time to move on. I made a quick scan of the park to make sure nobody else had entered. No one had.

"Let's get out of here."

We slowly walked off the diamond toward the gate. It was 3:45 pm and still warm. We exited the park and headed south on 18th Street, back the way I had come an hour ago. Jimmie tossed his cigar onto the cinder parking lot.

"Where are we headed?"

"Let's walk to the downtown area and see what happens." It seemed like as good a plan as any. What other options did we have? Though we had been drawn to the ballpark, it was obvious that nothing was happening there. No game we were supposed to see. No person we were supposed to meet. No nothing, as best I could tell.

Since the Michigan Avenue viaduct was still standing, we crossed it and headed east on Michigan Avenue toward downtown. We walked several blocks in silence. While I wasn't disinterested in

14

the surrounding landscape, I hardly noticed at all. My mind had, once again, wandered into the realm of "what is going on here?" Actually, the question I was really pondering was, "How long am I going to be stuck here, and what am I going to do about it?" Jimmie had taken his "transfer" from St. Louis to Sheboygan pretty much in stride, but even he must have been struggling with our dilemma, for he hadn't spoken a word for blocks. It really wasn't so difficult for him. He could always find transportation back to St. Louis and resume his life. What could I do?

We crossed 12th Street, moving into the business district of Michigan Avenue. For some reason, Michigan Avenue has always fascinated me. Maybe, it's the feeling that this is a very old part of town. That feeling was confirmed as I really started to look around and take note of my surroundings. This could have been the Michigan Avenue of the 2000's. Many of the buildings looked remarkably the same as I knew them. There were just more of them. Tiny shops butted against each other, all up and down the street. It was a comfortable street, just what you'd expect from 1933 middle America.

"Hey, I've seen that picture." I only half-heard Jimmie say these words, the first he'd uttered in a good ten minutes. We had stopped in the middle of the 1000 block, and I had been gazing into the window of Economy Cleaners. A sign in the window read, "Felt hats cleaned and blocked, 50 cents." I had been smiling at the idea that this was an age when men still wore hats and that there was a service to help keep them looking good.

"What did you say, Jimmie?"

"Across the street, the picture house. I've seen that picture."

The "picture house" was one that I had known as the Strand Theatre. I had never remembered it as being open. It had been an empty theatre for years. As a kid, I would walk past it and try looking inside. You couldn't see much, but it always attracted my interest. It's been re-modeled into the KBAER shop. In August 1933, it was the Star Theatre, and it was showing "Hell Divers" starring Clark Gable and Wallace Beery.

"You've seen that show?" I asked.

"A couple weeks ago, an off-day in Chicago. Pretty good, lots of action. 'Course I like just about anything with that Wallace Beery in it. You seen it?"

"Not yet. But I agree with you about Beery."

Our discussion of movies ended, we started walking. We'd only gone a few steps when I smiled to a stop. On my right was a

15

vaguely familiar sight. It was a small shop with a plain white and black sign above the window that merely said "Johne." I remembered seeing this store on my trips down Michigan Avenue in the late '50's and early '60's. I never did know what kind of a store it was. I wanted to go in and finally find out, but Jimmie wasn't interested, and we moved on.

I mentioned earlier, that this was a crowded Michigan Avenue, shop-wise. In quick succession we passed Pfister's Bakery, Economy Cleaners, Johne's Store, Weinkauf Electric, Michigan Avenue Grocery, and New Deal Oil Mart, Trilling Hardware (much smaller than now), Rickmeier Fedler Electric, and several others I couldn't retain in my ever-failing memory. And these shops were only on the south side of the street, the side on which we were walking. I noticed one unusual store across the street on the 800 block. Dietz Music and Confectionary, it was called. I remembered a Dietz Music from the late '50's maybe, but where did the confectionary come from?

"I'm starving. Let's go in."

Again, I had been taking in the surroundings and almost missed Jimmie's declaration. But I didn't miss this one and noticed he was looking into a small diner called Carlton Lunch. I hesitated, at first, thinking the Federal Reserve notes in my wallet might not go over too well here.

"C'mon, I'm buying."

That settled it, I was hungry too. And, besides, I wanted to see if food actually did taste better years ago, before the preservatives and additives invasion. We walked into the small diner and took seats at the table near the east wall. We looked at the paper menu and waited for the waitress to come over and take our order. And waited. And waited.

A young couple entered and sat at the table next to us. The waitress came over, greeted the couple, and took their order.

"Miss, we're ready to order now," Jimmie said to the waitress, but she walked right by us.

"What's going on here?" Jimmie complained. I could see he was getting perturbed over this, and I didn't blame him.

"I'm going to get some service over here." With that, he got up and walked over to the waitress who was now standing at the counter. He reached out his hand and tapped her on the shoulder, or tried to. He let out a loud gasp as his hand went clear through her shoulder. He staggered back a few feet and looked back at me, a horrified look on his face. I was absolutely frozen for about ten seconds. Regaining only a fraction of my senses, I arose and walked to the couple at the next table. I repeated Jimmie's gesture and watched in shock as my hand slid unobstructed through the girl's shoulder.

"Can you hear me?" I almost screamed at her. No response. Jimmie was next to me now, and we wordlessly stared at each other. After a few seconds, we turned and hurried out the door. There were people walking up and down the street, just as there had been the whole time prior to this. Until then, I hadn't thought much of the fact that we hadn't spoken to anyone else the whole time we had been here. Now, it was obvious why. For these people, we didn't exist. They couldn't see us, hear us, or touch us. On the street again, we tried talking and touching other people with the same results. It's an eerie feeling watching your hand glide through a person's body as if that body didn't exist, which, of course, for us, it didn't.

Jimmie took out another cigar, nervously lit it, and took several quick puffs to get it going. Smoking that stogie actually seemed to calm him a little. I, too, was a bit more rational. Maybe we both just needed a few minutes to adjust to this new reality. In any case, it was Jimmie who finally spoke.

"I know I've asked this before, but what is going on here. One minute I'm walking down the street in St. Louis, and the next I'm in some town I've been to once, in a ballpark I've played in once. I meet a guy, you, who had the same experience I did. We don't know why we're here, how we got here, or how we're supposed to get to where we belong. And now we find that all the people in this town are ghosts. Or are we the ghosts? Are these people real? We can hear them, we can see them, but we can't touch them. And to them, we don't exist at all. Again I say, what's going on?"

I don't know if he actually expected a rational explanation from me or was merely thinking aloud. But I felt I had to respond.

"All I know, Jimmie, is that somehow, for some reason, we've been shifted to this very spot. We don't seem to belong here since we don't materially exist in this place. That's really all I know."

Of course, he was the only one who had been shifted spatially. I had been shifted temporally. I figured I had a bigger problem than he did.

"What do we do now?" he asked.

"We wait."

"Wait? For what?"

I shrugged my shoulders. "Do you have a better idea?"

He took a long drag on his cigar and lowered his eyes in resignation at our plight. I know he didn't have any other course of action, so we continued to walk. I suppose he could have decided to take a bus back to St. Louis and continue on with his normal life, but I think he instinctively knew that that wouldn't work. We both had been brought here because of an unusual occurrence, and it would take an unusual occurrence to get us back where we belonged.

We were nearing 8th Street when we heard the clatter of a street-car approaching from behind. It was a single car motoring slowly along the tracks in the center of the street. I watched in fascination as it followed the tracks from Michigan Avenue onto 8th Street and lumbered south on 8th. As a kid, I had seen the tracks still embedded down the center of 8th Street, though the streetcar had ceased operation years earlier. I noticed now that the tracks were embedded into an area of concrete running down the center of the street, while the outer edges of the road were comprised of red bricks. The street itself, 8th Street, that is, was virtually littered with cars, all of them looking to me like ancient model T's. It must have been some feat keeping your car out of the way of that streetcar, but I suppose they were used to it.

"You married, Don?"

He surprised me with the question. We hadn't gotten very personal in the short time we had been together, mostly, because we had been pre-occupied with our predicament. For my part, I was still in awe of him. This was the great Jimmie Foxx walking next to me. Under normal circumstances, there would probably be a thousand baseball-related questions I would like to ask him. But these weren't normal circumstances. Of course, if they were, I wouldn't be walking next to him in the first place.

"No, I'm not."

"No? That's a shame. I think everyone should be married. I'm married. Helen's her name. Great gal. Five years we've been married and I'm still crazy about her. Got a boy, too. James Jr. Great kid, love him to death."

The expression on his face as he spoke these words underscored his sentiment. Here was a man who, seemingly, had it all. He was young (about 26 at this time), strong, good-looking: a devoted family man who happened to be one of the greatest baseball players of all time. I wondered, had I been walking with one of the current superstars, would the conversation be as congenial, open and familiar? Somehow, I doubted it.

"What do you do for a living?"

I had to think fast as he had caught me off-guard once again.

"I work for the park system in Milwaukee."

"Really? And what do you do for them?"

18

"Oh, a variety of things. Things like cutting grass, keeping ball diamonds in shape, painting equipment. Stuff like that."

It wasn't far from what I had once down for a few summers here in Sheboygan. Still, I hoped he didn't press the issue. He didn't.

We were on the west side of 8th Street, heading south. This was the city's main drag, if you will. The antique cars were clattering down the brick street at the robust speed of maybe 20 mph. And they were all single headlight, hard top sedans. No SUV's. No mini vans. No convertibles. No cycles. And, apparently, no mufflers. These were noisy vehicles motoring slowly along. And there were lots of them. This was one busy street.

It was after 5:00 pm now, and most of the stores and shops were closed. I couldn't help smiling as I looked down the length of 8th Street. Two and three story brick buildings dominated the landscape. Up head, I could see such sights as the still familiar Sheboygan Theatre sign and a huge Richman Clothing sign that hung out over the sidewalk. Across the street, the Prange's sign did likewise. In addition, a huge H.C. Prange Co. sign perched high atop the four story brick Prange building. Just past Prange's, the Security 1st Savings sign and building was clearly visible, even though we were several blocks away. The scene was right out of a local history book. And I was living it. Sort of. I couldn't help smiling at the quaintness of it all.

We had stopped in front of the Badger Sales Co. It appeared to be some type of factory outlet store. Jimmie was staring into the window at the merchandise, clothing mostly. I couldn't believe that a well-dressed, clothes conscious guy like him would be interested in that stuff. I sure wasn't, and I turned to my right, for some reason, to look back at the way we had come.

"I don't feel so good," I heard him utter.

"What?" I replied automatically, and turned back to my left. But he was gone.

19

It had taken a few moments for me to recover from Jimmie's disappearance. I knew, of course, that his vertigo had returned and that he was back in St. Louis. Alone again, I walked on down 8th Street. I started noticing the people more, rather than just the buildings, trying to compare them, somehow, to the people of my time. I could only really compare them by appearance. A few differences were obvious. The people seemed to be shorter, better-dressed, and slower in gait. The men generally wore long, casual-type pants and some type of sport shirt. Many wore hats. There were straw hats, fedoras, felt hats, and derbies. I even saw one man wearing an Ivy League cap, at least that's what I've always called it. Some men were even attired in full-dress suits. There were no 21st century touches such as tank tops or T-shirts, shorts, athletic shoes, or sandals.

The women were unanimously clad in dresses and casual shoes. Again, many wore some type of hat, accompanied by earrings, necklaces and the like. Surprisingly, I didn't see one single child, except for a few babies in arms. Where were they all?

All the above observations were what I expected to find in this era. The relaxed attitudes of mainstream America would come much later. No tattoos. No body piercing. No public swearing.

I had gotten to a place called Sheboygan Dry Goods, directly across the street from Prange's. It was a fairly large general merchandise type of store. All the shops were closed and I had been peering into one of the windows. I turned to continue walking when it hit me. A minute or so later, once the vertigo had receded, I found myself holding onto a lamppost in front of the Mead Public Library. I was back. Or forward. Whatever the terminology, I was in my own time again. It was 5:15 pm. I had been "gone" for two and one half hours.

I walked over to the water fountain in front of the library, and took a long drink. It's quite a shock to be living in 1933 one minute, and then in 2005, the next. Surprisingly, there was less activity on 8th Street now, than there had been. At that moment, I didn't care about any of that. I just walked home.

It was almost 6:00 pm by the time I got home. Finney was happy to see me, screeching and whistling and climbing around his cage. Hugo just wanted to go out. I grabbed a can of soda out of the refrigerator and sat down heavily in my old, worn-out rocker. I had been on my feet for maybe three hours, and was exhausted. It didn't take long for me to start questioning what had happened; or, to be more specific, whether it had happened at all. It's funny how the human mind works like that. A person may go through an incredible experience and, a short time after being removed from that particular environment, start questioning whether it had actually happened. And my experience was so remarkable, it didn't take much for me to start questioning it.

But I knew it had happened, and despite my mental and physical exhaustion, I did something very intelligent. I grabbed some paper and a pen and wrote down as much as I could remember. Notes, mostly. Hardly an organized and coherent account of my experience, but enough fact and figures so I wouldn't forget them. Remember, I said at the start that my memory isn't what it once was. Besides, I had to make those notes to keep reassuring myself that what had happened was real.

I was in bed by 9:00 pm, not an exceptionally early time for me, really. I figured I wouldn't be able to sleep, considering all that had happened, but I didn't know what else to do. It couldn't have taken five minutes for me to fall into a very deep sleep.

I've always found it interesting how the daytime can put a person at ease and make him feel better about things. Sunny days are particularly good at this, and the next day was absolutely beautiful. I was once again certain about my "trip" and by early afternoon, the usual questions rolled through my mind. How did this happen? Why did this happen? Why Jimmie Foxx? Why did he move spatially while I moved temporally? Could this be reversed? Why 1933? Why couldn't we be seen or heard by the locals? What could I do about this? Did I want to do something about it? And the two most important questions: Would this happen again, and, if so, when would I be? And, what if I couldn't get back?

Believe me, thoughts like that can just about drive you crazy. So, just to clear my mind, I hopped on my bike and started pedaling. Predictably, I rode over to Michigan Avenue. I had to see the 2005 version and compare it to that of my 72 year ago walk, yesterday. Modern streetlights, no streetcar tracks, fewer shops, a little more wide open. I rode my bike slowly down the same sidewalk I walked yesterday. Ok, not exactly the same sidewalk. I remembered the numerous small shops that lined both sides of the street. I got to the little restaurant that had been Carlton Lunch, and peered inside. It's El Camino now and, of course, looked very different, indeed. I saw no reason to go inside, so I got back on my bike, turned right on 8th Street, and retraced my route of yesterday, back home.

The next several days were interminable. I struggled to keep my mind on my work, all the time wondering if the vertigo would return. It didn't, but the experience of the previous Saturday had left me shaken and off-balance. I spent some of my spare time digging through my library of baseball books in search of everything I could find on Jimmie Foxx. There wasn't much, besides the stats I found in Total Baseball. 1933 was Foxx's Triple Crown year. He hit .365 with 48 home runs and 163 RBI's. He's listed as being six feet tall and weighing 195 pounds. I had noted that he wasn't really a huge man, more solid than anything. He's said to have had incredible power. His triple crown came in his ninth major league season. He was twenty five years old. Except for a few other bits of information on him, that was all I could find.

Another Saturday rolled around, and I repeated my early morning ritual of the week before. I had been agonizing all week over the possibility of trying to go back again. Maybe, I thought, if I repeated my movements of the week before, I could get back. But did I want to go back? Did I dare go back?

I did everything the same. I wore exactly the same clothes, left the house at exactly the same time, and followed exactly the same route. There was never any real doubt in my mind. Despite the risks, despite not even having control over it, I knew that I had to at least try.

I walked past Kiwanis Park, up the hill toward Erie Avenue. It was another beautiful day, similar to last Saturday. I considered that a good omen. Crossing Erie Avenue, I neared the spot where the vertigo had hit last week. I recognized the tree I had held onto and actually got nervous as I approached it. And then I was there, on the exact same spot. I closed my eyes and waited. Nothing. For some reason I was surprised. I really thought it would happen again. Undaunted, I walked on. Maybe if I got closer to the park, it would happen there. But it didn't. I walked all the way to the park, or where it had been, without incident. I walked around the old park

22

area for awhile, and when it became obvious that nothing was going to happen, I headed home.

The human mind is an absolute marvel. It's workings and machinations are utterly baffling, sometimes. I was certainly proof of that. One Saturday, I find myself seventy two years in the past, not knowing how I got there, what I'm doing there, or whether I'd ever get back to my own time, and the next Saturday, I'm disappointed that I can't go back. I actually felt betrayed. I had considered myself something special. I mean, how many time travelers can there be in the world, anyway? In short, I found my reactions to the events of the past week, quite interesting, and surprisingly.

I was down the entirety of the next week. I managed to do my job, get my runs in, and interact with others in a way that didn't arouse suspicion. But my mind wasn't into any of it, or my heart. My thoughts, and spirit, were seventy two years in the past. At times, I was convinced that I would never get back. Other times, I was equally certain that I would. One thing I was absolutely certain of: it wasn't up to me. It was totally out of my control. I simply had to be patient and accept what came. Or what didn't. And despite all this, I still couldn't keep from trying.

The following Saturday found me taking the same walk along the same route. I didn't wear the same clothes or depart at the same time, however. I figured it wasn't important. I was right.

I was standing near what remained of the left field wall when it hit. I found myself holding onto the brick wall, or trying to. Once again, the vertigo had struck suddenly, without any warning. Upon regaining my senses and stability, I turned around and took in the park. It was virtually unchanged from the park I remembered, not from my last visit, but from my youth.

A press box was perched atop the grandstand roof behind home plate. The dugouts looked better, stronger maybe. The field, itself, was in much better condition. I could literally feel it under my feet as I walked from outfield in, toward the infield. The scoreboard in centerfield was new, too. Light poles stood scattered throughout the park. And, of course, there was the wall. I had noticed the new, brick wall immediately. It hadn't escaped my attention when I had "reappeared." And it was new. The familiar Wrigley Field-type ivy had yet to be planted. Only ten minutes, and I had the year figured out.

I remembered from my park history that these park improvements had occurred in 1948. The wall ivy hadn't been planted until 1949. Using my shrewd sense of deductive reasoning, I quickly concluded that this was summer, 1948.

He must have been watching me the whole time. I had surveyed the entire park and had never noticed him sitting in the corner of the first base dugout. I couldn't help smiling as we met near the first base line.

He was wearing a white, short-sleeve shirt, open at the collar, blue slacks, and black oxford shoes. His slicked back hair had only a few touches of gray at the temples. He was, perhaps, ten pounds heavier, but he was forty now and had been out of baseball for several years. It was so good to see him again. He was my constant in these unfamiliar times.

"Hello, Jimmie," I said and offered my hand, I remembered our last handshakes but still looked forward to receiving his hand into mine. Once again, he crushed my small, pudgy hand with his strong, massive one. But I didn't mind. It almost felt good. I was so glad to see him.

"I was wondering if you were going to show up," he said. "I've been sitting in that dugout for, oh, must be twenty minutes, or so. Thought maybe I missed you. Heck, I was just getting ready to leave when, there you were, just like that. Damndest thing I've ever seen, actually. It was like, poof, and there you were."

He was glad to see me, that was obvious. He had mercifully released my hand, but he was still smiling as he awaited my response. I hardly knew what to say. How do you explain a magical appearance?

"So what has it been, about fifteen years?" This came from Jimmie, not me. After only a few seconds thought, I realized that my reappearance was no different from his, and he knew it.

"Yes," I replied, "exactly fifteen years, I believe. How have you been?"

"Great. I don't play ball anymore, of course, you probably know that. I'm sales manager for a beer distributor in Philly now. Get to meet a lot of people. Lots of traveling. Of course, I never expected to do this kind of traveling again."

We had, almost subconsciously, started walking out of the park. Just outside the main gate, I stopped to read the newly erected plaque dedicating the park to the servicemen of World War II. The North Side Park finally had a name, Memorial Park. A few years later, when the American Legion purchased the park, it would be known as Legion Memorial Park, or to its friends, simply Legion.

Jimmie and I exchanged solemn glances and continued walking. "Where we headed this time?" Jimmie asked.

Nineteen forty eight was much closer to my own time, and I wasn't interested in just seeing what Michigan Avenue looked like. I wanted to visit a familiar haunt. Besides, I wanted to spend less time sightseeing, and more time talking to my baseball legend friend. "Follow me. I want to show you something."

We walked in silence for awhile. Turning left on Superior Avenue, we walked east for a couple blocks. It was Jimmie who broke the silence.

"You know, after fifteen years, you've hardly changed at all."

He had caught me off-guard, but, thinking quickly, I took off my cap and replied, "Oh yeah? A lot less hair this time." Jimmie let out a great big booming laugh. I continued, "you haven't changed much either. A little gray at the temples, but otherwise about the same."

Jimmie just smiled and magically produced a huge stogie from somewhere and set it on fire.

"You still smoking those stinky things?" I surprised myself with this barb, but I felt close enough to him, that I could get away with it. I was right.

25

"Stinky things? That's a genuine rich aromatic scent. At least that's what it says on the package. You don't mind, do you?"

"Not really." Actually, I liked it. It was a part of him. In a way, it was a signal that he was comfortable in my presence.

I don't know when Jefferson School was built. The 1890's, I think. It's an old school, even in 1948. A square, two storied brick creation that has escaped the wrecking ball more than once. It stood before us now, minus the new addition, minus the gymnasium that I had always known. Just the main school. It looked old, even now. I knew that eventually it would give way to a new school, but I hoped I wouldn't see it.

I had stopped on the sidewalk along Mehrtens Avenue staring up at the main entrance in the middle of the south side of the school. Years later, the entry would be bricked over and the main entry moved to the east side, off of 15th Street.

"This our destination?"

"Yup, my alma mater, Jefferson School."

"You went to grade school here?"

"It's a long time ago, now. But I have a lot of memories of this place."

We walked up the steps to the school level. I couldn't help but reach out my hand and lightly touch the already old brick building. Jimmie was watching me closely. I could only smile and say, "Let's walk around back."

We made a quick tour of the grounds. There were still lots of trees on the northwest stretch of the grounds. And, of course, the old playground equipment was still there; jungle gym, monkey bars, those steel horizontal bars that you could spin around on. Much of the grounds would be re-landscaped when the new addition was built in 2001.

Within minutes we were back at our starting point. Since there were no benches on the grounds. I suggested to Jimmie that we pull up a step and have a seat. It was time to talk.

A lady was walking her dog along the sidewalk below us, and though it was a warm day, she was wearing a full dress. I couldn't help smiling.

"What do you think?"

"Huh?" He had caught me by surprise. Again.

"What do you think, about our ability to do what we do? Or whatever you may call this. You've had fifteen years to think about this, and I'm assuming you have. Think about it, I mean. Have you come up with anything?"

26

Actually, he'd had fifteen years, I'd had two weeks, but I wasn't ready to explain the differences to him.

"Not really," I finally replied. "How about you?"

"Nope, not a thing. And I certainly couldn't talk to anybody about it. I mean, how can you explain this to anyone? They'd throw me in the loony bin. Can you see the headlines, 'Baseball great magically shifted in space.' I looked through newspapers and magazines for any articles about people who may have had a similar experience, but never found one. Not one. I still look, but I don't expect to find anything anymore. And then it happened again. I must say, I'm not as spooked as I was last time."

I was proud of Jimmie. He had thought it through and handled it well. Checking the newspapers and magazines was something I hadn't though of, not that it could have helped me much.

"So you haven't had this experience again since the last time we met?"

"No. You?"

"No, but I agree with you about not being as spooked this time. I'm not as worried about getting back to where I belong. I really believe we'll be moved back before too long." I had to careful with my wording, since I wasn't ready to divulge the temporal differences between us.

He nodded his head slowly and took a long drag on that stinky rope of his.

"You have no answers then either, do you?"

"No answers, but I'm convinced of one thing. This is happening for a reason. I mean, this is no coincidence that we have both gone through this twice and have arrived at the same spot at about the same time. Eventually, we're going to find out what that reason is, but, at least for now, I have no idea what."

Jimmie took one final drag and flipped the stogie into the street, quite a flip, actually. But then, he'd had a lot of practice at flipping cigars. After a few moments he slowly stood up, arched his back and sad, "Boy, I'm sure not used to sitting on cement steps. C'mon, let's walk some more. Gotta work out the kinks."

I got up, and we began to walk. We were both deep in thought for awhile, pondering our recent conversation.

"You seem to know this town pretty well. Where should we walk?"

I had just the place. It was only a few blocks away and I couldn't resist the temptation of visiting a childhood haunt. I knew it would be there in this year, so I told Jimmie to follow my lead.

"I tried looking you up a few years ago."

"You tried looking me up?" I repeated.

"Sure, I was in Milwaukee visiting my old roomie, and I was going to look you up, but I didn't know your last name. I don't believe you ever told me, did you?"

I hadn't, but I didn't see any reason to withhold it so I told him.

"How do you spell that?"

I told him.

"Say, you live in Milwaukee, do you know Al?"

The Al in question was Hall of Famer and Milwaukee native Al Simmons. I knew from my research that he was Jimmie's roommate for awhile. It was exciting hearing such a name dropped in my presence. I almost felt honored thinking that Jimmie actually thought that I might know the great Al Simmons.

"No, I'm afraid I don't," I replied. "I just know he was a terrific ballplayer."

"Sure was. And a great guy, too. I sure was sorry when he got traded to Chicago that year," he said sadly. "I missed him. We weren't the same after that. Mr. Mack started breaking up the team and pretty soon, there was nothing left. Of course, by that time I was with the Red Sox and had new teammates. I was still sorry to see it happen. I grew up with the Athletics. And Mr. Mack was a fine man."

It was interesting listening to him talk a little about his playing days and teammates. I wanted to continue talking, but we had arrived at our destination.

"Why are we stopping?" Jimmie asked.

"We're here."

Jimmie studied the drab brown shingle building on the west side of 14th Street just south of Michigan Avenue.

"What is it?"

"It's Hermann's Grocery Store. I used to buy stuff here. Let's go in and say hi to John."

"As if he could hear us," Jimmie replied somewhat cynically.

We walked up the couple steps, opened the old screen door and entered the small neighborhood grocery store. There was always something about Hermann's Store that made me feel good. The place had an aura, an aroma about it that was unmistakable. John was waiting on an old man at the front counter. I led Jimmie over to the ice cream cooler to check the two flavors of ice cream John always had on hand. I opened the cover and looked in at the two large round ice cream tubs. Chocolate and vanilla today.

28

"It's the first thing I always do when I come here, check the ice cream," I smiled. "Not much variety today."

Jimmie followed me across the room to the free-standing candy counter. It was all there. The candy cigarettes, the tiny chocolate bars, the candy raisins, the candy dots on strips of paper. I smiled in memory of it all. Jimmie looked at me quizzically, but said nothing. John's customer had left, and we were alone in the store. The tall, thin storekeeper, who had always reminded me of a beardless Abraham Lincoln, was checking over some receipts.

"It's good to see you again, John," I said. "How have you been?"

I thought he was going to shoot through the ceiling with fright. He quickly looked around and stammered, "Who's there? Who's there?"

Jimmie let out a low gasp; I stopped breathing. We slowly backed toward the door and silently exited, leaving poor John in his state of shock.

"He heard us," Jimmie whispered, once outside. "How could he hear us? Nobody could hear us before. Is he special, or something?"

I took a deep breath. "Let's think this through," I said quietly. "Until we got to Hermann's Store, we weren't close enough to anybody for them to hear us. John paid no notice of us when we entered his store. And nobody else seems to have noticed us."

We were slowly walking west on Michigan Avenue, being careful of our conversation now, should someone be near. This unexpected development had us doing some serious reassessing. Jimmie fired up another stogie, his way of staying calm, I guess. A young boy was walking toward us pulling a coaster wagon. I automatically moved to the edge of the sidewalk. Jimmie held his ground and said, "Hi there, young fella."

The kid dropped the handle of the wagon and turned around searching for the voice. When it became apparent that there was no one nearby, he grabbed the handle, turned the wagon around, and hustled back the way he had come.

"I hated to do it, but I had to make sure," Jimmie said, now totally composed. "So, now they can hear us, but they can't see us, eh?"

I was about to respond, when the vertigo hit. Far away I could hear Jimmie calling my name. And then I was back.

I was sitting under a tree, a large scrape burning my right forearm. A teenage skateboarder rolled past, giving me a funny look. I didn't care. This was a bad vertigo, maybe the worst yet. I rested a few minutes against the tree just to recover from the "trip," then slowly got up and walked home.

The boys were happy to see me, and I them. I grabbed a soda from the fridge and repeated my procedure from last time, writing down everything I could remember. Jimmie was right, it just wasn't as spooky this time. That was the outstanding feature this time. And yet, we could be heard this time; heard but not seen. What was that about? At the moment, I didn't care. These "trips" take a lot out of a guy. I hadn't kept close track of the time, but I was certain I was gone a little longer this time. I didn't care about that either. I was tired and went to bed.

The next few weeks were tough. I was able to function okay. The work got done, the miles got run, the house got cleaned, the dog got walked, etc., etc., etc. But I was restless, uneasy, and expectant. I followed Jimmie's lead and kept my eyes and ears open for unusual reports of other possible time travelers, but of course, there were none. I was glad, actually. It made me feel special, unique.

The two week mark came and went without incident. I didn't really think this was an every other week adventure, but I wasn't absolutely certain either. But now I was. And the days passed, uneventfully.

It was late September, a Sunday morning. I had gotten home from church, changed clothes and decided to pick up a few things from K-Mart. I left the boys in charge and headed out the door. I never even made it to the car.

When I recovered my senses, I discovered that I was sitting on a bench at the baseball diamond at Kiwanis Park. This was new, and unexpected. I knew immediately, of course, that I was back in time somewhere, but the spatial shift unnerved me. It couldn't stop me. I had to determine when I was.

I crossed the road and headed over to the playground area of the park. There appeared to be some activity at the northeast baseball diamond, and I decided to investigate.

Two teams of kids were warming up, getting ready for a game. A few people were sitting in the bleachers behind the third base bench and a few more were nearby, ready to watch the game. The kids looked to be about nine or ten years old. The team on the third base side was wearing dark blue shirts, and, across the diamond, the team on the first base side was wearing green shirts. I decided to stay and watch a little of the game. I didn't have anything better to do. I was about to climb into the bleachers when I just froze. And I mean froze. My heart started pounding and my breathing quickened. I recovered quickly and took a seat. I knew when I was.

I hadn't seen him, at first. He was seated to my right, on the first bleacher, ground level, if you will. He was wearing an off-white shirt and gray slacks. His slicked back, once black hair was now mostly gray. A cane was propped between his legs. I knew he would be here. It was good to see "the Beast" again.

I was about to go over to him, when a lady sat near me on the bleacher, smiled at me and said, "Do you have a son on one of the teams?"

I suppose I should have been shocked, but I wasn't. From the start, this had been a different visit and being visible to the local wasn't surprising. Maybe I'd almost expected it.

"No," I answered, "Just an interested spectator. Excuse me, there's someone I know in the front row." With that, I got up, walked down the bleachers, and over to where Jimmie was sitting.

"Hi Jimmie," I said as I sat next to my old friend.

"Don," he proclaimed, wrapping his left arm around my shoulder, in a friendly embrace. "I knew you'd be here somewhere. You know what?" he whispered. They can see us now, too."

"I know, I was just talking to the lady when I saw you over here."

"Does that mean we're a part of this world now?"

"I don't know," I said truthfully. He had removed his arm and was studying me closely.

"You never seem to age. I mean you always look the same. Me? I was twenty four when we first met. I'm fifty nine now. And I look it. I fell a few years ago, and I've needed this cane ever since. But you, you never change. How do you do it?"

I would have to tell him this time. There was no reason to hide it anymore. I had done some quick figuring. If Jimmie was fifty nine as he claimed. That would make the year 1967. But it wasn't. It was August, 1963.

"The game is about to start," I replied. "Let's watch the game, and we'll talk later."

The green shirts took the field. Their pitcher was a big kid, much bigger than anyone else on either team. And threw some serious heat. The blue shirts went down in order. The green shirts did likewise in the bottom of the first. The game continued on with no scoring. It was a well-played game for a bunch of nine and ten year olds. Solid pitching, good defense, heads-up play. Except for an occasional "nice throw," or "good pick-up," Jimmie and I were silent, content to simply watch a good, competitive game.

The blue shirts were up in the top of the fourth. I leaned forward, nervous in anticipation. With two out and nobody on base, one of the blue shirts connected, the ball shooting into the gap in right center. The centerfielder tracked it down and relayed it into the second baseman. The runner had rounded second and was trying for third. The second baseman turned and threw the ball to the waiting third baseman.

I had been watching the third baseman closely the whole game. He was of average size and build, with sandy hair under his black White Sox cap. He hadn't had much action as yet, but now he had a play. It was going to be a close play. As the runner approached third and started to slide, the third baseman extended his glove to catch the ball and apply the tag. But the ball bounced off the end of his glove and fell harmlessly to the ground. The runner was safe.

"Ach, should've had it," Jimmie muttered. "I don't know if he'd have gotten him, though."

Silently, I agreed. The next hitter hit a come-backer to the pitcher. It looked like the green shirts would be out of the inning. Inexplicably, instead of throwing to first to end the inning, the big pitcher threw home to get the runner coming home from third. The catcher, perhaps surprised by the pitcher's decision, dropped the ball. It was 1-0 blue shirts. Jimmie just shook his head.

It stayed 1-0 until the bottom of the fifth, the last inning. With one out, the sandy-haired third baseman came up, hoping to atone for his drop the previous inning. He walked on four pitches. He was the tying run. But a strikeout and a pop up later, and it was over. The blue shirts had won 1-0.

Jimmie and I got to our feet. In front of us the blue shirts were jumping around and yelling. They were the Kiwanis Pee Wee League champs and would advance to the city-wide playoffs. The green shirts were packing up their gear and walking off. I felt badly for them. Again. I still don't know how I could have dropped that throw at third.

We started walking toward the playground area of the park, pausing to have some water at the water bubbler. Jimmie was looking at me when I had finished drinking.

"Do you think we would have been able to drink anything last time? Or eat anything?"

I had been thinking the same thing. Not having an answer to his question, I shrugged my shoulders, and we continued walking. We found an empty bench near the swinging wooden horses, and had a seat. Across the way, a few of the victorious blue shirts were frolicking in the small, in-ground wading pool that had been extremely popular in it's day. I wondered why they took it out. Probably in a liability issue, but I was only guessing.

We sat in silence for several minutes. Kids were everywhere, on the swings, the teeter-totter, the merry-go-round, the swinging gate. I remembered it all so well. As I said much earlier, the park held many fond memories for me. A little melancholy had started seeping through me. Jimmie brought me back.

"How old are you, Don?"

"Fifty one," I replied truthfully.

"So, last time, you would have been what, thirty two?"

My friend still thought he was in his own time, 1967. He wouldn't think so for long.

"No, I was fifty one."

Jimmie took a long drag on the stogie he had fired up upon sitting down on our bench. The cigar appeared to be a different brand from the others, smaller, thinner. Maybe he was trying to cut down. I knew it wouldn't matter. Unfazed, Jimmie continued.

"And the first time, you were..."

"Fifty one," I said quietly.

Another deep drag and another long, slow exhalation of smoke. He said nothing for a long while, being content merely to gaze off in the distance somewhere. Where he was spiritually and emotionally, I couldn't say. But I knew he believed me. This time, it was me who broke the silence. It was time to explain. I tried to gather my thoughts so that my explanation wouldn't sound totally ridiculous to him. A losing proposition, if ever there was one. But I had to try.

"Needless to say," I started, "I haven't been totally truthful with you. The reason I haven't changed much is that, for me, it's only been about seven weeks since we first met. While you have been traveling through space to our meetings, I've been traveling through time. I've never lived in Milwaukee. I've always lived right here in Sheboygan. I'm sorry I lied, but I knew what was happening, and I didn't think I could tell you until now."

Jimmie was still staring off into space. But he was listening to every word I was saying. And believing them too, I knew.

"We've been together three times now on three trips, or whatever they are," I continued, "and each one was different. The first one, 1933, no one could see or hear us, remember? We were distinguishable only to ourselves. The next one, 1948, we could be heard but not seen. And this one, we're totally a part of this world, totally discernible in every way. But that's not all."

Jimmie still hadn't reacted in any way, an occasional drag on his cigar, his only movement. I knew that was about to change; I was ready to deliver the kicker.

"This is the first time I not only traveled in time, but also in space. In the past, I always reappeared in the same physical spot; a different time, but the same spot. But this time, I reappeared about a mile from where I started."

I paused one more time. I looked at my silent friend, and concluded my speech.

"It's also the first time you've moved in time."

Jimmie stiffened and quickly turned his head toward me.

"What do you mean I've moved in time?"

"You said before that you were fifty nine, correct?"

"Fifty nine, right."

"That would make the year 1967, right?"

"That's right. June 16, 1967. Isn't it?" Jimmie asked, not too certainly. I slowly shook my head.

"It's August, 1963. I'm certain of it."

I felt sorry for my old friend. This was something he could not have anticipated. He was prepared for almost any explanation for our unusual trips, but this was a little too much.

"Are you absolutely sure?"

I nodded.

"That game we just watched? The third baseman for the green shirts? The one who dropped the throw, that was me. That game was played the first week of August, 1963. I had just turned nine years old."

"Nine? You? You were nine?" He was having a terrible time assimilating it all. I felt badly for him. "Then you're from, from, ah, I can't figure it."

"In my time, it's late September, 2005."

Jimmie slumped forward on the bench and absently dropped his cigar onto the ground. He brought his hand up to his face and wiped his eyes. I didn't see any tears, but there might have been a few. I gently put my arm around his shoulder. We remained in that position for what seemed like several minutes. Finally, Jimmie sat up straight and looked at me.

"So what was all this about? Just a way for us to watch you play a game as a nine year old in 1963? That's it?"

"No, that's not it," I responded. Some how, I knew that wasn't what this was all about. "This is leading to something, but I don't know what, yet. But we're getting closer. The two of us are converging. We're both traveling in space and time, now. And we're a total part of this world. But we don't belong here, in 1963, I mean. I can feel it." And I could. "But next time, next time we'll know. I can just feel it."

"Next time? Do you think there's going to be a next time? I'm fifty nine years old. My health hasn't been too good. I walk with a cane now. I can hardly..." Jimmie stopped abruptly. He turned to me and continued. "You know all about me. You know how much time I have left. Don't you?"

My silence effectively answered his question. "It's almost over for me. There won't be another time."

"Yes there will. We'll be meeting again. I know it."

Jimmie stood up slowly, the cane helping him to do so. I got up with him. Many of the kids had gone now. Only three or four were still playing in the playground area. Jimmie turned to me, his face leaden with sadness, and said, "I hope you're right."

I smiled and reached out my arm to put it around my friend, but it was grabbing for air. Jimmie had gone. A few minutes later, so had I.

It's winter now, and I haven't made any more "trips." But I will. I know I will. Historically, Jimmie Foxx died just over a month after our last visit. But I know better. He's out there somewhere, and I'm going to be seeing him again. We have a destiny to discover.

"I'm preparing for it as best I can. Several weeks ago, I went to a coin dealer and "bought" some pre-1930's money, about fifty dollars worth. I carry it with me at all times. I figure I'll need it for my next trip. It will allow me to exist in a by-gone time until I can make some money of my own, somehow.

I've also spent the last many weeks organizing my notes and writing this manuscript. Like I said, I don't remember things like I used to, so I want to get this down while I still can.

Besides, time is short; spring is just around the corner. Baseball season. A time for taking "trips." I've stored this manuscript in my little fire safe, along with other important documents such as the title for my car and the deed to my house. Take care of Hugo and Finney for me. I don't know if I'll be back. Don't worry. You know where I am. You just don't know when.

PART II

1

About six months ago, my cousin Don disappeared. Vanished. Just like that. The police were called in, of course, but except for more-or-less ruling out foul play, were unsuccessful in discovering any serious leads. After a few weeks, his mother, my aunt Joan, hired a private detective, but he didn't have any luck either. In the mean time, things needed tending to.

He doesn't have a family, as such. I mean, he never married or had any kids. He lives alone, except for his dog and his bird. We took Hugo, the dog, to live with us. He'd been over several times when Don went away, so we were pretty used to having him. His mother took Finney, the bird. She's had several birds, so she knows how to take care of them.

Other things had to be done, too. We had to clean out the refrigerator, not that there was much to clean out. Any other dated food we either took, or threw out. Bills needed to be paid. Monthly utility bills, insurance bills, a stray medical bill. Nothing large, fortunately. Still my aunt isn't able to pay her bills as well as his, so our family has helped her out on this. Fortunately, his house is paid for, so there's no monthly mortgage payment. In return for our help, my aunt has let us use his car, a 1997 Hyundai. Having just gotten my license, the car has really come in handy.

This whole thing has been pretty traumatic. Don was an only child, and my aunt is taking it pretty hard. "What could have happened to him," is something we've heard her mutter over and over again. Nobody has the answer. And it isn't because we haven't tried. Besides the official channels, the investigations, the questionings, from the beginning, we've searched his house for clues. A scrap of paper with an address on it, a phone number hi-lighted in the phone book, anything. But nothing. We did find an awful lot of money. For some reason, he kept a lot of cash on hand. He also had a fair amount in his checking and savings accounts which, after endless red tape, my aunt was able to access. This has helped us immensely in paying the steady stream of bills.

We did find one other item of interest. While going through the house for the umpteenth time, my aunt came across one of those fire safes, only this was more in the shape of a briefcase. It was buried in the corner of his closet, which is probably why it took us almost four months to find it. Inside were the usual things you'd find in a fire safe/briefcase; his will, the deed to the house, etc. Also inside, however, was the rather lengthy manuscript of a story he had written. It's the one you've just finished reading. We've all read it too, obviously. My aunt, my mom and dad, my sister, and myself. We all thought it was pretty good. Don liked to write things on occasion. And we knew he was a sucker for time travel, so it seems pretty natural that eventually he might try his hand at a time travel story. Well, like I said, we all thought he did a pretty good job with it. Of course, none of us took it seriously. Not even me. At least, not until the parcel arrived.

It arrived a couple days ago, Wednesday, an early dismissal day from school. My parents were still at work, and my sister Molly, was away at college, so I was home alone. I hadn't been home ten minutes when the front doorbell rang. At the door was a well-dressed man of about thirty, carrying a briefcase.

"My name is Arthur Jameson from the Law Firm of Hammer, Spaulding, and Flywheel here in town" he began. "I'm looking for Mr. Craig Mand."

"I'm Craig," I replied.

"Perhaps, I'm looking for your father, or even grandfather."

"I doubt it. I'm the only Craig Mand around here." Mr. Jameson looked confused and didn't seem to know what to say. Finally, he thought of something.

"Maybe you could provide some form of identification for me."

"My license is in my bedroom. I'll go get it. You can come in the house and wait."

Once I had gotten my wallet and showed him my license, he was finally resigned to the fact that I was indeed the one and only Craig Mand. He then opened his briefcase, withdrew a brown paper wrapped parcel about the size and shape of a magazine, and handed it to me.

"On behalf of my lawn firm, I'm obligated to deliver this to you personally. If you will just sign this form, which basically says that you received the package on today's date, and thereby, releasing Hammer, Spaulding, and Flywheel of any further responsibility in this matter."

I signed the form.

"Thank you. Well, that ends quite a saga," he said, shaking his head.

"What do you mean?"

"Our firm has had that bundle for more than fifty years, long before my time, obviously. The story goes that a fella brought that in to our office sometime in the '50's with instructions to hold onto it and deliver it to you on today's date. It was an unusual request, but he paid us enough to make it worthwhile. How he knew our firm would survive this long is beyond me. And you! Needless to say, I expected a much older man."

I didn't know how to respond after his story, so I merely repeated that I was indeed the person he was looking for. That evidently settled the matter for he started walking to the front door. I followed and let him out. Outside, he turned, shook my hand and said, "Thank you, Craig. Good luck. And just between you and me, I'd love to know what this is all about."

"Me, too."

He smiled, got into his car and drove off, I went into the house, grabbed the parcel off the kitchen table, and headed for my room, anxious to discover just what was in the package.

I just stared at it for awhile. It was wrapped in brown butcher paper and tied with a thin brown twine. The edges were taped, but I could see that some of the taping had been re-done. The paper looked old, and smelled old. I started thinking about the story Mr. Jameson had relayed about the delivery in the '50's. I had a feeling I knew what was in the package, and I was afraid to open it, in case I was right. I put the package on the bed, let the dog out, then back in again, went to the fridge for a Snapple, then back into my room. I carefully cut the twine and peeled open the brown paper away from the contents.

It was a manuscript, all right, like I thought. Maybe fifty or sixty pages of neatly printed lines on white typing-type paper. I knew almost immediately who it was from. My hands were shaking, as I began to read:

Craig:

How have you been? I've been thinking of all of you quite a bit.

I guess the first thing I should say is that I'm assuming you've gotten this. I wasn't sure how to handle it, but this seemed to be the best way. I can only hope that somebody at the law firm didn't throw it away immediately. I mean, it was a pretty odd request. Still, I paid them enough, and it is a reputable firm, at least they've stood the test of time, so I'll assume you've received this. What other assumption can I make?

Second, if you haven't found my first manuscript by now, it's in my fire safe in my bedroom closet. Read it before proceeding with this part of it. I'm guessing you've already found it and read it. And maybe laughed at it, too. I've given you six months to find it and to get used to my absence. I could have had this delivered anytime, but I thought it best to wait awhile.

Third, you might be wondering why I sent this to you and not to someone else. A couple reasons, actually. I figured you might be the one person who would take that first manuscript seriously. Plus, being a baseball player and fan, I knew you would really appreciate the baseball theme of what I'm sending you.

Finally, a few words on the manuscript itself. Through the time frame of this story, I tried to keep notes and record the facts as best I could. Every night, or at least several times a week, I would jot down my observations on our actions and surroundings. At first, I didn't know where any of this was leading, but by the time you're through reading this, you'll agree with me that everything has come together and been explained. Or, maybe there's more to come. But, I figured it was time to organize my notes and set them down into, hopefully, a coherent story.

I've tried to give you an accurate picture of the Sheboygan of this era, a little flavor, a little ambience, if you will, of what it's like to be here. Looking over the manuscript, I'm not sure I succeeded in that very well. I guess I'm just not a very descriptive writer.

I've also had to omit a lot of stuff. I couldn't put down everything that's happened. That would make this way too unwieldy, and probably more boring than it already is. I've gone into detail on some things and slid over others, concentrating on our first few months here. You'll see why.

Well, that's it for my intro. Do what you want with the story, though, I don't know what you can do with it. You could try to get it published, but there might be some problems there. I suppose you could claim it as original fiction and take your chances. How you handle it with the family is up to you. You have good judgment, use it here. Enjoy my story. It should clear up the mystery. At least for you. I don't know if anyone else will believe it.

> Until later?,
> Don

I couldn't help but smile as I finished reading his "intro." It was vintage Don. I finished the Snapple, got up to close the bedroom door, laid back on my bed and turned the page.

PART III

1

The winter wasn't too bad. The weather people kept telling us that it was a "mild" winter with above average temperatures and below average snowfall. That was fine with me. Winter is my least favorite season, and the sooner it ends, the happier I am.

It had "ended," more or less, by the beginning of April. At least, the ground was free of snow and the temperatures had moderated nicely. It had been a quiet, uneventful winter. No problems at work. Acceptable miles had been run week in and week out. Books had been read, more than usual. I tried to find as much as I could on Jimmie. I got lucky and was able to order a recent biography on him through a baseball literature catalog I occasionally get. It's the only bio of him I've ever seen, so I jumped on it. Like I said, I was lucky on that. Or maybe not.

Like I said, I'm convinced all that happened to us is for a reason. Those three trips into the past were what I now call "acclamation visits." In other words, they were simply to get us to know each other and to get used to the time travel experience with all it's socio-cultural trappings and paradoxes. So, maybe finding the sole biography on Jimmie just now wasn't a coincidence. Maybe it was all part of the grand design.

I missed him. The winter may have gone along uneventfully, but that doesn't mean it was a happy time. Reading Jimmie's bio was particularly difficult. Naturally I rejoiced in his many triumphs and despaired at his occasional failures and difficulties. But the whole experience just saddened me. I remembered his equanimity and acceptance of me and of our predicament. I remembered his genial, outgoing nature. I remembered his sadness of our last meeting. I remembered his cigar. I missed it all. Even the cigar.

It was the first week of April, a Saturday. I had run an encouraging ten miles, completed all post-Saturday run obligations, and had just completed a highly successful power nap. I walked over to the window and looked out. The sun had made a welcome appearance after several dreary, over-cast days. My indoor-outdoor

43

thermometer said 58 degrees. I had to check this out. I walked out the front door, down the steps, and out onto the sidewalk. It was beautiful. Sunny and mild. Spring. Baseball season. I looked up at the sky and smiled. It was my last view of the year 2006.

I was sitting on a park bench. How long I had been "out," I didn't know. It didn't matter anyway. I was sitting on a bench in the middle of Fountain Park. Once I had recovered from the inevitably brief disorientation of the vertigo, the Fountain Park location was easy to discern. It was an incongruous park, really, located practically in the center of Sheboygan's business district along 8th Street. The one square block park was more heavily wooded than I remembered, with the bandshell located in the middle of the park itself, rather than at the southwest corner. I had remembered a bandshell in this location, but it looked different. This one was bigger, I think. Maybe not.

I got up and took a brief walk. I walked along the paved walk path cutting through the park. As I got nearer the bandshell, I became convinced that it was, indeed, larger. I walked completely around it, strolled over to the fountain at the east end of the park, then back to my bench, and sat down. And waited.

A quiet pop, that's all there was to it. I was expecting it, but I was still startled. The shock passed quickly because there he was, sitting next to me on the bench. It took him a few seconds to get his bearings, but I couldn't wait and instinctively gave him a big hug. I don't know if I've ever given another man a hug, but I couldn't help it. It was so good to see him.

"Jimmie," I said somewhat stupidly. "It's great to see you again!"

"Don?" Wow, look at you," Jimmie Foxx said finally, after extracting from my unexpected embrace.

"What about me?" I replied, suddenly alarmed. What did I have, three eyes, green teeth, no chin?

"What about you? Heck, you can't be any more than, what, twenty years old. And where are your glasses?"

For the first time, I actually took stock of myself. Attire-wise, I was wearing black oxford shoes, black slacks, a blue long sleeve sport shirt, tan spring jacket, and one of those beige Ivy League caps. And no glasses. I had been wearing glasses for forty years, and, amazingly, I hadn't even noticed that now. I had no more need for them. And I was lighter too, I could tell. Maybe ten pounds. I hadn't been that heavy before; my running had kept my weight in the 145-155 pound range. But now, I couldn't be more than 140, tops. And I felt good. Nothing hurt. No sore knee. No bad ankle. No stiffness. And hair. I had hair again. I had taken off my Ivy League cap and was running my fingers through it.

"This is incredible! I hadn't even noticed some of this stuff until now. Man, I feel good." Then it was my turn. "And you, you can't be any more than twenty yourself."

It was, indeed, the young, strong, handsome Jimmie Foxx of our first meeting, not the older, hobbling man of our final one. He was attired in apparel similar to mine, but without the hat. He looked great.

For awhile, we just sat on that bench, looking at each other. Grinning. We felt like a couple of school kids who had just gotten away with something. Or maybe it was more like we had been specially selected to embark on a grand adventure. We had passed the preliminary entrance exams. And were now ready to begin our journey in earnest. We both sensed it, and we were pumped.

As if to confirm my assessment, Jimmie suddenly leaped to his feet, and, in a surprisingly modern gesture, pumped his fist and almost screamed, "This is terrific. I feel great. No more pain. Heck. The last thing I remember, I could hardly move. I was 59 years old and felt like 80. And now look," he exclaimed as he practically danced around in place. Finally, he'd had enough dancing and sat back down next to me.

"How long have been here, before I arrived, that is?"

"Maybe fifteen minutes."

"This park, it's downtown, right?"

"Good memory. It's called Fountain Park, right in the downtown district."

Jimmie nodded his head briefly, and looked around, "Do you know what year it is?"

"Not really, But judging from the cars and the appearance of the few people I've seen, I'd guess maybe the early '40's." Jimmie looked around again and gave me an agreeing look. After a few more minutes of surveying the landscape and trying to digest our circumstance, Jimmie verbalized what we'd both been thinking.

"So what do we do now? I mean, we've certainly been sent back here for a purpose. We've already experienced three trips back in time and now we've been rejuvenated, dressed in these period clothes, and dropped back into Sheboygan, Wisconsin in some long-ago year. That's great and all that, and I'm certainly happy to be given a new lease on life, so to speak, but, well, what do we do now?"

46

Jimmie had summed things up pretty well. I figured it was time to get down to the practical basics and take stock.

"First, as unobtrusively as possible, we have to find out what today's date is. Maybe we can find a newspaper, or something. Second, I think we just have to go about starting a life here. We're here to stay this time. I may be wrong, but I doubt that somebody is just going to show up with our special assignment. We're just going to have to settle in and see what happens. I'm absolutely convinced that our "Mission" will be revealed naturally rather than by some special emissary."

Again, Jimmie nodded his head and replied, "Sounds good. I agree."

"Good." Then I remembered the old-time money I made a point of always carrying with me. I told Jimmie about our limited, but workable resources.

"Great idea. I wish I'd have thought of it. At least we'll have fifty bucks to work with."

"Oh no. Maybe with these new clothes, my wallet didn't make the trip." I was almost panic stricken. If the wallet wasn't in my pocket, we'd have nothing to live on. Jimmie gave me his best frightened look. He knew the problems we'd have without that wallet and its money. I nervously reached my left hand to my back pocket. The wallet was there, or a wallet. I reached in and slowly extracted the wallet. It wasn't my old black bi-fold. This was a new brown alligator skin wallet. I gave Jimmie a wary look.

"This isn't my wallet," I said, as Jimmie gave out a low groan. "There'd better be some money in here or we're in big trouble." I opened the wallet and looked inside.

"Oh my God!"

"What? What is it? Are we broke?"

I was stunned. I gave him a shaken glance, then reached inside the wallet and extracted a sizable wad of bills.

"Whoa," was all that Jimmie could gasp out. We exchanged wary stares. This was something we hardly could have expected, or even hoped for. Somebody, or something, definitely had a plan for us. "Are they good?"

"They look good to me. All silver certificates, and none after 1943." I had taken a minute to flip through the bills to check this out, and now I started counting. There were ten five dollar bills, fifteen tens, ten twenties, and one hundred dollar bill. Five hundred dollars.

I just stared at the wad of bills for a moment, still stunned by our seeming good fortune. Finally, I put the money back into the wallet and was putting it back into my pocket when I saw Jimmie holding a similar wallet.

"The daily double," Jimmie offered, still obviously startled.

"Good God. This is incredible. Is this ours?" Jimmie's wallet contained the exact same breakdown of bills as mine. We had one thousand dollars between us. A lot of money for the 1940's.

"I guess. Who else's would it be?"

"I don't know. Maybe there's something else in here, an ID, or something."

Jimmie slid the bills back into the wallet, and opened the snap on the flap that held the picture sleeves in place.

"Sure enough. This looks like some kind of identification card. Somebody named Jerry Wolff. I knew it was too good to be true."

"Let me see that card," I said, suspiciously.

State of Wisconsin
Jerome Ebony Wolff
6'0"   195 Pounds
October 22, 1924
Sheboygan, Wisconsin

It looked convincing to me, although I had no idea if that type ID existed in the 1940's. And yet, I didn't know what it possibly could be good for; there was no address, no phone number, and no social security number.   It was simply a limited form of identification.   Finally, after about thirty seconds of perusal and pondering, I caught on. Why it took so long, I can't say. I would have to have my wits about me in this brave, old world.   Or, maybe I should say, we should.

"What's your middle name?"

"My middle name? It's Emory."

"Emory.   James Emory Foxx.   Pretty clever.   Very clever, really," I said, truly impressed.

"Clever?" What's clever?"

48

"Here's your ID back," I replied, handing back the card.

"My ID? This is supposed to be me?"

"Well, sure. Take a look at it."

Jimmie looked again at the card, more closely this time.

"Son of a gun. James Emory Foxx. Jerome Ebony Wolff. You're right, this is pretty clever. Guess I'll have to get used to my new name. What's your name?"

State of Wisconsin
Daniel John Parker
5'7"   145 Pounds
April 20, 1924
Sheboygan, Wisconsin

"Hi Dan, nice to meet you. I'm Jerry," Jimmie offered, hading back my ID. "I guess we better remember these new names and start using them."

"I guess."

Judging from the sun angle, it was probably late afternoon, and we were starting to feel the chill of what must have been an early spring day. It was time to embark on our new lives.

"We're going to have to find a place to stay, at least for awhile," I said, finally.

"Any suggestions? You know this place a lot better than I do."

"The Foesté."

"The Foesté?"

I turned slightly to my right and nodded at the large four story hotel about half block to our south.

"The Foesté Hotel. You stayed there when you were here with the A's in 1932. Remember?"

"Vaguely," Jerry replied. "That was another lifetime ago."

49

"You'll probably remember it better than I will," I countered, rising from the bench. I had taken only a step or two when I tripped and fell against Jerry's back.

"What the heck?"

Regaining my balance, I looked down at the beige canvas duffel bag that caused the trip.

"What in the world is this?" I gasped as we both sat back down to investigate our most recent discovery. "This wasn't here five minutes ago. It wasn't even here five seconds ago."

"Well, it's here now, and it's obviously for us, so let's check it out."

Jerry pulled the bag up onto the bench between us and pulled back the zipper that ran the length of the approximately two foot long bag.

"Eureka! We've struck oil," Jerry exclaimed, as he started to withdraw the bag's contents. We were now the proud owners of one catcher's glove, one first baseman's glove, or trapper, as it used to be called, one regular fielder's glove, one pair of baseball spikes, and one pair of gray baseball pants, one white with blue sleeves baseball shirt, one blue baseball cap, three pairs of blue baseball stockings, and six baseballs. None of it new, all appearing slightly used and ready for action.

"Looks like we're here to play a little baseball," Jerry concluded.

"What do you mean we? This is all for you."

"You think so?"

"Of course. You're the ball player, not me. I'll bet the apparel fits you and not me."

Jerry quickly tried on the cap and spikes. A perfect fit. The cap was at least a quarter inch too large for me. I didn't bother with the shoes. Jerry stuffed the gear back into the duffel bag, smiling the whole time.

"Looks to me like we're all set," Jerry said, arising, and slinging the bag over his shoulder. "Let's find some digs."

We walked through the park and over to 8th Street.

"You know," I said, "it's probably best if we don't reveal too much to people. At least, not at first, not until we get or bearings. Then there are a few other things we'll have to discuss."

"Like what?"

"Later." We had reached the Foesté. We climbed the four steps to the front door, opened it, and walked in.

Dark. That was what struck me first. It was dark in the Foesté Hotel. Not pitch dark, like it was night, but, well, dark. The décor was definitely not the indifferent, off-white malaise of the late Twentieth Century. This place had character. High ceilings. Chandeliers. All natural, dark-stained woodwork. High windows, rounded on the top. Purple tied-back drapes. Immense, deep red colored area rug. Green plants everywhere. I loved it.

"You know, I do remember this place. Very elegant. Good service," Jerry finally offered, after we had spent a minute or two in a cursory examination of the Foesté. We walked further into the lobby past a man sitting at one of the numerous easy chairs scattered throughout.

"Pardon me, sir, but is that today's paper?" Jerry had stopped next to the man and was gesturing toward the newspaper that the man was reading.

"Yes, it is," the man replied.

"Would you mind terribly if I just took a quick glance at it?"

"Not at all. In fact, you may have it. I'm finished with it, and besides, I have to run." The man handed the paper to Jerry, arose from the chair, and walked out the front door.

"Thank you," Jerry called after him. "Friday, March 29, 1946," He whispered. "About what we thought."

We walked over to the check-in desk where, hopefully we would find that a room was available. A short, middle-aged man wearing a white shirt, black tie and black slacks was waiting.

"May I help you gentlemen?"

"Yes, do you have a room available for my friend and me?" I replied, hopefully.

"Certainly. We have a very nice room on the second floor with an easterly exposure, or several on the third floor, facing to the north."

"The second floor room will be fine." I really didn't care where we were put, and I wasn't about to inquire about the price.

"Very good. Room 223. Here is the key. If you both please sign the register. The charge is $3.00 per night. May I inquire as to how long you will be staying?"

"We're not sure, exactly. Possibly a week. We'll be looking for a nice flat to rent."

While we were talking, I signed my Dan Parker in the guest book and scribbled in "Milwaukee" as my place of residence. I hoped it wouldn't come back to haunt us, but I figured I better put something there or it might arouse suspicion. Jerry followed my lead, quickly realizing we didn't have much choice.

"That might be quite difficult, I'm afraid," the clerk continued, "what with the housing shortage and all."

"Housing shortage?" There's a housing shortage?" I asked, innocently.

"Of course," the clerk responded, warily. Has Milwaukee escaped the nation-wide, post-war housing shortage?"

"No, of course not. I didn't realize it had gotten this far," I recovered.

"Oh yes, even little Sheboygan has been affected," he retorted, satisfied with my answer.

I thanked the clerk, took the key and walked away, glad to have escaped the confrontation. Jerry had been silent throughout the encounter with the clerk. As we were ascending the steps to the second floor, I glanced over to him and said, "See what I mean about being careful?"

"Sure do. But you got out of it nicely."

"Hell, I didn't know there was a nation-wide housing shortage."

"You do now," he replied, chuckling.

We had reached our room. I slid the key into the lock, turned it to the right, and opened the door.

It was a comfortable looking room. On the left, two single beds flanked a nightstand with a table lamp. A single dresser stood opposite the beds. A small desk with a chair was against the east wall under the window. A lone leather easy chair stood in the far left corner. That was it. Cozy and comfortable. It was just what we needed, at least for now.

Jerry dropped the bag on the floor next to the dresser, tossed the newspaper onto the far bed and strode over to the window above the desk. I sat on the edge of the near bed and stared down at the floral print carpet.

"'The Southerner' is playing at the Rex," Jerry offered, after a few minutes of surveying the street below.

"'The Southerner'?"

"Zachary Scott and Betty Field."

"Never seen it."

53

"Me neither." Jerry sat on the edge of his bed and joined me in staring at the carpet. The initial euphoria of our new lives and the endless possibilities had quickly given way to the realization that it was early spring 1946, and we were going to have to find a way to get by in this world. It was easier for Jerry, because he had been this way before, so to speak. This was all new to me. Or old. We would have to acclimate ourselves to our new surroundings quickly, and we'd have to be careful while doing it.

"Toss the paper over here, let's see what's happening in the world these days. Plus, we need to check on a few things."

Jerry flipped over the newspaper, and I quickly scanned through it. There wasn't anything earth shattering. Something about re-locating highway 141 around Haven, whatever that was about, and a long article on the lumber shortage. I quickly discovered that the 1946 "Sheboygan Press" was a personal paper. A lot of comings and goings of ordinary people. I figured that could only help us. I finally made it to the sports section and found what I was looking for.

"Indians sign Hurler," I read out loud.

"Terrific," Jerry replied, unimpressed. "After Feller they don't have much."

"Not the Cleveland Indians. The Sheboygan Indians, of the Wisconsin State League. It says here they've signed some guy named Leslie Orr, twenty-one-year-old right hander from Prairie Du Chien. He played briefly for the Indians in 1942 when he was seventeen. Let's see, what else. Yup, thought so. He was in the service during the war in the far east."

"So what does that have to do with us?"

"It has everything to do with us. Like I thought, it means that the Sheboygan Indians are looking for players for the upcoming season. And you, Jerry Wolff, are going to try out for the team. Think you're good enough to make it?" I smiled.

"Why in the world do I want to play for the Sheboygan Indians? I could play for the Yankees or the White Sox or any other team in the bigs. Why do I want to play here?"

"You're forgetting our situation," I replied instinctively. "If you were supposed to play for the Yankees or White Sox you would have found yourself in New York or Chicago, not Sheboygan. You were meant to play for the Sheboygan Indians," I said, pointing to the duffel bag on the floor. "Why, I don't know, but I'm sure we'll find out."

"You're right," Jerry said, resignedly. "But, you know, this could be fun. Not much pressure, not much exposure. Hey, I like it.

54

And besides, I could be in the bigs next year, or the year after for sure."

I had to give him credit. Disappointment never lingered long in the heart or mind of my friend. Still, I couldn't resist one last little shot.

"Hopefully, you have the skills of a twenty-one-year-old Jimmie Fox and not of a twenty-one-year-old Don Jackson."

"Ha!" Jerry scuffed. "Don't you worry about me. We're here for a purpose, remember? We wouldn't be here if I couldn't play like I used to."

He had me there. Besides, I wasn't really worried about any possible discrepancy of skills. I was excited, actually. Who wouldn't be, in my situation? An opportunity to see the young, strong Jimmie Foxx play baseball? Playing against vastly inferior competition? I could hardly wait.

"Does the paper say when these tryouts begin?"

"No." I had read through the article again, but there was no mention of tryout dates. "It must be pretty soon. We'll find out tomorrow somehow."

"Great! I'm ready to go right now." Jerry was pacing the room excitedly. He looked like he was about ready to lace up his spikes and take a little B.P. Finally, after a few minutes of telling me how he was going to send baseball missiles into distant lands, he settled down and sat on the edge of his bed. I had been sitting on the edge of my bed the whole time, and now he was directly across from me, looking as if he had something to say. He did.

"You know, Don, or, Dan, I mean. I gotta remember that. Anyway, you know we've been spending all this time talking about why I'm here, and what I'm going to do. But, what about you? I mean, why are you here?"

Jerry's blunt query had left me dumbfounded. In the several hours we had been here, I had never questioned my raison d'etre. And now I had absolutely, positively no answer to the question. "I don't know," was all I could reply, rather stupidly.

Jerry sensed my bewilderment and tried to cheer me up. "Maybe you're here to be my support crew. You know, like a manager or something. Heck, this is your town. Sure, it's a little before your time, but you still know your way around here. And you probably know some people, or, at least know of them. You can be a big help to me in doing what I have to do. And besides, maybe you'll have another purpose, something that we'll find out later."

His short speech had, indeed, cheered me up a bit. I really had to marvel at Jerry's ability to think on his feet, so to speak. His analysis was right on, and I told him so. "Maybe my role will be to support you, financially. I don't think Wisconsin State League baseball players make too much money. That $1,000.00 we have won't last forever, not after we do some shopping in the next few days. I'm going to have to find a job. I think I'll move from the sports section to the classifieds and see what job openings are available to a young, male, baseball groupie."

I settled back on the bed and set out to see my calling.

"Cab driver's wanted. Apply at 1131 Penn Ave."

"Man wanted to clean tavern mornings. Apply Steiner's Tavern. 1527 N. 8th St."

"Young man wanted -19 years or over for clerking in store. Apply at Badger Paint   and Hardware Store. 912 N. 8th St."

"Man wanted for general work in rug cleaning plant. Apply at 435 N. 9th St."

I couldn't help chuckling at the last one. Jerry had been listening to my potential career opportunities. "Anything interesting?" he queried.

"The paint store job has possibilities. I knew a little about paint, maybe not 1940's paint, but I could probably get by. I suppose I could check it out, but it really doesn't do much for me. That's about all I see here, so... Hello!"

"Something good?"

"Listen to this: 'Night clerk wanted. Immediately. Good salary. Apply Foesté Hotel." I tossed the paper onto the nightstand, and stared up at the ceiling. "I do believe I've found my destiny."

"So, how do you know you're going to get this hotel job?" Jerry inquired the next morning as we were attiring ourselves in the only clothing we had. "There are a lot of men out there looking for work. They'll probably be flooded with applicants. You don't have much of a chance, if you ask me. Do you even know anything about clerking?"

"Nope."

"Great."

"I've as good as got the job right now."

"And just how do you figure that?"

"Jerry, you're forgetting the most important factor. Fate. Destiny. Pre-determination. Whatever you want to call it. Look what's happened. We show up here, at the end of March, just as baseball season is about to start. It's perfect for you. And here I am in the Foesté Hotel just as they're looking for a night clerk. It's perfect for me. This is no coincidence."

"Oh. Hey, you're probably right. This is great. You'll have a steady job and I'll be playing ball. We'll have it made." Jerry had perked up considerably, but I know that despite everything I had said, we were still a ways away from his projection.

"Before we have it made, we're going to have to do some shopping. We're going to need clothes, shoes, toiletries, and who knows what else we see that we may need."

"I'll say. I need a shave already. But first I need something to eat. I'm starving."

"Me too. No wonder. We haven't eaten anything since we got here. Let's get some breakfast, and then do some shopping. Then we'll do some job hunting."

That decided, we locked the door behind us, walked down the steps to the lobby, then exited onto 8th Street.

We spent the morning spending money. Two blocks of walking found us in Kresge's, where Jerry insisted we have breakfast. Kresge's is my kind of store, a traditional 5 and 10 cent store where seemingly all and every gadget, trinket and whatnot can be had for next to nothing. Which is about what our hearty breakfast cost. Two orders of ham and eggs, toast, and coffee set us back less than a buck.

I liked Kresge's. I remembered it, somewhat, from early in my previous life. Just like Hermann's store, I loved the odor of it, the ambience, if you will. It was almost a combination of hot dogs, plastic and shoe polish.   We picked up a few toiletries and miscellaneous items, then proceeded across the street to Prange's.

Jerry loved Prange's. Prange's had everything, high quality merchandise at reasonable prices.   Jimmie Foxx had been a fashionable, snappy dresser, and his newest incarnation was no different.   After nearly two hours of browsing and selecting, we finally had our haul: two pairs of shoes, sixteen pairs of socks, six pairs of underwear, five pairs of slacks, four knit sport shirts, two belts, two ties, and three slack suits, which is a shirt and pant combination. Including our Kresge purchases, the total bill came to $51.65. Jerry really liked the slack suits and insisted on an extra one. We figured this initial spree would be enough to get us going. Other needs would undoubtedly arise within the next few weeks, and we would have to make more purchases. I was certain Jerry would be back soon for a couple more slack suits. And my prospective new job might necessitate additional spending. It couldn't be helped. We were in good financial shape, though that future would hinge on my ability to secure the night clerk job. It was time to go job hunting.

Back in the room, I changed into a pair of dark blue slacks, light blue knit sport shirt, and black wing tip shoes. I had washed my hair and brushed my teeth and felt like I was ready to make an impression.

"Break a leg." This from a reclining Jerry Wolff. He was lying on his bed, paging through yesterday's paper.

"Thanks. Care to go alone?"

"No thanks, I'm going to explore my new home town." He tossed the paper aside and snapped to his feet.

"Really? Just don't spend too much of our money." Jerry and I had decided to split the money evenly. And that included any future income we may earn. We felt that we were in this together, and we would split everything we had. At least we'd split it as best and as evenly as we could.

"No problem. I'm only taking $5.00 alone. Just for any possible incidental expenses." I knew that $5.00 wouldn't be in Jerry's wallet for long, but I didn't mind. Like I said, money wasn't a big concern. At least not yet.

Henry Boatwright wasn't much taller than me, and though he wasn't portly, he wouldn't qualify as being svelte, either. Jerry had gone off to explore the town, and I was standing in front of the assistant manager of the Foesté Hotel, or, as I would soon be informed, the Hotel Foesté. I knew it was Henry Boatwright by the name tag proudly positioned on the upper left side of Henry's chest.

"May I help you?" the assistant manager of the Hotel Foesté inquired.

"Yes, I saw your help wanted ad in the paper, and, if the position isn't filled, I'd like to apply for it."

"The position has not yet been filled. In fact, you are the first person to apply. Quite surprisingly, actually, considering the number of men out of work these days." He spoke in a short, clipped manner, totally in keeping with the position he held. As he spoke, I was well aware of his scrutiny of me, instantly evaluating my possible merit for the honored position of night clerk, Hotel Foesté. "Please follow me."

Having passed my first test, I walked around and behind the reception desk into a small office, almost a back room, really. I sat down at a rickety wooden desk and filled out a very elementary application form. I waited a few minutes for Henry to return from his post at the front desk. He sat down on a creaky wooden chair next to the desk and read over my responses on the form.

"Have you ever worked in a hotel?"

"No, but I think I could pick it up pretty quickly."

"I see." He paused for a few minutes, obviously mulling over his options. "We are in a bit of a bind here at the moment. Our night man resigned abruptly two days ago, and a couple of us have been working long hours to fill in. Would you be able to start tonight?"

"Absolutely. What would my hours be?"

"The night clerk starts at 10:00 p.m. and is on duty until 6:00 a.m. Being the night clerk, your duties would be light; answer the phone, whether it's an outside call or room service, greet anyone who may come to the desk and help them in any way possible, some cleaning of our office and counter area. Tasks like that. Things are pretty quiet on the late night shift. We usually have entertainment in the lounge, but that would seldom concern you. The night clerk is really just a babysitter, a night watchman, if you will." Boatwright's manner indicated that the night clerk position was one that was well beneath him. But it wasn't beneath me. This sounded like a gravy job, and I wanted it. I felt like I was close to getting it, but I had to close the deal.

"This sounds like a very good position, and I'd like it very much. You'll find that I'm always on time and am very responsible and conscientious. You won't be sorry that you hired me." I was laying it on a little thick, but I figured it was what Henry Boatwright would appreciate.

"Welllll," Boatwright uttered thoughtfully. "You look like you'll do, and, since you can begin immediately, I have decided to award you the position."

"That's great. Thank you very much."

"Your pay shall be 45 cents per hour to start. You will be expected to wear black or dark colored trousers, a white or light colored shirt, and a tie. You are to report to this office ten minutes before your shift is to begin. And, since we are short-handed, for the present, you may be expected to work every night. We are hoping to hire another man soon, possibly in a part-time situation. But for now, you shall be the night clerk. That's assuming, of course, that you work out."

"Don't worry, Mr. Boatwright, you won't be disappointed." All of Henry's conditions were agreeable to me, the pay was fine, I supposed, and working every night wasn't going to be a problem. What else did I have to do? It sounded like a pretty easy job, and we'd have a steady income. Plus, I'd be working in the grand old Foesté Hotel, or should I say the Hotel Foesté?

Henry had me sign a few more forms and reminded me to be in the office by 9:50 p.m. I informed him that I would certainly be here at the appointed time, and we bade each other a good day.

I walked back up to my room. It was almost 2:30, and I decided I better get some rest if I had to work all night at my new job. Jerry wasn't back yet from his exploration, so I laid on my bed and, surprisingly, fell right to sleep.

Jerry rolled in about 4:30. I heard him walk over to his bed and plop down heavily, sighing as he did. His entry had awakened me, and I rolled onto my left side to look at him.

"I'm going to like this town," Jerry offered. "Lots of charm. Hey, how'd the interview go?"

"I start tonight."

"Terrific! We have an income. Let's celebrate. I found a great little restaurant over on that street over there. I'm starved. Let's go, you can tell me all about your new job." Jerry had jumped off the bed and was combing his hair.

Jerry's discovery was a little restaurant called Quality Lunch, a part of the Herziger Sausage Company, located at the end of 13th and Superior Avenue. While sitting at a table near the west wall, I could see why Jerry had recommended the place. A sign on the wall near us proclaimed, "Tender, juicy steak with all the trimmings - 20¢," which, of course, we both ordered. While we were eating I told Jerry of my meeting with Boatwright and the particulars of my new

60

job. He agreed that the job was suitable and could provide us with a steady income until his baseball career could be launched.

The 20¢ meal was well-worth the price, and we both decided that Quality Lunch would be a regular stop. We would have to sample the cuisine of the other area eateries, but the tiny diner on Superior Avenue would definitely be a keeper.

We walked briskly back to the Foesté where I was able to nap another hour and a half. Jerry woke me up at 9:30. I got washed, dressed in appropriate attire and called a "See you later" to Jerry.

"Have fun," Jerry chuckled, as I walked out to start my new job.

Henry Boatwright, himself, greeted me at the front desk as I arrived promptly at 9:50 p.m.

"Mr. Parker, welcome." Henry actually shook my and as I walked around the front desk to greet him. "It is very good to see that you are perfectly punctual. This is not something I have been able to say to everyone I hire." I could see that he was relieved to see me, probably having been rescued from spending all night at the front desk.

My formal training for the position of night clerk, Hotel Foesté took all of twenty minutes. Henry had me pin on a simple name tag with "Night Clerk" printed on the front, then proceeded to instruct me on my duties. He showed me where things were located, what to do when the phone rings, how to deal with customers or residents, how to check in guests, and a few other related instructions. He gave me a phone number I could call if I had any problems. Then he left. Amazingly, I was now in total charge of the Hotel Foesté.

I spent several minutes familiarizing myself with my new work area. For the next half hour or so standing behind the front desk, giving my best dignified and important impersonation. By midnight I decided to take a break. I went into the back room and took a seat at the rickety old desk. I poured a coup of coffee from the pot on the small table across from the desk. Henry had assured me that plenty of hot coffee would be a definite aid in my new position. In the first hours of my first night, absolutely nothing had happened. A few people had come and gone from the lounge on the other end of the lobby. It was Saturday night, after all. But no one had needed any assistance from the night clerk. The phone hadn't rung and nobody had approached the desk.

The night passed quickly. I had one phone call, a drunk who had the wrong number. Two people had come to the desk to inform me that I was new on the job, information I hardly needed. No one had asked for a room. Once the lounge closed at 1:00 a.m., I had virtually nothing to do. That suited me just fine. I could do nothing with the best of 'em.

At 5:45 a.m., I was standing proudly at my position behind the front desk awaiting my replacement. A few minutes later, a tall, sad faced man entered through the front door and walked slowly around the desk and said, "You must be the new night clerk. My name is Samuel Phillips. Mr. Boatwright told me there would be a new man." He spoke indifferently, barely looking at me, even as he shook my hand in introduction. He was tall and thin, and moved with a slow, ambling gait. I followed him into the back room, where he took a name tag from the left top desk drawer. "Clerk" was all it said. "I help out here once in awhile," Phillips offered in way explanation. "With all the men looking for jobs, you would think the Foesté wouldn't need my help. But they do. I don't understand it." It seemed like it took five minutes to get these words out; but I didn't care. My first night was now over, so I tossed my pin into the drawer, said good-bye to Samuel Phillips, and walked up to my room.

I quietly opened the door, not wanting to awaken a certain to be asleep Jerry. To my surprise, he was already up, dressed and staring out the window onto 8th Street.

"Howdy, partner," Jerry greeted me cheerily. "How was your first night?"

"Great. The toughest thing I had to do was tell a drunk he had the wrong number. I'm going to like this job."

"Hey, you need an assistant? I'm temporarily between assignments."

"Thank you very much, but I think I can handle it. Besides, this should have been my busiest night, a Saturday. It should really be hectic tonight."

Jerry just laughed. He was obliviously in very good humor. So was I. I had an easy job, bringing in a small but steady income. I was twenty-one years old. My best and only friend was Jimmie Foxx, AKA Jerry Wolff. Spring was coming. Soon I would be seeing my friend do what he does best, hit a baseball. Life, or whatever this was, was good. This was going to be fun.

We quickly settled into a routine. After my shift, Jerry and I would have breakfast at one of the numerous small restaurants that surrounded the Foesté. On 8th Street alone, we patronized Coney Island Lunch, Gmach's, Schmidt's Restaurant, the Sheboygan Dry Goods Restaurant, The Kresge Restaurant, and the small restaurant inside Bock Drug Store. On Michigan Avenue we visited Avenue Lunch, The Snack Shack, as well as our personal favorite The Quality Lunch. After breakfast, I would return to our room for a few hours of sleep. Later in the afternoon, Jerry and I would walk around town, familiarizing ourselves not only with the immediate surrounding area, but points a little farther out as well. We walked east to Lake Michigan a few times. Jerry was fascinated with the vastness of the seemingly endless water. He'd grow silent for long stretches as he gazed contemplatively at the waves as they methodically slapped against the shore. By 5:00 p.m. or so, we'd have supper at one of our favorite haunts, and then I'd take a brief nap before my late night shift. What Jerry did while I was sleeping, I never did quite discover. I know he was doing some light work-outs; sit ups, push ups, even some short distance running. I suspect he was doing some more extensive local discovery, maybe even making a few contacts. Jerry was a very out-going guy, and I'm sure he was meeting a lot more people than I was. I didn't mind. I figured we might be needing some of his new associates somewhere down the road.

Anyway, that was our routine for the next several days. We either found, or purchased a copy of "The Sheboygan Press" every day. In this way, we were able to inform ourselves as to what was happening locally and nationally. We didn't want to slip up on any generally understood news items. Personally, we were also trying to find new lodgings. We couldn't stay at the Foesté forever. I was making $3.00 a day, before taxes, and the room was costing $3.00 a day, which meant that all incidental expenses were coming out of our original $1,000.00 stake. Our daily search of the classifieds proved fruitless. There was nothing that looked at all promising. Then on Thursday the 4th, a new ad appeared, one that looked like a winner:

Huron Ave- Room and Board for 2 gentlemen. Garage if desired. Phone 1054-J

We had to act. There was a post-war housing shortage and this place probably wasn't going to be available for long. We didn't have a phone so Jerry and I walked down to the lobby. The regular second shift clerk was on duty at the desk. Bob Schmidt was about average in every way; average height, average weight, average hair, average everything. We had gotten average friendly with each other in the few days I had relieved him as clerk.

"Hi Bob, how's business?" I greeted him

"Hello, Dan. Oh, about average. You're a little early, aren't you?" he replied, smiling.

"A little. I was just wondering if I could use the phone for a minute. I know it's not normal policy, but this is pretty important." It was a little thick, but I felt it would be worth it.

"Well, I suppose it's ok. Just don't tell Mr. Boatwright. Use the one in the back room."

"Thanks, Bob." We walked into the back room and quickly dialed 1054-J. After the third ring, an older lady's voice greeted us with a customary hello.

"Hello, ma'am. My friend and I saw your ad in the paper about room and board for two gentlemen, and we were wondering if that is still available."

"Yes it is, but I must say that I've decided I can't provide the board. After I placed the ad, I realized I just can't do that anymore. I hope that's all right.

She had such a sweet and kindly voice, that I would have said yes even if it wasn't.   "That's quite all right. We are really just looking for a nice place to live."

"Oh, good. I didn't mean to mislead anyone." She actually sounded relieved. Heck, we were the ones that were relieved; at least we would be if we could get this place.

"We are very interested in seeing your place. Could we see it? And how much is the rent?" Jerry had been prodding me about the rent, so I had to get the question in.

"Without the board, I'm asking $20.00 a month, if that's ok?"

"That's fine," I very truthfully replied. "Could we possibly look at it tomorrow morning?"

"Oh, yes. I'm here all day. Is 9:00 good?"

"Yes, that will be fine." She gave me the address on Huron Avenue and I bade her a good day. I had to be on my best behavior, trying to make a good impression. Jerry and I didn't know the details of this apartment, but the location was perfect, and we wanted it.

We thanked Bob Schmidt for allowing us access to the hotel phone and went back, expectantly, to our room. Sixteen hours later, we presented ourselves to our prospective landlady. Her name was

64

Mrs. Blumberg, and she was the spitting image of Mary Gordon, the actress who played Mrs. Hudson in the old Sherlock Holmes movies. Old? They could still be making those movies, though I didn't think so. She led us up the stairs on the back of the house. The door opened into a relatively small, but well-appointed kitchen. Small refrigerator, an even smaller gas stove, table against the south wall, a few cabinets, virtually no counter space. The kitchen led into a small living room containing a small couch, an old-style rocking chair, and a couple of end tables. The simple bedroom held the two single beds framing a wooden nightstand holding a small table lamp. And there was a bathroom, something not all structures contained, I was surprised to learn. There were towels in the bathroom, and pots, pans, dishes, and silverware in the kitchen. It was perfect.

"Are you gentlemen from Sheboygan?" Mrs. Blumberg inquired in her usual grandmotherly way. Even as good-hearted as she appeared to be, she was attempting to deduce if we would be responsible, reliable tenants.

"We're actually from Milwaukee," I replied, citing our agreed upon company line. "But I'm familiar with Sheboygan, having visited here many times. I'm currently employed by the Hotel Foesté as night clerk. Jerry, here, will be playing for the Sheboygan Indians this summer."

"Oh, how delightful. I've never had a baseball player for a tenant. Came close once, in '39, but he ended up staying with a teammate of his somewhere else. It will be good to have the Indians back again." We had learned from the paper that the Wisconsin State League, in which the Indians were a member, had shut down for the war. This would be the first year of baseball in Sheboygan since 1942. "What position do you play?"

"I can play any position, Mrs. Blumberg," Jerry replied truthfully, "but my best position is first base."

"Oh my! You look pretty strong. I'll bet you can hit a lot of home runs."

"Sometimes. When I get hot," Jerry said with a smile. I had to turn away for fear of laughing in the dear lady's face. Having composed myself, I told Mrs. Blumberg that we were interested in the flat, if she would have us.

"Normally I ask for references, but I can tell that you're good boys, so I'd be delighted to have you."

We insisted on paying her for the full month of April, even though it was the fifth. She said we could move in any time we'd like, so we walked back to the Foesté, packed our few belongings, paid the bill, and walked back to our new home on Huron Avenue.

My Friday night shift marked the end of my first week as night clerk of the Hotel Foesté. I had learned a lot in my first week, not so much about being a clerk, for my duties continued to be light, but about the hotel itself. The mailing address was 930 North 8th Street, though there were three entries off Ontario Avenue to the North. The hotel contained 153 rooms, three dining rooms, and banquet facilities for 400. It was a hotel in the grand old tradition, being the permanent home for at least ten people. The hotel was also the home for a beauty shop, a public stenographer, a physician, a real estate agent, the Sheboygan Gas Company, and the Hotel Foesté Turkish Baths. Next door were the Hotel Foesté barber shop and the Hotel Foesté tap room. None of these establishments were open during my shift, which naturally made my job much easier. And quieter.

I was using some of my ample quiet time shortly after midnight of the sixth of April. A bachelor party had broken up about a half hour earlier in one of the dining rooms, and the hotel was comfortably quiet. I was sitting at the desk in the back room with my feet propped onto the edge of the desk, drinking my third cup of coffee and reading the latest issue of "The Sheboygan Press." No new prospective Sheboygan Indians had been signed that day, but the Wisconsin State League schedule had been released by Herman D. Long of Eau Claire, president of the league. It would be a 112 game season with most of the home games being played at night. Conflicts with other outdoor sports attractions had necessitated the shift to mostly night baseball. I couldn't help wondering what those "other outdoor sports attractions" might be. Perhaps, I'd find out one day. Anyway, the article went on to say that the team would be covering between 5,500 and 6,000 miles of chartered bus travel. The article concluded with an apropos comment from Manager Joe Hauser about his high hopes for the coming season.

I folded the paper and laid it on the desk. I had finished the coffee and was thinking about the upcoming season. Jerry and I had yet to present ourselves to Manager Hauser, offering Jerry's services to the local nine. I figured it was about time to do just that. Hauser ran a successful sporting goods store in town and was in the process of re-locating his shop from 522 North 8th Street to 916 North 8th, just a few buildings south of the Foesté. The grand opening was set for Friday and Saturday, one week hence, and Jerry and I were planning on attending. The first team workouts were scheduled for Wednesday, April 24, and I was thinking that it might be in our best interests to meet Mr. Hauser sooner than next Friday.

I was pondering all this as I reached for the pot to pour my fourth cup of coffee. My hand never made the pot. In fact, I almost dropped the cup, itself. I quickly set the cup on the desk, stood up and started walking around. I was actually shaking a little.

Joe Hauser. Why hadn't I thought of it before now? We wouldn't have to meet Joe Hauser. At least Jerry wouldn't. He's already met Hauser, exactly one lifetime ago, as Jimmie Foxx. Jimmie played with Hauser for a couple of years with the Philadelphia A's in the 1920's. Joe would recognize him immediately.

"He's going to recognize you immediately," I explained to Jerry at breakfast the next morning. We had stocked our shelves with groceries from Bensman's store the previous afternoon. Jerry had insisted on purchasing four boxes of the cereal Kix, which currently consisted of our entire breakfast. "He's going to recognize you right away!" Jerry was reading the back of the cereal box while shoveling in another spoonful of Kix. "Are you listening to me?"

"Sure." It was obvious he wasn't the least bit concerned.

"Aren't you the least bit concerned?"

"Nope, he'll never figure it out. Who would?"

"But won't he remember you from the old days? I mean, it's only been twenty years for him."

"That's right. Twenty years. Right now, Jimmie Foxx is almost forty years old, and Joe Hauser is going to know that. Look, I know Joe. At least, I knew him once. He's not the kind of guy who'll be able to put two and two together. Heck, who could?"

Jerry calmly kept on eating his cereal. He was ahead of me on this one. He was right, of course. How could a guy like Joe Hauser meet up with the twenty one year old Jerry and assume him to be the forty year old Jimmie Foxx? It might give him pause, but he'd never assume it was his old teammate. And yet, what will he think when he sees Jerry hit, field, throw, and run like the slugger he knew? While I hadn't thought of this dilemma in particular, I had had a week to ponder the paradox of time travel in which we had unexpectedly found ourselves. Jerry and I were pawns in some grand chess match, the rules and objectives of which, neither of us understood. And while we were thrilled and excited about our new lives and the possibilities presented therein, we, at least I, couldn't help feeling that

68

we were walking on eggs sometimes. That we would be "found out" at any moment. That we would be unmasked as shams, imposters. As quant as it was to walk the streets of Sheboygan, Wisconsin in April, 1946, to meet it's people and to interact in their lives, it was also an almost eerie sensation. I know Jerry felt the same way at times, because he has mentioned it to me. And yet, while we're in this together, it was different for each of us. While this was my town, and much of what was here I remembered from my previous life, there was absolutely no chance that anybody would either know me or recognize me. Don Jackson wouldn't be born for another eight years. But while nobody knew me, there were any number of people in town whom I knew. I had family in town, and I knew where they lived. Perhaps, surprisingly, I had yet to see anyone that I knew from my previous life. But it was only a matter of time. How would I react to meeting a relative or friend who may be twenty, thirty, or forty or even fifty years removed from our last meeting? How prepared mentally was I for such an encounter? I would find out soon; it was inevitable.

Jerry, on the other hand, had the exact opposite dilemma. While this was not his town, and except for Hauser, there was very little chance of his meeting anyone familiar, there were hundreds of people out in the world somewhere that he knew. And knew him. He had friends, relatives, neighbors, managers, teammates, business associates, one wife, one ex-wife, and one son. And one Jimmie Foxx. What must he go through whenever he thinks of his other self alive and available, somewhere. If I had a problem imagining how I would react to meeting a close relative who wouldn't know me from Adam, what torment must he go through when he thinks about the possibility of actually meeting himself? While that possibility is an extremely remote one, at best, it nonetheless, remains a possibility.

"Still, I suppose we'd better find out for sure. We should go over to his new store and meet him." Jerry had removed me from my reverie with his logical disclaimer. Of course, I had been thinking along the same lines.

"He's not in his new store, yet, is he?"

"He's not officially open yet, but he's spending most of his time over there getting ready. I've often seen him in there puttering around, not really seeming to be doing much."

"Could he be there today?"

"Probably. It's Saturday, but I doubt if that matters much."

After a few hours nap, and a much needed bath, I walked with my friend over to Joe's new shop near the Foesté. We had discussed

69

the possibility of disguising Jerry a little, maybe by combing his hair differently or growing a beard or mustache, but Jerry would have none of it. Like his former self, Jerry was strikingly vain about his appearance. He considered himself quite the ladies' man, and I'd occasionally kid him about it. He'd always taken it well; I wouldn't keep it up if he didn't.

It was about 11:30 a.m. by the time we got to Joe's place. It was handsome building. The obligatory glass display windows flanked the entry. Above the windows and entry, in cream and maroon glass was Joe's signature announcing the name of the store. It was a remarkably accurate replica of Joe's autograph, maybe three feet high and six or seven feet long. Even when he was into his 90'sJoe always had a bold, clear autograph. I had seen it many times, and it was remarkable.

Joe was in the shop, all right. We could see him bending over some boxes near the north wall.

"Do you want to speak for yourself, or should I do it?"

"Go ahead. I'll chime in where needed." We were both dressed casually, with Jerry wearing his blue baseball cap, which we hoped might help disguise him a little. We walked up to the door and tried it . It was unlocked. We walked in.

It was a long and narrow building. Glass display cases lined the store from front to back, almost like soldiers in formation. Some of the cases had merchandise in them, most didn't, boxes were everywhere. Hauser was still bending over a couple of boxes, the contents of which appeared to be some type of apparel. He hadn't heard us enter, so we had to rouse him.

"Mr. Hauser," I uttered.

"Aargh, who is it? We're not open yet," he growled. He had turned around and was looking us over.

"I know you're not," I continued. "But we wanted to meet you before the grand opening. My name is Dan Parker and this here is Jerry Wolff," we extended or hands and Hauser tentatively shook each in turn. "We wanted to meet you because we know that you're the manager of the local Indians baseball team, and Jerry here would like to try out for the team."

"He would, eh?" Joe responded, eyeing Jerry carefully. "Where have you played?"

"Out east, mostly," Jerry answered, quite truthfully, really. "Maryland, Pennsylvania, places like that."

"Any teams I'd've heard of?"

"Doubt it. Semi-pro, most of 'em."

70

"Uh huh. What position do you play?"

"Almost any. First base, third, catcher. I can even pitch if needed." This was surprisingly true. Jerry told me once that he pitched in about ten major league games in his former life. He said he had an E.R.A. under two. Of course, he was wild as hell.

"How old are you?" Joe finally replied after a too-long pause.

"Twenty one." Another long pause. Hauser was studying Jerry closely. Obviously, he was making his decision. And yet, it was more than that. Could I see a hint of recognition in those narrow eyes? Or was I just paranoid? Jerry and I just stood there waiting for Joe's assent. I wasn't about to start begging unless he told us to get lost. He didn't.

"Well, I only have about five or six men signed up so far. Things are taking a long time to come together. Haven't had a team the last three years, what with the war and all. Most of these guys were overseas for two, three years. Now, they're scattered all over the country. Still, I expect to have a pretty fair squad once all our prospects return their contracts. But, I'm not afraid to give a young guy a chance. I'm not going to offer you a contract, but if you turn out to be something, we'll be sure to work something out. First work out is the 24th, Wednesday, 9:00 a.m.

"I'll be there." Joe was still studying Jerry, and I didn't like the way he was doing it. There was recognition in those eyes, I could just see it. Then, finally, it came.

"You look just like a fella I played with for a couple years in Philly, back in the '20's. It's amazing, you look just like him."

"Really?" Jerry responded, warily. "And who might that be?"

"Fella named Joe Boley. Ever hear of him?"

71

"Joe Boley? Joe Boley! Joe Boley couldn't carry my spikes! I hit 534 home runs in my career. He couldn't have hit ten! Joe Boley!" We were walking back north on 8th Street, or trying to. It was tough making forward progress with one of us ranting like a lunatic and the other laughing so hard it was difficult remaining upright. For some reason. Hauser's mis recognition had really set off Jerry. But, I knew Jerry's perturbation wouldn't last long. It wasn't his nature. I had heard of Joe Boley, of course. He was a light-hitting middle infielder with Connie Mack's great teams of 1929-31. Hauser was gone by then, but he certainly could have played with Boley a few years earlier, and Jerry was right, Boley wouldn't have hit more than ten home runs in his entire career. "He better not call me Boley during these workouts, that's all I've gotta say."

"Once he sees you hit, all comparisons to Joe Boley will fly right out the window." I had recovered myself, and decided it was time to calm down my indignant friend. It worked, though, like I said, Jerry didn't stay in a snit for very long.

"Yeah, well, once he sees me play, he'll quickly realize I'm not Joe Boley." Jerry had calmed down considerably. In fact, he was actually smiling. "Hey, where the heck are we going?" We had turned west on Michigan Avenue and were crossing 11th Street. Across the street stood what, in a few years, would be called Dutch's Bar. In fifteen years, or so, my grandpa would be dragging the seven year old Don Jackson into Dutch's where I could have all kinds of fun sponging schluck of beer and playing bean bags and other assorted made-up games in the back room. Dutch's old German Shepard dog would lay in the southeast corner of the bar, and, sometimes, I'd go over and pet him, though he seldom moved from his spot. But now, it was the Joseph Murray Tavern. I had scouted out this part of town earlier in the week, and had noted this early edition of my old haunt.

"We're going to visit an old friend. At least we will if we're lucky." We walked up a few steps and entered the bar through the main entry oddly located in the northeast corner of the building.

As Don Jackson, I hadn't been in this bar in probably 45 years, but I can say quite certainly, that it hadn't changed much. Wouldn't change much, really. Same terrazzo floor, same tables along the east wall, same long, north to south bar, same smell. There were no bean bags, and no German Shepard dog, of course, but the place looked truly familiar. And that included the bartender. He was a short man, maybe 5'5" tall with a soft, round frame. He was probably in his upper 50's now. Dressed in light tan slacks and a white shirt with the sleeves rolled up to the elbow, he was washing a few glasses at the small sink, pausing occasionally to rub his left hand across the side of his mostly bald head. He dried his hands on a towel and walked over to the north end of the bar, where we had taken seats.

"Howdy, gents. What can I get you?"

"We'll have a couple of cokes," I answered.

"Why are we here?" Jerry asked me as the bartender went off to get our drinks.

"We're here to meet this bartender. You'll see." The stubby bartender returned with our sodas. "You're Winde Wangemann, aren't you?" I stated, more than asked.

"Sure am. Do I know you fellas?"

"Not really, but I know of you. You played for the Chairmakers, what, maybe twenty, thirty years ago? Infield, right?" I knew the answers, of course, but this was my way of introducing Winde to Jerry. Besides, I wanted to get him started.

"That's right," was Winde's surprised reply. "How could you know that? You guys can't be more than twenty one or two. You couldn't remember me."

"No, we don't remember you in the sense that we saw you play, but we've heard about you. My name is Dan Parker and this here is Jerry Wolff. Jerry is going to be playing with the Indians this year. Winde, here, was a tremendous ballplayer for the Chairmakers, the old name for the Indians." Winde's expression really brightened when informed that he was serving a ballplayer. After hand shakes, Winde started in.

"So, you'll be plying with the Indians this year, eh? What position?"

"First base, mostly. But I can play third, catch, or even pitch. I don't actually have a contract yet, but Mr. Hauser has allowed me to try out."

"So, you've met Unser Choe, have you?"

"We just came from his new store." Hauser was from Milwaukee originally, and after his major league career, became a minor league home run legend, hitting as many as 63 and 69 in one season. Underscoring his German roots, his fans called him "Unser Choe," or "our Joe."

73

"Never played for him myself, of course, but I guess he's an ok manager. Kinda grouchy sometimes. Won the league in '42, last time we had a team here. Not going to have much of a team this year, from what I know."

"Why's that?" Jerry asked warily.

"Well, the Indians aren't hooked up with anyone. In the bigs, I mean. The other teams in the league are hooked up with someone in the big leagues. Oshkosh is hooked up with Giants, Janesville with the Cubs. Like that. And Sheboygan isn't hooked up with anyone. These other teams have the big club send them players. Good players. We have to go out and find our own players. We get what's left. It hasn't hurt us in the past, but with the war, and all, it's caught up with us. From what I hear, we're going to be scrambling to come up with good players this year. Maybe you can help, young man."

"Maybe," Jerry responded calmly, but he was smiling slightly. Winde excused himself to serve beers to the only two other patrons in the bar, a couple of older men playing cribbage at the far end of the bar. Jerry and I silently finished our Cokes. Winde returned and talked briefly about his days playing for Bill Liebl and with Gummy Wilke, Buster Braun, Tommy Heilberger, and others I wasn't familiar with. He told us he led the Fox River Valley League in hitting in 1923, something I didn't know. This little-known and quite unimportant item actually impressed Jerry. At least a little. After maybe ten minutes of reminiscing, we got up to leave.

"Well, son," Winde said, "good luck to you. I hope you make the team and have a big season. What's your name again?"

"His name is Jerry Wolff," I answered, "and that's the last time you'll forget it."

74

Our second full week in 1946 passed by quickly and uneventfully, except, that is, for a semi-emergency trip to Bensmann's store by Jerry. We were out of Kix. I had worked fourteen straight nights at the Foesté. It was something I didn't mind at all and was greatly appreciated by Henry Boatwright. He's hinted a couple times that he might be receptive to moving me to the second shift clerk position, a move, he assured me, was a step up the Foesté ladder, but I politely re-buffed his efforts. I was quite happy as night clerk, and Henry hasn't pushed it much.

Besides rushing to the store for more Kix, Jerry continued his training regimen, working in some running with his calisthenics. He also has become a big radio listener. Every morning he turns on the radio at 8:00 a.m. to listen to "The Breakfast Club" hosted by Sheboygan's very own Don McNeil. Jerry was pretty excited when I told him that McNeil was from Sheboygan. I think he's beginning to feel like this is his town. Between 5:00 and 6:00 p.m. Jerry always has the local radio station WHBL tuned in for what are becoming his favorite shows. In that hour, in fifteen minute intervals, he listens to "Terry and the Pirates," "Dick Tracy," "Jack Armstrong," and "Sports Parade." I listen, too, of course, "Dick Tracy" being my personal favorite. After "Sports Parade" I usually take a brief nap before my shift at the Foesté.

Anyway, my fourteenth straight work day was Friday, April 12th. Henry relieved me promptly at 6:00 a.m. on the 13th, and, as usual, I walked slowly home. It was, without question, my favorite time of the day. It was only six blocks from the Foesté to our upper flat on Huron Avenue, but it always took a good twenty minutes for me to walk it. Normally, a bustle of activity, 8th Street at this hour was always empty and quiet. I enjoyed walking slowly north on Eight Street, occasionally stopping to look into a store window. Sometimes I would cross to the east side of 8th and go into North Side News, the only store open at that hour. North Side News would become Suscha News in my time, but this incarnation was considerably different. Maybe it was the Fountain service, a certain give-away that this was the 1940's and not the 1960's or later. I loved it. It was little early in the day for a soda or ice cream, even for me, but once in awhile I'd buy a newspaper or magazine, just to show my appreciate for the still all-too-foreign 1940's atmosphere.

I walked up the steps to our flat. Jerry had just finished squeezing orange juice and was pouring it into a couple of glasses. The bowls and spoons were in position. It was time for breakfast. Kix. Since I was, for the moment, the sole breadwinner, Jerry was perfectly content to do all of the shopping, cooking, cleaning, and washing. And I was perfectly content to let him do it. He was good at it. Besides, I knew this arrangement would be changing soon.

"Are you going to take a nap before we go?"

"Maybe just a quick one. If we get there by 11:00 or so, we can catch lunch somewhere downtown afterward." Jerry and I were going to the grand opening of Joe Hauser's new sport shop. We figured it would be good to keep Jerry's face in front of Hauser as much as possible before the tryouts. Besides, Jerry wanted to buy a few more pairs of baseball socks. And I needed a baseball cap.

The place was packed. This was the second day of the two day grand opening, but being a Saturday, the people, and fans, were out in force. The glass display cases, as well as the knotty pine walls were packed with sporting goods and apparel of all kinds. Hauser, himself, had attracted a small group of fans and well-wishers. He was obviously enjoying the attention.

Jerry found the socks he was looking for, and I selected a plain black baseball cap. We took our purchases over to the cash register for payment. The cashier was Joe's assistant, a fellow by the name of Harold Kaye. Kaye greeted us pleasantly and asked if we had found what we were looking for. We assured him that we had and paid for our merchandise. The crowd around Hauser had diminished to one, a paunchy, balding middle aged man who was in earnest conversation with the store owner and manager. An earnest conversation being no deterrent, we walked over to Joe. Jerry, as usual, was hanging back a little, so I had to carry the load.

"Good morning, Mr. Hauser. It looks like your grand opening is a huge success."

"Yeah," Hauser croaked, turning in our direction. "Say, we've met, haven't we?"

"Yes, we have. Last Saturday, right here, while you were unpacking boxes."

"Yeah, I remember. And you're supposed to be a ballplayer, aren't you?" Hauser directed somewhat sarcastically in Jerry's direction.

"That's right," I responded quickly. "His name is Jerry Wolff, and he's your soon-to-be star player."

"I've heard that one before," Joe came back, almost cruelly.

76

"I'm sure you have, but you'll be singing a different tune in a couple of weeks," I shot back almost as cruelly. He was beginning to irritate me.

Joe softened a bit. After all, we were customers, if nothing else. "Well..," he said, "if you're a ballplayer, maybe you'd like to meet a couple more. See those two guys in front of that display case? They've just signed up with the Indians. Why don't you go over there and introduce yourselves?" It was probably a good way to get rid of us, but we thanked him anyway and walked over to one of the display cases near the north wall. Two young guys were standing over the case admiring some baseball gloves. Coincidentally, one of the fellows was short, about my size, and the other was about Jerry's height, though not as muscular.

"Hi," I said, breaking their attention on the gloves. "Joe said you two fellows will be playing for the Indians this year."

"If we're good enough," the shorter one said, cheerfully. "We're signed up, but, heck, you never know."

"My friend here is hoping to play for them, as well," I returned. We exchanged introductions and handshakes. The shorter one was named Tommy Bartos, a double veteran, you could say. He was an infielder on the '41 and '42 Indians, as well as the veteran of the 9th air force division. The taller one was Buddy Krier, and, like Bartos a double veteran; 1942 Indians, and 1943-45 U.S. Army. A pitcher from nearby Random Lake, he pitched the Indians to the 6-5 victory over Green Bay in the final playoff game in '42.

Our conversation had moved outside to get away form the crowd inside Joe's store. After a brief lull, Bartos moved the discussion into a new area.

"So, Jerry, you're going to try out for the Indians, huh? What position do you play?" Bartos was eyeing Jerry curiously. Though he didn't know anything about him, Bartos was obviously intrigued by Jerry's size and physique. Being a ballplayer, he could see the possibilities.

"I can play anywhere needed. First base, third, catcher. I can even pitch, if needed." Jerry's stock answer and all positions Jimmie Foxx played a lifetime ago in the majors.

"Look," Bartos continued, "we've been holding some informal work-outs. Just a few of us who are in town. Me, Buddy, here, Charlie Schwab, Leslie Orr, Billy Dwyer, a few others, sometimes. You can join us, if you're interested. I'd like to see what you can do."

"Thanks, I'd love to," Jerry answered, smiling.

77

"Great. We're getting together this afternoon at 2:00 p.m. if you can make it."

"I can make it. Where?"

"Kiwanis Park. Know where that is?"

"I know where it is," I answered.

"Do you play, too?"

"Barely."

"That's ok. You can shag balls, if you want."

"Sounds great. We'll be there."

"Good. Two o'clock, then." Bartos and Krier walked off south on 8th Street. We walked north, back home for a quick, light lunch. My step was light as we made our way home. I couldn't keep from smiling. It was a beautiful Saturday afternoon. The sun was shining. A light breeze was blowing. And the adrenaline was flowing. I was about to see the great Jimmie Foxx in action.

It was maybe a mile from our apartment to Kiwanis Park. Jerry was decked out in the gray baseball pants, blue and white baseball shirt and blue baseball cap that were magically provided for us back in Fountain Park. Not being the ballplayer, I wore a pair of jeans, or overalls in the '40's vernacular, a plain white T-shirt and my new black baseball cap. I gallantly offered to carry the duffel bag on our walk to Kiwanis. We walked, mostly in silence, west on Huron to 17th Street, then south on 17th to Kiwanis. As we crossed Michigan Avenue, I, almost involuntarily, turned my head to the right. Yes, it was still there. The Michigan Avenue viaduct. Where it all began. At least, that's how I associated it. How long ago was it? A truly unanswerable question, if ever there was one.

Bartos, Krier and one other player were already at the park when we arrived. Krier and the other player were sitting on the first base bench putting on their spikes. Bartos was already standing, tossing a ball into his glove.

"Hi, guys," Bartos welcomed us. "This here is Charlie Schwab. Charlie, this is Jerry Wolff and Dan Parker." We shook hands. "Charlie plays first sack." That was for us. "Jerry can play anywhere. Dan doesn't play at all." That was for Schwab. I certainly couldn't argue with Tommy's logic; my attire betrayed me. As we were talking, another player had pulled up a seat next to Jerry on the bench. Bartos introduced us to Bill Scheskie, another veteran of the 1941 team. Scheskie was with Buddy Krier at some baseball work outs in Montgomery, Alabama, but both were released. A little smaller and shorter than Jerry, Scheskie played short and third.

"Dwyer can't make it. He thinks he's catching a cold and he doesn't want to risk being sick for the try-outs."

"Too bad," Bartos said to Jerry. "Billy's a real peppery player. You'd like him."

The obligatory play catch warm-ups opened the work-out. Bartos quickly corralled Jerry for his partner. I could see he was very eager to test the new guy. Krier and Scheskie paired up, which left Schwab with me. His initial disappointment was quickly dispelled when he saw how well I could catch and throw. From Bartos' description, he must have expected a total incompetent. The others also noticed and I could tell that they felt better about having me there. And that included Jerry. I was standing next to him, and it was

79

easy to see he was surprised. And impressed. This was the first time he had seen me with a baseball in my hand. He must not have expected much. Maybe in deference to Schwab, Jerry was using the catcher's mitt to play catch. I was using the fielder's glove.

After about ten minutes of catch, Bartos led us in some calisthenics and wind sprints. The five players were in pretty good shape and handled it well. I managed ok, but I didn't keep up as well with the others as I would have hoped. Still, nobody minded much, me not being a player anyway.

Infield practice was next. We actually had a player at every position. Schwab played first, Bartos was at second. Scheskie took short, and Jerry handled third. Krier did the hitting and I caught the throw in, Jerry and I having exchanged gloves.

It was quite an impressive display, really. Bartos was a slick glove man at second. He moved well and was a quick pivot on the double play. Schwab and Scheskie were more than adequate at first and short, respectively. And Jerry was nothing short of sensation at third, a position he seldom played in his previous life. Going equally well to his left and right, he made every play and every throw. And what throws! He had, by far, the strongest arm of the group.

"Man, that was terrific," Bartos called to Jerry as they were making their way back to the bench after infield practice. "Where have you been playing your ball?"

"Milwaukee, mostly," Jerry repeated the company line. Fortunately, Bartos didn't pursue it or we would have had to scramble for answers. I made a mental note to come up with more detailed personal histories for Jerry and me. I should have thought of this sooner, but I hadn't.

"Ok, let's have some hitting practice. Buddy, you hit first. Jerry you pitch to him. The rest of us find a position to shag." Bartos was a natural leader, not a bad quality for a middle infielder. I settled in left center field, next to Schwab in left. Bartos took short and Sheskie took third.

Jerry pitched to Krier and Schwab. He had a nice delivery and, generally, proved to be a good batting practice pitcher, laying most of his pitches in a good hitting area. Krier took over from Jerry and pitched to Sheskie and Bartos. All four hitters looked pretty good, starting slowly, then swinging harder the longer they were in the box. I handled the flies to me flawlessly. Schwab hit one over my head that almost rolled to the willow trees along along the banks of the Sheboygan River. The trees and the river acted pretty much like a wall in a normal ballpark. Schwab's poke to the trees was quite a shot.

Jerry was the last to hit. I'm sure Bartos wanted it that way, for some reason. Jerry selected a bat, took a few practice swings, and dug into the batters box.

There are things in life you can only dream about. Winning the lottery, running a 2:50 marathon, maybe, getting a date with Morgan Fairchild. Wistful fantasies that float through your mind when you're at peace enough to let them. But that's what they remain, fantasies. Hopeless dreams. Well, almost hopeless.

His stance was straight-away, feet planted about shoulder-width, arms held low, the bat actually resting against his right arm. My mouth got suddenly dry. Light chills slid down my arms. A fantasy became an actual reality. I was about to see the great Jimmie Foxx swing a bat.

"We'd better move back a little," I called over to Schwab in left.

"Yeah, right," he muttered, without moving back one inch.

Krier wound up and delivered his first pitch to Jerry. Surprisingly, Jerry squared around and dropped a perfect but down the third base line. Then he dropped another one down the first base line.

"We're not going to have to move back for those," Schwab called back sarcastically. I could only smile, not expecting a slugger like Jerry to be able to bunt so well. On the third pitch, Jerry took a nice, easy cut and rifled a shot between Bartos and Scheskie. Then one over Scheske's head. Then another. With a long stride and tremendous timing and bat speed, Jerry made it all look so effortless. And he was just warming up. After a few more line drives, Jerry started swinging harder.

The first was a rocket right at Schwab, who was barely able to get his glove up in time for the catch. The next one went sailing high over my head, landing at the base of a willow tree. The next one soared over Schwab's head, knocking a few leaves off a willow tree before landing about three feet into the river. The last one flew high over our heads, over the willow trees, landing, or rather, sinking into the middle of the Sheboygan river.

After that, Jerry cut down on his swing, content to fire medium range missiles in our direction. And then it was over. Jerry walked out of the box and tossed the bat on the ground. Bartos waved us in, and that was it.

Nobody said anything as the players changed their shoes. I was watching each of them. Silently lacing their street shoes, they appeared too stunned to say much.

"Where'd you learn to hit like that?" Bartos finally inquired quizzically.

"Milwaukee. Sandlots, mostly," Jerry returned evenly.

"How is it nobody's discovered you before? That's the best hitting I've ever seen, even if it was just batting practice."

Jerry's shrug opened the verbal volleys. With everyone raving and tossing questions Jerry's way, I, unobserved, walked out to third base and started pacing off the distance to the river. One hundred sixty steps. At two feet per stride, that was three hundred twenty feet, plus the ninety feet from home to third, making it about four hundred ten from home to the river, straight down the line. Jerry's final shot went maybe four hundred forty feet. With very little practice and old, soft baseballs.

Jerry was hungry after his workout, so we walked over to Herziger's for supper. In my brief absence, the fellows had invited Jerry to join them in their informal workouts. With the formal workouts less than two weeks away, the players were going to be stepping up their pace in an effort to be ready. Bartos had assured Jerry that more players would be joining them, as the try-outs got closer.

The word spread quickly. Monday's workout drew eight players, and Tuesday's, eleven. By Wednesday, the man, himself, paid a visit. Hauser sat by himself on the bleachers behind first base, saying nothing. Shortly after Jerry hit, he left. His uncharacteristic silence unnerved me. It must have been obvious that this was no Joe Boley he was observing. The bat flat against his right arm. The pronounced left leg lift. The slight hitch. The even, powerful stroke. The wicked follow-through. Was this a swing that Unser Choe Hauser could possibly fail to recognize? We could only hope his mind wasn't flexible enough to make the connection.

By Saturday morning, April 27, I had completed my twenty eighth consecutive night of work at the Foesté. Henry had asked a few times if I would like a night off, but I had politely declined. There was still no reason to take off. It was easy work, and I loved the working conditions. Who wouldn't love the Foesté? I almost wanted to spend as much time as I could there. I had to enjoy it while I could. In fourteen years, it would be rubble.

Formal work-outs had begun on Wednesday the 24th. Jerry was calm and relaxed while eating his Kix that morning. He was confident that his "old" skills had returned with him and well-aware that he was far-and-away the best player in the city. I walked with Jerry to the still-named Northside Park to take in the work-out.

It was a waste of time. About twenty five players showed up for the first practice. And one spectator. There wasn't much to spectate. Conditioning, throwing, and sliding drills dominated the day. A little fielding. No hitting. I spent much of my time admiring the recent improvements to the park. There was a new scoreboard in centerfield. The grandstand had been painted. New brick construction flanked the entry. Jerry later told me that the rest rooms were new, as was the knotty pine clubhouse which had more than twenty lockers. In short, once again, I was savoring the atmosphere of a shrine that was destined for oblivion. I didn't know whether to grin at it's glory, or cry for it's fate. In the end, I did neither. It was too cold. And windy. I left early. I managed to catch Jerry's eye and motioned that I'd see him later. He nodded and went back to work. I went home.

I skipped the next work-outs, waiting, instead, for the first exhibition game, scheduled for that Saturday, against Milwaukee Heil. A second game was scheduled for Sunday, also against Heil.

After the obligatory breakfast of coffee and Kix, Jerry decided to take a walk. I took a nap. I awoke at 11:30, Jerry having already left for the ballpark. I got dressed, had a quick bite to eat and headed out to the door, walking west on Huron Avenue to the Northside ballpark.

There was no admission, so I walked in, over to the third base side behind the Indians dugout. The players were just finishing their warm-ups, most hanging around outside the dugout. I had my choice of seats, so I sat in the third row of the grandstands. It was another gray, chilly day, which, perhaps, contributing to keeping the crowd down. Actually the "crowd" numbered fifteen. Hopefully, attendance would pick up a bit once the regular season started.

Before long, the Indians took the field. Amazingly, Jerry wasn't in the starting line-up. I could only speculate what that meant. With Jerry not playing, I didn't pay as close attention to the game as I expected. The Heil team jumped on the Indian starter, a guy named Brechen, for two runs in the first. The home team countered with three in their half of the first. It turned out to be a sloppily played slugfest, a typical initial exhibition game. Schwab, Bartos, and Scheskie all started in the infield and played well. The same couldn't be said for the catcher, a fellow named Woody Streski, who was conducting an on-going battle handling the offerings of the three Indian pitchers. It seemed he muffed as many as he handled cleanly. This would have been forgivable had he been a heavy hitter. Unfortunately, he couldn't do that either. I hoped Woody Streski wasn't the best catcher on the team.

By the bottom of the eighth, the Indians were trailing 14-12 but had runners on second and third with two out. Schwab was due up, but Hauser sent in a pinch hitter. Number three. Jerry Wolff.

I moved forward in my seat, the first time all game I was actually paying attention. Jerry walked slowly to the plate, took a couple of practice swings, and settled into the batter's box. The current Heil pitcher was a gangly right hander who threw pretty hard. He went into his stretch. And, trying to get ahead in the count, threw a fast ball in the inner half.

Jerry was ready. He whipped the bat through the zone and rifled a shot into the left centerfield gap, scoring both runners. Jerry trotted easily into second with a game-tying, two RBI double. Unfortunately, the next batter popped up, stranding Jerry's go-ahead run on second. Jerry played at first in the top of the ninth, but got no fielding chances. Neither team scored in the ninth, and it was mutually agreed to end the game in a 14-14 tie.

Hauser held a brief team meeting after the game, merely reminding the players about tomorrow's game. As the players slowly filed toward the clubhouse, Jerry walked over to me and said, "Wait for me, I won't be long." I nodded and sat back down in the grandstand. True to his word, ten minutes later, Jerry walked up the steps to the grandstand.

"Let's get something to eat," he said. "I'm starving."

"Me, too." It was late afternoon, and we hadn't eaten since breakfast. A bowl of Kix only goes so far.

84

We walked out of the park, down Superior Avenue, to Herziger's. The tiny restaurant had room, so we took a table along the west wall. We both ordered a hamburger, a bowl of chili, and a large coke.

"A couple of the fellas wanted me to go with them over to Avenue Lunch on Michigan Avenue for supper, but I politely declined," Jerry said, smiling," we haven't seen much of each other lately, so I figured we better touch base, so to speak."

It was true. I had hardly seen Jerry all week. Between the informal, and then the formal work-outs, our schedules weren't exactly conducive to sharing much quality time.

"What did you think of the game?"

"For a slugfest, I thought it was pretty boring. At least until you got into the game. Why didn't you start?"

"I'm starting tomorrow. Catcher."

"Catcher!"

"Why sound so surprised? I've done a lot of catching, even in the bigs."

"I know, but…"

"Hauser went with Streski today, just to confirm what he already knew; Streski can't play. He'll probably be cut soon. We can only carry twenty players. And that's only for the first thirty days. Then the team has to be cut down to fifteen."

"Fifteen? On the whole team?" It seemed like an awfully small roster, even for the Wisconsin State League.

The waitress brought our order, and we started to eat. Between bites we continued our conversation.

"We must have about thirty guys trying out right now, and a few more will be coming in next week." I could tell by Jerry's tone that something was bothering him. I asked him about it. He took another bite from his hamburger before responding.

"I know it's early and all that. I mean we've only had a couple of practices and one practice game, but… Well, I just don't think this team is going to be very good. We've got a couple pretty good players, Bartos, Scheskie. But, man! I know this isn't the bigs, but still. Once I start playing, I'm going to tear this league apart. I'll put up numbers they've never seen before." Jerry stopped talking briefly to finish his hamburger. "I guess what's puzzling me now, Dan, is why we're here. I thought I'd have it figured out by now. It can't just be so I can put up big numbers for a bad club."

I had no answer for him. Jerry's bewilderment underscores the differences between Jerry Wolff and Jimmie Foxx. I had noticed early that there were, indeed, differences. Jimmie Foxx would never be overly concerned with his purpose or destiny. He might question it briefly, but he wouldn't dwell on it. Jerry is genuinely puzzled by his purpose here. Even more noticeable to me were some of Jerry's habits. Jerry isn't nearly as outgoing and flamboyant as Jimmie. He also doesn't drink, isn't excessive in his spending, and hasn't even looked at a woman. And no cigars. That one I noticed immediately. A couple times I came close to asking him about these changes, but I couldn't bring myself to broach the subject. I probably will someday, but honestly, it isn't all that important. He's still a great guy and a good friend, and we both know that through it all, we are all we've got. Besides, I can't help wondering if I've changed in some way. I don't think so, but I'm probably not the best judge. Maybe it will be important some day. Maybe, but not today. We walked home and went to bed early.

I went to the Sunday re-match with Milwaukee Heil, a 5-2 victory for the Indians. Jerry started behind the plate, and not surprisingly, had a good day. He played flawless defense and threw out two runners trying to steal. He also went 3 for 3 with two doubles and a single. Hauser took him out after six innings and re-inserted Woody Streski. Who, again, was terrible. I can't help thinking he'll be gone soon.

The following Sunday, the Indians played their final exhibition game, this one against Manitowoc. In a typically sloppy early season game, the locals handled the visitors 17-10. Jerry caught the whole game and had three of the only seven Indian hits. After three exhibitions, I could only agree with Jerry's assessment of the team. This was an ugly game played between two very mediocre teams. The caliber of play had to get better. Jerry was so much better than anyone else, it wasn't funny. He was so good, I was, once again, concerned that Hauser might start smelling a rat. Or a Foxx. How could he help but see the similarities?

"Does Hauser smell a rat?" I asked Jerry bluntly, later that evening.

"I don't think so," Jerry replied, knowing immediately my object of reference. "He looks at me funny sometimes, but he's never said anything. Actually, he doesn't talk to me much. Except after today's game he told me I'd made the team and would be the starting catcher."

"You weren't worried, were you?"

"No, but there are a lot of guys trying out these days, and remember the team can only keep twenty players, and later, fifteen."

"That's really bare-boning it, isn't it?"

"Sure is, but this is the low minors, and fielding a team costs money. And it really hurts a team like the Indians. Remember, Sheboygan is the only team in the league that isn't affiliated with a major league team. So, we have to be more creative. Want to buy some tickets?"

"Tickets? Sure."

"Buck a piece. Sixty cents for the actual ticket and forty cents for the club, profit so to speak. Roth's idea. They're trying to sell 10,000 tickets to get the club on a solid financial footing."

"Roth? Is he the business manager?"

"Yeah, he and Hauser are holding this thing together."

"I'll take ten." I gave Jerry a ten spot and he forked over ten tickets. "Hey, how many of those do you have?"

"Fifty. Forty now."

"Maybe I can sell some of those for you at the Foesté. I'll check with Henry tonight."

"Great. That would be a great source of possible sales. It's even just down the street from Hauser's store."

Later that night, I checked with Henry Boatwright, who readily agreed to place a small sign near the check-in desk advertising the sale of Indian tickets.

"The Hotel Foesté is happy and proud to support such a worthwhile civic organization as the Sheboygan Indians," is how Henry put it. In the first two weeks, we sold over 500 tickets. This made Hauser and Roth very happy, and Jerry made sure they knew it was my idea to use the hotel for ticket sales, which made me a minor VIP with the Indians big-wigs. Since I hung around the park enough, they knew me and would actually even speak to me on occasion. What an honor. I suppose you have to take your respect when and where you can.

On late afternoon, Tuesday, May 14, I was sitting in the living room listening to "Dick Tracey" on WHBL, when Jerry walked through the front door and said, "Well, here it is. The final roster of the 1946 Sheboygan Indians." He walked over to me and handed me a sheet of paper with nineteen names on it. These names:

Bill Dwyer OF
Charles Schwab 1B
Leslie Orr P
Tommy Bartos 2B
Ray Kowalski IF-OF

Buddy Krier P
Bill Scheskie IF
Russell J. Woldon IF-OF
Orville Grub P
Wilbert Hackbarth 1B
Tom Tarpo P
Rog Forsterling OF
Jerome Hemauer OF
Al Grenert Util.
Jerry Wolff C
Bobby Holm C-OF
Bob Vales P
Lawrence Casper OF
George Landwehr P

Woody Streskie had been released earlier. No surprise. The team would play an 112 game schedule. Opening day was Thursday in Fond du Lac. It was about time.

"I want to thank you for coming to this first of two staff meetings of the Hotel Foesté. We, of course, would prefer to have held one, all-inclusive meeting, but we, understandably, need some of our people at their positions to continue with the top-notch service that our hotel has offered to Sheboygan and the surrounding area for more than fifty years."

Henry Boatwright was laying it on a little thick, perhaps, but I couldn't really blame him. About half of the staff had assembled into one of the three Foesté dining rooms to meet the new owners. The Reichert group had recently sold their interests in the Foesté to Buchholtz Hotels. As assistant manager, Henry had been selected to introduce the Buchholz brothers to the staff. In the month and a half I had been employed at the Foesté, I had never seen, met, or even heard of, anybody who ranked higher than Henry on the food chain, possibly because the hotel was in the process of being sold. And, I suspected, even with the Buchholz's on board, Henry's position wouldn't change much. They would need him, he was practically Mr. Foesté.

"And so, without further ado, I present to you the new manager of the Hotel Foesté, Mr. William Buchholz."

Polite applause greeted the middle aged, average looking man, who, thankfully, had little to say.

"Thank you, Mr. Boatwright. On behalf of my brother, Robert, I simply want to say how happy we are to be a part of such a fine establishment as the Hotel Foesté. We certainly plan no major changes, simply wanting to continue the excellent quality and service this hotel has provided for so many years. I realize that you have been a bit short-staffed for some time, so, hopefully, our presence will help lift the load a bit. As a word of warning; my family and I will be moving to Sheboygan and taking up residence here in the hotel. So, if you see three little girls tearing through the lobby wreaking all kinds of havoc, be patient. We'll corral them for you." The group chuckled at that. At least the new boss had a sense of humor. "Truly, the girls are very well-behaved and shouldn't cause any undo commotion. To finish, I'd just like to say it is good be here, and we're looking forward to meeting and working with all of you."

Another brief round of applause welcomed the end of his brief talk. We all mingled for awhile meeting the new owners. I was talking with second shift clerk Bob Schmidt, when Henry brought William Buchholz over. Henry introduced us, Buchholz immediately taking a moderate interest in me.

"Oh yes, Mr. Parker. I've been hearing about you," taking a quick glance at Henry. "You're new here, and you've worked how many nights in a row?"

"Forty nine."

"Forty nine. Well, that's quite a streak. You're one of these people I was indirectly referring to when I said we'd get a little relief for some of you."

"I don't mind at all. This is a great place to work. I almost can't imagine better working conditions." Again, a little thick, but I meant every word."

"Well, we will see what we can do. A third shift hotel position isn't the easiest to fill, so we're happy to have you. Keep up the good work."

"Thank you, sir. I will." We shook hands, and I excused myself as Buchholz turned his attention to Bob. It was 8:45 a.m. Saturday, May 18. With the meeting scheduled for 8:00 a.m. I had had two hours to kill between the end of my shift and the meeting. I walked slowly south on 8th street to Gmach's for breakfast, then back north to the North Side news to browse through the papers and magazines. Now I was tired, and I walked slowly home. Jerry would probably still be sleeping. The team had split it's two opening games in Fond du Lac, losing 11-1, then winning on Friday 6-3. Jerry's homer in the opener was the Indians only run. I hadn't heard the details of last night's game, only the score from a Foesté patron, shortly before the meeting.

The big home opener was scheduled for tomorrow afternoon, complete with parade and all the usual opening day ceremonies. The real home opener was today. The mental gymnastics behind this eluded me, and I didn't bother asking Jerry about it.

He was sitting in the living room reading yesterday's "Sheboygan Press." "Morning, good to see you again. How'd yesterday's game go?" I asked, plopping heavily onto the couch. "We won 6-3. Only had seven hits, they had eleven."

"And how'd you do?"

"Three for three. A homer, two singles, and a walk."

"Good job. That gives you six hits and two homers in two games."

"Yup. I have six of our eleven hits. My average is a cool 1,000." Jerry seemed indifferent to his quick start, probably expecting it all along.

"What's your impression of the team so far?"

"The pitching's been average, the fielding stinks and the hitting has been woeful. But it's only been two games. It might get better. I think some moves are going to be made. I can tell Hauser isn't happy with the make-up of the team. Say, why are you so late?"

"Meeting at the hotel to meet the new owners."

"They're not planning on making any roster moves, are they?"

"No, I think my job is safe. At least it will be if I get some sleep before reporting for duty. I'm going to bed."

"Coming to the game today?"

"Oh, yeah. I'll be there."

But I wasn't. My fatigue had kept me in bed until after 3:00 p.m., too late to catch the game. I'm usually good at getting up when I want, so I was pretty upset and disappointed at over-sleeping the first home game. Still, the grand opener was tomorrow, and I wasn't about to miss that one.

As it turned out, I didn't miss much in Saturday's game either, a 17-3 routing of the locals by Fond du Lac. Jerry had his third straight 3-3 with a homer game. After three games, he was the only bright spot on the team.

My fiftieth straight night at the Foesté passed uneventfully. A wedding reception in the banquet hall didn't concern me much. This was one easy job. After fifty night shifts, I've checked in six people wanting rooms, answered, on average, one phone call per night, given countless directions to various parts of the hotel, and had to call the police once when two drunks refused to leave the lobby after repeated requests to do so. I could get used to this.

I walked out onto Ontario Avenue (the staff never used the main entrance) and was greeted by a steady, annoying drizzle. This wasn't promising. The skies looked ominous. Today's grand opening was definitely in doubt.

I hurried home to find Jerry already up and looking out the living room window.

"Doesn't look good," was his greeting.

"Sure doesn't," I replied, shaking out my jacket. "We may not get this one in."

I went into the bedroom to change into some dry clothes. Jerry started some coffee brewing and got the bowls, spoons, milk, and Kix ready.

"What time does the parade start?"

"One o'clock. Dwyer's picking me up at noon."

"Picking you up? He has a car?"

"He and Jerry Hemauer are the only two players who have a car."

We finished our breakfast and washed the dishes. I kept looking out the small kitchen window while drying. "It's raining harder." The rain had, indeed, picked up. Because of all the planned festivities, I figured that if they were going to call off the game, they'd do it quickly. I told Jerry as much, and he agreed. We turned on WHBL to listen for any news. Since we didn't have a phone, there wasn't any quick and easy way for anyone to reach us.

We had only been listening for five minutes or so, when there was a knock on our door. It was Bill Dwyer.

"Just thought I'd pop over to tell you the game is off. The grand opening is now next Sunday, that's our next home game."

"Thanks for stopping by," Jerry said. "Care to stay and have some coffee?"

"No thanks, another time maybe. I've gotta go over and tell Bartos. He doesn't have a phone either. Oh, Hauser says be at the park tomorrow by 2:00 p.m. The bus leaves for Green Bay at 2:30."

"I'll be there." Dwyer said good-bye and went on his way. I went mine, too, in to the bedroom for a good long sleep. With no game, I could sleep well into the afternoon, which I did.

The next Saturday afternoon, I walked down Eleventh Street to the Joseph A. Murray tavern. I felt it was time to pay another visit to Winde Wangemann. With Jerry gone on a road trip, I was getting a little lonely, and I knew Winde would be good conversation. I hoped he was working. He was.

"Hi, Winde, remember me?"

"Sure do, you came in several weeks back, with that ball player, Jerry Wolff. See, you're right. I didn't forget it again. How could I, after the start he's had."

Jerry had indeed continued his hot hitting, though in limited competition. Three of the week's five games had been rained out. Victories over Green Bay and Janesville had pushed the Indians' record to 3-2, and Jerry's home run total to five, one in each game. People in town were beginning to take notice of the new Sheboygan Indian.

"That young man's getting to be famous awful quick. Lots of our customers have been talking about him, and they're all saying the same thing, 'who is this guy, never heard of him, where'd he come from?' And all I can tell them is he stopped in here awhile back and told me he was going to try out for the team. That seems to impress them, actually. You're his friend, what can you tell me about him?"

Knowing that area fans were eventually going to want to know all about the newest local sports star, Jerry had decided on a bare-bones, but believable tale. Winde would be the first to catch our spiel.

"I've only known him a few years. We met while working in a munitions factory out east. He was exempt from military service because of a severe sinus condition." This part was actually true. "We both played a little amateur ball there until about a year ago when we left the munitions factory and moved to Milwaukee. We got a couple factory jobs and played ball last summer in an industrial league. We heard that the Indians might be looking for ball players this year so a couple months ago, we quit our jobs in Milwaukee and came up here. That's about it." And that was it, Dan and Jerry's totally fabricated life story. We hated to lie, but we certainly couldn't tell anyone the truth.

The story was enough to satisfy Winde. He probably felt he had received an exclusive, something he could pass on to his customers. We talked baseball for awhile, with occasional interruptions due to Winde's bartender duties. I was about ready to bid my good-bye, when one final reminiscence stopped me short.

"Yup, Buster Braun was quite a pitcher all right. Pitched a long time for the Chairs, twenty years or more. Heck of a pitcher. White Sox were gonna sign him, but his arm went dead. He could've made it, I think. He pitched in that game when the three Athletics came to town, you know."

I did know, but I didn't want to let on. I almost breathlessly waited for Winde's take on it. "When was that?"

"Must've been '32 I think. Players did a lot of barnstorming after the season in those days. For some reason, Foxx, Simmons, and Cochrane came to Sheboygan for an exhibition game. Let's see, Foxx and Cochrane played for Two Rivers, and Simmons for Sheboygan. And old Buster pitched for our guys. Did good too, won the game 6-4."

"How did the three Athletics do?" I inquired, already knowing the answer.

"Well, Foxx and Simmons didn't take the game too seriously, and they only had one hit each, both homers. Black Mike played it like it was the seventh game of the World Series, went 5-5 against old Buster. Of course, Cochrane took everything pretty serious, I heard."

93

"So Foxx and Simmons hit homers, eh?"

"Yeah, that one Foxx hit. Never seen one hit that far in that park. Left center, high and outta sight. Someone said it landed on that street, what is it, Cambridge Avenue? But I don't know about that."

I smiled at the thought of it, and at what I might see yet this year. "Are you going to the game tomorrow, Winde?"

"Sure am. Gotta see your buddy. He must be pretty special."

"You have no idea."

The Indians lost Saturday's game in Oshkosh 15-1, Jerry's solo homer in the second accounting for Sheboygan's only run. That home run pushed Jerry's homer streak to eight, heading into Sunday's doubleheader grand opener versus Wausau. The second game was originally scheduled for Monday, but for some reason they moved it to Sunday, leaving Monday as a rare open date.

Jerry was in typical good humor that Sunday morning. "I think I'm going to have a good day today," he muttered, while devouring his second bowl of Kix. "I always liked twin-bills. You could really get good and warmed-up in 'em, get good and loose. I hit good in doubleheaders."

"And you don't otherwise?"

"Oh sure, but there's nothing like playing two. You going to watch the parade later?"

"I doubt it. I've got to catch a little sleep yet, you know."

"I know. If you're interested, here's the route." Jerry took a piece of paper from his back pocket and tossed it across the table to me. It was quite an extensive route. Starting at City Hall, it would head south to Penn Avenue, west to 14th Street, south to Georgia Avenue, east to 12th Street, south to Union Avenue, east to 8th Street, north to Michigan Avenue, and west to the park.

"Jerry, this is quite a parade. It must be a good three, four miles, easy."

"So I hear. I don't know some of those streets, but they tell me it's quite a distance."

"It is. I hope you'll be comfortable."

"I'll be fine. I've been in parades before."

"Well, have fun. I'll see you at the game. I'm going to bed."

A couple hundred people were in the park when I arrived, well before the parade of players and dignitaries. I've never been one for parades, so missing it wasn't much of a loss. I also knew there would be ceremonies celebrating the opening of the season, another event I could do without. But, I supposed, I could put up with it to watch the locals, and their star catcher, play two.

I walked over to my spot on the fourth row behind the Indians dugout on the third base side. It was light-jacket weather, so I took a seat and contentedly waited for the team to arrive. The newly-remodeled park was nearly identical to the one I played in and remembered, another lifetime ago. The brick outfield wall, light poles, scoreboard, dugouts, grandstand, even the field, itself, were identical. Only the ivy hadn't been planted yet on the outfield wall. That would come in a couple years. It was a truly beautiful park, more a stadium than a park. Like the Foesté, I wanted to grab onto it, somehow, latch on and never let go. So many times over the past several weeks have I had the same sensation. It's incredibly difficult to enjoy the ambience of a place like the Foesté, or the charm of a place like the park, without thinking of the destruction that awaits them. Perhaps, I've over-killed this quandary, but it's one of the very few draw-backs of our new lives.

After a few more minutes of sweet ruminations, the teams, dignitaries, and hundreds of fans finally arrived at the park. The fans filed into the stands, while the others proceeded out to the centerfield area where they formed a V in front of the flag pole. The flag was raised as the Sheboygan Municipal Band played the National Anthem. The group then proceeded back to the grandstand area, where players lined up along each foul line and the dignitaries fashioned a circle around home plate. Business manager Carl Roth served as emcee for a brief program of typically boring speeches by mayors, league executives, and other local big-wigs. Finally, Roth introduced Manager Hauser who gave a brief talk before introducing the players.

By this time, the park had filled up nicely. I later learned that about 2,200 people attended the grand opening, many of them, no doubt, there to get their first glimpse of the Indians newest star. Hauser's intro of the players was brief, only mentioning the player's name, position, and any past association with the club.

"Hi, pardner, mind if I sit here next to you?" I had been so engrossed with the introductions that I hadn't noticed Winde Wangemann walking along the aisle and up to where I was sitting. I was glad to see him and said so.

"Winde, of course, please sit down. Glad you could make it."

"Wouldn't have missed it. Had to work a little later than I thought."

A few minutes later, the Indians took the field, Jerry walking slowly from the dugout to the catcher's box behind home plate. I couldn't help thinking that in less than twenty years, I, or someone, would be doing the same thing. It was an eerie feeling, one I couldn't dwell on. Random Lake's Buddy Krier was the Indians starter, and he easily retired the side in the top of the first.

Tommy Bartos led off the bottom of the first with a soft single to center, then stole second on the first pitch. Bill Dwyer followed with a hard ground ball to the right of the second baseman who could only knock it down without making a play at first. It was surprisingly ruled an error, which couldn't have made Dwyer too happy. Bartos had moved to third on the play. For some reason, the Wausau pitcher pitched carefully to Wilbert Hackbarth, walking him on four pitches, loading the bases.

In twenty first century jargon, the park became "electric." There was an audible buzz in the air. People were clapping, yelling, shrieking, pleading. This was why many of them were here. An early season, present-day mighty Casey was stepping into the batter's box. Jerry took a few practice swings, and then settled into his now familiar stance. I was actually nervous, my heart pounding in my chest, my mind trying to will Jerry to hit the snot out of the ball.

"Well, this here is what I came for," was all Winde could say, but I could tell he was about as excited as I was.

I don't know if the Lumberjack pitcher had heard of Jerry's early season performance, though I suspect he had. It didn't matter since there was nowhere to put him. Pitching from the stretch, he tried nipping the outside corner with a slow curve but missed. He tried again with the second pitch but missed again for ball two. The crowed began to boo, not wanting to see their new slugger denied a chance to swing the bat. I had to give Jerry credit; those first two pitches must have looked awfully tantalizing, coming in there so slowly. They hadn't missed by much, but Jerry had a good eye and was a patient hitter, a rare combination in a power hitter.

Behind in the count 2-0, the Lumberjack pitcher couldn't afford to go to 3-0. The crowd was screaming and yelling in anticipation, hoping for one good pitch that Jerry could hammer. The pitcher slowly came to a set position, then delivered.

"Fastball," I muttered as he started his motion home. It was. And Jerry was ready.

The great Ted Williams once said that when Jimmie Foxx hit one it sounded like an explosion. He was right. The ball rocketed off Jerry's bat, high and fast and long, soaring far over the 391 foot mark in left center. The awe-struck crowd rose to their feet cheering and yelling like mad. Bill Dwyer at second, actually stopped half way to third, just to watch the ball climb ever higher, clearing the wall by a good sixty or seventy feet. For his part, Jerry simply tossed his bat away and rounded the bases at a moderate speed, head down, almost lost in his own world. This was, after all, 1946. There was no cocky bat flip, no egocentric admiration, no staring down the pitcher, no eternity to round the bases. In a seeming instant, Jerry was back in

97

the dugout accepting his teammates' congratulations.   Before descending the stairs into the dugout, he caught my eye and smiled. I could only return his smile and shake my head.

Winde hadn't joined in on the cheering and clapping. He was stunned, plain and simple.   As we sat down, he turned to me, an almost shocked look on his face.

"My God, that ball could have landed on Cambridge Avenue," he croaked. "I haven't seen a ball hit so far since…"

He didn't finish his thought. He didn't have to. Winde was connecting the dots. 1932 was fourteen years ago. Twenty five year old Jimmie Foxx had hit a similar shot off Buster Braun. Twenty five plus fourteen equals thirty nine. Way too old. Still, Winde knew that Jimmie had retired a year earlier, couldn't be the same guy. Could it?

All this must have been swirling around Winde's head while he silently watched the next three Indian hitters make out. I decided to say nothing. For now.

The rest of the game, afternoon, really, was anti-climatic. Staked to an early four run lead, Buddy Krier allowed only two runs and six hits in posting an easy 10-2 win. In the nightcap, seventeen year old George "Junior" Landwehr pitched well enough to garner an 8-5 Indian sweep. Jerry caught both games, going 6 for 8, adding another home run in the fifth inning of the second game, giving him homers in eight straight games.

Winde hadn't said much since Jerry's mammoth homer in the first game. Every time Jerry came to bat, he'd lean forward in his seat and study him as best he could. But he never commented on him.

We exited the park and into the cinder parking lot. Winde offered me a ride home, but I politely declined. He might want to "talk." I figured I might need some time to think about some possible answers to some possible questions. I told him I'd stop in at the bar in a few days and walked home. I needed to take a quick nap before my shift at the Foeste.

Jerry still wasn't home by the time I left for work at about 9:40 p.m. I wasn't too surprised. Today's doubleheader meant there was no game tomorrow, so I figured some of the players went out to do a little celebrating.

The Bucholtz's had promised to do some hiring, but, thus far, had only hired one part-time clerk. They did offer me a day or two off, but I declined, saying, truthfully, that I had nothing better to do. Like Henry Boatwright, the brothers didn't push it, probably glad to have a dependable employee in the night clerk position, hardly a plum job. About fifteen minutes into my fifty eighth consecutive day at the Foesté, one fifth of the team walked in through the front door. Jerry, Scheskie, Krier, and Bartos leading the pack, as usual, swaggered up to the front desk.

"How's our number one fan? What'd you think of today's action? Not bad, huh?" This was Bartos.

"Can I help you gentlemen?" I countered, feigning a mostly absent business demeanor.

"Yes. You can tell us what you thought of today's games, in particular, do you think that homer of Jerry's has landed yet?" Bartos again.

I had to give it to Tommy Bartos. He certainly was an engaging fellow, when he wanted to be. I went along with him. "I think without Jerry Wolff, you guys would be 0-8 instead of 5-3. And yes, I heard that the ball landed about an hour ago. What are you guys doing here? Come to keep me company?"

"Hardly. We were here earlier for dinner, great restaurant, by the way. Then we took a walk, right guys?" Nods all around. "We came back to see Arline." Bartos must have been the only one capable of speech.

Arline Terry was a young, very pretty brunette who played the Hammond organ in the hotel lounge. "Fashions in Melody" was the name of her act, and she was very popular. In fact, she had been held over by popular demand. I'd had a chance to talk to her several times during her stay at the Foeste, and had liked her a great deal. She was very personable, and I could see why her act might be popular.

"Enjoy the act," was my parting command.

"We plan to," Bartos voiced the sentiments of the group, all the while, sauntering over to the lounge. Jerry smiled and gave me a wink as he passed by. The guys looked pretty loose, or lubricated, more likely. Oh well, they earned it.

A few hours later, the show was over, and the crowd was filing through the lobby and out into the calm, mild night. The last to leave were the four Indians. They'd added a new teammate, Arline Terry.

"Hey, kiddo, we've got a new shortstop," Bartos yukked.

"So I see."

"We'd love to stay and visit, but we've got things to do, right guys?" General agreement from all, even Arline. As they were leaving, Jerry paused briefly.

"It's not what you think."

"Me? I don't think." But I did.

99

By the end of June, the team had settled into sixth place with an 18-22 record. Players kept coming and going with the only real constant being Jerry's hitting. After thirty eight games, Jerry was hitting .693 with 33 home runs and 65 RBI's. His season opening home run streak finally ended at 19 on Monday, June 10 when the Indians were shut out 4-0 by Appleton. Ironically, the streak ended on the night the park was dedicated "as a living memorial to the men and women of this country who served in the late war." Those words by Tom Kroos, the president of the Sheboygan Baseball Association, were part of yet another special ceremony at the park, complete with bands, dignitaries, and speeches. More than 1600 people braved rain, lightning, and generally miserable weather, to be a part of the dedication.

By 6:00 a.m. on Saturday, July 6, I had completed my ninety eighth consecutive night at the Foesté. The Bucholtz brothers had hired a couple more desk clerks, but neither was interested in subbing for me on the night shift. The brothers must have felt a touch guilty about not following through on their pledge to me because they gave me a 25¢ per hour pay increase. I took the pay increase and gladly kept my secret about the night clerk being the easiest job in town.

Jerry surprised me by meeting me in the lobby after my shift. They'd had a rare night off, a double header being scheduled for Saturday against Janesville.

"Hi, partner," Jerry greeted me. "How about some breakfast? Avenue Lunch should be open."

We had an atypical hearty breakfast, then decided to take a walk. It was a beautiful summer morning, so we walked over to Kiwanis Park. We walked past the playground area and over to the bleachers along the third base line of the northeast ball diamond. From these same bleachers we would watch the blue shirts play the green shirts. It was no coincidence. I could tell Jerry had something on his mind and wanted to talk.

"What do you do all day?"

"Huh?"

"What do you do all day? Since the season started, I haven't seen you all that much, and I was just wondering how you passed the time. Have you made any friends? Do you have a girlfriend?"

It was true that our schedules hadn't been conducive to spending any quality time together. Half the time he was gone on road trips, and when he was home, his time was spent mostly at games or with teammates. I had caught several of the home games, but with weeknight games starting at 8:00 p.m., it was tough for me to catch the game and still get to the Foesté by 10:00 p.m.

After thinking about Jerry's questions for a minute, I responded as best I could. There wasn't much to tell him, really. In the morning, after walking home, I'd have a quick breakfast (Kix, of course), then listen to the radio for awhile, going to bed, usually by about 8:00 a.m. I'd sleep until early afternoon, get cleaned up, and head outside for a walk around town. Sometimes I'd have lunch; sometimes I'd wait until late afternoon to eat. I loved walking around the downtown area, occasionally ducking into stores that might catch my interest. I was a regular at the Northside News, Kresge's, and Bock Drug.

I was always sure to be home by 5:15 so I could listen to "Dick Tracy." Currently, the Stooge and Mumbles were planning a jewel heist. I was confident Tracy would bring those rascals to justice. He hadn't failed yet. Jerry listened to my recitation in silence. He leaned back against the bleachers and let out a sigh.

"Sounds like you're not having much fun. Pretty boring, actually."

"Not really. I find it pretty interesting, actually. It's restful, relaxing, peaceful..." It was hard to describe the low-stress, comforting lifestyle of the '40's.

"No friends? No girl?"

"Just you. I've been meaning to go see Winde Wangemann, but haven't gotten around to it." I'd told Jerry about Winde's reaction to his mammoth home run on opening day. I had wanted Jerry's reaction to it, but he never offered it. I asked Jerry about Hauser. I figured, if Winde Wangemann is suspicious, someone like Joe Hauser has to be, as well.

"He doesn't talk to me much," Jerry responded. "Almost avoids me. I think I spook him a little. He knows who I look like, but also knows that I can't be him. That has to scare him some. He only talks to me briefly. Then just about game situations, never anything else, anything personal. Maybe he's just being protective of his minor league home run record. He has to know I'm going to beat it." In 1933, Joe Hauser hit 69 home runs for Minneapolis, a record that would stand until Joe Bauman would hit 72 a few years from

101

now. Hauser would dismiss Bauman's record, it being set in the low minors in Texas.

"A guy named Clements has been hanging around the team lately," Jerry said, shifting gears. "Robert Clements, I think it is. Supposedly, a field rep. for the Brooklyn Dodgers. He's been watching the team, touring the park, talking a lot to Roth and Kroos, things like that. Talk is, the Dodgers are interested in signing up Sheboygan as one of their Minor League teams."

"Of course, it's no coincidence that a Major League franchise becomes interested in little old Sheboygan the year you started playing for them."

"Hardly. The park improvements have helped, but I'm what they're after. If Brooklyn signs up the Indians, I become Dodger property."

"Do you think they'd move you right up?"

"I doubt it. They'd probably keep me here to keep the fans coming in. I mean attendance is way up, and it's not because they want to see a seventh place team. I just think my presence here would set the stage for a solid partnership in the future. And, they'll probably start sending players in to try to strengthen the team a little. There will be a real revolving door around here should they take over."

"And you know what next year brings."

"Jackie Robinson," Jerry realized immediately.

"And the Dodger teams of the next ten years will include players like Roy Campanella, Gil Hodges, Jackie Robinson, Pee Wee Reese, Duke Snider, Carl Furillo... And Jimmie Foxx."

Jerry slowly turned toward me and nodded. "I only played in the National League briefly, at the end of my career. It might be fun having another go at it."

The next morning, after a breakfast of Kix, orange juice, and coffee, I walked over to the Joseph A. Murray Tavern. Jerry had given the Dodger brass plenty to look at the day before, going seven for eight, with three home runs and ten RBI's in a double header sweep of the Janesville Cubs. After yesterday's talk with Jerry, and his subsequent performance, I knew it was finally time to see Winde Wangemann, and let him speak his piece.

The bar usually did a fairly good business on Sunday morning, and today was no exception. Winde was at the far end of the bar when I walked in, so I settled in at my usual spot at the north end and waited. After maybe thirty seconds, he spotted me and slowly walked over.

102

"Hi, Winde."

"Dan."

"I'll have a coke." Winde slowly walked over to fetch my drink. Placing it before me, he stood before me, waiting."

"I haven't seen you at the ballpark, lately," I finally said, truthfully.

"I've been to a few games. Sit on the first base side mostly. Your friend is having quite some season."

"Yes, he is. I told you he would," I replied, rather hesitantly. I was waiting for the outburst that wasn't long in coming.

"How is he doing it? Who is he? Where has he been? I mean, that home run he hit. I haven't seen anything like that since, well, since that day in '32 when those Athletic fellas were here. That stance, that swing, that power. Those home runs were just the same. He looks just like him, hits just like him. But it can't be him. The real Jimmie Foxx just retired last year, must be close to forty. This guy, tell me, Dan, truthfully, is this his son?"

"No, it's not his son."

"It's not, not him, is it?"

Winde was near tears, and I didn't want to lie to him, but how could I possibly tell him the truth? "How can it be him? Like you said, Foxx is probably forty by now." It was the best I could do. Not exactly lying, but not exactly answering the question either.

"You're hiding something from me, Dan. There's something awful fishy about all this."

I relented a little. I've never been a very good liar, and Winde was proving to be much more perceptive than your average bartender. Or average anything else, for that matter. Of all the people in town, all those who knew Jerry and seen him play, Winde was the only one who suspected. Or at least, the only one who let on.

"Winde, I wish I could tell you more, but I can't. Honestly, I can't," I said empathetically.

The little bartender slowly nodded his head, his suspicions at least partially confirmed. I finished my Coke and got up to leave.

"Look," I said, "There's plenty of season left. Maybe I'll see you at the park sometime."

"Sure, I'll be going to a few more games. I'll look for you."

"Good. I'll be watching for you." I left the bar feeling I'd done the best I could. I never saw Winde Wangemann again.

Jerry's hot streak continued well into July, though neither of us considered it a streak. With about half the season complete, Jerry's numbers were truly impressive: Batting average- .620, home runs- 52, RBI's- 109. Impressive, but not unexpected, at least for two city residents. Still, despite Jerry's performance, the Indians continued to wallow in seventh place with a record of 25-35.

Jerry's extraordinary hitting continued, and as we knew, the inevitable finally occurred. The July 20 edition of "The Sheboygan Press" said it all:

Indians Join Brooklyn

Dodger Field Rep. Robert Clements had, indeed, been in town scouting out the city and the Indians organization as a possible site for a Brooklyn farm affiliate. While the organization and the city and park were positive selling points, it was obvious to all concerned, it was Jerry as a commodity that drew the Dodgers interest to Sheboygan. "The Sheboygan Press" admitted as much in their write up:

Fresco Thompson, Dodger Farm Director, stated unequivocally, that Sheboygan's franchise and facilities were top-notch. He also did not try hiding the fact that Indian slugger Jerry Wolff was a major ingredient in the package.

The signing up of the Indians brought the Dodger Farm system up to twenty one teams, seven in class D. It also created a major sensation in the city of Sheboygan. People everywhere were talking of it. The clientele of the Foesté were talking about it for days. Most of the staff knew of my relationship with Sheboygan's most famous resident, as, indeed, Jerry was. In a few short months, Jerry had become a celebrity of the highest rank, and as his friend, I was treated with undeserved admiration and respect. Not that I minded. I was perfectly willing to accept any reverential looks people may throw my way.

It was a good time to be in Sheboygan, everybody was happy. The townspeople were happy, the players were happy, Joe Hauser was happy, Jerry was happy, and I was happy. I was twenty-two years old.

The rest of the season was anti-climatic. Jerry was accurate in two of his other assessments. The Dodgers were perfectly content to leave Jerry in Sheboygan for the remainder of the season. They felt it would help develop a solid fan base if he stayed. They virtually promised him an invitation to spring training next year. Dodger General Manager Branch Rickey was a shrewd judge of talent, which, to me, assured Jerry's rise to the Dodgers next year.

Jerry was also accurate with his revolving door theory with the Indians. The Dodger organization moved players in and out so fast, it was hard to keep up with them all. The end of the season Indian roster bore very little resemblance to it's season opening counterpart. Only Jerry, Bartos, Krier, Dwyer, and a couple others remained. The roster changes did nothing to improve the Indians' plight. The newest Dodger Farm team finished the season at 44 and 66, seventh place in the Wisconsin State League, one half game out of last. How a team with Jerry Wolff on it could be so poor was a mystery to me. Jerry finished the season batting .562 with 82 home runs and 202 RBI's, all records.

The season mercifully ended with a Labor Day doubleheader loss to Green Bay, 17-5 and 13-5. Two final exhibition games were scheduled to finalize the season. On Tuesday, the Indians lost a predictably lackluster contest with the La Crosse Stars 5-2. Jerry played third base and went three for four with a home run. A final game was scheduled for Saturday, September 7 against the local Pine Club team, proceeds to go to the players, themselves. Many of the Indians were planning on leaving town, but since we weren't going anywhere, Jerry agreed to play in the game. Or so we thought. By Saturday, we were gone.

We found ourselves, once again, sitting on a park bench, attired in period clothing, a duffel bag on the ground between us, and $500 in each of our wallets. We had the same names, but the year of our "birth" was now 1930, which, assuming consistency made this 1952. It was chilly and raw, probably making it early spring.

"Where are we this time?" Jerry asked, dejectedly.

"Not sure, but I can guess." I was just as down as my friend. I loved the Sheboygan of 1946. I loved the atmosphere, I loved the people, I loved the park, and I loved the Foeste. But, for all intents and purposes, they were all gone, unexpectedly gone. I had assumed that we had been planted there permanently, to pursue our new lives as we saw fit. Sitting on that park bench I felt foolishly naïve and frustrated. I wanted to continue working at the Foesté and enjoy the slower, more relaxed pace of life in 1946 Sheboygan. And I know Jerry was extremely disappointed by the transfer. He was looking forward to a restful off-season of celebrity status before joining the Dodgers in the spring. He truly had his heart set on playing with all those great Dodger players in Ebbets Field for years to come. And now he had a new city, a new challenge, a new team, maybe. We had to start the process all over.

"So, where do you think we are?" Jerry questioned, glumly.

"Milwaukee, I think," I replied, matching his mood." And if I'm not mistaken, were not too far from the downtown area."

"Milwaukee, huh? What are we doing here?"

"Beats me. But I suppose we better find out."

We were, indeed, not far from downtown Milwaukee. After walking for maybe fifteen minutes, we came upon the Pfister Hotel and decided it would be a good idea to check into a room and get our bearings. It worked last time.

Jerry confiscated a morning "Milwaukee Sentinel" from the lobby and took it up to our room. We paged through the paper, trying to acclimate ourselves to what was definitely March, 1952. It didn't take us long to figure it out.

"Looks to me like you'll be playing your baseball for the Milwaukee Brewers."

"Yeah, but who are they?"

"High Minor League team, associated with someone or other."

"So, the competition should be considerably better than last time with the Indians?"

"Should be."

The news perked Jerry up a little. He wouldn't be playing for the Dodgers, but he would be playing baseball. Assuming, of course, he would get the opportunity to play with the Brewers, which I hardly thought would be a problem.

After reading the sports section, I turned to the classifieds. It took only a minute to find the ad I knew would be there: "Night clerk wanted. Immediately. Good salary. Apply Pfister Hotel."

"Well, at least you have plenty of experience," Jerry muttered, chuckling.

"And I just have a feeling that I'll get the job."

"I wouldn't bet against it." After a few minutes, Jerry asked, "So where do those Brewers play?"

"Borchert Field, I think, but I don't know where it is."

"You say the Brewers are in the high minors, huh. I just finished helping the Sheboygan Indians hook up with a Major League franchise. What am I suppose to do with these Milwaukee Brewers?"

"The same, I suppose. I mean next year the Braves move from Boston to Milwaukee, you know."

"That's our purpose in all this? Help teams move from one city to another? So next we go to, what, Baltimore and then Kansas City, and then who knows where?"

"Seems that way," I replied some what forlornly.

"Well, I suppose there could be worse fates then that. Do you think we'll ever get back to Sheboygan?"

I had been thinking over just that question for the past several minutes.

When Jerry asked the question, I thought I had an answer. No, not just thought, knew.

"We'll be back, some day. I know it. Jimmie, the best is yet to come.

PART IV

1

Well, Craig, that's just about it. An improbable story, to be sure, but that's what happened, as best I could document it.

Needless to say, I got the job as night clerk at the Pfister Hotel, and it's just as easy as at the Foesté. It also proved to be surprisingly easy for Jerry to get a try-out with the Milwaukee Brewers. Making the team was no problem, and he's currently tearing it up for the local nine.

Anyway, that's not all of it. A few days ago, without telling Jerry, I decided to go back to Sheboygan for a visit. I finally decided what I wanted to do with this manuscript, and I wanted to find a reputable, established law firm to handle it for me. So, after my shift at the Pfister this morning, I took the train to my hometown.

Instead of taking a cab from the train station, I decided to walk. Before visiting a lawyer's office, I had a different visit I had to make. My very predictable visit was to the Foesté. I had to see it again. I had to walk down 8th Street again, past the still very familiar stores and shops, up to the entry of the Hotel Foesté, and into that marvelous lobby. And I had to see Henry Boatwright again. I had to apologize for my sudden, unexpected departure. They had been very good to me, and I felt I owed them an apology and an explanation, not that I could even make one up that would sound plausible.

It had hardly changed at all. I thought the wall coverings were new, but that was about it. Henry was talking with an older gentleman at the front desk. I waited for the man to leave, and then walked over.

"Hi, Henry," I offered shyly.

"Sir? Is there anything I can do for you?"

"Henry, it's me, Dan Parker. I used to work here."

"Dan Parker? I'm sorry, I don't know a Dan Parker, and we've certainly never had an employee by that name."

"I see," I stammered, somewhat shakily. "I'm sorry." I turned and quickly walked out of the lobby and onto 8th Street before the conversation got any stranger. Maybe I should have expected this, or at least something like it. Jerry and my situation was hardly what you might call normal, and unexpected twists should be, well, expected.

109

I had to be certain, so I walked over to the Mead Public Library, a few blocks away on 7th Street. At the circulation desk, I asked for a copy of "The Sheboygan Press" for July 20, 1946. After a few minutes, the lady brought up my request. I took it over to a nearby table to check out my supposition. I found the bold heading in the sports section, "Indians Join Brooklyn." I read through the accompanying article, the one I had read through several times only a few months earlier.

I was more saddened the shocked. There was no mention of Jerry Wolff or of his Herculean accomplishments in bringing the Indians into the Brooklyn fold. I returned the paper and asked for a couple more from "last summer", just for confirmation. Again, there was no mention of Jerry. Nothing in any of the game write-ups or box scores, which, of course explained why none of his current team mates or coaches had ever heard of him. Some one would have heard of him and remembered him after only six years. We thought it strange, but never seriously questioned it.

I will have to tell Jerry, I suppose. I will have to tell him that, for the record, Dan Parker and Jerry Wolff never lived in Sheboygan, Wisconsin in 1946. All those incredible on-field achievements never happened. All the wonderful people we met and knew don't know us from Adam. But we'll know it all happened. We'll know why Brooklyn wanted to sign up Sheboygan. That'll be good enough for us. It will have to be.

So, that's it Craig. Believe it or not. I'm finishing this at the library, before I seek out my lawyer. Then I'll take the train back to Milwaukee, back to my new, most recent life.

Who knows where Jerry and I might pop up after this period.

Maybe we'll run into each other again some day, Craig. But, if we do, you probably won't remember.

Free Dreams

PART V

1

I placed the manuscript on the night stand, leaned my head back on to the pillow and stared up at the ceiling. What was I to make of this. I had expected weird, but this was well, off the charts. And yet, I believed it. Don just wasn't a big time leg puller. What would he get out of it? A good laugh at my expense? Hardly.

Many a thought passed through my head over the next few days. I finished off the remaining two days of the school week in a state of mental numbness. Fortunately, none of my teachers or fellow students, seemed to notice. Not very flattering, actually.

Still, I didn't care. I was trying to decide how to handle what Don had written, as well as what to do with it.

By Monday morning I had a plan. I couldn't sit on this forever. I needed someone else to read this, someone with no family connections. After school on Monday, I went to one of those print places and had two copies made, just in case. In case of what I don't know, but just in case. After fourth hour English class on Tuesday, I asked my teacher, Mr. Collins, if I could see him briefly after school, and he agreed. I like Mr. Collins, and was interested to get his observations on Don's manuscript. Would he find it believable? (Probably not) would he consider it great writing? (Probably not) would be consider it laughable? (A definite possibility) Still, I didn't care. Holding onto it for my own private enjoyment (enjoyment?) just didn't seem to be the right thing to do. I don't know what Don really intended for me to do with it, but I just had to explore a few possibilities.

"Hi Craig, what's up?" Mr. Collins greeted me as I walked into his classroom after school. "You're not having a problem with anything are you?" he said with a smile.

"No, not really," I replied while taking a copy of the manuscript from a vinyl folder. "I would appreciate it very much if you could read this for me and give me your opinion.

"What is this exactly?"

"I'd rather you just read it and tell me what you think."

"Okay, I can do that for you. It might take me a few days, but I'll get it read."

"Thanks. There's no hurry. Let me know when you're finished. I'll see you in the morning."

"You bet."

With that, I left the room and headed home. I had actually been a little nervous about the whole thing. I felt a little reluctant to part with it, but deep down, I knew I had to do something. I needed another viewpoint.

A couple days passed without Mr. Collins saying anything to me about the manuscript. I wasn't surprised. I mean teachers have a lot more important things to do than read something like that. Heck, I figured it would take a couple weeks before he would get around to it. So I was surprised when after Friday's class he asked me to stop by after school.

As I walked up to his classroom after school, I expected the worse. Maybe he didn't even bother reading it. Maybe he read part of it and didn't bother reading the rest. Maybe he read it all and would be kind to me about "my" writing ability. Would he believe any of it? Hardly.

Mr. Collins was sitting behind his desk, paging through Don's manuscript. I walked over to a front row desk and sat down. And waited. Finally, after a few minutes, he got up from his chair and sat on the corner of his desk, one leg dangling alongside.

"How did you come up with this?" he asked, gravely. The expected question, but hardly the expected demeanor. A chuckle, maybe, or a shake of the head, but this was a serious question. I hardly knew how to react, so I simply shrugged my shoulders.

"This is quite remarkable, Craig, in many ways. It's imaginative. It's coherent. It's well-written. It's incredibly entertaining. I mean, this is really excellent."

Now I was really thrown for a loop. I think my jaw actually dropped. I wanted to say something intelligent, but the words just weren't there. "Thanks," was the reply I managed, and sheepishly at that. After a few seconds, I was able to compose my thoughts and ask the question I needed to ask.

"Did it sound believable to you?"

112

"Absolutely. You made the weirdly impossible seem very believable. An impressive feat of fictional writing."

"Thank you." So he didn't believe a word of it. Of course who would?

"Look, ah. Not many people know this but I have a friend who happens to be a literary agent. His name is Julius Marks. I think he'd be quite interested in this."

And that's how it all started. Mr. Marks loved the manuscript, found a publisher for it, quickly made a pretty sweet deal for me on it, and I got rich. The book has sold I don't know how many million copies, and was quickly made into a major motion picture.

To date, the movie has grossed over $150 million and climbing, while winning four Academy Awards including best picture, best director, best supporting actor, and best adapted screenplay.

I've been on Leno, I've been on Letterman, I've been on in NPR, I've been on C-SPAN, among many other talk and television shows. I've become a national phenomenon. Boy literary genius. The kid with the incredible imagination. I've long-since stopped trying to convince people of its truthfulness. Of its reality. Whatever. I was rich and famous. Just what everyone wants.

It was early June, a pleasant day, finally, after another chilly, rainy spring. Warm and sunny meant it was a good day to take my dog Fido (really) for a walk. I was back home again after the latest round of appearances and interviews.

My mom and dad, newly retired due to my financial success, were taking a cruise somewhere around Alaska. Don't ask me why. My sister, the doctor, had recently opened a practice in Milwaukee and was busy as heck. That was good, because she didn't need to tap into the Craig Mand treasure vault, not that I would have minded, I have plenty to last a long, long time, unless, I blow it, which I won't. Anyway, after finishing with Fido's walk, I had a quick lunch, and planned to rest and watch a little TV. Fame is great, but I was getting a little sick of the travel and the hectic pace.

I had no sooner settled into my favorite recliner and turned on the TV when the phone rang. I resisted the temptation let it ring and got up and answered it.

"Hello," I mumbled.

"Hi Craig, it's Don."

"Craig, are you there?"

"Yeah, I'm still here," I replied shakily. The last person I expected to hear on the other end would have been Don. I sat back down in my recliner and waited.

"Sorry I startled you, but there was no really good way to present myself to you."

"No, I understand. Jeez, I have about 1000 questions," I stammered.

"We have to talk. Three o'clock at the big tree. Can you make it?"

"Sure, right."

"We'll see you then."

And that was it. Short and sweet. Or maybe not so sweet. He seemed pretty terse. Could he be upset with something.

What could he be upset about? And what is he doing here? He did say we'll see you, that means Jimmie is with him. Jimmie Foxx. I'll actually get to meet Jimmie Foxx. Or will I? What if that wasn't Don on the phone? What if it was a crank call? No, settle down don't get paranoid.

It did sound like Don. No, I'm sure it was him. I had been pacing, so I sat down again. Three o'clock. An hour and one half away.

I managed to kill enough time and then hopped into my car for the ride over. I knew which big tree he was talking about. It was a large silver maple that had once been located in the extreme right center field corner of what had once been called Legion Park. The park had once served as the home-field for the local team from 1924 until the late 1970s when it was purchased by American Orthodontics for expansion of its company.

Most of the park was torn down except for part of the brick outfield wall. And, of course, the silver maple still stands. Why it had been accepted into the field of play is anyone's guess. Maybe just to give it some character. That's something the park always had, character.

I parked on Cambridge Avenue, just north of 18th St. and the big tree. I got out of my car and walked south on 18th St. to the big tree. No one was waiting for me. This section of 18th Street had no streets intersecting, so they had to be coming from either the north or south. And just how would they be coming? Car? Cab? On foot? It was 2:45. I was early, so I leaned against the tree and kept scanning left and right, over and over again hoping to spy something that might signal their imminent arrival.

I was getting nervous. What would they look like? According to Don's manuscript, both are about 22 years old and feeling good about it. I only knew Don when he was in his 40s and 50s, so this could be a real eye-opener. And the thought of meeting the young, strong Jimmie Foxx was almost intimidating. What do I mean almost? I started pacing looking each way for any hopeful sign. A couple cars rolled by on the seldom-used street, but no Don and Jimmie.

Finally, I saw two figures slowly approaching from the south. One was a little taller and stockier than the other, so I figured it had to be them, Don being shorter than Jimmie. As they drew closer, I became less certain. I had tried to prepare for anything, and that's exactly what I got. They were both smiling as they stopped in front of me.

I can only imagine the expression on my face, though it must of been really something, because it had them on the verge of laughter.

"Hi Craig, good to see you," Don said, shaking my hand and giving me a friendly pat on the shoulder.

"Good to see you too," I managed to stammer.

"And this, as I'm sure you know, is Jerry Wolff, a.k.a., Jimmie Foxx."

"Glad to meet you, at last," Jimmie said as he extended his hand for a firm but not painful handshake.

"This is really an honor," I croaked, a true fan to the end.

Don thoughtfully let me take in the sight before me before proceeding. And what a sight! My youthful, 22-year-old cousin was dressed in a navy blue T-shirt with dancing men on the front, dark tan shorts, sandals, and a well-worn, blue and white baseball cap that I recognized as an old Philadelphia Athletics cap.

Not bad. Modern. Cool. Sharp. On the other hand, I'll try to describe this. Jimmie was wearing an impossibly colorful Hawaiian shirt, beige shorts, sandals, a wide-brimmed straw hat complete with a purple hatband, and wrap-around black sunglasses. To complete the picture, he was smoking the longest Panatela cigar I've seen in this non-smoking era.

"I'm in hiding," Jimmie smirked, as if reading my mind.

"Sorry," I replied, "I wasn't expecting, I mean..."

"No problem," Jimmie came back, smiling, as he had been the whole time. He really seemed to be enjoying our encounter.

"What are you doing here?" I finally got out, one of the seemingly thousand questions I had for them.

"Vacation," answered Jimmie still smiling. I must have looked doubtful, for Don confirmed his friend's quick reply.

"No, really. At least it's the best we can come up with. We're not told anything, you know, but we are getting pretty good at surmising things."

"How long have you been here?"

"A while." Don was being purposely vague. Probably something they both were used to by now. "How are your folks?" He asked quietly.

"Good. They're on a cruise to Alaska right now."

"And Molly?"

"She's great. She just started her practice down in Milwaukee."

My cousin nodded slowly, somberly looking downward. "And my mother?" he whispered, as if afraid of not only the question, but the answer.

Don's mother had been frantic, at first, desperate to find her missing son. Since those early days, she's settled into sort of permanent malaise, still hopeful of locating her only child. I said as much to Don, not knowing how he would react to such disheartening news, but he just kept looking down, nodding.

"Are you going to see her?"

"We can't do that," he stated flatly.

"Why not. It would ease her mind tremendously knowing you were okay. She doesn't believe the story, you know. She thinks I just made it all up to help her feel better. But if you showed up looking like you do with Jimmie, here, with you, I think she'd feel better." Jimmie had taken off his sunglasses and was looking closely at his friend. Don raised his head and shook his head slowly. "That's not why we're here."

"How do you know? Maybe that's exactly why you're here."

"No, that's not why." Jimmie, not smiling anymore, nodded his head in agreement.

"This is why," and handed me a large manila envelope I hadn't seen until then. "The further adventures of Dan and Jerry, or whatever you care to call this one. By the way, how did you come up with the title Long Ago and Far Away?"

"It's a line in a Janis Ian song. I always liked the sound of it. I take it you've seen the movie?"

"We saw it a couple days ago. We kept hearing about this great movie that was currently playing that just happened to be about two guys who get transported back in time to 1946 Sheboygan. We quickly figured it out."

"We are pretty smart that way," Jimmie added with his engaging smile back in place.

"How'd you pull it off?"

I could see where they would be pretty surprised to find that Don's manuscript had not only survived it's travel forward in time, but that it had been made into a successful book and motion picture. To answer Jimmie's question would have taken more explanation and time that I cared to give. "Pure luck," I finally volunteered. "I showed it to my English teacher, and he knew someone who was a literary agent who managed to get it published. It just took off from there."

"Amazing. I didn't know if it would even get to you, much less this. I take it you're doing well on all this?"

"Very well," I nodded.

"Come on. Give. How well?"

"A couple million, and climbing."

"A couple million!" Jimmie gasped, dropping his cigar in the process. "Dollars?"

"Of course dollars. I got a nice payout on the book, plus a very small percentage of the movie profits. It's adding up. How did you like the movie, by the way?"

"We thought it was terrific. Very well done. And four Oscars to boot, including best picture? Truly remarkable."

"Hey, don't forget my acting Oscar," Jimmie quickly added.

"Oh, of course. We can't forget your Best Supporting Actor Oscar. It's been a running joke for the last few days."

"Yeah, well, that guy couldn't have done it without me. And why only a supporting Oscar? I was the star of the picture."

"Another running joke."

They were giving sly smiles to each other, and I couldn't help admiring their true camaraderie and friendship for each other. It was obvious they really liked each other. I suppose they would almost have to, to endure what they have probably been through together, adventures, I imagined, that would be detailed inside the manila envelope I currently held in my hand.

Jimmie lit another cigar to replace the one he had dropped, while Don, arms folded across his chest, was pawing at something on the ground with his foot. "So, ah, how are Finney and Hugo," he asked tentatively. Finney and Hugo where his pet cockatiel and cocker spaniel, respectively. After his disappearance, Finney had gone to live with his mother, while we took in Hugo. Sadly, both had died recently and the expression on my face must have adequately answered his question, for he simply turned away and walked a few steps back-and-forth, head down. Jimmie removed the cigar from his mouth and sadly looked down.

"Look, we have to get going. We still have things to do," Don finally said, composed once again. Jimmie was back to smiling, silently blowing smoke rings skyward. I didn't want our time to end; there was so much to talk about and yet, all I could think of saying was, "I'd love to see you hit."

"Perhaps you'll get the chance," Jimmie replied. "We'll be around for a while yet."

"You will?" I happily answered. "How do you know?"

"We are getting a pretty good sense of what we have to do in a certain place and how long we have to do it. It's just something we know," Don replied, while Jimmie nodded his head in agreement.

"How can I get in touch with you," I wanted to know.

"You can't. We'll call you in a couple of days, long enough for you to read what's in that envelope." Don and Jimmie in turn shook my hand and started to turn away.

"Do you need a ride somewhere?" I asked, hoping to find out where they were staying.

"No, we're fine. Oh, and Craig, please don't follow us, okay?"

"Sure, no problem." And I meant it. I watched as they walked slowly south on 18th St., and having nothing else to do, walked back to my car and drove off.

My head was a mental mess as I headed home. Being now late afternoon, I drove through McDonald's for a bag of nourishment. As I gnawed through my Big Mac and fries at the kitchen table, I tried to relive everything that happened. I had so many questions I had wanted to ask, but had asked virtually none of them. Heck, I had more questions now than before. I had wanted to ask Jimmie so many questions. Was Lefty Grove really so ornery? Could the Babe hit 'em farther then he could? What was it like playing in all those great old parks? How did he like Sheboygan? And on and on. Looking back, it seems that he had had a strange attitude toward our meeting. Well, not strange, really, but a sort of bemused bearing during the whole thing. He had that cock-sure grin during it all, as if he found it all pretty humorous. Or as if he knew something I didn't, which he certainly did. They called him the Beast because he could hit a baseball so far. Lefty Gomez claimed Jimmie had muscles in his hair. And yet, he didn't look that big. About 6 feet, 185 maybe, his listed playing height and weight. But compared to some of today's players, not that big. Still, I don't doubt that he could hit them as far as anyone. I sure hope I get the chance to find out.

And Don. He seemed so different, and not just because he was now about my age. Distant is maybe a good word for it. He and Jimmie have been through a lot, and even though he was back home in present time, both must feel an incredible amount of disconnect. Maybe they are growing weary of the time travel. Of course, Don always has the possibility of bumping into people he knows, hoping, probably, that they won't know him.

I wonder if that has happened already. Still, all the questions about his time in 1946 Sheboygan never got asked. And, I'm thinking that by the time I read the manuscript in the manila envelope laying on the chair next to me, I'll have a whole lot more questions to ask him. Then there's the one question that's been bugging me since they're departing. It's something Don said right at the end. "We still have things to do." What could two not-even-alive men have to do right now?

I wish I would have followed this up with Don, but he almost certainly wouldn't have told me. He wouldn't even tell me where they were staying or how to contact them. Way too many questions. I sure as heck hope I get at least a few of them answered.

I finished my Mac-meal and walked to the front door to bring in the mail. I was used to getting at least some mail, and today was no exception. Besides the usual junk mail, I had three solicitations for personal appearances, and two for radio interviews.

I also received a request for a donation to the local Sheboygan Athletic Association for use toward their ballpark improvements. Wildwood Baseball Park had replaced our venerated Legion Memorial Park as the local baseball park and, understandably, continually needed upgrades to make the park a comfortable and entertaining place to watch a ballgame. Since my success, I have received innumerable requests for financial assistance from seemingly every organization imaginable, but this one struck closer to home, so I will probably send them something.

I dropped the mail on the kitchen table, picked up Don's manuscript and sat down in my favorite recliner. And sat there. And looked at the manila envelope. And sat there. And looked at the manilla envelope. For some reason, I simply couldn't pull the manuscript from the manila envelope and start reading. I was a little afraid, I think. After reading of their previous adventures, I felt a certain degree of trepidation about learning of their latest.

Besides, I was tired. Tossing the manila envelope onto the couch, I flipped on the TV and started watching the Yankees-Red Sox on ESPN. Soon I was nodding off, and realizing my best bet was to just hit the sack, I turned off the lights and TV, and padded off to my room.

I dreamed I was pitching in the old Legion Park here in town. The park was torn down long before I was born, but the dream seemed to capture the atmosphere of the park as I imagined it. Dreams can be very hazy and illogical most times, but this one was remarkably clear. The hitters I was facing were various major leaguers, and I was doing very well; nobody could touch me. With two outs in one of the middle innings, I received the ball back from the first baseman after an out and turned to face the next hitter.

Standing in the batters box stood the smiling, cigar smoking figure of Jimmie Foxx. I toed the mound carefully and looked in for the sign. Fastball. Jimmie dug in and waived the bat several times across the plate. "Let's see what you have, sonny," he growled out at me, still chomping on his cigar, blowing smoke rings through his smile. I was determined to wipe that casual, cocky smile from his face. Imagine, him smoking a cigar while hitting. That would be like a high jumper jumping in his sweats. Pure arrogance. I went into my wind-up, reared back, and fired my best heater. Jimmie's bat whipped through the hitting zone, meeting the ball with a loud explosion. I turned and watched in awe as the ball sailed over the centerfield wall, over the houses along Cambridge Avenue, landing on the street somewhere. I turned back toward the plate, and Jimmie was still standing there, watching the result of his effort.

"Nice try, kid," he said, as he flipped his bat aside and started rounding the bases, smoke rings rising slowly skyward as he ran. After crossing home plate he stopped, took the cigar from his mouth and said, "Great park you had here. It'll be back." With that, he walked slowly toward the dugout.

I kept thinking about my dream over a nutritious breakfast of apple juice and a peanut pershing. It was a weird dream. Haunting. An omen maybe? Of what? Did Jimmie say, "It'll be back" or "I'll be back?" Does it matter? Maybe an answer will be found in the manuscript. Or, maybe not. I finished my hearty meal and settled into my favorite recliner. Taking the manila envelope, I slowly, cautiously, removed the papers inside.

Again, for some reason, I was somewhat frightened about what I was about to read. Something strange was going to be revealed in this manuscript. I could feel it.

I was never more right in my life.

Part VI

1

"I'm getting a little sick of this."

    We were sitting on a bench in Minnehaha Park in Minneapolis, Minnesota, September, 1960. Another minor-league baseball season had concluded, and, as usual, Jerry had put up some phenomenal numbers, this time for the hometown Minneapolis Millers. This was our fourth stop in our ever-predictable efforts to bring major-league baseball to cities looking to prove themselves "Big League."

    Since leaving the Sheboygan of 1946, we have spent summers in 1952 Milwaukee, 1953 Baltimore, 1954 Kansas City, and 1960 Minneapolis. The Braves, Orioles, and Athletics had followed us into town in each succeeding year, and, we both knew that in 1961, the Senators would leave Washington and be anointed the new Minnesota Twins. In each city, I was able to secure an easy night clerk job in a local hotel, while Jerry wowed the locals with hitting displays heretofore unseen on area diamonds.

    As much fun as it had been, it was beginning to get stale. Of course, we still had no control over our "comings and goings," but I knew where Jerry was coming from. We needed a break.

    "We need a break," Jerry decided. As they say, great minds think alike. Actually, I don't believe great minds think alike, but that's a discussion for a different time.

    "I mean, I like playing baseball and all that, but it just seems like we're going around in circles, you know?"

    "Yes, I do know, but I don't think there's anything we can do about it."

    "We can try. Hey, maybe the big boss knows about our concerns and will give us a bit of a break."

    "Maybe."

    "If not, what's our next move, you think?"

    Well, let's see in '58 the Dodgers and Giants moved to the coast. The Senators move from Washington to Texas. The Pilots move from Seattle to Milwaukee. And the Expos move from Montréal to Washington."

"That's still a lot of stops," Jerry offered, somewhat dejectedly.

"It is. But I don't think we're going to any of them."

"Huh? What? What do you mean?" Jerry replied, with more than a little bit of hope in his voice. "

"Just a feeling. I think if we were going to one of those places, we would have been gone by now."

"Hey, that's right. We always have been in the past," Jerry came back, excitedly. "So what do you think? Where are we going? Are we going to stay here? What do you think? Your instincts are really good on these things. What do you feel?"

Jerry was almost babbling now, but I understood his excitement. A possible chance to do something a little different had me intrigued as well. But, I didn't have any answer for him, and I told him so. He just nodded.

We sat on our bench a few minutes longer, then walked closer to the waterfall, a central feature of the park. We watch the falls for a few minutes, the water cascading down to the rocks below.

"Are you getting a headache?" I asked Jerry. He turned to me nodded and smiled.

"Me too." Lately, this was a sure sign the vertigo would hit, and we'd be on our way. We were right. A few moments later, the spinning started, and we were gone.

I arrived first, sitting on a, now expected, park bench, located in what appeared to be a grassy sitting area. Not a park really; a few trees, a bench or two, people milling around. It was warm. Summer. As usual, after a transfer, I checked my clothes and wallet. I was wearing a heavy, brown tweed suit, black oxford shoes, and a snazzy Ivy League cap. I checked my wallet, more of a pocketbook, really. One hundred dollars in older bills.

Interesting. As our travels increased, so, too, did our expense account. At our last stay in Minnesota, we had several thousand dollars to work with. My guess is that we had gotten our request for a brief vacation. We wouldn't be here long, however, wherever "here" was.

After a few minutes Jerry arrived, the soft "pop" signaling his presence.

He was dressed much like me; a dark gray suit, black shoes, derby hat, and a full brown beard. Having never seen Jerry in a beard, I was quite surprised, but thoroughly amused.

"Hi," Jerry uttered, after first checking our location and his appearance. "Do you know where or when we are?"

"Not really. The '20's or '30's I'd say, but where...?"

"This place looks a little familiar. I wonder if," and stopped. He looked stunned. Jerry got up slowly and turned around. "Damn," he whispered, obviously stunned by the site. I got up and turned also. And stared. Even a novice to the area like me, knew immediately where we were. We were standing near the corner of Lehigh and 21st St., Philadelphia, PA. Across from us stood a French Renaissance-style building, complete with thick white columns, arched windows, red-brown bricks, and a domed tower. It looked more like a church cathedral than what it really was, one of the most famous baseball parks in history; Shibe Park, home of the Philadelphia Athletics.

I turned toward Jerry to get his reaction. What must he be thinking? This was his home park for many years. The scene of so many of his greatest triumphs, back to life again, just for us. He was still staring, almost solemnly at the park. After several moments, he finally mumbled, "Shibe Park." I just nodded.

He looked at me with a combination of sadness, wonder and even fear stretched across his face. Just as I did, he knew what this meant. For our "vacation," we were to watch a baseball game. A baseball game featuring the Philadelphia A's and their great star Jimmie Foxx playing on their home field, venerable Shibe Park. He was about to watch himself play Major League baseball.

For the first time since we met, I saw him visibly shaken. A man who never seemed to be bothered by anything, was bothered now. I couldn't blame him. I would have been bothered too.

"What the heck is this?" Jerry was rubbing his face, finally noticing his new, thick beard. "I've never had a beard!" He looked so comical rubbing his hand over the beard, that my amusement over it returned.

"You look like one of the Smith brothers. No, I got it, James Garfield.""

"Who? This thing is spoiling my striking good looks."

One thing was certain about my good friend. He doesn't stay bothered long.

"I know, a disguise, right?"

"Probably. It seems we've been granted our request for a brief vacation."

"Brief? Why brief?"

"We only have $100 in our wallets." Jerry quickly checked his pocketbook and confirmed the amount. "We might only be here a day or two."

"Then I suppose we better get moving."

We crossed Lehigh and walked up to one of the numerous ticket windows. While Jerry looked down and avoided eye contact with anyone, I purchased two reserved seats for three dollars each. Located eight rows behind the first base dugout, the teller assured me we would have an excellent view of not only the field, but the hometown Athletics as well.

We left behind the hordes of fans walking up and down Lehigh, all of them rattling on about their A's particularly, and baseball in general, and walked through the turnstile and into the main concourse. Once inside, the feeling of having entered a church vanished completely. People scurried everywhere, chattering as they went. Hawkers made their pitch for popcorn, peanuts, ice cream, scorecards and pennants. With Jerry still staring at the concrete stadium floor, I bought a scorecard and pencil for $.25, and led my near-sightless friend to one of the stairways leading to the main grandstand.

"Come on, you can't keep staring down all afternoon. Nobody is going to recognize you in that get-up. Besides, we're here to see a ball game."

126

"I know. But this idea of watching me play ball, well, I don't know."

"You'll be okay. Besides, maybe we were sent here for a reason besides just a vacation. Everything has always worked out well in the past, hasn't it?"

"Yeah, I guess. But I still don't like it."

We walked to the top of the steps, and I got my first look at Shibe Park. What did I expect to see? An off-white infield and foul lines? A light gray outfield, scoreboard and stadium façade? Dark gray seats and bleachers? That's how all those old, long-gone baseball parks looked in the books I had back home. It's funny how modern-day people think of the old days as a series of black-and-white images, possibly broken up by a little drab coloring now and then. We fail to recognize that color has been around forever. It just hasn't been captured on film until relatively recently. And so it was with Shibe Park.

I stood at the top of the steps and gawked at the majestic beauty of this glorious ballpark. Lush, green grass spread throughout the infield and outfield, creating an image of almost velveteen beauty. The light brown dirt of the infield looked smooth as glass, a bad hop grounder a seeming impossibility. The dark green seats and bleachers were in perfect repair and immaculately clean. This was one great ballpark, as I knew it would be.

Being informed that we were holding up traffic, we quickly found our seats in the eighth row and settled in. I continued to marvel at the park. The whole park was basically rectangular in shape, completely double-decked except for the right-field wall, which was 12 feet of concrete. Fans across N. 20th St. could watch the games for free from their living rooms or from their roofs, at least until the mid '30's when Connie Mack built his famous "spite fence." Twenty feet of iron was erected atop the 12 feet of concrete already in place, denying the freeloaders of view of the game.

The park was quirky, like so many of the old-time, long-gone parks. The park's dimensions were 334 feet down the left field line, 331 feet down the right field line, and a whopping 468 feet to dead center field, thus giving the park that rectangular look. Despite the large dimensions, Jerry had told me that the ball always carried well and that he loved hitting here. He said this despite the fact that the pitcher's mound was a towering 20 inches high and that there was a lengthy 90 feet from home plate to the backstop, factors that favor the picture. It was a classic old ballpark, and I loved it.

"I think I remember this game."

127

Jerry's statement brought me out of my fascination with the park, and reminded me there was an actual game to be played between two actual teams, and an actual date. The program told us it was Saturday, August 29, 1931, and that the opponents were the New York Yankees. The Ruth, Gehrig, Dickey, Lazzeri, Gomez Yankees. Those Yankees. And I was about to watch them play.

"Hey, I said I think I remember this game."

Once again Jerry's statement snapped me out of what was proving to be a non-stop daze.

"Sorry. This place seems to have some kind of mesmerizing effect on me. You remember this game?"

"Actually, I remember the game just before this one, the famous 'Grove Tantrum' game."

"I thought Lefty throwing a tantrum was a regular occurrence if he didn't pitch well."

"True, but this one was a whopper. He was going for a record 17th win in a row but lost one to nothing, to the Browns of all teams."

"Hey, I remember reading about that. Al Simmons was out and the sub miss- played a fly ball and the only run scored."

"Jimmy Moore. Boy, did he feel bad. Simmons had a bad ankle and was back in Milwaukee. Boy, did Lefty let it rip in the clubhouse afterwards," Jimmie chuckled.

"He ripped off his uniform, threw bats, balls, shoes, gloves, his uniform, benches, water buckets, you name it. He broke chairs, lockers, shower heads. Then, typical Lefty, he blamed it all on Simmons for not being in left field to begin with. "Simmons would've stuck that ball in his back pocket" he said. Boy, was he mad. Anyway, I think this is his next start, against the Yankees."

I finally turned my attention to the field, where the pre-game warm-ups were winding down. I saw the great A's catcher Mickey Cochrane, glove in hand, walking toward the dugout. I saw his counterpart, Bill Dickey chasing after a loose ball near the home plate screen. I saw Yankee second baseman Tony Lazzeri trotting in from second base, followed closely by the immortal Lou Gehrig from first. And, I saw the one and only Babe Ruth swinging a couple of bats in front of the Yankee dugout. All of them, future Hall of Famer's, here in a time when the Baseball Hall of Fame wasn't even a thought, much less a reality. To say I was in awe of the entire situation would be an incredible understatement.

I asked Jerry about the numbers on the backs of each team's uniforms. Baseball historians are uncertain about the introduction of numbers on uniforms, so I was somewhat surprised to see them.

"I think this might have been the first year we had them. The Yankees had them a little earlier."

Jerry appeared to have gotten out of his funk and was watching the players, players he knew all too well, walk off the field toward their respective dugouts. A man with a large megaphone walked toward home plate, turned around and barked out the starting batteries.

"For New York, Gomez pitching, Dickey catching. For Philadelphia, Grove pitching, Cochrane catching." And that was it. No announced starting lineups, no national anthem, which made sense since we didn't even have a national anthem yet.

After a few seconds, the A's emerged from their dugout and ran out onto the field. I watched as Lefty Grove slowly, determinedly, strode toward the pitching mound. Surprisingly, there was not a huge crowd for such a game, and I could hear a few catcalls.

"Kicked over any water pails lately?" And "that was a bush stunt Grove, but you are a busher, aren't you?" There were also a few reminders about his appearance, his origins, his mother, observations not needing repetition here. For some reason, I got the impression that these remarks were coming from the Yankee dugout. Regardless, Lefty undoubtedly heard them, and he literally sneered as he delivered his warm-up pitches.

Mickey Cochrane fired the ball to shortstop Dib Williams, the umpire yelled out "play ball" and we were underway.

The game, itself, was vintage Lefty. And Jimmie. Firing bullets, Grove struck out Sammy Byrd, Joe Sewell, and Babe Ruth in the first inning, Lou Gehrig, Ben Chapman and Lynn Larry in the second, walked Bill Dickey, then struck out Tony Lazzeri and Lefty Gomez, before getting Byrd to pop out. Ten batters, eight strikeouts.

Meanwhile, Grove's counterpart, Lefty Gomez found early trouble, surrendering five runs in the third, highlighted by Jimmie's three-run triple. With one out and one on in the fifth, Jimmie strode slowly to the batters box, this time to face Yankee reliever Ivy Andrews. Next to me, Jerry sat forward slightly in his seat, an indication to me that something special may soon occur. I sat gazing at the batters stance I'd seen hundreds if not thousands of times before. I saw the basically upright stance, bat resting on his shoulder.

I saw the slight hitch in the swing as the ball rushed toward him, and, finally, I saw the ball rocket high and far over the left field wall for a two run homer. Beside me, Jerry was standing and chuckling, and I couldn't help giving him a high-five to celebrate. I had finally

129

seen Jimmie Foxx hit a long home run. Not Jerry Wolff. Jimmie Foxx. Against the vaunted Ruth-Gehrig Yankees. In Shibe Park. As good as it gets.

Lefty cruised through five innings before finding trouble in the sixth. With one out, Lefty gave up hits to Byrd and Sewell before walking the Babe. That brought up Lou Gehrig with the bases loaded. Grove tried sneaking a fastball by him, but Gehrig was ready and rifled a grand slam home run over the right-field fence. Lefty was immediately lifted for a reliever and stalked angrily towards the dugout where he proceeded to kick the water cooler, balls, gloves, and anything else not nailed down, before raging into the clubhouse.

Jerry was once again shaking his head and chuckling, "That's our Lefty. We kinda got a kick out of it, actually."

A's reliever Rube Walberg finished off the game in fine fashion, holding the heavy-hitting Yankees hitless the rest of the game, preserving a 7 to 4 is victory. Grove got the win, giving him a record of 26 and 3. Gomez took the loss, leaving him 16 and 8.

As soon as the game ended, I hustled down to the fence next to the A's dugout. About midway through the game, I had gotten a pretty good idea, and I was about to give it a shot. Stationing myself next to the dugout, I watched as the players trotted in towards their dugout.

"Hey, Jimmie. Jimmie," I yelled as Double X neared me. Only a little surprised, I watched as he came over to me. Extending my hand, I said "Hi, Jimmie, I'm a big fan of yours." With his customary big smile, he grasped my hand and crushed it into his, a phenomenon I had experienced many times before.

"Why, thank you. A guy can't have too many fans."

As he was about to leave, I called out, "Hey, Jimmie, I'd like to buy your cap."

"You want to buy my cap?" He asked comically. "What for?"

"Souvenir," I answered, truthfully.

"How much?" He smiled.

"50 bucks."

"50 bucks! That's a heck of a lot of money. I could buy 4 or 5 new caps with that. Easy."

"Deal?"

"Deal. I'm not supposed to do this, but for 50 bucks. What the heck." I handed over $50 from our stash, and gladly received his old, sweaty A's cap. "Wear it in good health," he chuckled and walked quickly into the dugout.

130

Jerry had been watching all this from our seats, not far from the dugout. "What was that all about?"

"I just bought your cap for 50 bucks."

"What did you do that for? You can't take that with you to our next stop."

"I feel lucky."

Jerry just shook his head, and we started walking out. Before leaving, I turned and took one last look at the shrine I knew I would never see again. I felt lucky to have seen it just this one time. Now, if I could only keep this cap...

We exited the park, crossed Lehigh, and sat back down on the bench in the small park where we arrived.

"That isn't going to fit you, anyway," Jerry volunteered, somewhat dejectedly.

"I know," I replied, while trying it on. All his clothes were way too big for me, having tried on Jerry's cap in particular, many times. "Maybe I can pin it, so it fits better."

"Good idea."

Throughout our "vacation," Jerry's attitude has been very difficult to read. For someone who I'd gotten to know exceptionally well, and who was so transparently genial, this was, indeed, a puzzling situation. I could certainly understand it, of course. For a man who had the career he had, to relive just one game, observing his young, strong self performing wonders at long-gone Shibe Park, seeing long-gone teammates and long-gone rivals, must've been, well, I don't know what.

At times he would sit up in his seat, intently watching the action, and others, he would sit back, and appear lost in thought, which he probably was. At present, he was sitting on our bench and staring straight ahead. What was he thinking?

"I hate this damn beard," he finally said, breaking the tension. So much for deep thought.

"I still think you look like James Garfield," I shot back, chuckling. "Just watch out for wide-eyed maniacs with a gun."

"And you look stupid in my cap. It's way too big for you. And it's dirty and sweaty too."

"Yeah, but it's still a great souvenir."

"Which you won't be able to take with you."

"I still feel lucky. Anyway, we'll find out soon."

I was getting the all-too-familiar headache that preceded our "departures." Jerry was too, I could tell. I took one last look back at Shibe Park, turned to Jerry and smiled. And then we were gone.

131

PART VII

1

We arrived together. A first. Usually one or the other of us would arrive ahead of the other, but not this time. If there was any particular significance to this, I could not tell. It was something I would wisely take note of.

The rest was all the same, mostly. We were yet again, sitting on a park bench, scattered trees surrounding us.

A few other benches were not so strategically placed, and were totally unoccupied. Cars were chugging down the surrounding streets at a respectful, modest speed. To our right, a lonely bandstand stood, a Spartan relic that appeared to have not been in need of its services for quite some time. It appeared to be about mid-day on a

late spring or early summer day. Judging by the car's rolling by, it was maybe the '50's. Or maybe earlier. It was a beautiful day. As

they say, the sun was shining, the birds in the sky were singing, the wind was blowing gently, and all was right with the world.

Jerry smiled at me. I smiled back. We were back where it had all begun. We were home.

We sat there smiling for what seemed like minutes, but probably wasn't. Finally, the smiling stopped, and the reconnaissance began. Jerry was wearing a short sleeve button-down shirt, brown slacks and black oxford shoes. After a quick check, I discovered that I was dressed similarly. Except for one thing.

"Hey, it made it," Jerry said, pulling off my cap. It was the white and blue Philadelphia A's cap I had bought just a few minutes (decades?) ago. "This is a first. I wonder what it means. Why don't you let me keep it. It fits better on me than it does on you."

"No, it's mine, I bought it. Come on give it to me."

"I think I'll keep it," Jerry laughed, pulling away from me as I lunged for my cap, now sitting perfectly atop Jerry's head.

"Come on give it to me, or I'll tell everyone you're a Kixoholic, " I half laughed, while trying unsuccessfully to get my cap back. Finally, after he felt he had teased me enough, Jerry surrendered it back. "I knew that Kixoholic threat would get you, placing the cap lovingly back on my head.

"You're going to have to pin that thing up or something, it looks silly on you now."

"I will. Besides, I don't care anyway. This is an incredibly rare souvenir. And the story behind it is literally unbelievable."

"I won't tell anyone if you won't. How much money you got?" Jerry said changing the subject to a more important matter.

Checking my trifold wallet, I discovered I had just over $1000, A sum matched inside Jerry's.

"Looks like we're gonna be here a while. But what for?"

This time neither of us had an answer. It appeared to be a summer day, too late to join the Sheboygan Indians again. Except for Philly, all our other appearances had occurred in late spring, just in time for Jerry to join the local team, but this was different. It was warm, the grass was green, the trees had leafed out. And we were stumped.

"Guess we better find out what year this is. I kinda hate to say this, but it looks pretty close to the last time. But I'm guessing it's not."

"Why not," Jerry countered. "It could be."

"It could, but I doubt it. I don't know why we would be sent back to Sheboygan, 1946 again."

"Yeah, maybe. But none of this makes that much sense to me."

"Let's go over to the news store and get a paper."

We picked up our always present duffel bags, walked out of Fountain Park, crossed 8th Street, and headed to one of our favorite stores.

We walked into a news store that hadn't changed a bit since last we visited, how many years ago? We casually walked down the few aisles glancing at magazines, pamphlets, books and assorted other periodicals. After a few minutes, we wandered to the counter area where the newspapers were located.   Jerry grabbed a "Sheboygan Press" and paid the lady at the counter.

"You fellas new in town?" She asked curiously.

"Yes, we just got in," I responded. "How did you know?"

"Oh, most of my customers are regulars, and you two just look like outsiders. No offense, mind you."

"None taken," I smiled. "We might be in town a while, so we may be back."

"Good. I can always use more customers."

I walked outside and joined Jerry who was slowly walking south on 8th Street trying to scan the paper while doing so.

"Friday, June 5, 1953," he said quietly as I joined him. We stopped and looked at a Sheboygan that could have passed for 1946. Hasn't changed much, has it?"

"Not much." Scanning 8th Street, it appeared that the stores were the same, the people dressed about the same, and the vehicles were only a little newer. The Sheboygan of this era certainly could not be regarded as a community of dynamic change. "Not at all," I amended.

"Well, here's something that hasn't changed, and glad of it. C'mon, I'm hungry."

We were in front of Kresge's and since it was pushing noon, we walked in and sat down at the restaurant counter. I swiveled my chair and looked back at the store filled with anything and everything. From knitting yarn to model cars to bin candy, it was all here. And it had the aroma to prove it.

"What are you looking at?"

What was I looking at? A sad, yet satisfying melancholy had overtaken me sitting in that chair. I was home. I was back home in a time when I didn't even exist yet.   Still, it was all so familiar. Sheboygan certainly hadn't changed much. Not yet. And I was glad. I was home. But for how long? And for what? This was new. I'm sure we'd find out. But I didn't care. I was home. And I liked it. What was I looking at?

"Memories."

"Well, stop dreaming and turn around and order. This young lady is waiting."

I turned back to the counter and witnessed, a vision. An angel. A goddess donned in a suitably appropriate white dress, holding a small order pad.

"And you, sir?" The goddess whispered.

"Ah, I'll have what he's having," is all I could stammer.

Jerry eyed me amusingly, his eyes practically twinkling with mischief, the way they get when he was about to have a little fun with someone. I'd seen that expression many times before.

"Catch your eye a little, did she?" Jerry chuckled.

"Um, she just has an interesting face is all."

And she did. A very distinct, fascinating face. Her wide eyes were set back in her head, giving her face a distant, vacuous look. As such, her nose and mouth jutted out just a little, but not too much. Just enough to catch your eye in an extremely pleasant way. Her short blond hair was tied up into an attractively short ponytail that pointed almost straight up from the top of her head. She was of average build and height which, translated for me meant... Sensational.

"Interesting face, huh. Well, you better pop your eyeballs back into your head before she comes back with our food."

Jerry was enjoying this so much, he was struggling to keep from breaking out into his loud, at times annoying laugh.

"What are we having anyway, I countered, trying to change the subject. I knew it was hopeless, because I could sense at least a day of ribbing from my best friend.

"Turn your smitten head and find out." The goddess had returned carrying our orders, placing them in front of us.

"Let me know if there's anything else you need," she sighed.

Stifling a cough, Jerry replied that we certainly would.

I kept one eye on my roast turkey slices, dressing with gravy, mashed potatoes, green peas, cranberry sauce, and roll with butter, and the other on my goddess. It's certainly not easy eating that way. Still, I somehow managed. Jerry, meanwhile, was single-mindedly wolfing down his food, pardon the expression. That was fine with me. I didn't want him horning in on my girl. One customer to a goddess, I always say.

We finished eating all too quickly, and Jerry generously agreed to pay our $1.18 bill. While he was at the cashiers paying, I discreetly left a five dollar tip for my new girlfriend. I was hoping to catch her eye to say goodbye, but she was waiting on some trucker-looking lout who was shamelessly flirting with her. Fortunately, goddesses aren't so easily impressed.

"How much did you leave her?" Jerry asked after I had rejoined him.

"How did you see that?" I asked, puzzled.

"I didn't see it. Hey, partner. I know you pretty well by now, you know. It's exactly something you would do. You don't have to tell me, if you don't want to."

"Five bucks," I confessed, sheepishly.

"Wow, she really did turn your head, didn't she? Five dollars on a $1.18 bill. You keep coming in here for lunch, and we're going to run out of money pretty quick."

"Very funny."

Jerry was enjoying himself, and, I guess, I couldn't blame him. I doubt if he'd ever seen me like this.

We were both smiling as we finished our visit to Kresge's. Jerry bought two packs of LaPalina Panatelas and we left. Reluctantly, for me. I made a needless mental note to be a regular patron of the Kresge's lunch counter.

I was a bit nervous as we approached the front door of the Hotel Foeste. What would it look like? Who would be working? Would I know them? Would they know me? Would it matter? Swirling questions that were answered the moment I walked through the door that Jerry was holding open for me.

Nothing. No change at all. It was the same Foeste that I remembered well. Has anything changed in this town in the last seven years?

We walked slowly over to the vacant check-in desk. Presently, a man came out of the small office to greet us.

Henry Boatwright was a little plumper and had a little less hair, but still carried himself with the same dignified air I had gotten used to so many years ago. It was good to see him again, but, of course, I couldn't tell him that.

"What can I do for you two gentleman?" Henry asked in his stilted, formal manner.

"We would like a room please, possibly for several days," I replied, anticipating the automatic second question.

We paid for a week in advance, signed the register, took the key from Henry's hand, and walked up to second floor to our room, number 225.

"Is this the same room we were in the last time?" Jerry asked, once we got settled into our room.

"It's one room down, I remember."

"Well, the view's the same. This time the Rex is showing "Peter Pan". What was playing last time?"

"'The Southerner" with Zachary Scott."

"Oh, yeah. Never saw it. Even now."

"Me neither." We both sat on the edge of our beds, looking around the room. It was virtually the same room we had last time, so there wasn't much new to look at. Still, we sat there.

"So." Jerry finally asked. "You're the brains of this outfit, why are we here this time?"

For once, I had no answer.

We spent the next several days buying some clothes, boning up on the news of 1953, and, generally, touring the city, reacquainting ourselves with our beloved hometown. Being quite familiar with the town, Jerry would occasionally go off on his own, which was fine with me. I ate virtually all my lunches at Kresge's ogling my new girlfriend as unsuspectingly as I could. Not being terribly outgoing, I was unable to discover my goddesses name. Jerry suggested we simply call her Mary, so that's who she became.

At the end of our first week, we were able to find a "furnished apartment for two, ground-floor, private entrance, utilities included," and moved in on Friday the 12th. We spent the rest of the day grocery shopping, settling in, and scanning the paper for, well, anything.

"The Indians are in town tomorrow night versus Wausau. Want to go?" I asked Jerry. We had been so busy doing not much, that we had not paid much attention to our former team.

"Sure, if you want to."

"Decided."

About 6:30 on Saturday we started walking to the ballpark. It was a nice evening, so we took our time, talking as we went, something we hadn't done much of since our arrival.

"So, how are you doing with Mary?" Jerry asked, semi-humorously.

"I've said hi to her."

"Hi! That's it? You should be on your third date by now?"

"I haven't quite gotten up the nerve yet."

"What's keeping you? We're not going to be here forever, you know. You gotta go out and get her. She isn't engaged or anything, is she?"

"No. At least there is no ring on her finger," something I had noticed immediately.

"Well, there you are. She's probably waiting for you to ask her out. She certainly can't help but notice you're in there every day."

"Not every day. Okay, every day." Jerry had given me one of his famous smirks, and I had to confess the truth. "I will, really. I sure don't have anything to lose."

"That's the spirit."

My uncle plays for the Indians this year," I offered, quickly changing the subject.

"Really. What's his name."

"Bill Adelhelm. He plays first base."

"First base, huh. Any good?"

"I think he's the best hitter on the team. He got up to B ball, I think. Seems to me he said he had hit .345 one year, or something like that."

"Pretty good. Never made it to the Bigs though, huh?"

"No. Being in the Dodger organization, he had Gil Hodges ahead of him, so he knew he'd never get a shot, so he quit. He would've had a much better chance in my time."

"A lot of good players never got a shot at it. I knew a lot of them. Sometimes you have to be as lucky as good."

We had reached the oh-so-familiar park, paid the pittance of an admission, and seated ourselves in my usual, 1946 seats behind the third-base, home team dugout. I was again wary of seeing people I had known in a prior life, but, walking towards seats, I had not seen any. The park, itself looked very much the same, except for the recently planted ivy on the outfield walls. Jerry noticed the improvement, and heartily approved of the planting.

The game itself was a good one. The Indians carried a 3 to 1 lead going into the eighth, when solo Wausau homers in the eighth and ninth sent the game into extra innings. Fortunately, Indian reliever Edward Knapp pitched one-hit ball for three innings, getting the game to the bottom of the 13th inning. In the bottom of the 13th, Indian shortstop, and future Dodger, Dick Tracewski singled, followed by a walk to center fielder Al Shaw. That brought third baseman Ray Mitchell to the plate.

If they walk this guy, your uncle can be the hero."

I only nodded, knowing my uncle was on deck. He had only gone one for six, so I was hoping he'd get a chance with the bases-loaded. It would be great watching my uncle get the winning hit.

It didn't happen. Ray Mitchell hit a shot to center bringing in Tracewski with the winning run. The players mobbed Mitchell as they ran off the field into the dugout in front of us.

"Too bad it wasn't your uncle. Good game though."

"You have any plans for today?" Jerry mumbled the next morning while finishing his second bowl of Kix.

"Not really."

"Looks like a nice day, how's about you and I taking a walk?"

About an hour later, we were out the door and on our way. We didn't say much of any consequence, being content to enjoy the day and our time together.

I let Jerry lead, and soon became aware of where we were going. We walked the short, winding hill along the river and ambled over to the northeast diamond of Kiwanis Park. As we sat in the bleachers along the third-base line, I remembered our other visits to this park and these bleachers. Each time was a significant event in our relationship. Jerry had guided us here for a reason. I sat and waited.

"Good game last night," Jerry finally commented

"Yup." I waited some more.

"I still don't know why we're here," Jerry questioned at last. "I mean all our other stops were obvious. Even Philly was a nice break and a sorta treat watching that game. All those memories. Geez." Jerry had become wistful, not an attitude he displayed very often.

"Maybe that was a little vacation for us. A real treat for both of us for different reasons. And, maybe this is the same."

"I suppose. But what are we supposed to be doing? With the money we have, it appears that we're going to be here a while. But why? I mean, watching that game last night gave me the itch to play ball again. But I don't have any equipment in my bag like the other times."

"I've been thinking about that, and I've got an idea. You remember that TV show 'Home Run Derby'?"

"Sure, I watched it all the time. Was only on for one year though. Wish they would have had that when I was playing."

"I bet. Anyway, what if we try to organize a home run contest before one of the Indian games? We could pitch it to Hauser. Tell him to promote it. Make a special day of it. The contest could feature two Indian players, two opposing players, and one wildcard entry."

"Call me Wildcard. I love it. Do you think Hauser would go for it? He's not the most imaginative, you know.?

"Why not? Attendance is down. The Braves are killing the minor league teams in this state. It's the last year for the Indians anyway, though he may not suspect that. Let's go over to his Sport Shop tomorrow and make our pitch."

"Great! I'll destroy the competition. Hey, Your uncle could be one of my competitors. You could meet him then."

"Exactly."

We sat back on the bleachers and gazed out over the park. Being a late Sunday morning, there was no activity. Nothing. Only us. Sitting in a bleacher, staring out over four vacant baseball diamonds. I wondered if that was why Jerry had intentionally

141

brought me here, to discuss our reason for being here. Somehow, I doubted it. I kept thinking there was more. There was more.

"So, ah, how are you doing with Mary?" Jerry asked almost disinterestedly."

"I'm working on it," I replied cautiously.

"Great. Great." I don't think he even heard me. Normally, he'd be kidding me about my pseudo-girlfriend, but now, his mind seemed to be elsewhere.

"Say, ah, I've met this girl. She's really nice, and I like her a lot. I've only known her a few days, but she's really special, you know? She's a waitress at that restaurant on Michigan Avenue. Can't remember the name. She's really nice, you know? I know we're not supposed to get involved with anyone. And we never have, until now. I mean, you're hot on your Mary, so we're even."

Jerry had gotten this all out in a matter of seconds. He actually took a deep breath when he had finished. So, this was what he had on his mind. It must've been bothering him for a few days, and he wanted to tell me about her to get my approval. I could hardly berate him, since I was perfectly ready to do the same thing with my Mary.

"So, what's her name, Mary?"

"Very funny. Unlike some people, I know how to put a move on a girl. Her name is Jane." By the tone of his response, I could tell he felt relieved.

"Jane, huh. Nice name. Jane. Well, enjoy her company. Just remember who we are, and don't do anything stupid."

"Right."

The next morning we walked over to Hauser's Sport Shop to make our pitch. Hauser stood staring at us, chomping on an unlit cigar. He didn't seem impressed with our idea.

"Home run contest, eh?" he finally got out.

"Yup. Promote it right, and you could get a good turnout, for a change. Make it half-price for the ladies. That should help. The Braves are killing you, and a good crowd would do you a lot of good. Emotionally, financially. Right?"

"Yeah, well. I don't know," he growled, still looking skeptical.

"And, besides," I countered, "my friend here would need some baseball gear. A couple bats, a glove, some spikes, some baseballs, warm-ups. You know a good sporting good store around here that could supply him with what he needs?"

142

That did it. Joe not-so-reluctantly now, scheduled the contest for Wednesday night, July 8, before the game with Fond du Lac. We bought all the equipment Jerry needed, plus a glove for myself, and told Joe we'd keep in touch. As we were about to leave, Joe asked the question I had been waiting for.

"Say, young man, where'd you get that cap?"

I had purposely worn my '31 A's cap to get a reaction out of Hauser and I was ready for him.

"Jimmie Foxx gave it to me," I replied with a smiling glance at Jerry, who was also smiling.

"Jimmie Foxx? Hauser shot back, startled. "How did you manage that?"

"It's a long story."

We walked back to our flat, chuckling at our exchange with Hauser.

"You really caught old Joe on that one. I've never seen Unser Joe as off-balance as he was there. Good one." Jerry was puffing contentedly on a stogie as we walked north on 8th Street.

"I didn't think he was going to say anything, but I knew he would recognize the cap. Maybe I shouldn't have done it, but I couldn't resist. Now he'll be thinking about that all day."

I doubt it. Joe doesn't think on much for very long. Still, that was a good one."

"Thanks."

"Well, partner, that was fun. But I have a little Chickie to see," Jerry offered after we had dropped off our stuff at the flat. "No, that's okay, I don't need any company."

"No problem. Besides, I'm starting to get a little hungry. I hear they have pretty good food at Kresge's lunch counter."

"So I hear. Maybe you'll meet your own little chickie over there. And maybe her name will be Mary."

"Could be. And this time, I'm going to do more than just eat."

"Good luck. Don't do anything I wouldn't do."

"No deal."

"Ha. If you say hello it will be a major advancement." "

"Says you. You'll see."

I was reading an 'Archie' comic book when Jerry rolled into our apartment, smiling and puffing on a long panatela. Flopping down on our ratty couch, he just smiled, waiting for me to say the first word.

"Well, how is Jane these days, as if I have to ask."

"Just great. She's the sweetest little thing in the whole wide world. Of course, I've told you that before. So how's Mary? I want a full progress report."

"I'm working on it," I replied very sheepishly.

"Told ya. You made no progress at all, did you?"

"I don't have to report everything to you. You don't tell me everything about your times with Jane," I came back, actually trying to change the subject.

"I don't need all the details. Just a brief recap will do. Besides, I tell you a little about what we do. You don't want all the details, do you?"

"Hardly."

"So. Once again, you accomplished nothing."

"Hey, I made some progress today."

"Like what?"

"I finally found out her name."

"Really. So what's Her name? "

"Mary."

After a few days, Jerry decided to practice for the home run hitting contest. We had been playing catch in the backyard just to loosen up, but that wouldn't help Jerry with his hitting, as if he needed any help. Still, we rounded up a couple neighbor kids for our ball shaggers and walked over to the Kiwanis baseball park. The boys were more than eager to assist, since they were promised five dollars each, plus an ice cream cone to follow.

"Why do you want to practice hitting mister? " the shorter boy, Stephen asked. "Are you going to play for the Indians?"

"Not exactly. There's going to be a home run hitting contest before an Indians game, and I'm going to be in it. And if you do a good job of shagging balls, maybe you boys can come and watch, on us." Jerry then went on to explain the why's and wherefore's of the contest, which interested the boys immensely.

We arrived at the diamond, and sent the boys out into deep left field. Jerry changed into his spikes, I climbed the pitcher's mound, and we were ready to go. I couldn't help but be reminded of the last time we did this, Jerry's "unofficial" try-out for the 1946 Indians. How long ago was that now? A very tough question to answer, for sure. After a few easy tosses to Jerry to loosen up, Jerry walked into the batters box and I started to pitch.

Like last time, Jerry bunted the first two pitches. "Why are you doing that?" I asked incredulously. "That's not going to help you in a home run hitting contest."

"Habit," Jerry replied smiling. "Okay, now let's get serious."

His next swings were fluid and easy, balls jumping off his bat into deep left field. The boys were very energetic in their fielding and returning the balls back to the infield, though I did have to run a little to get the returned balls, the boys being so far out in left field, that their throws came up well short of the pitcher's mound, even with a running start on their part. After hitting a few more mid-range missiles, Jerry got serious. Taking a harder swing, Jerry hit the next three balls over the awestruck boys' heads, into the Sheboygan River.

"Okay, enough of that," I called to Jerry. "We only have three balls left."

"Alright. Throw those three in here, and I'll take some easy swings to finish this off." And so I did. Our batting practice had lasted all of maybe 15 minutes. Jerry had lost the only three balls he had tried to lose. He was ready, though I figured he would have been ready without the practice.

We took the boys to the "Twin Whip" on the corner of 17th and Erie. We all ordered vanilla twist cones and walked home enjoying the day. A few blocks from home, we said goodbye to the boys, thanking them for their efforts, and promised to take them to the contest.

We were standing in front of Dutch's Bar, the former Joseph A. Murray Tavern of another age. For several days, we had been meaning to stop in, but had never made it. Until now. I knew that Winde Wangemann still worked here, so we took a gamble, and walked in.

As usual, our luck held, as Winde was behind the bar drying off a few glasses. Being only 11:15 the bar was empty, so we sat at our usual seats on the north end of the bar.

"What can I get you gents?"

"I'll have a beer, and my buddy here will have a Coke," Jerry answered Winde's query.

"Gotcha." Winde returned with the drinks, and we started talking.

"You fellas from around here? Don't recall seeing you in here before. Most of the guys coming here are regulars. You know?"

"Well," I began, "we're not really from around here, though we've been in here before, but it's been a while."

Jerry gave me a quick glance. I was tempting fate a little, but I didn't care. Nobody ever remembers us, so I thought I'd have a little fun. What the heck. I began regretting it almost immediately.

"You have, eh? You say you we've met before?"

"It's been quite a while."

"It can't be too long ago. You gents look like you're barely 21. I couldn't serve you if you weren't 21." Winde was eyeing us closely now, and I suddenly remembered that he was the one person who was suspicious of us the last time.

"We're older than we look," Jerry replied easily, bailing me out. Winde seemed to go along with Jerry's offhanded explanation, but for the remainder of our visit, he seemed a little wary. Why was he the only one that could sense something? We were going to mention to him about the home run hitting contest, but now, neither of us brought it up. Instead, I tried changing the subject.

"So, who are your regulars, you know, the guys you see a lot?"

"Well, let's see. There's Gus Mohr, Al Yurk, Alvin Kraemer, Slim Volbrecht, guys like that. You know any of them?"

"No, I'm afraid not," I lied. Actually, I knew them all. We talked a little more, then bid Winde adieu.

"Nice talking to you gents, hope to see you again."

"Thanks, same here. Sure, we might be back."

"You knucklehead. Why'd you have to bring up that 'we've been here before' bit? He picked up on our ages right away," Jerry admonished, once outside.

"I was just trying to have some fun. I didn't think that 'it's been a while' part would probably make us pretty young to be drinking in a bar."

"For sure. And what's with that guy? He always seems to be able to smell a rat. Remember last time?"

"I don't know, but I've been thinking the same thing. Maybe it's best if we stay away from Winde for a while."

"I don't need any convincing."

The next several days passed quite uneventfully. While Jerry was busy romancing his Jane, I spent a lot of time touring the city. Several days, I walked down to the lake, stopping to watch the new YMCA being constructed. I spent hours watching the workers put up a building I would become so familiar with in another time. It's always fun watching other people work. I stopped at City News a couple times to pick up some magazines, as well as at Hermann's Grocery Store just to say hi to John and buy some baseball cards. The '53 tops set was great; I even managed to get the classic Satchel Paige card. One day, I decided to stop for lunch at the Snack Shack on Michigan Avenue. This was where his Jane worked, and I figured it was time I met her. I was certain she was working that day because Jerry had told me he had something to do and wasn't seeing her. I was quite anxious to see this girl that had turned my buddy's head so much, but was disappointed when I was informed that she wasn't working that day. I had a bowl of soup and a Coke and left the Snack Shack with a huge letdown. I decided not to try again. If Jerry really wanted me to meet her, he would have arranged it by now.

By the next morning, I had decided I'd had enough. It was time to make my move on Mary. I figured, if Jerry could have a girlfriend, so could I. For all we know, maybe this was our last stop. No explanation for our 1953 Sheboygan visit had arisen, so maybe this was it. Besides, what did I have to lose? Right? My plan was this: I would have a late lunch at Kresge's, then wait outside for her to leave, then talk to her. I knew she got off at 2 o'clock, so I wouldn't have too long to wait. A great plan, if ever there was one.

147

I got to Kresge's a little later than normal and had my usual cheeseburger, fries and a Coke. Mary waited on me with her usual indifference. I wonder if she even remembered that I was in there nearly every day. No matter. Once I put on a few moves, she'd be all mine.

I lingered over my meal as long as I felt I could, then paid the bill and walked outside. It was 1:45 only 15 minutes to wait. I strolled nonchalantly along 8th Street being careful not to stray too far lest she come out a few minutes early, thereby missing her. I watched as a few people went in and a few people came out, consciously getting more nervous by the minute.

I was standing maybe 10 feet north of the door when she came out, arm in arm with a husky guy I had seen enter just a few minutes before. They talked animatedly as they passed me, heading north on 8th Street. I continued watching as they got farther and farther away. Finally, they turned left on Ontario Avenue and disappeared. It should have been a huge disappointment, and yet, I felt... Nothing. No letdown. No heartbreak. No disappointment. Nothing.

I contemplated my reaction as I, too, started walking north on 8th Street. It was a reaction I couldn't explain. After great thought, I could only come up with one conclusion. I wouldn't be eating too many more lunches at Kresge's.

The next morning I told Jerry about my "in absentia" rejection. He commiserated with me and decided it was his job to cheer me up. I told him I didn't need cheering up, but he waved off my denial.

His idea of cheering me up was a night on the town. He described to me the simple itinerary for the evening. I replied it wasn't necessary. He replied it was. I acquiesced. I concluded this was as much about what he wanted as what he thought I needed. So by 5:30 pm we were dressed up and heading for the ever popular 8th Street. Jerry had made reservations for two at the Sky Garden restaurant. He said he'd always wanted to eat at the top of Sheboygan's tallest skyscraper.

I must say, the meal was sensational. A thick T-bone steak, mashed potatoes, green beans, warm rolls, apple pie a-la-mode for dessert. After a steady diet of cheeseburgers, fries, soup, hot dogs and potato chips, this was quite a treat. And while I wasn't really "down," this was a great elixir for whatever I had, which was probably nothing. Still, I thanked Jerry for the meal, and we proceeded on to what he called the "special treat" of the evening.

"Have you ever been to one of these before?" Jerry smiled as we headed north on 8th Street.

"I've told you a dozen times that I haven't." Jerry was having his fun as he continued smiling as we walk.

"Oh, that's right. You did tell me, didn't you?" He was laughing now, and, though I was mildly irritated, I couldn't help laughing myself. "Hey, this is going to be great, you'll see."

"Says you. This is going to be really embarrassing."

We turned right on New York Ave. and headed for the Playdium. Jerry's "special treat" was a professional wrestling match featuring the dynamic double feature of Crusher Allen versus Swede Carlin, and Tony Borkin versus Bud Fuller. Jerry paid for our ringside seats, and we were ready to witness some fine, professional wrestling.

The first match was a real slam-bang affair. Crusher Allen came out in one of those Tarzan-like outfits that made him look more like Cheetah than Tarzan. The Swede meanwhile, was appropriately attired in traditional black wrestling trunks. After a seemingly endless series of head locks, flying mares, strangleholds, bodyslams and pile drivers ("it should be illegal, it is in some states"), the Crusher was able to pin the Swede, much to the displeasure of the latter. Claiming referee indiscretion, he immediately demanded a rematch. Allen-Carlin 2 would not be on my immediate list of things to see.

The second match was a real snoozer. Tony Borkin came out in a white bodysuit which made him look like anything but a wrestler. Meanwhile, Bud Fuller was wearing trunks that were far too revealing. Jerry kept snickering throughout the match, continually calling Fuller "Jumbo." In any case, "Jumbo" got pinned and didn't bother to protest. Neither did I, for the matches were over, and we were on our way home.

"Pretty exciting, huh?" Jerry offered.

"Sure was, I haven't been doused with that much sweat in a long time."

"One of the benefits of a ringside seat, my friend."

We walked silently toward home, Jerry puffing contentedly on a Panatela. I was debating about bringing up a subject that I felt needed addressing, but wasn't sure I should. Finally, I bit the bullet, so to speak. What the heck.

"Look. It's probably none of my business, but why haven't I met this girl friend of yours? I mean it's been almost a month now, and you haven't made any effort to introduce us. Is there something wrong with her,? Or odd? Or something? Let's face it. It's you and me. Whatever it is we're in, we're in it together. The real bond here

149

has to be you and me, not you and her, no matter how you may feel about her."

I had said more than I intended, but once I got going, I figured I had to get it all into the open. I didn't know if I had done the right thing or not, particularly considering Jerry's continued silence.

"Um, the thing is, well, first, there's nothing wrong with her. Believe me, she's great. She's beautiful and smart and personal, and well, you know. But, I don't know. There's something odd about all this. Eerie, almost. It's just this feeling I have that you two shouldn't meet, you know? I feel I have to keep her to myself, for some reason. I don't know. She'll be at the park tomorrow night for the home run hitting contest, maybe I'll introduce you two then."

My friend was struggling to find the right words, and I felt badly for him. Still, he hadn't cleared up anything. My suspicions about this relationship were deepening. And for some reason, I felt that a meeting between Dan and Jane was anything but imminent. I would prove to be right.

The next evening, we gathered up our ball shagging boys and headed to Memorial Park. Jerry was carrying his athletic bag which contained a couple of baseballs, gloves, spikes, and a couple small towels. The boys took turns carrying Jerry's bat. The home run hitting contest was scheduled for 6:30, and we got there plenty early. We left the boys to do what they pleased, and made our way to the third-base dugout.

"So you showed up, did you?" was our greeting from Hauser.

"Your fans are expecting a special treat, aren't they?" was my snappy reply. "And, before you ask later, my friend is not interested in playing for the Indians, are you?"

"Nope, I've done all that."

"Huh?"

"Never mind. I'm still not interested."

"Yeah, right," was Hauser's predictable response.

The format of the contest was very simple. Each of the five hitters would get 10 swings. Any ball not going out of the park in fair territory would be considering an out. Then the five hitters would get 10 more swings for a total of 20. Whoever hit the most home runs would be declared the winner. In case of a tie, the men tying would get five swings each to determine the winner. I didn't think the tiebreaker would be necessary.

The five contestants gathered near home plate, and faced the crowd. As each was introduced, the player stepped forward and doffed his cap. Representing the Fond du Lac Panthers were Miguel Ballester, a 5'8" burler from Cuba, and Joseph Tuminelli, a young fellow who was tearing up the State League with his hitting. For the Indians, Allan Mugford, a 6'6" 19 year old switch hitter, and uncle Bill Adelhelm age 23 from Brooklyn, New York, would hopelessly try to win the contest that almost certainly would go to the one and only Jerry Wolff, a.k.a. Jimmie Foxx.

Upon my insistence, I would pitch to Jerry. I offered to pitch to all five contestants, but Hauser nixed the idea and declared that each team would supply a pitcher for their own hitters. That was fine with us. It wasn't going to matter anyway.

Burler Ballester hit first and managed to deposit two balls over the left-field wall. Mugford hit next and, batting left-handed, also hit two home runs, the larger than the usual home crowd cheering heartily after each clout. To promote the attraction, the Indians had declared the game "ladies night," all women and children getting in for $.25.

By agreement, I insisted that Jerry should go last. That made Joseph Tuminelli the next hitter. The terror of the Wisconsin State League ripped four out of the park, bringing a look of smug conceit to his face. I smiled as I glanced next to me where Jerry was trying to keep from laughing.

Uncle Bill was introduced to a loud, and, somewhat raucous applause. At the time, my uncle was hitting .343 with 14 home runs, and I was pulling for him. He dug into the right-handed batters box and promptly hit two line drives foul down the left-field line. Disappointed, he stepped out of the box and took a couple practice swings. He hit the next two over the left field wall, the second one traveling way over. Jerry and I both applauded politely. Bill missed on his next four, but hit his final two out, for a tying total of four.

"And now hitting, representing Sheboygan Indian fans everywhere, please welcome, Jerry Wolff."

There was a smattering of applauses as Jerry amusingly doffed his cap and strolled toward the batters box, and I walked to the pitchers mound. Jerry didn't just want to win the contest. He wanted to put on a show, as usual. As such, he wanted to hit home runs to all fields, beginning in left field, and ending in right. I was allowed a couple warm-up throws, and we were ready to go.

I knew where Jerry liked his pitches and at what speed, and I had gotten quite good at obliging him. I laid the first one in on the inside corner, belt high. Jerry took a nice easy swing and rifled the pitch well over the left-field wall. I proceeded to lay "fat ones" in there, and Jerry continued to rocket home runs deep over the wall, moving steadily from left field toward right.

By home run number six, the crowd was really getting into it, cheering louder with each home run. Ball number seven would have easily cleared the right centerfield wall except for the large maple tree that intercepted it as it was going by. The crowd groaned, but Jerry just shrugged his shoulders and smiled. "I thought I could get it over that tree," was all he said. That would have been quite a blast considering that the tree was in the deepest part of the park, some 391 feet away. And high. It didn't matter. My friend deposited the next three pitches over the right field wall and calmly walked off to the side, the fans giving him a huge ovation.

152

I quickly walked off the mound, doffing my Cap as if I had actually done anything. The two Indian players walked over to congratulate Jerry, while the two Panthers just stared over in disbelief. For his part, Jerry cooly took it all in, knowing the contest was virtually over. After Jerry's first-round performance, the rest of the contest was mostly anti-climactic. The two Panthers hit two more home runs each, while Mugford hit three. Uncle Bill also manage three home runs, putting him in second place with seven. Jerry's nine homers had already won the contest, so he didn't have to hit in the second round. But Jerry hadn't performed before a crowd in quite some time, and he wasn't about to pass on the opportunity.

The fans cheered as they watched Jerry stride to the plate, hoping to see some real fireworks, in this, the unnecessary second round. My friend, being a natural ham, wasn't about to disappoint them.

I delivered a steady diet of Jerry's favorite pitches, and watched as all 10 of them easily cleared the left or left centerfield wall.

"I'm really going to let loose on this one," Jerry called me before his final swing. I could tell, even with his mighty blows, that he hadn't really been going all out. This was going to be epic.

I grooved a beauty, and Jerry took a mighty rip. The ball sailed over the 391 foot sign in deep left centerfield, over the house beyond that, landing somewhere on 19th Street. That ball must've traveled at least 480 feet. The crowd was stunned at first, but then let all the mightiest roared yet. The other four competitors just stood there and stared. Speechless.

"I got a hold of that one pretty good," Jerry smiled, deadpanning the understatement of the year. We shook hands with the other batters, congratulating them on their efforts.

Jerry was presented with a small trophy recognizing him as the winner of the first annual "Indians home run hitting contest." The event was such a success, that Hauser told us they'd be doing this every year. He even thanked us for coming up with the idea. We, in turn, thanked him for allowing us to participate. We walked to the Indians dugout knowing that this will be the first and last "Indians home run hitting contest." There would be no Sheboygan Indians next year.

Before we walked up to the grandstand, I wanted to talk briefly with my uncle Bill, but the team was ready to take the field, and I didn't get the chance. "Maybe after the game," Jerry said, reading my mind.

153

"Sure."

But the game was a drag, a long, boring affair that took forever to play. By the eighth-inning, the Panthers were up 5-0, and were in the process of putting up five more. We left. We found the boys behind the Panthers dugout and took them home. They were ready to leave anyway. The game ended up 10-2 Panthers. My uncle Bill went 0-4. I never did get to talk to him.

After the home run bout, Hauser inquired about obtaining Jerry's services for the remainder of the season, but Jerry declined. I knew he would, and yet, I was surprised. Passing up an opportunity to play baseball wasn't something he would normally do, but, like me, I think he sensed that this wasn't something he should be doing. We had gotten quite good at "sensing" things. Instead, Jerry spent even more time with his girl Jane.

Maybe this was something he "sensed" as well. Anyway, this left me to my own devices, so I spent day after day alone to explore and enjoy my old hometown.

I spent a couple days watching building construction. I walked down to the lakefront for more looks at the building of the new YMCA. They were in the early stages of it, but it was always fun watching other people work. From there I would walk all the way to S. 24th St. to take in the early work on the new James Madison school. They were building it on what, a couple decades earlier, had been an airfield. Maybe they should have named to Charles A. Lindbergh school. And, maybe they would have had Lindy not become a Nazi lover.

The school was quite a ways from the YMCA, and from home, but I didn't mind. The weather was consistently fine, and I didn't mind walking. Besides, I didn't exactly have a full agenda.

When I wasn't watching people work, I was roaming, relaxing, and contemplating. I spent parts of many days sitting at the Northside beach, watching the swimmers and the sunbathers. In a few years, I would be romping through the sand and sliding down the slide stuck several yards into the lake, just like the kids were doing now.

A couple times I walked to Kiwanis Park to watch the little leaguers play baseball. For some reason, I enjoyed watching games at the southeast diamond the best. Perhaps, it was because, along with the northwest diamond, it would be eliminated in a few decades. As much as it pained me to say it, baseball's popularity would decline substantially in the not-too-distant future, and the number of ballfields needed would shrink accordingly.

I went to a couple movies in those late July days. I saw "Peter Pan" at the Sheboygan, and "Moulin Rouge" at the Wisconsin. I liked the latter but not the former, maybe because it seemed too much of a kids show. Jerry actually accompanied me to "Moulin Rouge" and enjoyed it also. For a while, when he wanted to be playful, he would call me "Toulouse".

With Jerry often gone, and with substandard cooking skills, I spread my patronage to a variety of restaurants. I never went back to Kresge's or the Snack Shack, but that still left Erie Eat Shoppe, Gmach's, Thimmig's, Quality Lunch,   and my personal favorite, Avenue Lunch on Michigan Avenue. I would also make regular stops at Hinze's Ice Cream Parlor for the obvious reasons. Occasionally, I would rough it and eat in.   I can open a can of spaghetti and meatballs with the best of 'em.

The days slowly melted away, possibly victims of the midsummer heat. I developed a never-before love of comic books. "Archie", "Popeye", "Little Lulu", "Woody Woodpecker", manly things like that. I'd read them over and over again until the new issues would come out. It's not like they took too long to read. For some reason, I just couldn't get into any other kind of reading material. Maybe, it was something I "sensed."   Or, maybe, it was just a comic book era.

The time was like something out of a Norman Rockwell painting.   I kept feeling I was in the middle of "To Kill a Mockingbird," only 20 years later. But, eventually, the tranquility ended. The city was gearing up for its huge centennial celebration. And, for some reason, I couldn't have cared less.

The City Fathers had set aside the week of August 9 as a celebration of the hundredth year of Sheboygan as a city. As such, a wide variety of activities were planned for the entire week, with each day represented by its own theme. For example, Sunday was "Freedom of Religion Day, Monday was "Governor's Day'" etc. Thursday was declared "Bratwurst Day," the first of what would be many such celebrations in future Augusts.

It seemed as though the entire city shut down for the week. There were bands, drum and bugle corps, parades, fireworks, games, contests, concerts, street dances, barbershop quartets and three performances of a play entitled "Salute to a Century". And eating and drinking.

On Monday, Gov. Walter J. Kohler gave an address in dedication of the opening of Kohler Memorial Drive. Later that evening, the governor crowned the centennial queen, Jenna Senkbeil, and gave awards to her princesses. On Wednesday, the local kids marched in a lantern parade from downtown to Vollrath Bowl. On Thursday, the Bratwurst Queen was crowned by Academy Award-winning actor Charles Coburn. It was quite a week. And, for some reason, I still couldn't have cared less

For some reason. Actually, I knew the reason, and it disturbed me. My close friend had been acting oddly lately. He was quiet, and sullen, and moody, and secretive. He hadn't wanted to be in my company much, and I didn't know why. I didn't think it was anything I had said or done, so I was a bit stumped. And concerned. One morning I decided to try to get him out of his funk.

"What you say we go to the parade today? We haven't been to a parade in a coon's age; it could be fun."

"I don't know. Don't feel much like it," Jerry replied, glumly.

"You're not seeing Jane today, are you?" He already told me he wasn't, so I thought it would be a chance for some quality time together.

"No, but…"

"Great. Finish your Kix and we'll see what's going on in the great outdoors."

Jerry grudgingly got dressed, and we headed out to see what this Centennial day had to offer.

We made our way over to 8th Street where all the activity was taking place. It was a short walk to downtown, but we still encountered dozens and dozens of people heading in the same direction. It was certainly a festive atmosphere. Fathers and mothers talking animatedly, teenagers frolicking and kidding, children caring American flags, beating each other over the head with them, and Jerry and I walking solemnly onward, wondering with each step, why were we were even bothering.

"Aren't you afraid you're going to meet someone you know, with all these people?" Jerry was looking for an excuse to turn back, but I wasn't about to let him find one "

"Not really. We're protected, remember? Besides, I haven't even been born yet, just like last time."

Jerry shot a quick nervous glance my way, but immediately pulled it back. We made it to 8th Street, and looked for a good spot from which to watch the big Centennial Parade. We settled for a spot, appropriately enough, near the Hotel Foeste.

The crowd was getting to be two or three deep, eventually topping out at maybe six or eight deep in spots. Still, we had a good spot, so we waited quietly, uncomfortably, for the parade to reach us.

A parade, is a parade, is a parade, I suppose, and this one was, well, a parade. Drum and bugle corps, bands, clowns, dignitaries (same thing?), floats, the usual. Still, it was a good parade, though I didn't think Jerry saw much of it, or, at least, not much registered.

Finally, the Queen's float arrived, slowly being pulled by a flower encased Buick convertible. Or, maybe it was a Chevy. I don't know much about cars. Anyway, Queen Jenna and her Court, all attired in delicate white gowns, were waving elegantly to the local masses. Jerry actually snapped to attention as the float passed by. All was not lost; he still had an eye for the ladies.

"This is sooo beautiful. Look at those gowns. They're sooo beautiful."

"Really. And the queen. She just looks like a queen. I would just love to ride on a float, just like her."

"Oh, Mary Alice, you're such a dreamer."

I had been aware of the two pretty, teenage girls standing near us, but hadn't paid their constant commenting much notice. But now it was I who snapped to attention. I paid no mind to the taller blonde, but the shorter brunette now caught my eye. Short, dark brown hair, slightly built, beautifully tanned skin, athletic looking, as a dancer. She was an absolute doll, and I couldn't resist.

"So, are you girls enjoying the parade?"

"Oh, yes," the taller one exclaimed. "It's so beautiful and exciting."

158

"The Queen's float was particularly attractive, didn't you think?"

"It was just lovely," the shorter one commented. "I think it's every girl's dream to someday be a queen and ride on a float like that. It's so romantic."

"Honestly, Mary Alice, you're such a dreamer."

"Well, you never know," I smiled. "Maybe someday you'll get your wish. In fact, I'll even make a prediction that you will."

"That would be too much to ask for, but, I hope you're right."

"I'm pretty confident," I replied, staring into her beautiful dark eyes. It was easy to be confident; future first runner-up Miss America's get parades thrown in her honor.

A little young for you, aren't they?" Jerry had been watching our verbal exchange, and had to get his two cents in. Of course, he was never one to miss a pretty face. Or two.

"Depends on how you look at it, right? Actually, I semi-recognized the short, dark one and just had to say a few words."

"Semi-recognized, huh? And why did you feel you just had to talk to her?"

"Because in a few years, she'll come this close to becoming Miss America," I replied, holding my thumb and forefinger about 2 inches apart.

"Yeah, right."

"I'm not kidding," and I proceeded to tell him a little of the Mary Alice Fox story. "In fact, in exactly six years, she'll be riding in a parade something like this one, traveling south on 8th Street, just like today."

"That's pretty amazing," Jerry said, trying to get a final look at Mary Alice as she walked away, north on 8th Street. "That's quite a claim to fame. Was she still living in your time?"

"Shortly after the pageant, she got married and moved to California. She was still living the last I knew."

Jerry just nodded as we made our way back home. The parade over, our big day on the town was over as well.

The next few days passed quietly, somberly, Jerry still stuck in his funk. As much as I hated to admit it, I was beginning to join him. It pained me to see him in such a state, and I was unsure as to what to do about it. Several times it appeared as though he was about to let it out and tell me what was bothering him, but he always held it back. And why were we even here, Sheboygan, 1953? It wasn't for Jerry to play baseball. It wasn't so he could win a home run hitting contest. It wasn't to experience the city's centennial.

159

I pondered all these things as I sat on a park bench in Fountain Park, very near to where it all began, you could say. I looked over to the popcorn wagon on the corner, where a couple of kids were buying, popcorn, what else? I thought we'd have it by now. Why were we here? Why in the ever loving HELL were we here? I was about to find out... In a big way.

As all good things must, the grand Sheboygan Centennial celebration came to an end, and the city returned to normal. Jerry was hanging around the apartment more often than usual, another sign that something was up. I continued to wait him out. I knew him well enough not to press the issue. He would tell me in his own good time; he couldn't last much longer. The time came a couple days later, a Friday. We had both just finished our Kix, Jerry staring down at his empty bowl.

"Whad'ya say we take a walk. We, ah, haven't done that for a while. Unless you have something else to do."

Assuring him my morning (and life) was open, we washed the dishes and walked outside. We took the oh-so-familiar walk to Kiwanis Park, site of probably all our serious discussions. There was no need to question our destination; it was a given. It was a pleasant late August morning, and we walked slowly, silently to the park. I wish I could say we were enjoying the conditions, but it was more like walking the last mile to an execution. At least, I felt that way, and for Jerry, it was probably worse.

We trudged over to the bleachers on the third base side of the north east diamond and sat down. All the Little League games were over, and the whole park had a school's starting-soon abandonment feel about it. I remembered the other discussions we had, sitting in this very spot. How many years ago, ahead, was it, would it be? I waited for Jerry to open up. I prepared myself for anything, yet, I couldn't even imagine what it could be. I waited some more. I was ready. Or so I thought.

"We, ah, have a problem," Jerry started, slowly.

"We do," I replied in the same tone, more of a statement than a question.

"Yes, we do, we have a little problem. Well, maybe not so little, really, I guess." He was searching for words, a way to say what had been bothering him for weeks. He was not in his element, so to speak, and I felt sorry for him. I was determined not to get upset, no matter what the bombshell maybe.

"Go on, I'm listening."

"Well, Jane, you know Jane?"

"Only by reputation."

"Well, Jane is going to have a baby," Jerry almost whispered, feeling, no doubt a whole plethora of emotions as he did.

"A baby," I said, just as quietly. Jerry simply nodded. "And I don't really have to ask who the father is, do I?" This time Jerry slowly shook his head.

"There's more."

"More? It gets worse?" Jerry nodded again, probably afraid to let the other shoe to drop. The "baby" revelation was a shock enough, so I was almost afraid to hear the rest. Still, Jerry and I were friends, and whatever "trouble" he may or may not be in, I was going to stand beside him.

"You see, her name really isn't Jane. It's Joan...Joan Jackson."

I just sat there, staring straight ahead at the lonely baseball diamond, a diamond that so long ago, or, more accurately, so far in the future, the blue shirts had defeated, (will defeat) the green shirts 1-0 in the Kiwanis Pee Wee League Championship game.

I recognized the implications immediately, of course. If there is a word far more powerful than "stunned," I would use it now to describe my state of being at that moment.

"The baby is due in April? April, 1954? Possibly April 20?" I whispered.

"Possibly."

Now it was my turn to nod. We sat quietly for the longest time, both of us trying to assimilate the far-reaching implications of all of this.

"How can this be, Dan? How can this happen? This can't be. You're here now. We met how many times in this city before I even knew her. This is ridiculous! Maybe it's some other kid born in April, 1954. I mean, no evidence of our presence has ever lasted before. So, I mean, I just don't get it. This is impossible."

Through all of his ranting, Jerry was making some good points. And yet, he, like I, knew that it wasn't only possible, but probable.

It explains so much. All of our travels, all of our stops, were leading to something, something much more than playing baseball, working in hotels, and visiting long-ago baseball parks. It explained our reason for being here, and why I never quite was able to meet the mysterious Jane. It explained the father I never knew, and never, ever heard about. It explained why it was us two, Don Jackson and Jimmie Foxx who so unexpectedly, unexplainably, had been joined together in this surreal, extraordinary ride. It explained well, pretty much everything.

162

"What are we going to do about this? What can we do about this?" Jerry pleaded. "And it's not just all this, but I've been getting headaches again. You have too, haven't you? I can tell. And you know what that means."

It was true, I had been getting the occasional headache, and I certainly knew what it meant. We would be leaving soon, very soon. But if this was the reason for all of our traveling, what was to be our next stop?

"There's nothing we can do, is there?" Jerry asked sadly.

"Nope. Not a thing."

"I haven't seen her in a while. I feel bad about it, but what could I tell her, what could I say?"

I could only shake my head slowly in response. We sat there somberly, each of us feeling the enveloping dizziness. Finally, I placed my arm around his shoulder. We looked at each other, smiling sadly. Father and son.

And then we were gone

PART VIII

1

I spent the next few days moping around the house taking only an occasional trip outside to walk Fido. As anyone can imagine, Don's manuscript left me shaken and awestruck. Heck, if my 22-year-old cousin hadn't placed it into my hands himself, I wouldn't have believed a word of it. I mean, how outrageous is this? I'm supposed to believe that my cousin Don, who I knew in this age as a 50 or 60 something human being is actually the son of baseball Hall of Famer Jimmie Foxx ? And that this is a result of some strange rendezvous occurring in the early '50's when Don, or Dan was already 22 years old? And that's why I never heard anything about my uncle, my aunt Joan's "husband?" And that I'm really the nephew of the great Jimmie Foxx? And that, well, all sorts of other stuff? This is way beyond me. And yet, I have to believe it, because it makes too much sense, answers too many questions. Nobody's going to believe this. Maybe that's why the two are laying low. I can only imagine what's going through their minds, both of them wanting to see my aunt Joan for different reasons. But they won't. They can't. Still, I'd sure love to be there if they did.

Like I said, I stayed around the house for a few days, waiting for their call. They said they'd get back to me, and I sure didn't want to miss the call. Boy, did I have the questions now. Because of my current fame, I receive a lot of phone calls, and I usually blow most of them off. I just kept waiting for that one special call.

A couple of days later, an article in the local paper drew my attention. In short, it said that the Sheboygan Athletic Club was delighted to disclose that they had received an anonymous check for $500,000 to completely renovate Wildwood Athletic Park, the only condition being that the renovation would be in "the style and form of the old Legion Memorial Park." That meant ivy-covered brick walls with the correct Legion Park dimensions, a Legion correct grandstand, dugouts, etc. "The Sheboygan Athletic Club is only too happy to adhere to these conditions. A close replica of the old Legion Park will bring excitement and nostalgia to the Sheboygan baseball

164

scene. "The paper went on to say that a minor condition was that the donors remain anonymous. Anonymous, huh? Maybe to the general public, but not to me. "Things to do," Jerry had said. That will be one less question I need to ask when I see them. "It'll be back, Jimmie had told me in my dream. Another mystery solved. Or was it?

The call finally came the next morning.

"Craig, it's Don."

"Don, yes," I replied, actually breathing heavily.

"Kiwanis northeast diamond, 1:30. Got it?"

"Yes, got it." And that was it. Short and sweet. Maybe they could feel that they wouldn't be here much longer. I sure hope not; there was so much to talk about.

They were already sitting in the second row of the third-base bleachers, the site of all of their important discussions. I felt I was on hallowed ground when I came up and sat next to them.

"Craig, good to see you again," Don said happily, slapping my right knee in fun.

"We'd have called you sooner, but we've been busy."

"I saw how busy you've been in yesterday's paper."

"See, I told you he'd figure it out," Don said, elbowing Jimmie as he did.

"I never doubted it for a minute," Jerry chuckled, somehow blowing smoke rings from another impossibly long cigar.

"Anyway, we just wanted to say goodbye. Our time is short."

"Short? You just got here. I have a million questions. I mean, is Jimmie really your dad? That can't be! And..."

"I know. There are questions galore, not just from you, but from us also," Don interjected soberly. "But the headaches are back, and we'll be leaving soon. It appears we had just enough time to see you, give you our latest update, and make an "anonymous" donation.

"Where did you get the money for that?"

"Knowledge-aforethought, kid," Jimmie answered. "It pays to know little bit about the future."

"Oh, I see. But don't you want to see your, well, I mean, you know," I stammered.

"We can't," Don whispered. "At least not now."

I let it pass. I knew this was a subject neither wanted to talk about. At least, not now.   "I was hoping to see you hit, uncle Jimmie."

"Jerry. Jerry is still better," Jerry corrected. "Besides, maybe you'll get to see me play sometime."

165

I got the feeling he knew something I didn't, an understatement, to be sure, but both of them gave out the impression that they knew a lot more than they were revealing. About everything. "So, if all this is about, well parentage, where could you be going to next?

"We never know for sure, but let's just say we both know, instinctively, that there are places that need us, that can benefit from our presence, whether we become a part of the history books or not. We're kind of like ephemeral, roving ambassadors, hopefully, influencing the past in a beneficial way."

"So, we probably won't ever see each other again," I replied sadly.

"You never know kid," Jerry chuckled again while jumping off the bleachers to the ground. Don and I did likewise, and I stood staring at both of them.

"It was great meeting you kid," Jerry said, offering his hand. He was actually gentle with his handshake as was Don with his.

"Take care of, well, you know who."

"You guys know something, don't you?"

"We know a lot kid," Jerry replied, blowing one last smoke ring before tossing his spent cigar onto the ground.

"Patience, Craig."

They stood next to each other, staring straight ahead.

Then they got this weird, glassy look on their faces, started to shake a little, and then…disappeared. Just like that, gone.

I sat heavily on the front row of the bleachers, trying to take it all in. It wasn't the disappearance that had shaken me, though it certainly did. It was their attitude, what they said, and the way they said it.

"Maybe you'll get to see me play sometime."

"You never know kid."

"We know a lot kid."

"Patience, Craig."

What did it all mean? They knew something, alright. Would they be coming back soon? How soon? For them, time meant nothing. The past was the past. Or was it? Or, maybe I'd be joining them. That would really be something. Joining cousin Don and uncle Jimmie on their adventures would be more than awesome. I am about their age. Wow! How cool would that be? But, hey, I'm getting carried away with all this. It's something that couldn't possibly happen.

On the other hand, I have been getting a few headaches lately.

166

Chasing Tomorrow

PART IX

1

Well, the weeks rolled by, and the headaches stopped. I suppose it's not often that someone hopes they have headaches, but this was one such time. Actually, I knew I would. I figured I wasn't going anywhere without my cousin and uncle. Patience, my uncle Jimmie had advised. If their hints were correct, I might have all the time in the world. Eventually.

In the mean time, I made a couple decisions, the big one being I decided to buy a house. I had been considering this for some time, long before my meetings with Don and Jimmie. I temporarily changed my mind when I thought I might be going with them but quickly realized that I just couldn't wait on that happening. I found a nice two story house just a touch north of town that I liked a lot. Nothing special: three bedrooms and two full baths up, living-dining room, family room, kitchen-dinette, half bath down, and a moderately sized family room in the lower level. It had a nice two car garage, patio/deck, and a modest back yard. It also had a nifty backboard and hoop on the garage which was a bigger selling point than it should have been. As much as I like baseball, I'm also a basketball fan, having played varsity ball in high school. I still love shooting around all by myself. Maybe it's one of my ways to relax and unwind. Anyway, I bought the house.

Being young, single and still living at home meant I needed to furnish my new house. Being young, single and rich meant that wasn't a big problem. Still, my folks donated a few items, and I gathered up a few other things from various sources. Then I had to go grocery shopping for maybe the first time in my life. My cart was overflowing for hopefully the only time ever. After only one week of haggling, acquiring, buying, moving and shopping, I was a proud new home owner. The whole business cost me just over $250,000. I paid cash for everything.

Now that I had my house, I had to figure out how I was going to pass the time. Most of my friends were either still in school or had just started new jobs. My only job was pretending to write. The hoopla over "Long Ago and Far Away" was subsiding which left me with a lot more time on my hands. I was still getting royalties on the book and movie, but the cross-country appearances had slowed to a trickle. That was fine with me. It was exciting for awhile, but it got old very quickly. Naturally, my publisher was on me to write a sequel, which is where my "pretend " writing comes in. I convinced him I was working on it, even sending in small portions of my cousin's latest manuscript, a little at a time. I wanted to drag this out for as long as possible, certain there was going to be more to come. That certainty was what kept me in Sheboygan. I could have gone to live anywhere I wanted, but I wanted to be where my cousin and uncle could find me. I kept waiting for the parcel or phone call or the visit, but none was forthcoming. "Patience," I kept hearing my uncle caution. It's tough to be patient when you're twenty two years old, have a cousin and newly-discovered uncle bopping around through time and space, knowing that some day soon you could be joining them.

Anyway, once I got the house in order, I started looking for things to do. I cut the lawn a couple times with my new lawnmower. I painted the two spare bedrooms. They must have been kids bedrooms by the look of the walls. This was a pretty easy job considering there was no woodwork to paint and nothing in the rooms. I didn't see any reason to furnish them yet, so I didn't. The same with the lower family room. A main floor family room was enough for now. I may have money, but I don't intend to spend it unwisely. I'll get around to furnishing the entire house when and if I need to.

Once the chores were done, I was looking for something else to do. I took many a walk with my dog Fido, who was extremely happy to have me around more. He also likes the new house having already dug a very workman-like hole near the back patio. I rode my bike a lot, though never very far from home. Biking isn't my favorite recreational activity. I took a trip to Milwaukee to visit my sister Molly for a couple days. That was a case of she was happy to see me and happy to see me leave. What I enjoyed the most was shooting baskets in the driveway. I would leisurely shoot hoops almost by the hour. It was a great way to relax. And wait. And wonder.

It was the middle of July and I was again shooting hoops. And thinking.

Where were they now? Were they in another city, in another park, watching another baseball game?

Two mid-range jumpers and a left handed lay-up.

Maybe they were at the old Polo Grounds watching Matty throw his famous fade-away. Or Sportsman's Park watching Rajah spray hits to all fields.

Two missed jumpers from the key, then a made left handed hook from the near left side.

Or maybe they were at Detroit's Bennett Park watching Ty Cobb slide into second, spikes raised. Or maybe Chicago's Old Comiskey watching "Old Aches and Pains" Luke Appling foul off pitch after pitch until he got a good one.

Three made jumpers from the top of the key and a missed scoop shot from the right side.

More than likely they were back in Sheboygan, literally "back" in Sheboygan. But when? Maybe 1953, so my uncle Jimmie could be with my aunt Joan.

Another missed left handed hook.

How could Jimmie Foxx be my uncle anyway? Right, in my day, he's dead. And Don? How could he be twenty two when he was born in 1954? And yet, I saw them. I met them. I talked to them and shook hands with them. They're real. They're physical. I touched them. They're not spirits. But what are they? Celestial time travelers roaming through time and space performing minor acts of good? Celestial? What or who is the guiding force behind all this? It doesn't appear they know. And yet, their instincts are growing keener with every "trip." And where do I fit into all this? Am I just a conduit for my cousin's stories?

"You're Craig Mand, aren't you?"

I was so startled, I think I might have jumped and looked up, possibly expecting a heavenly answer to all my uncertainty.

"I'm over here, not up there."

Standing on the strip of grass between my driveway and the one to the north stood a girl of about my age, smiling.

I ambled over to where she standing to say hi.

"I'm Marci Jones," she greeted me pleasantly. I accepted her out-stretched hand.

169

"Craig Mand," I confirmed.

"I thought so. I live next door here with my parents," she said, nodding to the house next door. "My parents told me you had bought this house and had moved in. They were fairly excited, actually, having a celebrity as a neighbor. Personally, I'm not as impressed with today's celebrity-based culture."

I only responded with a wry smile and nodded. She was maybe 5'4" tall, slim build, shoulder length blonde hair and beautiful golden brown legs that were thoughtfully displayed under a fashionably short pair of white shorts. She had a delightfully mischievous look on her face, even as she was dissing me. I've never had a problem attracting girls, and since my recent fame, they've practically throwing themselves at me. I've repulsed virtually all of them, only settling on a few dates here and there. I've gotten to be quite leery of the opposite sex. Still, this girl was a real looker.

"I'm sorry I startled you," she offered, again with an almost impish look on her face.

"That's ok, I was just lost in thought for awhile there. It happens a lot when I shoot hoops."

"Thinking about your next book, the sequel to your first masterpiece?" Again, she seemed more amused than truly inquisitive.

"Something like that," I semi-lied. I had quickly gotten bored with the whole conversation. She didn't seem to care for me or my book. After months of being on the book and movie pushing circuit, I've gotten good at separating what I call the "genuine" from the "phonies." It may be a cruel way to look at the world and at people, but I really can't help it. Now that I'm mostly rich and famous, I definitely have to watch my back. And front. And yet, she had a beautiful smile and an adorable way of raising her eye brows in what I took to be amusement. Ok, I was quite attracted to her. But I was still wary.

"I've been gone most of the Summer, in Minnesota being a counselor for disadvantaged children. More of a baby sitter, but still, it's something I consider worthwhile and enjoyed.

"I see," was all I could answer. "Are you still in school?"

"I graduated this Spring. In a few weeks I start my new job."

"Which is?"

"Third grade teacher at Jefferson School," she replied rather proudly. "It's something I've always wanted to do. I am so looking forward to it."

"I see," again. "So you're going to be around awhile, or do you have an apartment of your own?"

"No, I'll be here," she smiled. "I have a huge student debt, and it's much cheaper to live at home until I can get a little more financially stable. Some people aren't independently wealthy, you know, and actually have to work for a living, and watch their pennies." An obvious shot, still, she was smiling when she said it. I could only give a brief, indifferent smile. I was about ready to put an end to this introduction. There wasn't much more I could think of to say.

"Well, maybe we'll have to get together some time." It was a throw-away line, but she didn't take it that way, or at least she pretended to. It was getting tougher and tougher telling the difference between when she was serious and when she wasn't.

"I HAVE a boyfriend."

"Good for you," I deadpanned. I didn't particularly care if she had a boyfriend or not.

"You certainly give up awfully quickly," she came back.

"I'm not particularly in the market for a girlfriend."

"Oh, I see. Well, maybe I can work you in some time," she smiled, eyebrows rising. She gave a cute little turn and walked deliciously toward her house. I gave a not-so-cute turn and walked slowly back to my garage where I took a few more shots. I was thinking of her as I hoisted up a few long -range bombs. She was quite charming in an intriguing sort of way. Part fascinating and part maddening, kinda like most girls. I didn't know quite what to make of her, and I wasn't sure if I even wanted to try. Still, we were neighbors, and, I suppose, I'll be seeing her now and then. I don't know if the thought excites me or not. Still, did I mention she's quite a looker?

Over the next few weeks, I got better acquainted with my new neighbors, the Joneses. Marci's mother Martha works as a dental hygienist and is a real fitness buff. She has a membership to the YMCA and likes to run, swim, walk and do those dance/stretch exercises that women do. I don't know what you call them. The father, Doug, is a banker here in town and likes almost all sports except soccer. He played football and basketball in high school and claims to have me watched me play at North High. I liked him immediately and invited him over to shoot hoops any time he liked, and since he doesn't have a basket of his own, he quickly accepted. They were a very handsome couple, the mother being merely an older version of the daughter.

After a few dates, I got to know Marci fairly well, if that's really possible after only a few dates with a girl. Any girl. She recently graduated from UW - Stevens Point with a degree in elementary education, which makes sense since she'll be teaching third grade this year. She's into fitness, though not to the extent that her mother is. She plays a reasonably good guitar, hates going to bars which she hardly ever does, and is a moderate sports fan. The so-called boy friend she claimed to have isn't really a boy friend at all, but rather a casual acquaintance she threw at me to "keep me off-balance." I was happier than I would have thought when confessed to this minor fib. She had to confess that she really liked "Long Ago and Far Away," which made me feel good. She also had to confess that she was very impressed with the author and his vivid imagination and writing skills. This pleased me even more, though despite her positive impression of me as a person, she wasn't the least bit impressed with my fame or my fortune. I believed her, and that made me even happier because she was a very easy girl to like. And have I mentioned that she is a real looker?

"How did you think of the rest of your book? I mean the first part was true, right? Your cousin did disappear one day, and left that story behind." We were sitting in an Applebee's one evening when she started asking me questions about the book. It was the first time she had brought up the subject. "Then you added on to that story and made it into a book. How did you do it? Why did you do it?"

These were questions I had tried to answer during my many interviews and talk show appearances, but I could see why she would want a personal answer from someone who was rapidly becoming her boyfriend.

"I just felt it was something I had to do. I don't know if Don planned to continue with it or not. It seemed to me that it was a good start, so I did some thinking and research and came up with the rest. It seems like it fits pretty well and something he might have come up with." This was pretty much my stock answer but saying it to her in a personal, face-to-face setting seemed so much more, well, intimate I guess. I sensed that she felt the same way.

"And you haven't seen him since?" she asked quietly.

"Nope," I just as quietly lied. And it wasn't really a lie. The Don Jackson I knew really doesn't exist anymore. The cousin I saw was a new creation mostly.

"It sounds as though you were pretty close to your cousin."

"We were, despite our age difference. We liked the same things and sorta thought the same way."

"He sounds interesting. I would like to have met him."

I had been debating for some time as to how much of all this I could, or would, tell her. Nobody knows the truth about any of this, not even my family. And yet, I was beginning to trust this girl. I think she just might understand and believe me. Plus, what if my cousin and uncle showed up again some day, like I expect them to. What would I tell her? My decision has been not to decide. I'll make the decisions as the circumstances present themselves. Don always said I had good instincts. I will employ them as they are needed. But for now, I had to play it safe. Or maybe not.

"Maybe you will someday," I replied mischievously.

She gave me a quizzical look.

I just smiled.

173

4

The day after my latest date with Marci, I drove Fido over to the dog run south of town. I try to do that at least once a week, as long as the weather is nice. He loves to romp around the open field with some of his doggie buddies. After about an hour we hopped back into the car and headed home. Since I had nothing else planned for the day, I decided to take the scenic route, or, maybe more accurately, the historic route. I drove north to 24th Street and stared at the current James Madison Elementary School. Don had walked here several times in 1953 to watch it's construction. Where did he stand? What was he thinking about?

I continued driving north, over to Kiwanis Park. I stopped the car and Fido and I got out and walked over to the infamous third base bleachers of the northeast diamond. Being late August, there was no one around, so we sat in the now historic spot, and looked out onto the expansive park. I imagined what the park would have looked like with four baseball diamonds instead of the current two. I imagined watching the blue shirts playing the green shirts in that famous game so long ago. I imagined Don and Jimmie talking on the several occasions they were sitting here on this very spot. I almost felt I was on some sort of personal, hallowed ground.

We then drove over to the ultimate hallowed ground of the local baseball scene. I never saw the original Memorial Park, but even to me, the semi-occupied building planted on the space looked totally foreign. I parked the car in the lot, and we walked to the stone commemorating the approximate location of home plate. Standing there and looking north, I imagined what the famous park would have looked like. Short down the lines, stretching deep into the power alleys, then straight across deep center field. This was where Don met Jimmie for the first time. I imagined the meeting. Despite Don's description, the experience must have been more mind-blowing than he recorded. I took Fido over to the large maple tree that still stands. It's tough imagining this large tree actually being in play inside the playing field. Part of the brick wall still stands as a reminder of what once was. Of course, this spot was my own historical marker, being the place I met Don and Jimmie. Was it only a couple months ago? Why did it seem longer? I couldn't help thinking that a couple generations of young men had missed out on a lot when the park was torn down. And that included me.

174

Before heading back to the car, Fido left his mark on the tree, an appropriate salute, I felt, for what was, and should have been.

Before leaving, we walked over to the plaque that was placed at the park's entry in 1946. It memorialized those that fought and died in World War II. It's what finally gave the park a name:

Sheboygan
Memorial
Athletic
Park

Dedicated to the Memory
Of the men and women of
Who served in
World War II

It was thoughtfully preserved and embedded into a large rock just north of the parking lot. Showing respect, Fido sat down and stared at the plaque. He left no mark this time.

I parked my car in the garage and let Fido out to run around. Walking over to the front door, I opened the screen door and picked up the Manila envelope I expected to be there. How did I know it would be there? I can't explain it. I just knew that after our history tour of the city that it would be there. I called Fido into the house, and we had a light lunch. Meal time over, I let Fido out into the back yard and followed him out onto the patio. I took a twenty ounce bottle of Diet Coke along and plopped down onto one of the comfy lawn chairs. Marci was, by now, busy with school meetings and setting up her classroom, so I wasn't concerned about being interrupted. I wasn't too thrilled about having to explain to someone what I was reading. I took a deep sigh, opened the envelope, took out the contents, reminded Fido to be a good dog, and began to read.

175

PART X

1

Hello, cousin, we're back, as you obviously know by now. And, we're probably going to be here awhile. We've rented a house in town, and wait till you see where. Sorry about the hasty departure last time, but now we'll have plenty of time to talk. Jerry's looking forward to a little hitting practice at Kiwanis Park, if you're still interested. This looks like a nice house you have here; can't wait for the official tour. Anyway, here's a brief summary of our latest adventure. It's not much, not nearly as extensive as our other trips. Still, it should give you an update of where we've been, and a possible pre-cursor of what may be yet to come. We'll give you a day or two to read this, and then we'll be back, hopefully for a nice long visit.

Don

By the way, you knew this envelope would be here today, didn't you?

Only a few sentences, but boy were they packed full of interest, and suspense. Was I still interested in batting practice with my uncle Jimmie? Jimmie Foxx? That's Don's subtle sense of humor for you. Where were they living, and what had they been up to? And how did they know that I knew the envelope would be here today? Probably in the same way I did. Only they were a lot better at it than I was.

I shuffled through the the pages he had written. There weren't nearly as many as in the past times. I took it to mean we would be doing a lot more talking, like he said. I hope so. The thought of hanging around with my cousin and my uncle was pretty thrilling. Superstars known only to me. Kinda like Superman and Batman almost.

I was anxious to get started reading, but felt it just be better to go inside where I could read in private. Marci might get home early and pop over for a visit, something she did quite often. I called Fido into the house, settled into my recliner, and proceeded to peruse the latest chapter of Don and Jimmie's extraordinary adventure.

Same park bench, same park, same city, maybe even the same year. The cars looked the same, as was the people's attire. It was chilly. Both Jerry and I were wearing heavier coats. This was unusual as we usually arrived in warmer Spring-like weather. My not-so-wild guess was that it was early 1954, and that we were here to witness the arrival of baby Donald.

"I think we've been here before," Jerry deadpanned while pulling a cigar from his inside coat pocket. "Don't tell me, Sudlersville, Maryland."

"You're pretty funny for so early in the day." Sudlersville was where Jerry, aka Jimmie Foxx was born.

"Why is it always about you? Why don't we end up in my hometown and get to relive my old memories?" Jerry was puffing contentedly on his cigar and wasn't the least bit upset. He liked it here. Still, he had a pretty good point, one I had no good answer for.

"When you meet the man in charge, you can ask him."

" I will. Not that I mind, of course."

" I don't mind either."

" Then it's settled. Neither of us minds." He was smiling, almost happy to be back. So was I.

We sat on the park bench for awhile, looking at our so familiar surroundings. After a short while, I was starting to get cold. It was time to get moving.

"Let's get the usual out of the way," I said. "Date, time of day, find a place to stay, etc."

"And something to eat. I'm starving."

"A revelation if ever there was one."

"You're pretty funny too. Let's get going."

Jerry was scanning the paper he had just purchased at the news store. We were walking south on eighth street, trying to decide on a place for lunch.

"Tuesday, April 13, 1954," Jerry offered.

"One week."

"Huh?"

"One week to the birth of, well, you know who. It's why we're here, you know."

"I know. A week, huh? What do we do til then?"

"Find something to eat for starters."

177

"How about this place?"

We were once again, standing in front of Kresge's. Why did it seem we were always standing in front of Kresge's? I know that's an exaggeration, but it sure seemed that way. I didn't have much desire to have lunch at Kresge's. Jerry could see my doubt and responded accordingly.

"C'mon let's try it. It's been almost a year. She's probably not working here anymore. If she is, we'll pick up a few things and go somewhere else.

"Deal." It was 11:30am, and the place was starting it's lunch time rush. We both looked over to the lunch counter where no Mary was in sight. Relieved, I followed Jerry to the counter where we sat down on our usual stools.

"So, what do we we do now?" Jerry mumbled while finishing his third hamburger.

"Are you finished, or are you going to have a couple more?"

"That's enough for now. I don't want to spoil my supper," he responded seriously.

"Oh, right." Throughout all our traveling, Jerry's appetite has never been adversely affected.

"I suppose we better find a lovely, economical flat just perfect for two time traveling gentlemen like us."

"I've been thinking about that. You know we're not going to be here too long. A couple weeks, maybe? What if we just live at the Foeste for the duration. We could pay by the week, so when we take our departure, nobody would be out anything." I was going to add, and that we wouldn't be missed, but I guess that isn't really a consideration, is it?

Jerry pondered it for a few moments and agreed with my suggestion.

"At least we won't have to worry about breakfast," Jerry offered as we walked north on eighth street.

"I wasn't worried about breakfast."

"You would have been had you given it any thought."

"What thought?"

"If we stay at the hotel, how are we going to have Kix for breakfast?"

"Oh, of course. How thoughtless of me not to think of that. So, why shouldn't I worry? Did you solve a potential problem?"

"Certainly. I noticed that they have small boxes of Kix at Kresge's. Guess where we're having breakfast every morning?"

"Ah, Kresge's?"

178

"Heh, heh. You catch on quick."
"I'm good that way."

"Gee, haven't we been here before?"

We had just plopped down onto our beds in Room 227 of the Hotel Foeste after checking in with the seemingly ever-present Henry Boatwright a few minutes earlier. This room was down from the one we had last time, and two down from the time before that. It looked the same, of course, and had an easterly exposure as did the others. Jerry's dead-panned comment belied the obvious for a brief moment. I couldn't help feeling we were in an endless loop, constantly checking into the Foeste and, eventually, disappearing. Maybe, that's what we were in somehow, a bizarre, off-center endless loop that keeps playing over and over again. Still, I know better; and yet, I couldn't help wondering how many more times we'd be checking in and out, so to speak.

"You're very observant."

"Thanks. I get that from you."

"And witty, too."

"Ditto."

"Thanks. I'll take that as a compliment."

"Would I give you a compliment?"

"Only if necessary."

"There you are."

We couldn't help smiling at this mindless banter. After all our time together, I still treasured my time with Jerry, and always will.

We spent the afternoon walking the city. We decided not to stop in a few former haunts: Hauser's Sport Shop (no reason to), Dutch's Bar (not ready yet), Jetzer's Five and Dime (saving it for later). The one store we did enter was Hermann's Grocery Store on North 14th Street. Jerry wanted a mid-afternoon snack, an ice cream cone. We walked into the oh-so-familiar store and headed to the ice cream cooler. Today's two flavors were chocolate and vanilla. We debated for several minutes over our selection, finally splitting the difference. Jerry took chocolate and I had vanilla. Not wanting to spoil our approaching supper, we limited ourselves to a single scoop each. We forked over the fourteen cents to John's wife Rose, and walked back out onto 14th Street.

After a hearty chicken dinner at Thimmig's Restaurant, we decided we'd had enough for one partial day and headed back to the Foeste.

I was laying on my bed, head propped on the pillow watching Jerry standing silently looking out the window, smoking another impossibly long panatela. I knew what he was think about, and I felt badly for him. How would he handle the situation? How would she react? Would the meeting be tearful and joyous, or acrimonious and hostile? I decided to open the discussion.

"Are you going to see her tomorrow?"

"See who?" Jerry feigned ignorance.

"Who do you think?" I came back a little too emphatically.

"Oh. Yeah, I guess," he came back meekly.

"You scared?"

"Me, scared?" This time feigning bravado. "Why would I be scared?" He sounded scared, and knowingly it, started pacing the floor.

"You know, I've been thinking."

"About time."

"Very funny."

"About time."

My last barb brought a smile to my worried friend's face.

"No, really. In the past, what we've done wasn't remembered, or lasting, or anything. Right? So what if it's no different this time? I mean all those records I set playing ball in the minor leagues disappeared the minute we did. Nothing was left. Maybe this is the same. Maybe Jane, or Joan, I mean, isn't pregnant at all. Maybe if I went to see her, she wouldn't remember me or know me at all."

Jerry was getting worked with hope, and with good reason. He'd brought up a good point, one I hadn't thought of. Maybe. Maybe. And yet...

"It's possible, I suppose. But that doesn't explain a few things."

"Like what?"

"Well, like the fact that I'm about to be born in a week. Someone's the father, and you're the logical candidate. I suppose it could be someone else if your existence last year never really happened, at least not permanently."

"Huh?"

Huh, was right. This was getting confusing. Despite our experience, time travel paradoxes were still nearly impossible to decifer and understand. A few times we had tried to make sense of it all, but had not been terribly successful. Besides, we wouldn't have to think about this for long.

"By tomorrow at this time we'll have our answer, won't we?"

Jerry's hopeful expression had turned dour again.

181

Neither of us slept well that night, so we got up early, took a brief walk, then went to Kresge's for an early breakfast. Jerry's meager two bowls of Kix told me the depth of his angst over his upcoming meeting. I also wasn't very hungry and for a different reason, though I didn't know what that reason was. Maybe it was a concern for my friend's predicament. Maybe it was an uncertainty over my upcoming "birth." Or, maybe it was a latent disappointment over not seeing Mary behind the lunch counter. In any case, all I had was a cup of coffee and a sweet roll. Usually Jerry was a big talker during breakfast, or any other meal for that matter, but not today. We ate in silence. And slowly, Jerry trying to drag out the mini-meal for as long as possible. Inevitably, it ended, and we walked outside onto 8th Street.

"I suppose I better get going," Jerry offered lamely.

"I suppose. C'mon, I'll walk with you part of the way." It was 8:30 and the day was promising to be at least somewhat pleasant. Weather-wise, that is. The particulars of the day may prove to be something else. We walked silently north on 8th Street, then west on Michigan Avenue. We crossed 14th Street and stopped.

"Good luck," I offered.

"Look, maybe you could come with me. I could introduce you as..."

The look on my face stopped him in mid-sentence.

"I know. This is something I have to do myself."

"I expect a complete report later."

"Yeah, right," Jerry muttered as he sauntered off for his meeting.

I decided to walk the few steps to Hermann's Grocery Store. Just like I would one day, I gravitated to the candy case. As I had several times before, I had John load up a bag of some of my favorite old-time candy. Candy raisins, candy cigarettes, candy dots on a strip, lik-m-ade, black licorice, Lunch Bars, small candy ice cream cones, and two packs of baseball cards. I paid John the twenty three cents and asked him how he thought the Braves would do this year. He said they would be pretty good if they could fill the hole in left field. I replied that I thought they would fill it nicely. That Aaron kid looks like he has a future. He said he hoped I was right, but wasn't sure. I just smiled.

I spent the next few hours resisting the temptation of spying on my friend, and instead, walked around the city. Not much had changed, of course, since our last visit, so deciding my twenty three

182

cents worth of candy and an earlier sweet roll wasn't enough, I walked to Kresge's for a more substantial meal.

I sat on my usual stool and stared down at the unneeded menu.

"What would you like today?" A sweet voice asked.

"I'll have a cheeseburger, fries and a coke," my usual, more substantial meal.

"I haven't seen you in here lately," the sweet voice replied.

I looked up, and there was my goddess, my angel in white, a slight smile gracing her lovely, yet mysterious face.

"I've been gone for awhile," was all I could mumble.

"Your friend too?"

" Yes we always travel together. He has another appointment at the moment." I had re-gained my composure a bit, and I watched as she smiled again and walked off to deliver my order. I tried not to watch as she went about her duties, but I couldn't help it. I had an incredible attraction to her, but I didn't know why. She was hardly a classic beauty. I think it was the high cheekbones and the set of her eyes. They gave her a continually mysterious, far-away look. Almost lost. I thought how much I wanted to find her, and lead her to wherever it was she was hoping to be. But I kept thinking about our situation as well as her bruiser boyfriend, and settled in to the hopelessness of it all. I would have to settle for a visual appreciation only.

Before long, she brought my order, and, again, I thought I detected a hint of a smile on her lovely face. I downed my more substantial meal, all the while stealing glances at my princess. All too quickly, I was finished eating. Funny, I didn't remember eating anything.

"Thank you," she said as she handed me my check. Was that another faint smile I saw? I paid the check, left another huge tip, and regretfully walked out of the store. We're those really smiles I saw, or just wishful thinking? I concluded that it really didn't matter. This pseudo-relationship wasn't going anywhere. Still, if Jerry could have a girlfriend, why couldn't I? Of course, look what became of that. Me!

I spent the next couple hours walking around the downtown area. I stopped in to Hill's Department Store and it's adjacent Piggly Wiggly. As I walked down the aisles, I could only smile at the prices, prices to which, by now, I had grown quite accustomed; milk, 66 cents a gallon; butter, 69 cents per pound; beef roast, 45 cents per pound; sirloin, 49cents per pound; ground beef, 69 cents for two pounds; Post Sugar Crisp, 19 cents a box. And though people make considerably less these days, for us, the amount of money Jerry and I found in our wallets was more than enough to last us a long time, even without working.

I made a few other stops, most notably a quick visit to the old library on seventh street. I hadn't been there since my research check in 1946, the one that cued me in on our permanent insignificance. I just looked around awhile, then left. Not many pleasant memories here.

At last, I wandered over to our bench at Fountain Park. The park was quiet, and I sat down to ponder.

I thought of Jerry and his seemingly impossible predicament. How was such a thing possible? Could he really be my long-lost father? What was my mother's reaction to his re-appearance? Was this really the point of all our traveling? Or is there more?

I thought of Mary and why she had such a powerful effect on me. Did I know her somewhere from my original past? I don't think so. But what is it? It couldn't amount to anything. Or could it? Of course, she had a Dick the Bruiser clone for a boyfriend. That's tough competition. I don't even think I'm in the competition, if there is one. What is it about women, that they can have such a strong influence over men? Is it an acquired trait, one coming from strong, eternal, outside influences? Or isn't it just something in our DNA? Are men just born with an irresistible tendency to be total fools over the opposite sex? History is loaded with examples: David and Bathsheba, Antony and Cleopatra, Solomon and Sheba, Burton and Taylor, Mickie and Minnie, Foxx and Jackson, Jackson and Mary something. I guess we're just two of a long line of men who have come under the intoxicating spell of a woman. It's agonizing. It's frustrating. It's debilitating. It's painful. It's...wonderful.

"Hi, may I sit down?"

I was so deep in thought, I hadn't heard her approach. Despite my surrender of all hope, my special vision of loveliness stood beside me, actually wanting to sit with me.

"Yes, of course," was all I could mumble.

"Thanks." She sat down next to me, far enough to be 1950's proper, yet close enough to be semi-intoxicating. She maintained that distant look, and I wondered why she was here. In spite of my infatuation, I had quickly recovered my composure and was determined that she should make the next move, the first move, really. After the few moments that passed like a few hours, she did.

"I was surprised to see you before."

"Like I said, my friend and I have been doing a little traveling." She had asked her question in a quiet voice, and I had responded in kind. I wasn't going to be intimidated, something I had been all too often in my previous life. She may have been my superficial dream girl, but I wasn't about to act the fool. I could be a fool without acting, but this time I was having none of it.

"My name is Mary, Mary Smith."

"Dan Parker," I responded, and we both shook hands. Her hand was soft, yet solid, a combination regarding her sex and her job.

"I suppose you're wondering why I've come to see you."

"Yes, I am." I had turned slightly to my left to get a better look at her. I was enjoying the view, and the closeness of her made it all the more appealing, and exciting.

"I don't know, really. It's just that you seem so interesting, mysterious maybe. And you always give me such a big tip, so I though maybe...I don't know."

She was clearly struggling for the right words and wasn't succeeding. I wanted to think she hadn't been in this position before, actually going after a fella. Was she actually going after me? Maybe it was just an act. I could be pretty dense sometimes. And what about Dick the Bruiser, or was he out of the picture? I figured in my position, I didn't have time to play the cat and mouse relationship game.

185

"The last time I saw you, you were walking arm-in-arm with some Neanderthal type."

"Oh, him," she said softly, after deciphering my not so subtle reference. "I don't see him anymore. He wasn't very nice to me."

"I'm sorry," I replied, only half meaning it.

"Actually, after him, I swore off boys. And I haven't had a date in over six months. But, you seem a little different. I don't know why I feel that way since I hardly know you, but I do."

Her face was staring down onto her folded hands in her lap. I guessed that this was no act. And if it was, so what? It's not as if this had the makings of a lasting relationship.

"So you're not looking for a boyfriend, but you find me interesting, is that it?"

"Kinda," she replied sheepishly.

"Of course, those big tips I left you were more than a mild indication of my interest."

"Either that or you just have a lot of money."

"Maybe it's both," I smiled.

"Maybe," and she smiled back.

"Look, ah, I've gotta go. I have something I have to do." She stood up, and I stood up with her. "I get off at 2:00 again tomorrow, if you're interested."

"I'm interested. I'll see you tomorrow."

"Tomorrow," she replied sweetly, then turned and walked north, out of the park. I watched her for a few moments, then sat back down on the bench and pondered what had just happened. After about forty minutes of pondering, I finally arrived at a conclusion: I had no idea what the hell this was all about. Satisfied with my conclusion, I got up and walked back to the Foeste to rest. It had been a much more eventful day than I had anticipated.

186

Jerry was staring onto eighth street, smoking yet another panatela. I closed the door, took off my shoes, and dropped heavily onto the bed.

"Hi," Jerry said glumly.

"Hi," I replied tiredly, yet expectantly. "So, how'd it go?"

"Ah, well..."

"You didn't see her, did you?"

"I meant to, really. I was standing on the front porch, and I wanted to knock on the door, but I just couldn't. I convinced myself at the time that nobody was home, so I left. I've been walking around since, feeling terrible about it. I'm sure she was home, but I just needed an excuse. I'm just putting it off. Now I'll have to go through all this again tomorrow." He had turned from the window and was dejectedly pacing the floor.

"Why am I not surprised?" I said calmly.

"I meant too, really. I just couldn't."

I had more sympathy than disappointment for my friend. Maybe, were I in his shoes, I would have failed too.

"You hungry?" I asked, as if I didn't know the answer.

"Hungry? Oh, what time is it?"

"About 4:20."

"In the afternoon?"

"When do you think?"

"I just, I mean I didn't realize it was that late. I must have missed lunch."

"You missed lunch?" I exclaimed. "You. Missed lunch? C'mon, let's get out of here and get something to eat. We need to do some talking."

As we walked north on 8th Street, I told Jerry about my encounter with Mary. I knew he'd be interested, plus I figured it would be quite therapeutic considering the kind of day he'd had. As expected, the news perked him up immediately.

"So, now you're also headed toward the quicksand, eh?" Jerry gave a little chuckle and, as usual, puffed away on his panatela.

"That's not very encouraging."

"Hey, don't get me wrong, it's a wonderful trip. And we all take it, sooner or later."

"Still, you just stuck a little pin in my balloon."

187

"Don't mind me. Just keep in mind the kind of day I've had. Still, when I think about her, I get a good feeling inside, you know?"

"I know."

We turned left on Michigan Avenue. I figured supper at Avenue Lunch was just the thing we needed. Jerry hadn't eaten since breakfast, plus they had the best baked beans in town. I told Jerry where we were headed, and he heartily agreed.

"Great idea, I'm famished. They have the best baked beans in town, you know."

"I think I'll have two servings, plus maybe a cheeseburger."

"That's quite a bit for you, plus, you had lunch."

"True, but I don't remember eating it."

After a total of three steak sandwiches, one cheeseburger, four orders of beans, two heaping piles of fries, and three cokes, we were finally ready to leave. We assured the lady behind the counter that we would be back again, and stepped out onto Michigan Avenue.

"'Paris Playboys' is playing at the Rex," Jerry stated glumly. We were back in our room, positioned in our usual locations. "I'll bet it's not about our life stories."

"Certainly not the Paris part. Or the playboy part," I responded just as somberly.

Jerry inhaled deeply on his latest panatela and exhaled a huge cloud of thick, aromatic smoke onto the air of our not so spacious room.

"I'll have to go see her tomorrow, but I don't know what to say to her. I mean, she's going to ask me where I've been and what I've been doing, and I won't have an answer for her. That's why I couldn't go through with it. I didn't have a story to tell her, you know? I don't want to lie to her, but I sure can't tell her the truth either."

Jerry had, quite cogently, actually summarized not only his predicament, but mine as well. As much as I was looking forward to seeing Mary tomorrow, I knew that I had no answers should she start asking questions. It was obvious we both needed a story, the same story, if our relationships with the girls was going to go anywhere. And even though Jerry's situation was different from mine, we were both in a bind.

"Any ideas Einstein?"

"No, but let's think and talk this through. We both need stories and we'll need them by tomorrow. I think I have it a little easier. Mary doesn't really know me, and I could tell her any reasonable story, and she'd have no reason to question it. But you have a relationship going, one involving a baby."

188

Jerry stubbed out his cigar and sat on the edge of his bed. "So…?"

"I just think we have to be as vague as we can," I finally decided. "I'll tell Mary that my work moves me around quite a bit, and if she asks what my work is exactly, I'll say it's something I can't get into right now. I think you should take the same approach with my mother, or maybe I should say with Joan. I'm guessing she's going to be so happy to see you, she's not going to ask too many probing questions."

"I guess that sounds ok. But if she does ask a lot of questions, I'll just say my work doesn't allow me to reveal too much, right?"

"Right. We'd just be two mysterious guys doing mysterious work. They'll probably think we're secret agents, or something."

"Maybe we are."

After a restless night, each of us for different reasons, Thursday morning saw us ambling over to Prange's for a modest breakfast. While Jerry nursed a cup of coffee and a mud pie, I did the same with coffee, orange juice and a peanut Pershing. We were killing time until our walk to see Joan. I had agreed to accompany him this time as moral support, and by the way he was pawing at his meager breakfast, I could see that he needed it.

By 8:30 we had dawdled long enough. I paid the check, and we started walking north on eighth street.

"I feel a little better about this having you along, you know?" Jerry finally muttered after we had walked two blocks.

"I know. It'll be alright. She'll probably be so glad to see you, she won't even ask any probing questions," I repeated my reassurance from last night.

"You think so?" Jerry asked hopefully. "I really do want to see her. It's just those questions that bother me."

"Just stick to our plan, and you'll be fine."

"I hope so. Do you think she's going to want me to marry her?"

"Oh, yes. That's for sure." Jerry groaned in response.

We walked the rest of the way in silence, our pace slowing the closer we came to the house. Finally, inevitably, we were standing on the sidewalk in front of Joan's house, my first home. Jerry glanced at the house, then looked back at me.

"Maybe if I had told her more about myself last year, I wouldn't be going through some of this now, you know? But she never asked too many questions."

"If she had, you would have had to make something up, just like now."

"Yeah, I guess."

After another moment, Jerry gave me a wink and said, "Well, here goes."

Displaying a sudden surge of confidence, the old Jerry Wolff walked to the front porch, gave a few quick raps on the door and waited. Although the house faces north, the front door actually faces west, so I positioned myself in such a way to be virtually unseen by anyone answering the door. After only a few seconds, Jerry turned to me and shrugged his shoulders. I motioned to rap again, which he did. Shortly, I saw the door open, followed by a shriek. Two female arms flew around Jerry's neck, an embrace Jerry eagerly returned. Jerry turned his face my way and smiled. I smiled back and slowly walked away. It would be ok. Jerry and Joan would be happy, at least for a while. Maybe longer. I could feel it. I was getting quite good at feeling things.

I spent the nearly five hours before meeting Mary just walking around town. My weakness for variety stores led me to spend some time in both Jetzer's on Michigan Avenue and Woolworth's on 8th Street. I certainly didn't need anything but that didn't stop me from purchasing a few typical five and dime store items; a paddle with a rubber line and a ball on the end, a medium size squirt gun, one of those square games with fifteen tiles and sixteen spaces that you have to arrange in order, an extremely discounted Milwaukee Braves cap, and a whole bunch of cheap candy. I took my booty back to the room and killed time until 2:00pm.

I entered Kresge's a few minutes before 2:00pm and glanced over to the lunch counter. Mary was wiping off part of the counter when she looked up and noticed my arrival. She flashed me her sweet, subtle smile then walked to the other side of the work area and disappeared into the kitchen. Very shortly she re-appeared, apron-less now, and headed my way.

"Hi," she smiled in greeting.

"Hi," was my clever reply.

"Well, shall we walk?"

"Absolutely." I held the door for her as we exited onto 8th Street. As we started walking north, she naturally and comfortably slipped her hand into mine. As she did, I started briefly. It was like a swift electrical shock had jolted my hand. She had felt it too for she chirped, "Oh, what was that?"

"A sign of our mutual magnetic attraction," I replied suavely and confidently. This had to be one of the very few times the right words came at exactly the right time. Mary gave me that cute little smile of hers, and we continued walking.

We walked the downtown for a while, occasionally pausing to look into shop windows. Mary gazed at several pairs of shoes in the window of Nobil's Shoe Store, as well as a couple of attractive dresses in People's window. At each store she would wistfully sigh, "I'd like to go into this store someday, but I know I can't afford to buy anything anyway." I made a mental note to remedy this problem real soon.

We continued walking and talking, Mary doing most of the talking. The information didn't exactly spew from her lips but gradually I got a little better picture of whom I was infatuated. She graduated from Central High School last year but hadn't found a suitable full time job as yet, thereby explaining her part time waitress job at Kresge's. She lived on the near north side, not far from where Jerry and I had lived a couple times, with her divorced mother. Her mother, as well as her older brother, worked at the KOHLER Company, she in the office, he in shipping. The brother had recently found an apartment and had moved out, leaving the girls alone in the house. Evidently, neither seemed to mind.

We had been walking for an hour and a half with no particular destination in mind. I was just happy to be in her company, not caring where we were going or how long it would take to get there. And, for some reason, I sensed she felt the same way. We were walking west on Michigan Avenue when we approached Hinze's Ice Cream Parlor.

"Oh, I just love this place. Let's go inside and get something. I'm kinda hungry, and I love their banana splits."

"A banana split at 3:30 in the afternoon?" I questioned.

"Any time is a good time for ice cream."

I couldn't argue with that, so we walked into an empty store and sat at the counter. The owner, Harvey Hinze, slowly walked over and asked for our order. Mary ordered her banana split, while I selected a chocolate sundae. The orders came, and as we ate, Mary opened up a little.

"I guess I've mentioned that this is only about the second date I've had in the last year, or so, since that guy, you know, the one who wasn't so nice to me. This is a date kinda, isn't it?"

I assured her that it was for me.

"Well, anyway, I've been pretty down on boys since then. Maybe I shouldn't be, but I am. And it's not just me. I mean, my best friend had this boyfriend last Summer that she was just crazy about, but then he left her, just like that. She hasn't seen him since. And now she's having this baby any day now, and he's nowhere around. I feel so bad for her. I'm so upset. I think it's just terrible, don't you?"

"Yes, yes I do," I answered warily. "What's your friend's name?"

"Joan. Joan Jackson. Do you know her?"

Our mid-afternoon snack over, we walked hand in hand west on Michigan Avenue, then north to her house. We continued with some occasional small talk, but the heavyweight disclosures were over, praise the Lord! One bombshell per day was enough. At last we stopped in front of a modest, one family home.

"This is it," Mary said. "It isn't much, but I've lived here my whole life, so I'm used to it, and I like it."

"It looks fine to me," I replied, meaning it.

"Look, ah, I'm not available tomorrow. It's Good Friday, so I'm not working and then there's church and other things I have to do so..."

"No, I understand. I think I have some things I may have to attend to also." It was a defensive reaction; I couldn't think of anything I may actually have to attend to.

"Oh, ok. How about Saturday? I'm working my normal shift. I mean if you want to see me again."

" Of course I want to see you again," I answered with more emotion than I intended, but sincerely felt.

Mary looked down and actually shuffled her feet for an instant.

"I've been down on boys lately like I said," she began slowly, " But I really like you. You seem so nice. Quiet, but nice. I hardly know anything about you, you've been so quiet. Still, I get the feeling you're a good person, so different from many of the boys I've known. Maybe Saturday you can do the talking, and I'll do the listening."

"Deal," I said with a smile. It wasn't something I would be looking forward to, but standing so close to her, staring at that lovely and expressive face, I would have agreed to anything.

"Deal," Mary repeated while flashing a larger than normal smile. "Saturday, then," Mary whispered, leaning over to give a quick kiss on the cheek. She turned quickly and trotted to the front door.

How one person can be remarkably elated and stunningly depressed at the same time I cannot explain, yet, that was my state as I walked back to the Foeste. My time with Mary had left me ecstatic beyond words. She was everything I could want in a girl. Plus, I felt I was only scratching the surface, so to speak. She was sweet and gentle and sensual and a whole lot of other things all assembled into one irresistible female. And, she was available. And Joan's best friend. And un-possessable. An echo of a long ago time and place.

I picked up a paper at the news store and slowly walked back to our room, my mood alternating between total joy and absolute misery.

I had my paddle ball up to sixty eight when Jerry entered the room and interrupted my concentration. My friend tossed his jacket onto the bed and then followed suit, landing heavily on the bed. I was sitting on the edge of my bed, paddle ball in hand, waiting for the re-cap of his day. Nothing. Waited some more. Nothing. Finally, I'd had enough. The waiting was over.

"Well, are you going to give me the 'Reader's Digest' condensed version, or not?"

"What a day! I'm beat."

"Enough already. Give!"

"Well, she sure was happy to see me, though I guess you saw that. We talked mostly. We took a little walk, but she wasn't comfortable, so we cut it short. I met her mother, of course, and she made us lunch. They wanted me to stay for supper, but I told them I had business to attend to."

"You and me both."

"Huh?"

"Tell you later. Keep going."

"That's about it, really. Just a lot of talk. She wanted to know where I'd been and what I'd been doing and if I was going to stay and on and on. I kept to our story. I said I was called away unexpectedly and couldn't get back to her. I told her that I couldn't tell her more because of my job. She seemed satisfied with that. She kept saying 'at least you're back now,' over and over again. Of course, she wanted to know if I was staying this time, and I said that I didn't know. I think she thinks I'm some kind of spy, or something."

"Are you seeing her tomorrow?"

"They wanted me to go to a Good Friday service with them, but I told them that even though it was Good Friday, I needed to attend to some business here in town. I am invited for supper Saturday night. Her mother's going to make some special German-Russian dish."

"Did she talk about marriage?"

"She only brought it up about a couple hundred times."

Jerry was sitting on the edge of the bed now, facing me. I could tell he was happy to see her and be with her, but was definitely concerned about the future.

194

"How can a guy feel so wonderful and so miserable at the same time?" Jerry finally posed. We'd been together a long time now. Our emotional responses were beginning to merge. "How'd your meeting with Mary go?" Jerry asked after after taking his usual spot near the window and torching up a new cigar. I quickly gave him the highlights. Jerry nodded somberly and continued staring out the window. "So, my girl and your girl are best friends. That's just great. What next? At least they're not sisters. Then you'd be crazy over your aunt."

I had to wince at the thought of that one. Where was all this leading, and why had I asked that same question about twenty times since all this began?

"Enough of this. Let's go down to the bar. I need a drink."

I silently agreed, and together, quietly, we made our way to the bar.

Only a few people were seated at various tables as we entered the Hotel Foeste bar. We took a couple seats at the bar and waited for the bartender to come over to take our order.

"What'll you have tonight gents?" The slightly overweight, middle age bartender asked upon noticing our arrival.

"Whiskey sour," Jerry ordered. "Make it a double."

"Rum and coke, not a double."

"Rum and coke? You don't drink."

"I'm thinking of starting."

"I'll give you lessons."

"I'd appreciate it."

I took a few sips of my rum and coke and decided it tasted fine, except for the rum. Jerry and I chatted for a while on topics less important than our personal predicaments. While we were talking, I kept glancing over to the silent piano not far from us. I would talk and glance, talk and glance. Finally, I hopped off my stool and strolled over to the piano and sat down on the bench. I stared at the keys for a few seconds, then brought my hands up and began to play. My fingers glided over the piano keys neatly and knowingly, smoothly and effortlessly. I started with a touching version of "As Time Goes By" then slid seamlessly into the romantic "Misty." By this time, Jerry was standing next to me, smiling a semi-dumbstruck smile. Most of the patrons had also moved to tables closer to the piano. After "Misty," I got a little frisky and pounded out a spirited "A Hard Days Night," then the haunting "Year of the Cat." I concluded with Glenn Miller's "Moonlight Serenade," a particular favorite of my mother.

195

I sat on the piano stool for a few extra minutes acknowledging the polite applause and marveling at what I had done. I had never played a piano before in my life. Leading the applause was my good friend who was shaking his head in wonderment, even as he was puffing away on his latest cigar.

"I didn't know you could play the piano, " was his expected comment.

"I don't."

"That sure sounded great to me."

"I'm a quick learner."

"I caught those two ringers you threw in there, though I didn't recognize the second one."

"'Year of the Cat" by Al Stewart. A little after your time."

"Boy, you could have a lot of fun with that stuff."

"Yeah. I could be Lennon and McCartney before Lennon and McCartney."

"Maybe you're the reason they were so successful."

"Good grief, don't even go there."

We finished our drinks and started to leave. A tall, well-dressed, distinguished looking gentleman stopped us at the entry to the bar.

"Very nice playing young man," the man said smiling.

"Thank you."

"My name is Winston Niles, assistant manager of the Hotel Foeste." We shook hands.

"Dan Parker, and this is my friend Jerry Wolff." Niles and Jerry shook hands.

"Would you be interested in playing for us nightly? We have an opening for someone of your ability and would appreciate your helping us out. Business is always better with entertainment. We'd make it worth your while."

"Thank you Mr. Niles, but my friend and I aren't going to be in town long, so I'm afraid I can't help you out. Thank you for the offer though."

"I see," Mr Niles replied, obviously disappointed. "Well, I'll tell you what. You can have free use of the piano for as long as you're in town. You can entertain the customers we do have. How about that?"

"I'd appreciate that, thank you."

"What in the hell was that all about? Suddenly you're Liberace?"

We were back in our room, stationed at our usual positions. Jerry's astonishment was, obviously, quite valid. And, of course, I had no good answer for him.

"It was just so strange. I kept looking at that piano, and I knew that I just had to go over there. Suddenly, I just started playing. It was so easy. I'm as amazed as you are. I sure don't know what it means."

"Is it supposed to mean something?"

"I suspect it will. Everything happens for a reason, especially to us."

Jerry continued to look out the window, smoking away on another cigar. I finally got around to looking through the paper I had picked up earlier.

"Your new-found piano playing talent may be fine, but we still have a little female problem to deal with."

"I know. I'll have to come up with something a little more substantial than I have now, by Saturday. Mary's expecting some serious biographical information, and I don't have a clue as to what to tell her."

"You could be really vague, like me. We could be a couple of real mysterious cats, you know?"

"We ARE a couple of real mysterious cats."

"No big news there."

"I suppose that's the avenue I'll have to take, but it's so misleading. It's almost like lying, and I feel terrible about it."

"Yeah, and lying to someone you care about is the worst."

Jerry continued to puff away while I continued skimming through the paper. I was just about finished when something jumped off the page, and I couldn't help letting out a little chuckle/groan.

"What is it? Something actually amusing?"

In an incredibly appropriate way, yea. Guess what's playing at the Sheboygan Theatre right now?"

"I couldn't even begin to guess."

All I could do was smile and shake my head. The irony was perfect. Who says God doesn't have a sense of humor.

"Pinocchio" I answered.

Having had our fill of lies for one day, we passed on "Pinocchio". We also passed on attending a Good Friday church service, not because we weren't willing, but because we didn't have appropriate attire. This was the 1950's after all and people "dressed up" to go to church. We also passed on visiting Dutch's Bar figuring it wasn't in good taste to sit in a bar on this Holy Day. Instead, we picked up a few papers and magazines at City News, and kept a low profile.

Saturday morning dawned chilly but passable. After a quick breakfast at Prange's, we walked to Joan's house. Jerry was less anxious this time, definitely more excited than nervous. Standing in front of the little house on Huron Avenue, I felt a wave of nostalgia coast through me, a wave through someone who was about to be born, yet knew so much of what was about to happen. A paradox inside a conundrum wrapped inside an enigma, as they say.

"Have a good time," I wished Jerry. "Enjoy your supper. I know I would."

"Thanks. Same to you with Mary."

"I am so looking forward to seeing her again regardless of what she may think of my explanation."

Jerry just smiled and started walking down the narrow walk leading to the back of the house.

"I'm a back door friend already," Jerry called back.

"You should be, you're virtually family." With that, Jerry turned right toward the back door, and I wandered slowly off to the west, not having any idea how I would kill five hours until my meeting with Mary.

It was a very slow kill, indeed. It always is when you're really looking forward to something. I roamed around the city for a while, probably doing as much thinking as roaming. As usual, whenever I did some serious thinking, or some serious talking with Jerry, I had many more questions than answers. The only significant decision I made was things were rapidly coming to a head, and Jerry and I would need to have another of our serious talks.

Finally, I killed enough time to wander over to Kresge's for an early lunch. I thought about going somewhere else, but concluded Mary might not be happy about not patronizing her place of employment and losing out on another of my generous tips.

Mary was at the other end of the counter when I sat down on my usual stool. Another waitress started walking my way when Mary noticed me and rushed to cut in front of the other girl.

"I'll take him," Mary said to the other girl. The girl merely shrugged and walked away.

"Don't tell me. Cheeseburger, fries and a coke, right?" Mary smiled.

"Right," I replied, returning her smile.

"I didn't know if you'd stop here for lunch today."

"I want to take advantage of every opportunity I have to see you." Mary liked that and told me she'd get my order in. I watched her the whole time she was taking and delivering other orders. She had such an easy grace in her movements, that special "something" that made me so incredibly attracted to her. I'm sure other guys would never have seen it or responded to it the same way I did. At least I hoped so; I wanted exclusive rights without anyone else nosing in. Exclusive rights, huh? For how long?

After a few more minutes, Mary eased her way over with my usual order.

"Here you are, sir."

"Thank you, miss." Smiles on both ends. She paused for just a moment, turned away to continue with her tasks. I ate very slowly, prolonging my stay in her orbit for as long as I could. Unfortunately, it doesn't take long to eat a cheeseburger and French fries, and all too soon my plate was empty.

I paid the check, leaving Mary a $5.00 tip and told her I would be back by 2:00. That still left another hour and one half to kill, so I picked up another paper and retreated to our room.

The time finally officially dead, I arrived at Kresge's a couple minutes early. Mary must have been in the kitchen or somewhere, for she wasn't behind the counter. I was looking in a different direction when she snuck up behind me, put both hands on my shoulders, and gave me a quick peck on my right cheek.

After cordial greetings, we started walking north on 8th Street. We exchanged a few pleasantries and talked about minor issues for a short while. It was chilly and breezy so we decided to cut our walk short. "Maybe we could find a place to sit down for a while," Mary suggested. "I've been on my feet a lot and wouldn't mind sitting down."

"Good idea. I know just the place." We weren't far from the Foeste, so we headed in that direction, arriving only a few minutes later.

199

"You know, I've never been in here," Mary said as we entered the lobby. "This is lovely, so elegant and old fashioned, sort of." We sat down on a couch facing the reception desk, the area in which I had spent so much time in another life. Linear time-wise, it was an eternity.

We sat silently for several minutes, hand in hand, content to be in our own special place. I would have to explain myself eventually but was in no hurry to do so. I was perfectly content to sit this way for hours.

"Do you remember my telling you about my friend Joan, you know the one who's having a baby?" Mary finally said, interrupting my reverie.

"I remember," I answered cautiously.

Well, I talked to her yesterday, and guess what? Her boyfriend is back."

"Is that so?"

"Yes, and she is so happy. She has been so down for so long, depressed almost, but not really. I'm so happy for her. I hope he sticks around this time. The baby's due any day now, and it would just be awful if he disappeared again. I asked her about that, but she wouldn't tell me much."

"Hopefully it will all work out for both of them," I responded carefully. This wasn't a subject I wanted to pursue, but, I didn't want to abruptly change the subject either.

"Speaking of disappearances," Mary began slowly, "you were going to tell me about yourself and where you've been." The subject had been changed for me. I was glad she had not, as yet, connected the dots between disappearances.

"My name is Dan Parker, I'm twenty two years old, I was born and raised here in Sheboygan, currently I am residing here at the Foeste with my friend." I had to start with the basics, things that couldn't be found to be a verifiable lie. Now, I had to improvise. "My friend and I make our living in a field that I am not at liberty to divulge. It involves a great deal of travel, sometimes at a moment's notice. That's all I can really tell you..". And it was. Everything I had said was true, vague but true. I honestly wished that I could have told her more, told her everything, but I couldn't. Maybe someday.

"I see," Mary said softly, "So you're here now but could leave at any time."

"We could," I whispered sadly.

"And you don't know when that could be."

200

"No, but we usually get an advanced notice, though sometimes not very much of one."

"What about now? Have you gotten an advanced notice this time?"

"Not yet. But we don't think we will be here for much more than a few more days." Maybe I shouldn't have said that last line, but I just felt I should prepare Mary for what was almost certainly an instant departure. We were still holding hands, and I could feel her grip tighten with every word I uttered. I had been looking down into my lap the whole time I had been talking, but now I raised my head and gazed at her sweet face so close to mine. I wanted so very much to kiss her but couldn't work up the courage. Why, I couldn't say. My feeling was that Jerry and I would be gone in a few days, and I certainly didn't know if I'd ever see her again.

She gradually released the pressure on my hand and turned her face toward mine. Her eyes were moist, and she forced a smile that didn't take. I smiled back, a smile as unconvincing as hers, staring into those damp eyes did convince me that I was hopelessly lost over her. I think I would have done anything for her, had I the power to do so, which, of course, I hadn't. But I decided right then and there to somehow find a way to be with her always, a brave declaration coming from someone with limited powers and abilities. There had to be a way. Just as Joan was in Jerry's life for a purpose, so Mary had to be in mine, or so I told myself.

"Are you thirsty? Would you like something to drink?" I finally asked, just to relieve the the tension.

"Yes, I would, thank you," Mary answered with a brief giggle thereby validating my intention.

The bar was nearly empty as we entered and sat down on a couple of bar stools.

"Rum and Coke again, is it?" It was the same bartender from a couple days ago. Good bartenders have good memories.

"Yes, but hold the rum."

"Oh, I get it," he chuckled. "And for the young lady?"

"She'll have the same."

"And hold the rum."

"Right."

We were both feeling considerably better as we started sipping our Cokes sans rum. The discussion turned to more innocuous subjects like the weather and the recently begun KOHLER strike. Mary's family was affected by the strike, and it was a great concern to her.

201

"Are you going to play something for us again tonight, sir? You play very well, and I know the management would love to have some regional nightly entertainment."

"Thank you, but I don't think I can make any long-term commitments," I said, or short-term, I thought.

"That's a shame. Everybody's spirits pick up around music. Mine sure do."

Mary had been listening to our conversation with a startled yet pleasant expression. She hadn't said anything, but her smile made me feel much better about the day.

"Look, I'll play for a few minutes, how about that?

"That would be wonderful, sir."

Sitting at the piano, I thought about what I wanted to play. It wasn't as easy as it sounds considering most of the music I knew hadn't been written yet. Not that it mattered. This was something I could have some fun with while impressing Mary at the same time. Mary was watching me expectantly, her sweet smile gracing her lovely face. I began with my old stand-by "As Time Goes By," following with Scott Joplin's "The Entertainer." Then I went futuristic, once again pounding out "A Hard Day's Night" then Billy Joel's "Piano Man." Mary had pulled up a chair, listening delightedly to every note. A few other people sauntered in and stood around the piano, smiling as I played.

I brought my informal performance to a close with another version of "Misty." I knew "Misty" was written by Errol Garner in 1954 but was uncertain of the time. It's possible I may have "inspired " another song. Being a visionary was getting to be fun.

After the final note, I dropped my hands to my lap still amazed at my new talent. A small crowd had gathered by now and were all applauding more enthusiastically than necessary. Leading the ovation was my goddess. Her face beaming brightly, she lit up my world more than she could ever know. As I rose from my seat, she stepped forward and threw her arms around my neck, pressing her appreciative nineteen year body tight against mine.

"That was wonderful," she exclaimed. "I didn't know you had such talent. You ARE mysterious, aren't you?" I wisely refrained from saying she had no idea, and just smiled instead. Just another humble superstar.

A few complements were tossed my way as Mary and I walked out of the bar. Once again, Winston Niles was there to greet me with his standing offer.

"You're very good, you know that? We would still like you to play whenever you would like. We, of course, would prefer a regular schedule so we could advertise your performances. What do you say?"

"Like I said Mr. Niles, I can't make any long-term commitments, but I'll tell you what. Tomorrow is Easter, so let's skip that. But, I'll come in Monday and Tuesday evening from about six until nine. How's that?"

"That's great. We'll make up a few placards promoting your performances. We'll just take it one day at a time after that, if that's ok by you."

"Sounds good."

"We can work out remuneration later."

"Fine." We shook hands and after introducing Mary, we left the Foeste and walked towards Mary's house. The weather had gotten colder and windier, so we moved along rather quickly, saying little.

"Tomorrow's Easter, and I'm busy all day." We were standing in front of Mary's house, ready to say good-bye. The cold and the wind promised this to be a quick parting.

"I understand. Are you available Monday?"

"Oh yes. I work the same shift. I am so looking forward to hearing you play again. I can come, can't I?"

"Absolutely! I might not do it if you weren't there." Mary smiled shyly at that. "Plus, if you're interested, we'll do a little shopping beforehand."

"Shopping? What kind of shopping?"

"You'll see." We were silent for several moments, then Mary stepped toward me and threw her arms around my neck in an almost desperate hug.

"You'll still be here Monday, won't you?"

"Oh yes, I'll be here," I smiled. "Happy Easter."

"Happy Easter to you too," Mary smiled again and trotted toward her house. I waited until she was safely inside then started walking back to the Foeste, stopping to pick up a paper on the way.

I was laying on my bed scanning the paper when Jerry came plodding in. Throwing his jacket on the bed, he followed it, falling heavily onto his back.

"Those snitzers wiped me out," he groaned.

"It's schnitzels. You had schnitzels for supper?" I asked enviously. "I love schnitzels."

"Me too. Boy, did I eat. You're grandma sure can cook."

"So you liked it, huh?"

203

"Let's just say there aren't any leftovers."

"I'm not surprised. I know how you can eat." Jerry sat up with a groan, then stood up and took his usual position near the window. "I see you're not too stuffed not to light up another cigar."

"A man can never be too stuffed for that. It's like a dessert, or a second dessert tonight. Apple pie with whipped cream was my first."

"How'd you get away so early? It's barely 6:30."

"I promised to go to Easter service with them tomorrow, then stay for dinner. I might just be hungry by then."

"You'll be hungry by bedtime. You don't have anything dressy to wear to church."

"Your grandpa said what I had on is fine and that he would lend me one of his ties."

"Sounds like you'll have a fun-filled Easter with the family."

"I'm looking forward to it. They've taken to me real well. Of course, they expect to be celebrating a wedding any day now, right after the baby is born. They're all pretty excited, but I'm still being vague, you know, happy but vague. I'm not going to be able to keep this up for much longer. I feel like such a rat."

"You're not the only one," and I cued him in on my visit with Mary.

"It seems to me, we're both between a rock and a hard place. How long do you think we're going to be here? I'm thinking three or four more days tops."

"Sounds about right."

"Then what? Do we head back, or forward, I mean to Craig's time?"

"Probably."

"And what are we supposed to do there?" Jerry's irritation was increasing with every sentence, and I couldn't blame him. I was right there with him, though I wasn't as demonstrative about it. Not having an answer to his question, I simply shrugged my shoulders.

We were silent for the longest time. Jerry was content to puff on his cigar, while I went back to my paper. It was Jerry who broke the silence.

"So, what are your plans for tomorrow? I feel kinda bad leaving you on your own so much."

"It's understandable considering your situation. The paper says it should be a fairly pleasant day tomorrow, so I thought I'd do some walking. I've got a lot of thinking to do."

"About what?"

204

"I'll tell you tomorrow. Try not to stay too long. We need to have another of our heart-to-heart talks." Jerry just nodded, probably understanding just where I was coming from.

"What other interesting tidbits of information does your paper offer?"

"The KOHLER strike is heading into it's third week."

"Your grandpa told me all about it. What else?"

"Nixon says we may have to fight in Indochina if the French pull out."

"Talk about old news," Jerry uttered sarcastically.

"Let's see. Aha! Romy Gosz and his Goslings are playing at the Playdium tonight. Wanna go?"

"Not tonight. I'd rather listen to Dan Parker at the keyboard."

"You'll have to wait until Monday night."

"I'm looking forward to it. Say, what time were you born on Tuesday? I mean...". Jerry chuckled at the sound of his question.

"7:22am."

"7:22am?" Jerry replied in dismay. "That could mean an all-nighter on Monday."

"Could be."

I plan to be with her the whole time, you know, even if I do feel kinda like a cad. Say, do you think you'll get some publicity for your performance?"

"Maybe, but I doubt it. I'm hardly a name performer."

"Not like Romy Gosz."

"Certainly not like Romy Gosz."

"Anyway, thanks for the update on all the news that fit to print."

"No problem." I couldn't bring myself to tell him that "Pinocchio " had been held over.

Jerry was long gone by the time I rolled out of bed at seven o'clock Easter morning. He hadn't told me what time the service was, so I had to assume it was a sunrise service. I decided to have a light breakfast in the Hotel Foeste coffee shop. Slowly sipping my coffee, I started planning out my day of meditation. By the time I was finished eating, I had decided on a plan. My plan was that I didn't have a plan, so I just decided to wing it.

The newspaper had been right, it was a pleasant mid-April day, a good day for walking, and thinking. The streets were mostly deserted as I started roaming along 8th Street.

I stopped in front of "People's," the ladies dress store. The dresses that Mary had admired a few days ago were still in the window. One was a yellow print sun dress, while the other was a red checked dress similar in style to the yellow dress. I imagined Mary in each dress, uncertain in which she would look better. Each vision was glorious.

We will be leaving soon, probably a day or two after the birth. Would we be back? And if so, when? Would I ever see Mary again? What happened to her? Is she still living in Craig's time? She would be my mother's age, in her eighties, if still alive. We were going back to Craig's time, both Jerry and I knew it. Would she be there? What would she look like? Would she remember me? It wasn't lost on us that both Joan and Mary had remembered us from our last visit in 1953, one year ago. This was definitely a first. That means they would remember us when we leave this time also. Of course, there would be a concrete, seven pound reminder of our presence. Does that mean that other people we have been in contact with would also remember us? My grandma and grandpa? The Foeste bartender? Winston Niles? Others? I'm thinking yes, they would remember us. What would be the implications of that?

I walked on. Gone. All gone. As I passed by the stores and shops of April, 1954, I soon realized they were all gone. Hill's Department Store, Joe Hauser Sport Shop, People's Clothing Store - gone. Gmach's Restaurant, Kress-Hertel - gone. Tic Toc Tap, Penney's, Woolworth's - gone. Prange's, Kresge's - gone. Monkey Wards, Nobil Shoes, Sears - gone. Hotel Foeste - gone.

I was drifting now. Seeing Easter service parishioners leaving Holy Name Church, I decided to turn west on Michigan Avenue. I loved Michigan Avenue almost as much as I loved 8th Street. Of course, the scene was the same. The smaller shops are gone; Johne's Men's Furnishings, Bensmann's Grocery Store, Hinze's Ice Cream Parlor, Jetzer's Five and Dime, Avenue Lunch, etc, etc, etc. Only City Bakery is still around, an anchor in a city of change. That's the nature of life, I mused. Nothing is static. The world and the people in it are always moving forward. Well, maybe not always.

I turned right on 11th Street. A block and a half away stood Horace Mann School. Later, it would be called the little red schoolhouse. It was a classic two room schoolhouse. I would attend senior kindergarten there in five years. Miss Barry. She always reminded me of the Old Maid in the card game. A tad cruel, but true. The building would still be standing in sixty years, but wouldn't be used as a school.

I continued west on Huron Avenue. At 13th Street, to my left was Christianson Motors. Eventually it would morph into Seefeldt Dodge, but now it was a Studebaker dealer. As a kid, I thought they were the ugliest cars around. Now, of course, I love them. I decided to turn off my mind for a few minutes and check out some of the cars

The lot was loaded with used cars, cars of all makes and models. I naturally gravitated towards the Studebakers, of which there were plenty. They ranged from a 1948 Champion convertible for $495, to a 1952 Champion Vista four door for $995. My favorite was an aqua green 1950 Champion four door for $595. All the cars came with climatized, whatever that was, a heater and a radio. I couldn't help but run my hand over the hood and roof just to be sure that it was actually before me. The Studebaker was gone now too. This was getting to be a depressing stroll in the park, so to speak. Despite seeing no Studebakers running the streets of my former time, I promised myself that one day I would get one. And I knew I would.

I moved on, farther west on Huron Avenue. A few houses past 14th Street I paused to look across the street at the family home. There was no activity, not even a car in front of the house. I stood staring at the house for quite some time, then, not wanting to be around when the family got home, walked on. Crossing Superior Avenue, I walked another block to Jefferson School. My Jefferson School. My mother's Jefferson School. My grandma's Jefferson School. It would be several decades before it would be torn down, relegated to the rubble of a former, simpler age. I ran my hand along the coarse bricks so that, like the Studebaker, I could convince myself that it really existed.

Leaving another bit of my history/future behind, I strolled back to Superior Avenue, then across the viaduct to 18th Street. The day had warmed up nicely and despite my remorseful reminiscences, I was starting to feel a little better. And then I saw the park, and my sadness returned.

As I expected, the door was unlocked. I entered into a lonely, forlorn edifice, if I'm allowed to ascribe human emotions to an inanimate structure. To be sure, I couldn't help feeling the same way. The park was empty, of course. No, not empty, really. Vacant. And despite being a "thing," it was lonely. There would be no baseball played in Sheboygan's Memorial Athletic Park in the year 1954. The Indians were dead, never to be resurrected except in memories and yarns. The local Kingsbury team would begin play next year. This was a break between eras, and the park was responding in kind. The early Spring grass was already too long and uneven. The infield dirt and baselines bore the marks of muddy footprints, prints that may have been made last season. The incongruous tree in right centerfield was beginning to bud, but still looked neglected and abandoned.

Standing on the pitcher's mound, I stared down at the eighteen inches of a home plate that once felt the weight of Mickey Cochran, Al Simmons, Gabby Hartnett, Ernie Lombardi, Chick Hafey, Billy Herman, Joe Hauser...and Jimmie Foxx. And hundreds more. It wouldn't feel anybody's weight this year.

This is where it all began. I was sitting in the third base dugout, in the exact same spot when so many years ago, I first noticed my soon-to-be best friend Jimmie Foxx entering the park. It seems so long ago now. So much has happened. So many stops. So many baseball games. So many laughs. So many serious, confusing talks. And I am so worried.

It's something that's been bothering me since we arrived. I've seen enough time travel shows and movies to know that when it comes to something as bizarre as time travel, almost anything goes. Anything's possible. It's all in the mind of the author. Or screenwriter. Or director. One line of thought is that a person cannot meet himself. Should that happen, one of the two will immediately disappear. Now I know that I've already met myself, so to speak, when Jimmie and I watched the blue shirts play the green shirts way back when, but I can't help feeling that was different. It was part of a series of trial runs, as I like to call them. What if when that baby is born at 7:22 on Tuesday morning, I disappear, my usefulness ended? What if Jerry disappears as well, leaving the life of Donald Jackson to play out, just as it has to? Maybe this is what this has been all about, a fun little game just to get us to where we were all the time.

I realized this was all a lot of far-fetched conjecture, and yet it would explain everything as well as anything else. I would relay this on to Jerry later to get his thoughts. Lately, he has been getting as thoughtful about our situation as I have.

I sat a while longer in the dugout, letting other thoughts and ideas pass through my mind. Since I had all day, and since it was only 12:00pm, I toured the park, walking through the grandstand, sitting in various seats, walking all along the outfield wall, again brushing my hand along the bricks and ivy, just to make sure it was still there. My tour brought me back to the entry, where I turned to give the park one last look, and yes, I couldn't help but think, Legion Memorial Athletic Park - gone.

This had gotten to be way too depressing a morning, and I was determined not to let the rest of the day follow suit. Still, I couldn't help but pass by the house on my way back downtown. Again, standing across the street, I saw the family's light green Mercury standing alongside the curb. I was able to look in through the living room window and saw some activity but couldn't make out any identities. Getting a little bolder, I jaywalked the street to get a closer look. Jerry and my mother were sitting on the couch, hand in hand. I could tell that they were talking, Jerry dominating the conversation, as usual. My grandpa was standing in the middle of the room, talking on the phone, left arm flailing away. Unlike my grandma, he could talk as well with his arms as with his mouth. My grandma was not in view, probably preparing Easter dinner in the kitchen.

Suddenly, I wanted desperately to walk to the front porch, knock on the door, and say hi. Jerry could easily cover for me. Why not? What harm could it do? I could make the excuse that I just wanted to meet my good friend's girl. I wouldn't even stay for dinner, just a quick greeting, then gone. It would be something I would treasure, well, forever, however long that may be.

But I didn't. I instinctively knew that it was something I shouldn't do, that instead of treasuring it, I would regret it. I couldn't logically explain it, but I just knew. Darn it all! I wished it was the other way around.

My decision made, I sauntered east on Huron Avenue, past the haunted house on the corner, crossed 14th Street, and headed back to downtown. Being a Sunday, there was no paper to pick up, so I went back to the Foeste. The Rex Theatre was playing that irresistible double feature "Gypsy Cult," followed by "Tennessee Champ."

209

Somehow I was able to resist this tantalizing draw and settle for a commendable Easter Sunday dinner in the Foeste Coffee Shop. Physically satisfied, but emotionally drained, I made my way back to my room.

I was composing my play list for Monday night when Jerry got back.

"Congratulate me, I'm engaged."

"Congratulations. Anyone I know?"

"Hardly. She has beauty, and class, and style, and grace. Certainly not your neighborhood."

"So, what does she see in you?"

"A mirror image, my man. A mirror image."

"How many have you had?"

"Only a couple. Your grandpa and I had to toast the engagement, you know."

"Of course. So when is the happy day?

"A few days after the baby is born. I made a bold prediction that it would be born early Tuesday morning."

"Karnak the Magnificent. That all sure sounds wonderful, but, if I may ask, where will the prospective groom be on this joyful day?"

"Alright, I haven't gotten that far yet. Something we need to talk about, right?"

"I'd say."

"Well, so much for me. What did you do all day?"

I gave Jerry a summary of my day, what I had done , and more importantly, what I had thought. Standing at his usual spot at the window, smoking his usual cigar, Jerry soberly contemplated all that I had said. I think everything I said he had been expecting. Except one.

"Do you really think we might disappear once that baby is born?" Jerry was actually taking my theory seriously. By now, he knew that just about anything was possible.

"Not really. I'm just trying to cover all possibilities, which in and of itself is impossible."

"Maybe we're going to stay. How about that for a possibility?" Jerry had turned toward me and I could tell, was starting to get demanding. "Why can't we stay here? I like it here! I'm sick of traveling all over the place not knowing what the hell is going on. I want to stay here, and watch my son being born, and marry his mother, and live my life out right here, just like everybody else. I could make a good living here too. I wouldn't have any trouble hooking on with the Braves, or the Cubs, or anyone else, you know that. And you would grow up having a big leaguer for a daddy. You know you'd love that! And I could grow old just like everyone else instead of staying young forever. And you could too. You could be my best friend just like you are now. I could have my family and still have you. Think of what a kick it would be, watching yourself grow up. Think of all the knowledge you could impart, knowing what you know. How about that for a possibility, huh?"

It seemed Jerry had spit all that out in one breath, he was talking so quickly. And while his scenario had some rational holes, I had to admit that the picture he had painted had a most definite appeal. And yet, we both knew we were destined to return to Craig's time very soon, though for what reason, neither of us could say. Jerry could say though, because he wasn't finished ranting.

"And who's in charge of this operation, anyway? We've wondered about it but never talked about it. What's the total point of all this? Sure, we've talked about the little reasons, but that's supposed to be it? Do we just keep going on and on like this?" Jerry was sitting on the end of his bed now, our faces literally inches apart. At least he wasn't blowing cigar smoke at me. "And another thing. Ah, I've lost my train of thought. Let's go down to the bar. I need a drink.

Jerry had settled down somewhat by the time we got to the bar. Outside the entry stood a sign announcing my upcoming performances. Had I not had so much on my mind, the promotion might have gone to my head, for the sign made me out to be an up and coming young talent. Well, maybe it went to my head a little bit.

"Are you including a few new songs in your set?" Jerry inquired.

"Of course. That's what's going to make this fun.

"Wish I could be there, but I might be otherwise disposed."

"I'll be thinking of you."

"Sure you will, with Mary sitting dreamy-eyed right in front of you."

"Ok. Let's just say I'll try to give you a passing thought.

We walked up to the bar and gave our order. "Whiskey old fashioned sweet, hold the olives," Jerry said.

"Rum and Coke, hold the rum," my usual order.

"What's that sir?"

It wasn't the usual bartender, so he wasn't in on my witticism. "Just Coke is all." I conceded.

"Right."

211

We took our drinks to a corner table, away from the few people in the bar. Jerry took a swig from his drink, and I did the same from mine. Neither of us talked for several minutes, then Jerry started up again, though not in quite so agitated manner.

"I like it here. I don't want to go back, or forward, or wherever. What is Joan going to think, running out on her again? She remembers me, remember, just like you say. People are remembering us. And what about Mary? You don't want to leave her, do you? She'll remember you, and she'll be miserable. And so will you, right? And what are we going to do when we get back, or forward? I mean I like Craig and all that, but it seems to me our purpose there is over. And after that, what? So we come back here yet again? And when? And why? I'm not liking this one bit."

I had been taking this all in, nodding gently, agreeing with everything Jerry said. We both knew that the only way we could live here is if we aged along with everybody else, otherwise there would be a twenty two year old Don Jackson and a twenty two year old Dan Parker living at the same time eventually. And still that wouldn't work because even if we aged, the memory of a twenty two year old Dan, now forty four, with a still twenty two year old Don, would be too striking. This was getting far more confusing and complicated than I could handle. But, it wasn't our decision to make. Although we have a little bit of say in our fate and future, ultimately, it's out of our hands. So far, it's all worked out for the best. It's only been lately that we've begun to seriously question our fate and gotten demanding over it.

I shared these thoughts with Jerry who reluctantly agreed and understood most of what I said. Not that either of us was happy about it.

"So where does that leave us?" Jerry inquired finally.

"I think we'll just have to go with it and see where it takes us. We've come out alright so far. Besides, we don't have much of a choice anyway, do we?"

Again Jerry reluctantly agreed. We finished our drinks and headed back to our room. What I didn't tell my friend was that suddenly, I started feeling good about things. Everything was going to work out just fine

I spent the next day just killing time. Jerry had left early again, planning to spend the entire day and night with Joan. The baby would be born at 7:22 tomorrow morning, and he figured he'd be pulling an all-nighter with her. So, I was on my own again, at least until 2:00.

Mary was just getting off her shift as I walked into Kresge's. She came running around the counter and threw her arms around me in a most welcome embrace.

"I didn't think you were coming, you're usually so early," Mary said in an extremely relieved voice. "I thought maybe you were gone already."

"Not yet, maybe a couple more days," was all I could answer.

"I see. Are you sure?"

"Pretty sure. But let's not think of that now. C'mon, we have somewhere to go." I took her hand and we exited Kresge's and walked towards "People's."

"Why are we going in here?" Mary questioned as I held the door for her to enter.

"I'm going to buy you a present," I answered bluntly.

"What kind of present?" She came back with a smile.

"I noticed you looking at those dresses in the window, and I'm going to buy them for you." After a somewhat half-hearted denial, Mary agreed to try on the dresses she had been admiring. Fortunately, the store had them in her size, and as she emerged from the dressing room wearing each, she couldn't help but notice my delighted approval.

"I just don't feel right accepting these from you," Mary mildly protested as the sales lady was wrapping them up.

"Please don't protest. I want to buy these for you. Money isn't an object for me. Besides, I expect you to wear one of them tonight to my performance."

"Ok, I will," she smiled again. "Any preference which one?"

"Surprise me. You can wear one tonight and the other tomorrow."

"Ok," and again that smile.

After walking and talking for a couple hours, I walked her home. She told me she would meet me in the lobby of the Foeste at 5:45. I offered to pick her up, but she said that wasn't necessary.

I was only waiting in the lobby for a few minutes when Mary entered. Under her light jacket was the red dress, looking absolutely stunning on her, considering it was just a simple Spring dress. She gave me her brilliant smile as she approached, and I gave a gentle kiss on the lips. I'm pretty shy on such things, but I figured there wasn't much time, so what was I waiting for? The kiss, at least on my end, was electric.

"It's about time you did that," Mary said smiling, and proceeded to return my affection. I was literally gasping for air, and Mary started to giggle.

"Your hair is down. I don't think I've ever seen it like that. I like it," I said, trying to recover a bit.

"I only wear it up when I work."

"Well, shall we?" I remarked, taking her hand in mine. "My expectant audience of about six people await."

"There will be more than six people, won't there?"

"On a Monday night? To watch and listen to a nobody play the piano? Let's just say I don't expect standing room only."

There was standing room only. Mr Niles was at the door to greet me. "Looks like we have a healthy turnout for your opening performance," he said with a smile while shaking my hand, no doubt mentally calculating the added liquor sales for the evening. "Now then, about your remuneration."

"All I ask for is free soft drinks for me and my girl friend, plus a seat up front for her. That's all I want."

"That's all? Are you sure? We are prepared to do quite a bit more than that. You see the crowd. We are going to make out quite nicely on this."

"That's just fine, but I'm just an amateur, and I'm not asking for any more."

"Very well then. We've anticipated your bringing a guest, so we saved a seat at a table right in front. Oh, by the way, do you sing as well as play?"

"A little, but I'm not promising anything."

"That's fine. We have a microphone positioned about mouth level that you can adjust accordingly."

"Fine." So far, it was a very fine evening.

Mary hung up her jacket, kissed me on the cheek for luck and was guided by Mr. Niles to a table right in front of the piano. My friend the bartender was on duty tonight, and he immediately delivered two rum and Cokes hold the rum. I brought one over to

Mary, smiled, then went to stand next to the piano as Mr. Niles made the introduction.

"Good evening ladies and gentlemen, and welcome to the Hotel Foeste. We are pleased tonight to introduce to you a young man we heard playing our piano a few days ago and were very impressed. Subsequently, we invited him to perform for us, and he has agreed to play two shows for us, tonight and tomorrow night. So, please give a warm welcome to a very talented young man, Mr. Daniel Parker."

During the introduction, I had been scanning the crowd, trying to gage the general clientele and mood of same. They seemed to run the gamut from younger couples in their twenties, to middle aged couples and singles, to senior citizens. They all looked eager and expectant, happy to enjoy some live entertainment after forty long days of Lent, even if it was only me. For myself, I was happy not to recognize one familiar face, not that it would matter.

"Thank you very much Mr. Niles," I began. "I'm heartened to see such a turnout on a Monday evening just to see me. Tonight I'm going to play a few songs you're probably quite familiar with, as well as a few you've probably never heard before. A few ballads, and a few, ah, non-ballads. We'll start slow."

I sat down on the piano bench, adjusted the Mike, and began to play. I opened with what I already considered to be my standard first three songs: "The Entertainer," "As Time Goes By," and " Moonlight Serenade." These were very well received by my audience, more so than I would have expected. I got the impression that this was a group that was starved for entertainment. It was time to shake things up a bit and see how they would respond to a big time look into the future. Besides, I was ready to rock.

"Thank you very much,". I replied to their applause after the third song. "Now that we've warmed up with a few mellow oldies, it's time to shift gears. Are you ready?" A mild response. I needed more. "Are you ready?" I practically screamed. This time an enthusiastic reply came crashing back at me. "Ok, hold on, 'cause here we go!"

One, two, three o'clock four o'clock rock
Five, six, seven o'clock eight o'clock rock
Nine, ten, eleven o'clock twelve o'clock rock
We're going to rock around the clock tonight...

I proceeded to belt out Bill Haley's "Rock Around the Clock," a year early to a suddenly lively and energetic crowd. Playing up-

215

beat rock and roll only using a piano isn't exactly ideal, but I managed to pull it off ok. Maybe better than ok judging by the enthusiastic reaction I received upon playing the final note. I wasn't sure what kind of reaction this song would bring, but it certainly appeared that, at least in Sheboygan, Wisconsin, people were ready to embrace rock and roll.

"Did you like that?" I called into the microphone. Cheering and applause answered my question. "Want another one like that?" Same response. "Ok, hold on, 'cause here we go."

You shake my nerves and you rattle my brain
Too much love drives a man insane
You broke my will, but what a thrill
Goodness, gracious, great balls of fire

For the next few minutes I gave them my best Jerry Lee Lewis impersonation complete with standing up while playing. I really got into it and so did my crowd, Mary in particular. She was the one I cared about, so I was able to feed off her enthusiasm. The people were literally on their feet for most of the song, shaking and jumping and clapping and generally having one heck of a good time. The response after the song was dynamic, electric, you name it. Who would have guessed staid, 1950's Mid America would respond to music years before it's time?

"Thank you," I almost had to scream. "How about one more?" Cheers all around. "Ok, we'll dial it back just a bit."

I started plunking the familiar, for me, opening notes to Bob Segar's "Old Time Rock 'n Roll," and then sang:

Just take those old records off the shelf
I'll sit and listen to 'em by myself
Today's music ain't got the same soul
I like that old time rock 'n roll

And off I went.

Bob Segar went down as well as Bill Haley and Jerry Lee Lewis. I motioned for the people to settle down, an act that proved to be quite futile. Finally, the commotion died down, and my new fans returned to their seats.

"Again, thank you. I didn't know how you'd respond to a few of these songs, but I guess I know now, don't I?" Again, more clapping and shouts of approval. "We're going to slow this down a

216

little." Several shouts of disagreement rolled my way. "Hey, easy, I'm not as young as I used to be." The people greeted this statement with laughter, no one laughing more heartily than me, though nobody else could even guess why.

I spent the next hour and a half, or so, mixing in my newer (as in, not yet written) songs with several moldy oldies, all of which were very well received. My gaze often locked in on Mary, who was thoroughly enjoying herself. That in itself was payment enough for my performance. Mr. Niles was still positioned near the door, though he was now surrounded by people unable to get all the way into the room. I don't think his smile left him all evening as he watched waitresses scurrying back and forth with one drink order after another. For myself, I had gone through three rum and Cokes hold the rum, and was ready for a restroom break. But the clock was rapidly inching it's way toward nine o'clock, and I figured I could wait. Still, it was time to wrap this baby up. The air had been thick with smoke all evening, and it was starting to get to me, so I launched into my final two songs, both directed at my beloved:

> Look at me
> I'm as helpless as a kitten up a tree
> And I feel like I'm clinging to a cloud
> I can't understand
> I get Misty just holding your hand

I stared at Mary for the duration of the song. We both knew that I could be leaving in a day or two, and I think the words of "Misty" had a strong emotional impact on us both. I thought I detected a tear or two rolling down her cheek. Maybe not. Maybe they were rolling down my cheek.

The people could sense that this wasn't just another performance, rather a declaration of affection from one person to another. When I softly ended with the words:

> I'm too Misty, and too much in love,
> Too Misty, and too much in love

they gave me a solid, respectful, appreciative response.

"Thank you," I managed to croak. Once the applause ended, and I was able to compose myself, I concluded my first ever performance.

217

"Thank you so much. This is my first performance ever, and I'm delightfully surprised by your reception. I want to end tonight with a song you may not know, but is one which I like a lot. It's called "Sister Golden Hair."

The classic song by "America" has always been one of my favorites, and I played it with enthusiasm, all the while staring at my very own "Golden Hair Surprise." I ended with a flourish, and my new fans responded accordingly.

"Thank you very much," I yelled into the mike. "I'll be back tomorrow night, same time, same place." I had stood up and was waving my arms in appreciation. Shouts of "encore" and "more" filled the room, another unexpected development. "Ok, ok, one more. I'll take a request."

"The clock song," "yeah, the clock song again." The shouters appeared to be unanimous, which was fine with me. I loved playing and singing the soon-to-be Bill Haley classic.

"Ok, one more time."

One, two, three o'clock, four o'clock rock...

I belted it out with all I had. Everyone was standing now, most of them trying to figure out how to dance to it. Most were jumping and shaking their arms and clapping and making movements I certainly couldn't describe. I finished with gusto, and the room went wild with cheers.

I stood up and raised my arms to acknowledge the ovation. As I moved from the piano, Mary rushed to greet me, throwing her arms around me in a very gratifying embrace.

As the people started my way, Winston Niles reminded them of tomorrow's performance. "Remember folks, Dan will be here tomorrow night from 6:00-9:00 for one final show. Don't be afraid to tell your friends and neighbors about this spectacular new talent. Good night and drive home safely."

By this time I was swamped with people, all asking questions or asking for autographs. I was able to dodge most of the questions, but I signed my name to anything pushed in front of me; napkins, menus, business cards, you name it. Finally, after maybe twenty minutes, I excused myself and told them I would see them tomorrow. Many said they would be back.

"That was great Dan, just great!" Winston Niles was shaking my hand, slipping a twenty dollar bill into it as he did. "I know you didn't ask for much, but here's a little something to show our appreciation."

"Thank you. I do appreciate it."

"What a crowd! If the word spreads, we may see an even bigger one tomorrow."

"Could be," I replied somewhat indifferently.

"We would certainly love to have you here longer than tomorrow, if you're available."

"I would but I think I'll be going by Wednesday."

"Too bad," he replied, obviously disappointed. "If you're ever back in town, you're welcome to play here anytime."

"Thank you, I'll remember that."

I tossed on my jacket, helped Mary with hers, and hand-in-hand we exited the Foeste, and headed north, on our way to Mary's house.

"Are you really going to be leaving by Wednesday?"

"Pretty sure."

"Do you know when you'll be back?"

"No."

"Do you know if you'll even be coming back?"

"No."

This brief exchange was uttered in a most somber tone. Neither of us wanted to face the reality that in less than two days, I would be gone, uncertain as to any possible return. In short, I may never see her again, and I couldn't stand the thought.

"You look lovely in that dress."

"Only lovely?" she murmured with a slight smile.

"Lovely is my highest compliment."

"Oh."

We were standing in front of her house, our arms wrapped around each other. The weather was still quite pleasant, but it was getting late, well after 10:00pm, yet I couldn't bring myself to let her go. We had one more day together, and every second grew more precious. Still, it had been a long day. The performance had taken a lot out of me, and I was dead tired.

"Tomorrow night I want you to wear the yellow dress, ok? We'll go out to eat and then head over to the Foeste. I'll stop over about 4:15."

"Ok. Where are we going?"

"Kneevers Hotel. It's not too far, and I've heard it's very good."

"I've heard that too, though I've never been there."

219

"Good, it's settled then." We kissed goodbye. I could feel the desperation in her lips, if such a thing is possible. We said our goodbyes, and I walked quickly back to the Foeste.

Being dead tired didn't translate to being asleep in my bed. I hadn't seen Jerry all day and didn't expect to see him until some time tomorrow. Having rejected the possibility of disappearing at the birth of the baby, my mind was seriously engrossed in other areas. Both Jerry and I had long ago accepted our uniqueness, having things fall our way, our ability to do things just as we wanted, so my expertise on the piano plus the ability to know the lyrics to all the songs as well as having a good enough voice to sing them came as no surprise to me. Indeed, the rapturous response to my performance came as much from this phenomenon as from my actual talent. I didn't care. It was great fun, and I was looking forward to Tuesday night's show.

Somewhat. Tomorrow would be my last day with Mary. Or would it? Lying on my bed, unable to sleep, I contemplated the possibilities. Tomorrow the baby would be born. 7:22am. Was that really what this was all about? I was starting to doubt it. Throughout this whole odyssey, more and more has been revealed to us as time went on (so to speak). We understood more now, we could sense more now than at the beginning. And, so far, everything had worked out for the good, for our benefit. We had been to places and done things we never could have dreamt of. And yet, here we were. Uncertainties abounded. I felt as though we were at the tail end of a long, complicated mystery with the solution about to be revealed. And maybe that solution had been right in front of our eyes the whole time. Tomorrow would be the day. Tomorrow I would get it. Tomorrow we would get it. Things would be ok. I could feel it.

I had a light breakfast in the hotel coffee shop. As expected, Jerry had not come back last night. I didn't envy what he must be going through. Also, as expected, I didn't sleep very well. My mind kept racing ahead to what I knew would be an important and eventful day.

Despite dismissing the "disappearance at birth" theory, I still kept glancing at my watch at regular intervals. 7:03. 7:07. 7:12. I was getting nervous, as much for Joan and Jerry as for myself. 7:14. 7:17. 7:19. Let's get this over with already. I was staring at my watch as the minute hand landed on seven twenty two. Nothing. At least nothing here. Plenty was happening at Memorial Hospital. So much more than I could have ever imagined.

Being yet alive in this world, I started my day. I had a list in my mind of what I wanted to do, and I knew some of it would take some time, so I got right on it.

I called for a cab at 4:00. I had had a busy day and didn't feel like doing any more extensive walking. Besides, the weather was getting a little cooler so I wanted a little comfort before my Tuesday performance.

Mary was waiting for me at the front door. She was wearing the yellow dress with a light Spring jacket over it. As usual, she looked sensational.

I kissed her gently, took her hand and walked her to the cab.

"A taxi cab? Something special for our last night together?" She was subdued but not bitter.

"Yes," was all I could reply. She was right, after all.

I had never been to the Kneevers Hotel, though I had heard enough good things about it to want to try it out. I was no connoisseur, but I wanted Mary to enjoy it. After all, this just could be our final time together.

The place had a very old feel to it. The bar was to the left, guarded by a huge heavy-looking scale. Drinking not being on the agenda, we by-passed that in favor of the restaurant to our right. We hung our jackets on coat hooks along the west wall and took our seats at a table in the center of the room. Being a Tuesday with inclement weather, there weren't many other people in the restaurant.

The table was covered with big blue flowers on a a white table cloth.

White cloth napkins stood tall in front of us, though no menus were in sight. We were only seated for a few minutes when Carol, our waitress strode over with water and a smile.

"Good evening, welcome to the Kneevers Hotel. What can I get for you today?" She asked politely. "Our specials today are chop suey and hash, though we also feature our standard roast beef and roast pork."

"Do you have a menu we can look at?" I asked.

"We don't have printed menus here."

"I see," I replied not minding one bit. This place had real charm. Natural charm, not manufactured. We both ordered the roast beef which came with mashed potatoes, carrots, soup, bread and dessert. I didn't bother asking the price figuring it would be ridiculously cheap.

Mary and I talked generalities, neither wanting to get to the emotional substance. Soon two bowls of hot chicken dumpling soup was delivered followed by fresh caraway rye bread, a huge bowl of mashed potatoes plus the main course. There was enough food in front of us to feed a regiment. Mary didn't seem fazed by this abundance, but I was astounded. Wisely avoiding any comment, I grabbed my fork and started to dig in. Fortunately, I had eaten very little during the day, so this feast was a welcome sight. I managed to get through everything without much trouble, while Mary was right behind me.

"And what would you like for dessert this evening?" Carol questioned after we had finally stopped eating. I started chuckling, and Mary followed suit.

"Are you up for some dessert, my dear?"

"Sure, why not?" Mary smiled. I ordered the cherry pie, always a favorite, while Mary selected a cheesecake.

Our delicious dessert finished, we sat in silence for a few minutes. I knew Mary was upset at my leaving and wanted a more substantial explanation than the flimsy ones I had given her. I decided to bring up the subject myself.

"Look, I know I haven't given you much information on what I do and why I have to go. I wish I could tell you more, but right now I just can't. Believe me, I wish I could."

"You're not a gangster or something are you? Running from the law?"

"No," I chuckled, "I'm not a gangster or anything. It's much more complicated than that."

"Are you married with a wife and kids somewhere?" Mary was getting more dejected by the minute. Her head was down, her glorious smile nowhere in sight.

"No, it's nothing like that." Her head came up and the smile made a brief appearance. I took her hands in mine, stared into her beautiful blue eyes and calmed her apparent fears of another girl. She smiled broadly at that. The fear that there might be someone else obviously ran much deeper than I could have imagined.

We talked for a short while, then Carol came back with the check. As payment for this marvelous feast, the Kneevers Hotel expected $1.50 in return. I calmly took a bill from my wallet.

"How many employees are working in the restaurant right now, Carol?"

"Only four tonight, two in the kitchen, and two waitresses. Of course, Tuesday's not a busy night. On weekends we have a few more."

"Here, you take this," I said, handing over a twenty dollar bill. "This takes care of the check plus something extra. Share this with the others, ok?"

"Twenty dollars! This is way too much. I can't accept this."

"Sure you can. Everything was so great, it's worth it."

"Thank you so much! And I'll be sure to share it with the others."

"Great. Goodnight."

Despite the inclement weather, we decided to walk back to the Foeste. Mary was approving yet leery of my generosity, again questioning my means of support. Again, I was vague, promising to tell her everything someday. Would that someday ever come, I wondered. For some reason, I thought that it would. Maybe.

We entered the Foeste at 5:45, or tried to. People were everywhere. Dozens and dozens of them. We tried to make our way through the swarm to get to the bar, but weren't successful.

"Why are all these people here? Is something wrong? Has something happened? Maybe you're show has been cancelled for some reason." Mary's concern was real, and she was border-line frightened. I didn't have an answer for her, but I was looking forward to this second performance. Stuck in the middle of this mass of humanity, we were suddenly rescued by Winston Niles who had somehow spotted us and was forcing his way through the crowd.

"Thank goodness I found you. Follow me." We followed Mr. Niles as he forced his way forward. Shortly, we were at the bar where my bartender friend had two rum and Cokes hold the rum ready for us.

"What's with all the people outside?"

"They're all waiting to get inside, my boy," the bartender answered.

"This is all for me?" I cried incredulously.

"Sure is," Mr Niles answered. "Word about you got out quickly. We really don't know what to do with them all. We'll try to turn the sound up a little so they can hear you out there. As you can see, there's no more room left in here."

No more room was right. All the tables were taken plus every standing room space was occupied. This was truly incredible. Almost. This was going to be a blast, and I was ready to go.

"Of course, we saved the usual spot for the young lady," Mr. Niles offered, pointing to the seat right in front of the piano.

"Thank you, we appreciate that."

Once again, Mary kissed me on the cheek for luck, then took her front row seat.

After a spirited introduction and a rousing reception, I thanked the people for attending and sat down to start playing. I began with my standards though I mixed up the order a little. Following this warm-up, I picked up the pace with a few up-beat, not yet written classics. I was about half way through Billy Joel's "Piano Man," when I noticed a minor disturbance near the entry. Jerry had pushed his way through the crowd and was waving for me to come over. Pronto. I nodded and finished the song, a delight to my new fans.

"Thank you very much." I acknowledged. "I'm going to take a brief break. I'll be right back."

The crowd let me pass through to where Jerry was standing. We walked to the front entry of the hotel to get some privacy, which still proved to be difficult. Jerry gave me the update on his last twenty four hours or so. He was surprisingly coherent considering how upset he was. I listened to his account calmed, again surprisingly, considering the content of his story.

"Well, what do you think? What's this all about?" Jerry was agitated and confused, and I couldn't blame him. I was right there with him. For a while. Then the fog cleared. At last. Finally. Beautifully. Brilliantly. Everything was right in front of me. The confusion was gone. The unexplained was gone. The doubt, the angst, the frustration, all gone

"What are you smiling at? This is not what we expected."

224

I gave Jerry a very brief summary of my conclusions, then sent him off with a specific set of instructions. I stood near the entrance of the Hotel Foeste with what was probably an incredibly silly grin on my face. I didn't care. Our odyssey was just about over, and I was liking the ending.

My silly grin and I walked slowly back to the bar. The people were milling around awaiting my return. They gave me a polite round of applause as I grabbed another rum and Coke hold the rum from the bar and brought it back to the piano. Mary was wearing an uncertain smile as she expected me to continue my act. Instead, I walked over, bent down and gave her a sweet, soft kiss directly on her inviting lips. Her smile broadened which I'm certain corresponded with mine.

I finished my second performance in high spirits. All the songs were upbeat, which the crowd approved of heartily, particularly the now classic "Rock Around the Clock " which concluded the set.

After the obligatory thank you to the patrons, thank you from Mr. Niles, promise to come back soon, autographs, small talk and even a few photographs, I got Mr. Niles to call us a cab. I had the cab driver wait for me as I walked Mary to her front door. She desperately threw her arms around me, certain she would never see me again.

"I may never see you again," she sobbed, underscoring my intuition.

"Yes, you will," I smiled confidently.

She looked at me quizzically. "What do you mean? I mean, are you sure? Or are you just trying to make me feel better?"

I drew her even closer to me and kissed her. Then I kissed her again. And again. "I WILL be back. I'm certain of it now."

"You are?" she replied sheepishly. "How do you know?"

"Still another question I can't answer right now. But, I will be back."

"When?"

"I'm not sure, but my guess is maybe in two weeks, or so."

"Really?" she said brightly.

"Will you wait for me?"

"Silly question. I'll wait for you for as long as it takes."

Again we kissed, but this time I knew it wasn't goodbye. "I'll be back," I smiled. She was still standing on the porch waving as I looked out of the window of the cab. The cabbie drove off, and I sat back, physically and mentally and emotionally exhausted.

225

We were sitting on a park bench. In Fountain Park. Again. The bench was like an old friend to us now. We were either saying goodbye to it, or hello to it. It didn't matter which elements of both sadness and expectancy were ingrained in each. If my intuition was correct, this would be our penultimate trip. Would we miss our bench friend eventually? It would always be here, of course, and if not this one exactly, one very much like it, located in a very similar spot.

After packing our bags, Jerry and I had a light breakfast in the coffee shop, then checked out. I took one more look at my beloved Hotel Foeste. Would it be my last? I didn't think so.

"Are you sure about all this?" Jerry muttered hopefully.

"Nope."

"Great," Jerry came back, not so hopefully.

"But it's the only way it makes sense."

Jerry turned toward me and gave me what I took to be a reassuring smile. At least, I hoped it was reassuring. It didn't matter. In an instant, we were gone.

PART XI

1

It was early evening by the time I had finished reading, only being interrupted by two visits outside with Fido. Since we were both hungry, I fed Fido, then made a small meal for myself, constantly going over in my mind what I had just read. Why did Don's manuscript always raise more questions than it answered? How did Don suddenly get the ability to play the piano and sing well enough to fill a bar after only one performance? This had to be heading somewhere, but where? And what was going on with Don and Mary? I didn't see that coming. But the big question is what did Jimmie say to Don that night that cleared everything up for him? That's the big mystery, and I knew it would drive me crazy thinking about it until they cleared it up for me.

I spent the rest of the evening staring at yet another baseball game on tv, still rolling over those questions around in my mind. I made it to the seventh inning of a Tigers-Red Sox game when I finally gave up and went to bed. For some reason I was exhausted, more mentally than physically. Still, it was enough, and I fell right to sleep.

I slept fairly well considering everything that was on my mind. I woke up early and, since it was a nice day, took Fido to the dog park again. Afterward, we drove to the downtown area where I parked the car on Ontario Avenue, just south of Fountain Park. I spent the next hour, or so, imagining. Fido and I walked around the park two or three times, trying to imagine what the park looked like the times Don and Jimmie had been here. We stood on the northwest corner of eighth and Ontario staring across the street, trying to imagine the Rex Theatre across the way, then trying to imagine the Hotel Foeste just across the street. It must have been a grand structure, much more imposing than the motor inn currently occupying that space. I tried to imagine Don inside the Foeste pounding away on the piano while countless people rocked to songs that hadn't even been written yet. I tried to imagine how Mary looked as she sat right in front of my cousin flashing her glorious smile. And I tried to imagine Jimmie and Don talking near the entry to the hotel, the discussion that cleared everything up.

While I was doing all this imagining, Fido had been sitting obediently at my feet, silently paying homage to all that happened so very long ago. Or so I imagined.

On the way home, we stopped at the family house on Huron Avenue, the Jackson family home of the 1950's. I had been told of it, and had seen it, but had never been inside it. It wasn't much of a house. It was incredibly small, certainly by today's standards. I wondered how four people could live in such a place. Don once told me that the house was built in 1874, which could explain it's size. Maybe it was huge for 1874. Anyway, my imagination took hold of me again, this time trying to picture Uncle Jimmie knocking on the front door, then having my Aunt Joan welcome him with open arms. Maybe I was standing on the exact same spot where cousin Don witnessed the whole scene. I felt a sudden chill as the imagination almost became all too real. All of this was becoming all too real. Once again Fido was sitting quietly next to me, intuitively knowing this was a special place. If Don thinks I have good instincts, wait until he meets my dog.

The rest of the day dragged by. I shot a few hoops, watched a little tv, re-read parts of Don's manuscript, and half-listened to Marci's re-cap of her last couple days getting ready for her first day of school. Like a child on Christmas Eve, I went to bed early, knowing the next day would be exceptionally special. Better than Santa Claus, my cousin and uncle would be coming, and I wanted to be ready. But how could you be ready for two time traveling relatives with a whopper of a tale to tell. I didn't sleep for crap.

228

"You're going to meet a couple very interesting fellas today, Fido," I said while pouring some dog food into his dish. Fido perked up his ears, probably more in anticipation of his breakfast than in any potential meeting. I placed his dish on the floor then took a cup of coffee to the kitchen table. I seldom drink coffee but decided to brew a pot for my cousin and uncle. I knew they were coming today, and I had to admit, I was more than a little nervous. There were so many questions and, suddenly, I wasn't so sure I wanted to know the answers.

Fido finished eating his doggie food, walked to the front door and sat down. That was not a normal occurrence. Maybe thirty seconds later the doorbell rang. My dog's instincts were getting to be better than my own.

"How're you doin' cousin? Don beamed, as I let my honored guests into my house.

"Just fine, but confused," I came back.

"Heck, I'm that way all the time," Jimmie fired back.

I shook their hands, then introduced Fido who welcomed them with great enthusiasm. The enthusiasm was returned since, as they told me, they hardly ever come into contact with dogs in their travels.

"Now, before we get down to business, we demand the nickel tour of your new place here," Jimmie insisted. Fido and I gave them the nickel tour, and they were suitably impressed.

"Very nice, Craig," Don complimented, "comfortable without being opulent. Just what I would expect from you."

With this compliment comforting my ears, we headed into the kitchen where I poured ourselves some coffee, then sat at the kitchen table for what I hoped would be an enlightening conversation.

We spent the next several minutes engaged in small talk; what I'd been up to, how old was Fido, how was the family, things like that. I somehow refrained from blurting out some of the multitude of questions just waiting to be answered.

The coffee finished, Don suggested we sit outside, the morning being exceptionally pleasant.

"Now that I'm through with the coffee, you wouldn't have any beer around would you? Jimmie kidded as we were about to sit outside. "I think I may need one."

"I don't buy expensive beer," I replied. "I have Pabst in cans and Budweiser in bottles."

"I don't drink expensive beer. I'll start with a Pabst, no glass."

I asked Don if he wanted anything, but he said he was fine, and I sat down in one of my comfortable lawn chairs. Don was to my right with Jimmie to his right in sort of a semi-circle. From somewhere, Jimmie pulled out a grotesquely large cigar and set it on fire. He was wearing another of his Hawaiian shirts that had to have incorporated every imaginable color in it. Brown sandals, tan shorts and a wide-brimmed Panama hat completed his attire. I would describe his look as impressively casual. Don was similarly clad in gray shorts, his Jimmie Foxx A's cap and a dark gray t-shirt with an appropriately large question mark on the front. It was time to get some answers, and they were ready.

"So, did you read what we dropped off?"

"Oh yes, I sure did."

"Any questions?"

"Any questions!? Only about a hundred of them."

"We thought you might have a few," Don came back soberly.

The time had come. I was about to get some answers to the long list of questions stamped in my brain. It was time to get serious. I opened my mouth to speak, but nothing came out. I had drawn a blank. Nothing was transferring from my brain to my mouth. I must have been some sight trying to come up with something, instead just sitting there with a blank expression on my face.

"Just remember, we don't have all the answers," Don confided. "But we do believe that the fog is lifting, so to speak. If we're right, our situation has cleared considerably."

My cousin's brief caveat had given me just enough time to organize my thoughts. I decided to start slowly.

"Tell me, how did you learn to play the piano so quickly? Did it really just come to you? You never played the piano before, did you?"

"No, I never played. The best way to describe it is to equate it to you knowing there would be a package between your doors the other day. You had no advanced notice, you just knew it would be there, didn't you? All of a sudden, I knew I could play the piano. How I got the ability is one of the things I can't answer. It's just like so many other things we've been blessed with along the way. Everything has gone our way as you've undoubtedly noticed from your reading."

"Is that why your audience was so enthusiastic to your performance of songs that hadn't been written yet?"

"Undoubtedly. Staid, conservative Sheboygan of the 1950's wouldn't normally be expected to go crazy over songs of a style totally foreign to what they were used to."

"Is all this a case of divine intervention?"

Don paused for several moments while trying to formulate an answer. "Jerry and I have discussed this many times without ever coming up with a concrete answer. You know our story, you've read the progression of our story and the so-called breaks we've received. Something or someone is guiding or dictating our lives, but other than that, we're not even sure we want to know the details."

"So, what's the point of all this?"

"Ultimately, we don't know. At first, of course, we thought we were just instigators, or at least Jerry was. He was the big factor to get a certain team or city to the next level, baseball-wise. But now, obviously, the field has changed. Now it seems to be all about us. But, as to the point of it all, we simply don't know. Maybe we'll never know. Would it even matter?"

"I see," I said even though I didn't, at least not totally. Our discussion had finally led me to the big question, the question that I hoped would clear things up for me, as it had for Don.

"Ok, so with this in mind, what did Jerry say to you in the hotel that cleared things up for you."

Don took a quick glance my way, then stared straight ahead. Jimmie suddenly found the concrete of my patio fascinating. I waited. Finally Don nodded to Jimmie. "I think you better take this one."

My uncle continued to lean forward in his chair, head down, staring at nothing in particular. I waited some more. I had all day. I sensed a bombshell. I was more than right.

Jimmie leaned back in his chair, took a huge puff of his cigar and slowly exhaled a long column of smoke. He tipped his hat back slightly, took a deep breath, stared straight at me and said, "The baby died Craig, about three hours after he was born. The doctors did what they could, but it was hopeless. They tried explaining the problem to us, but we really couldn't understand it. I stayed with Joan and her family the rest of the day then went to see Dan later that evening and told him what had happened."

It had taken Jimmie some minutes to get all this out, and he spoke with great sadness and distress as he did. I thought I was ready for anything, but I sure wasn't ready for this!

231

"I don't get this at all," I started slowly and quietly. "The baby died, but you're still here. How is this possible, and how does this clear things up?" I stated this calmly and under control; this was no time for ranting and raving. Jimmie sat back in his chair and continued blowing smoker rings.

"Your turn," he mumbled to Don. My cousin also sat back and tried to explain away the dilemma.

"Here's how I look at it," he began. "I had a big time problem with there being two Don Jacksons in the world. Even though I would be a special case, there would still be two of us. He would be growing every day, while I would be standing still, so to speak. I had already sensed that our traveling days were just about over, and that we would be staying in 1954, or so. Having two of us around would be awkward, to say the least. Jerry, here, would be concurrently my best friend as well as my father, trying to raise me from a baby on. Try unraveling that in your mind. We couldn't. But when Jerry told me that the baby had died, as tragic and as sad as that was, it opened up everything for us. We would be free to continue our relationships with the girls, as well as trying to carve a life out of our new situation. It became clear to me that, though we would be leaving that time, we would be back soon and this time to stay. And this time we would be really part of the era. No more traveling. No more uncertainty or instability. No more existing without leaving a mark or a memory. We could live normal lives, more or less. "

"But how can you live normal lives? Neither of you even have a credible birthday. Or any birthday."

"I suspect we will be entering a new time line. Everything we've done and has happened will remain the same. But when we go back, we'll be starting over starting in 1954. What I'm not sure of is this: will we be a part of a whole new time line where everything is different, or will we be merely injecting ourselves into the current time line, your time line, making our presence felt in what little way we can."

"I'm not sure I get that."

"Ok. If we stay in the current time line, John Kennedy still becomes president, the Beatles still become famous, Neil Armstrong still walks on the moon, etc. We may change a few things, like Jerry here changing the history of baseball a little, but most everything else will stay the same. But if we become part of another time line, Kennedy, Armstrong, the Beatles may not even exist. Get it?"

"Yeah, I get that. What do you think it will be?"

"I think we'll be part of a whole new time line, with knowledge of the other. It's started already with the death of the baby. Had he lived, like I said, there would be two of us in this time line. Now I can have it all to myself."

"What about me? Will I be in the new time line?"

"Good question. I'm still thinking about that. The best I can say is that it's possible. A whole new time line doesn't necessarily preclude current time line people from being there. I just don't know."

I thought about what Don had said. While much of it made sense in a general sort of way, the details were way too complex and complicated to have any clarity in my one time line brain. I would have to do some more thinking on this. Many more questions I'm sure will pop up.

"Look, this is all real fascinating and all that, but why don't we lighten things up a little. Either that, or I want another beer."

"Agreed," Don replied, standing up. You gave us a tour of your house. What you say we give you a tour of ours?"

"Can Fido come along?"

"Absolutely. I'll drive."

"You have a car?"

"Oh yes. We have a car alright."

Don wasn't kidding. Standing in my driveway stood a blood red, 1950 four door Studebaker Champion. It was stunning. Mint condition. New tires. The thing practically glowed. Fido and I slowly walked around the car in pure admiration, Fido wagging his tail approvingly.

"Wow, where'd you get this ?" was all I could say.

"Connections, kid," Jimmie answered while tossing his spent stogie into the street. "Connections."

I knew exactly what he meant, of course. Fido and I hopped into the back seat, and Don drove off.

"We actually wanted a two door with a manual transmission, but I guess we can't have everything," Don offered matter of factly. The car rode beautifully. It felt so solid and strong. I could see why my cousin expressed so much admiration for it in his manuscript. We had been driving for some minutes before I took notice of where we were actually going. After another minute or two I "sensed" our destination, and when we pulled up in front of the house on Huron Avenue, I was proven right.

"We have arrived," Don proclaimed, "though I doubt it was a surprise, was it Craig?"

233

"I had a feeling," I replied, somewhat truthfully.

Fido wagged his tail happily as we walked to the front door. "There used to be a couple trees there," Jimmie said, pointing to the area between the sidewalk and curb.

"That doesn't help Fido much," I shot back while Jimmie just chuckled.

Though the house was small, it had a distinct old world feel to it. The living room was in two parts, a front room and the main living room. The kitchen was surprisingly large with glass doored cabinets along the north wall. The open stairwell was situated between each living room. Upstairs opened into an empty room of no conceivable use. The west bedroom was of modest size, while the north bedroom was tiny, maybe nine by nine. The bathroom was of average size with the usual fixtures. As I walked the tour, Don and Jimmie gave me a running commentary. In the '50's, the bathroom didn't have a bathtub, so young Don took his baths in the kitchen sink; the open area above the stairs was Don's "bedroom," the living room had a gas space heater; the kitchen had contained an old cast iron stove that weighed a ton, etc. Based on their descriptions, I could just about imagine what the house looked like back then.

"Well, that's about it," Don said finally. "We'll dispense with a tour of the basement, or dungeon, as we call it."

I gave one last look around. It was modestly furnished, but very homey in appearance. I liked it and so did Fido who was showing his approval by happily exploring every accessible area.

"So, what do you think?" Don asked.

"I like it. I like it a lot."

"Great, glad to hear it," Don came back with more relief in his voice than satisfaction. "C'mon we'll show you the back yard." The guys ushered us out the back kitchen door into an area that measured the width of the house by maybe seven feet long. "Not a lot of room for the family, is there?" Don joked. This wasn't a backyard, this was an "area." "The charm is in the house, not the landscaping," Don joked again.

After another quick walk-through of the first floor, Don locked up, and we were ready to leave. "Wanna drive?" Don asked, dangling the keys in front of me.

"Really?"

"Sure, why not? It's pretty easy to drive, actually."

I snatched the keys from Don's hand and settled into the driver's seat. Jimmie and Fido sat in the back seat, the two having quickly developed a mutual affection..

"Ok, here we go." I turned the key in the ignition, moved the the handle on the column to drive, and off we went. The car was a dream to drive. The steering wheel was wider than I was used to, and it didn't steer as easily, but that was minor. The thing felt so solid. We cruised around for some time, the three of us talking while Fido stuck his head out the open back window. It was so cool catching the stares of other drivers as we motored along or stood waiting at a light.

"This is so cool," I kept uttering, or words to that effect.

"I take it you like the car then?"

"What's not to like?"

"Good," again more relieved than anything.

We continued to drive around town, stopping occasionally to investigate a point of interest. We had lunch at Sparky's Hot Dog Stand, which particularly delighted Jimmie and Fido. Jimmie wolfed down four kraut dogs and two chili dogs, though he gave Fido generous portions of each. We bought a dozen extra hot dogs of various varieties for later. I suspected Jimmie and Fido would be devouring most of them. It's no wonder they got along so well.

"I'm planning a fry out for tomorrow, if that's ok with you." It was early evening, and we were back sitting on the patio. Don and I were relaxing with a couple of Diet Cokes, while Jimmie was enjoying his second Pabst and puffing contentedly on yet another enormous cigar.

"As long as you have plenty of brats available for consumption," Jimmie answered.

"Oh yeah. Brats, burgers, beans, potato salad, ice cream for dessert, the works."

"And beer?"

"Plenty of that too."

"I think we'll be available to help you consume those delicacies." Jimmie was waxing poetic, and Don was getting quite a kick out of it.

"What you say we work up an appetite beforehand by hitting a few baseballs around?"

I eagerly agreed to my cousin's suggestion. "I have gloves, bats, a bag of balls, everything we need."

"Great. Jerry and I will stop over about eight. That'll give us plenty of time to get in our workout and still get back here in plenty of time to fry out. Plus, you'll get another chance to drive the Studebaker."

235

The thought of finally seeing the great Jimmie Foxx hit a baseball, paired with the opportunity to drive the Studebaker again made me down-right giddy.

"Hi. I heard voices, so I thought I'd investigate." Marci had come around the side of the house and was standing on the patio in front of us. Don and Jimmie stood up respectfully. I stood up in shock. I knew this meeting was possible but was startled by the suddenness of it. Oh well, this could get interesting.

"Hi, welcome," I greeted her, recovering my composure rather quickly. Marci, this is my, ah, friends Dan and Jerry," I introduced, proud to remember using their new names. They shook hands in turn, then we all sat down. I cringed to think where this conversation might go, but, like I said, it could get interesting.

"Do you mind if I smoke?" Jerry asked considerately.

"Well, as a matter of fact, I do."

Jimmie nodded and continued to blow perfect smoke rings. Don chuckled softly. Marci gave me a funny look. I shrugged my shoulders. Fido chased a squirrel out of the yard. Yes, this could get very interesting.

"So, do you still go to school, or do you have a job or...?" Don asked.

"I just graduated in the Spring from UW-Stevens Point. In a few days, I begin my first full-time job, teaching third grade at Jefferson School," Marci proclaimed proudly.

"Jefferson School, huh? I went to Jefferson School, the old one, not the new one."

"Really. You don't look old enough to have gone to the old one." Jimmie stifled a cough and quickly continued puffing away. It was easy to see he was having one heck of a good time with all this.

"I was there just before they built the new one."

"I see. Are you one of those that were sorry to see the old one go?"

"Yes, I was."

"But this new school is so much nicer. It has so much more to offer than the old school. From what I've heard, that building was just about ready to fall apart."

It wasn't that bad. That building had a lot of character."

"Unfortunately, character doesn't educate children."

"And new doesn't always equate to better," Don came back mildly, no doubt thinking of the Hotel Foeste.

After a pause, Marci wisely changed the subject, somewhat. "And what business are you in, or are you still in school?"

236

"We're in the insurance business," Don answered without missing a beat.

"Insurance business," Marci stated flatly. "What kind of insurance?" She sounded skeptical. For my part, I was curious to hear the answer.

"Baseball insurance."

"Baseball insurance? What's that?"

"We see to it that baseball teams remain solvent. It isn't easy to keep a professional baseball team afloat financially. We see to it that a team can be successful in as many ways as possible."

"I'm not sure I understand."

"That's ok miss. Hardly anybody else does either," Jimmie consoled her, finally contributing to the conversation. He was certainly enjoying all this. Marci furrowed her brow, then looked at me.

"I don't get much of it either," I confessed shrugging my shoulder. I was getting quite proficient at shrugging my shoulders. "Hey, I'm sorry. Does anybody need another drink?" I asked, standing up while changing the subject.

"How about A drink," Marci chided for forgetting to offer her a first drink. Jimmie shook his empty Pabst can, while cousin Don said he was fine. I returned with the drinks, Marci ordering a Diet Coke also, and sat back down. I was determined not to let the conversation drift back to Don and Jimmie's background, or foreground, for that matter, but there wasn't much I could do as Marci continued to ask questions.

"Are you both from Sheboygan?"

"I am. Jerry here is originally from Maryland. We met during the course of our business."

"And you live here now?"

"Sometimes. We spend a fair amount of time on the road."

"So you're only here for a visit?"

"Yes. We'll be leaving again in a few days."

"I see. How long have you known Craig?"

"My whole life. He's my cousin."

"Your cousin?" Marci replied, quite surprised at Don's minor revelation. "Why didn't you tell me he was your cousin?" she shot at me with a deliciously mischievous smile. I went into my shoulder shrugging act and confessed truthfully that I hadn't thought of it.

"Let me take a wild guess," Don said. "You thought we were a couple of gold digger hanger's on, trying to take advantage of Craig's fame and fortune. Am I close?"

"Very. I'm sorry, it's just that Craig has told me of those people he's had to deal with since he's become famous. I must come off as an old mother hen, or something."

"Hardly old, my dear. By the way, how is it that you know cousin Craig?" Jimmie was comically throwing Marci's suspicions back at her.

"I just happen to be his next door neighbor," Marci replied, acknowledging the kidding for what it was.

"Ok then, I guess you pass."

"Thank you," Marci smiled back. " I take it, then, that you've seen Craig's movie?"

"It's not really really MY movie," I corrected unsuccessfully.

"Well, it's mostly your movie. You wrote the book, you wrote the screenplay, that's most of it"

"Yes, we've seen Craig's movie," Don answered.

"Did you like it? Almost everyone does."

"Oh yes, we were very impressed."

"I particularly enjoyed the performance by the actor that played Jimmie. I thought he stole the show." Jimmie was definitely getting into this.

"He was good. He won an Oscar, you know."

"And it should have been in a lead role, not supporting," Jimmie feigned indignation.

Things lightened up considerably after that. We talked about the Studebaker, Marci's upcoming school year, the state of modern day baseball, and other innocuous topics. As Marci got ready to leave, I invited her to our brat fry the next day, and she accepted.

"I don't like brats much, you know, but I'll have a hamburger."

"Great. Come over any time late morning. We're going to be hitting the ball around a little beforehand."

"Really? Can I come along? I don't have to hit, but I can shag balls for you. I have my own glove, too."

"You certainly can come along," Don answered. We're going to pick Craig up about 8:00. We'll be taking the Studebaker, so you'll get to have a ride in it."

"Oh, I'd love that! I'll be ready." Marci gave us all her sweetest smile, then walked back home.

"Well, we needed an extra ball shagger," I noted, thinking the guys might object.

"Prettiest ball shagger I've ever had," Jimmie said, probably truthfully. Don said nothing, just sat there with a pensive look on his face. "My beer is gone. That means it's time for another one, or it's time to go. I vote we go. We have a fun day planned for tomorrow, and I want to be at my best."

Don agreed, so we walked to the driveway, said our goodbyes, and I watched as the guys drove off in the Studebaker. I thought Jimmie wasn't the only one who wanted to be at his best tomorrow.

As I expected, the guys were early and casually dressed for a little baseball. Jimmie was checking out the bats, while Don and I loaded the rest of the equipment into the trunk of the Studebaker.

"Hi," Marci said brightly, also arriving early. She was wearing white athletic shoes, short, pale blue shorts, a blue Hank the Dog t-shirt, and a pink Milwaukee Brewers cap. She looked adorable, and she knew it. "No cigar today?" Marci chided Jimmie.

"Never when I play ball," was Jimmie's totally serious response.

I looked at Marci's glove before loading it into the trunk. It was a very nice blonde, Rawlings fielder's glove that fit my hand nicely. "I'm impressed with your glove," I told her.

"Thank you. I've played a little."

This time Jimmie drove, with Marci and I in the back seat. The Kiwanis Park diamond was empty which, considering the end of Summer, was not a surprise. We warmed up briefly, then started to hit.

"I see they put up a sissy fence since I was here last." Jimmie was referring to a decorative wood fence located several yards in front of the river in left and left center field.

"I don't think it was put up with you in mind," I replied.

"Doesn't seem to make much sense having it there, I mean it doesn't do anything, does it?"

"I suppose somebody thinks it looks good."

It was decided that Don would hit first, with Jimmie pitching. I knew my cousin had played some ball when young, and he showed it by hitting some nice shots out to Marci and me. We were positioned in medium left field, and I was impressed by some of the plays Marci made.

I hit next with Don pitching. I got some good wood on a few, but wasn't as consistent as my cousin.

As much as I enjoyed hitting, I was really just killing time until I could watch Jimmie hit. It was agreed that I could pitch to him, and I was a little nervous as I walked to the mound and stood astride the rubber. I threw a few warm up pitches, then threw my first pitch. I was prepared for a rocket right at me but had forgotten that Jimmie always laid down a couple bunts first. His bunting over, Jimmie dug in awaiting my first pitch. A nice easy swing produced a sizzling liner to left field. Then another. And another. Then he got serious. My next pitch was a waist high "fast ball" that he promptly lofted over the sissy fence into the cypress trees. Then he hit one over the trees into the river. Then another. Then four more. With each blast, Don and Marci simply turned around and watched it sail well over their heads. Finally, Marci tossed her glove on the ground and sat down on it. "You don't even need a ball shagger for him," I could hear her yell.

After a few more missiles, Jimmie tossed his bat down and declared he'd had enough. I had gotten what I wanted, a chance to pitch to the great Jimmie Foxx. Ted Williams was right, the ball did sound different coming off his bat, just like the explosion Williams had described.

"Now I think Marci should hit a few. She did her part shagging balls, now she should get a chance too."

" I didn't have to shag many balls with you hitting," Marci remarked admiringly. "I've never seen hitting like that." Jimmie and Don just smiled. I thought, "If you only knew."

Marci readily agreed to hit a few, with me pitching and Don and Jimmie shagging. Marci wasn't kidding when she said she had played a little. Not wanting to insult her, I threw medium speed pitches instead of lobs. She hit several nice shots into the outfield, causing Jimmie to shag a few down. Her last hit was a blast back at me which I fortunately snared in the webbing of my glove. She gave me a dirty little smile while tossing down the bat. "I told you I've played a little," she said anticipating our responses.

Before leaving, with my phone , I took a picture of Jimmie in his batting stance at the plate, then had a passing lady take a group shot of us at the same location.

The guys let me drive again, so with Marci seated next to me, I took a nice casual tour of the city. Marci loved the car as much as I did which is unusual, I think, for someone of her (our) age. Finally I stopped at the site of the old Legion Park and snapped a couple pictures of the three standing next to the home plate marker. I'm glad I did.

Marci wanted to change clothes when we got home, so I started the fire while the guys relaxed with a couple of drinks.

The four of us spent a very pleasant afternoon eating brats, burgers, and beans while laughing at many of the jokes and stories the four of us shared. Not surprisingly, Jimmie was an excellent story teller. Some of his baseball stories, while hilarious, drew perilously close to "I was there" reality. A couple times I noticed Marci giving inquisitive looks at Jimmie. I could tell she was getting suspicious, but for some reason, I didn't care. We continued to talk and laugh for several minutes, and then it broke.

"You know, you two look remarkably similar to the two leads in Craig's book. Even the names are the same. And the way you hit today," Marci said directly to Jimmie. "Are you the models for Craig's main characters?" She was fishing, and we all knew it.

"There is a resemblance," was all Don answered.

"Uh huh." With that skeptical response, Marci pulled out her Smartphone and started to tap and click. We were sunk, but again, I didn't care. "Let's see, Jimmie Foxx, born October 22, 1907 in Sudlersville, Maryland, died July 21, 1967 in Miami, Florida. Hall of Fame 1951." Then she looked from her Smartphone to Jimmie and back again several times. "This is impossible. It just can't be. Are you really Jimmie Foxx? You should be dead."

Don had been sitting back in his chair, relaxing, showing no emotion or distress whatsoever. Jimmie, as usual, had been contentedly blowing smoke rings from yet another enormous cigar. "Take over kid," Jimmie smiled over to me.

There was no point denying it anymore. I had to trust her, and I did. I stood up and ended the mystery. "Marci, I'd like to introduce to you to my cousin Don Jackson, and our friend Jimmie Foxx."

Again, as a courtesy, Jimmie and Don stood and approached Marci who was too stunned to move.

"Nice to meet you, my dear," Jimmie stated, shaking her hand. Don did likewise while offering a semi-formal bow.

"You mean every word you wrote in that book is true, it all actually happened?" Marci was torn between belief and disbelief, which under the circumstances, would be about normal. "That's Impossible! You just can't go bopping around through time and space like that!"

"We can, and we do," Don stated calmly. "As for the why's and wherefore's, well, we're understanding more and more of it as it goes on. We would also appreciate it if you kept all this to yourself. Of course, you'd probably sound pretty foolish if you told anyone about us. Can we count on you to keep our little secret?"

"Yes, of course," Marci promised. "I guess I should be honored, but, I can hardly believe this."

"That's alright miss. It took us awhile to get a handle on this ourselves," Jimmie observed seriously.

"And those installments Craig has been sending to his publisher were actually written by you?"

Don nodded. "I wrote every bit of it with instructions to Craig to do what he wanted with it. I think he's decided wisely, don't you. We brought back another installment of our latest adventures. He'll have plenty of material for quite some time. And it's not over yet."

Marci continued to ask questions while Don, mostly, patiently answered them as best he could. After maybe an hour, and two Jimmie cigars, the conversation finally started to wind down. I had added very little, content to let Don and Jimmie handle everything. After a considerable pause, Marci asked one final question.

"So, are you here to stay, or are you going somewhere else? Or don't you know?"

"We'll be here for a few more days," Don answered. "Then we'll be off again."

"Do you know where, or when you'll be going?"

"We'll be going back to 1954. And we'll be taking Craig with us."

I looked at Marci. Marci looked at me. Don sat back in his chair looking totally relaxed. Jimmie smiled slightly while continuing to blow his smoke rings.

"Craig's going with you? Are you sure?" Marci asked incredulously.

"Oh, yes," Don replied confidently. "As I said, we've learned a lot about our comings and goings. By now, we know pretty much when we're leaving, where we're going, when we're going, the works. We'll be leaving in a couple days, and Craig's going with us. He won't be gone for long, no more than a day probably. Then he'll be back.

"Are you sure? Marci asked again, more than a little relieved.

"Quite sure. And he won't even be missed."

I didn't know what to think. I was excited to think that I'd be going back to the Sheboygan of 1954, seeing all those great, long-gone places that Don described. I'd probably meet Joan and Mary too. And yet, I was nervous as well. What would the "trip" be like? What would it feel like? How big of a shock would it be? Would I really be coming back? A lot for my brain to process in so short of time.

The shock of this sudden revelation started to subside, and we started talking about all kinds of things, most of it related to my "trip." Where should I go? Who should I meet? Should I bring a camera? What should I (or could I) bring back? Would I like it better then than now?

While we were discussing these, and many other questions, I couldn't help noticing that Don was spending an inordinate amount of time staring at Marci. In fact, he was doing less talking, and more staring. It was a quizzical stare, a stare of uncertainty almost. When at last there was a lull in the conversation, Don changed the subject.

"I know Craig's introduced us, but I'm afraid I've forgotten your last name."

"It's Jones, Marci Jones. Pretty plain isn't it? Jones. My family has a long history of very common names. My mother's maiden name was Brown, while my grandma's maiden name was Smith. And the girls all have first names beginning with M. I'm Marci, my mother's name is Martha, and my grandma's name is Mary. How plain can you get?"

"Your grandma's name is Mary? Don asked unevenly.

"That's right, Mary, Mary Smith. Pretty blah, isn't it?"

I shot a quick look at the guys. Don was leaning forward, silently staring down at the ground. Jimmie had suddenly stopped blowing his smoke rings and was also staring at my cousin. Don said nothing. Marci noticed our reactions.

"What is it? What did I say?"

"You suspected, didn't you?" Marci had walked home shortly after our assurances that she had said nothing wrong and that we were just somewhat amazed at the commonness of the names. She wasn't buying it but was polite enough not to press the issue. Besides, she probably knew she'd get the truth out of me eventually.

Don slowly nodded at my question. "I suspected it from the start but thought it would be too much of a coincidence. You'd think I'd have learned by now. In this life, there are very few coincidences."

Nobody said anything for the longest time. The sun had mostly gone down, and we were sitting quietly under the patio night lights. Marci's revelation had created a whole new set of questions, most of which, Don assured me, could not be definitively answered. What would happen if Don went back, married Marci's grandmother, and had children? Would Marci still exist? How? Since Don was obviously not Marci's grandpa. In this time line, Mary had married a man named Brown. Would all this support Don's theory of a different time line?

It had been a long, exhausting, eventful day. The fellas acknowledged as much as they bade me good night. Way too much information was swirling around in my head when Fido and I finally hit the sack. Amazingly, I fell right to sleep.

The next day sped by. Don, Jimmie and I spent considerable time cruising the city in the Studebaker while talking over all that happened. One day I didn't see them at all. They had business to attend to, they said. I didn't question them on it. Marci was back preparing for her first day of teaching which was only a couple days away.

Early one morning, a Friday, the fellas rang my bell. Fido excitedly greeted them, while I made a pot of coffee. They had brought along a bag of donuts, and, it being another pleasant day, we decided to have our breakfast on the patio.

"Sure is a beautiful day," Don remarked.

"Yup, sure is," Jimmie echoed while polishing off his fourth donut.

"It's too bad we won't be around long enough to enjoy it."

"Yup, sure is."

"Why, where are you going?" I answered naively.

The guys looked at me with blank expressions on their faces. I finally got it.

"Today?"

"Our day has arrived at last."

"Yup, sure has," Jimmie repeated while reaching for a fifth donut.

I was suddenly frightened. The time had seemed so far off, even though it really wasn't. "How long do we have?" was all I could think of to say.

"Couple hours yet, probably."

"Oh. Do I need to do anything?"

"Nope, just follow our lead."

The couple hours slowly passed until Don announced it was time. We were still sitting on the patio, Don on my right and Jimmie on my left. "Just for insurance, take our hands in yours." It felt odd to do so, but I wasn't about to say no.

"What's going to happen?" I asked.

"You're going to feel a headache, then you're going to feel the dizziness, then you're going to black out, then you're going to arrive."

And that's exactly what happened.

I won't go into great detail about my visit to 1954. Don had done such a good job describing everything about it, that for me to give my account would be merely repetition.

We arrived sitting on a park bench in a remarkably different Fountain Park. I was dressed in period clothes of black slacks, light blue sport shirt and thin Spring jacket. The guys were similarly attired. They also had a fairly large suitcase positioned at their feet.

Almost immediately upon arrival, I stood up and looked around, trying to take in the whole ambience of what almost seemed to be a foreign city.

"So, what do you think?" Don asked with a smile.

"Cool. This is so cool," was all I could say.

The guys smiled, picked up their bag, and we headed to their traditional first stop, the news store, to pick up a paper.

It was Tuesday, May 4, 1954. It was 1954 I kept reminding myself as we crossed North 8th Street and entered the glorious Hotel Foeste. It was as wonderful as Don described it. It was elegant. It was stately. It was ornate. It was something I didn't see in my time. I saw the famous check-in area where Don had spent so many hours in 1946.

After checking in, the fellas walked me over to the bar where Don had drawn huge crowds while singing and playing the piano. The guys were planning on staying at the Foeste until they settled in. After dropping off their bag in their room, we set out to tour Sheboygan, 1954.

The guys were eager to reunite with their girls, but were gracious enough to indulge my fascination with the city. Across from the Foeste, the Rex Theatre marquee announced that their current double feature included "Casanova's Big Night" starring Bob Hope and Joan Fontaine as well as "Blackout " with Dane Clark.

The next several hours included stops at Prange's, Hill's Department Store, Woolworth's, Montgomery Ward's, Jetzer's Five and Dime, plus a few others, none of which were still in business in my time. As fascinated as I was by these places, I almost felt more sadness at the thought of their transiency. It took this visit to truly relate to the fellas' feelings about being in surroundings that would be so different, so quickly.

We had lunch at Avenue Lunch on Michigan Avenue, where I got to sample those great baked beans Don had mentioned. He was not inaccurate in his assessment.

From there we headed west, crossing the infamous Michigan Avenue viaduct as we made our way to the park. I was particularly interested in seeing this landmark, having heard so much about it.

"This is so sad," Jimmie muttered, as we walked through the unlocked door and stared out at the park. The Sheboygan Indians were no more, and the park had the expected forlorn, neglected look. The grass was high, weeds thrived everywhere, ruts and pebbles graced the infield, litter blowing every which way. And yet, I could see it's beauty. The ivy covered brick walls, the large, covered grandstand, the small, well-used dugouts, the bizarre dimensions of the outfield, designed, like many old parks, to fit into the existing neighborhood. Jimmie was right, it was sad. He had played here when it was in it's glory. Great condition. Great crowds. Great games. Great players. And yet, it was still here. It would be great again. For awhile.

We slowly walked around the park. I stood on the pitcher's mound and pretended to throw a few pitches to Jimmie, standing in the batter's box, pretending to swing at my offerings. After my pitching efforts, I stood in the batter's box myself and took a few swings, running around the bases like a kid. After touching home, I walked to the home team, third base dugout and sat on the bench, looking out at the field. I could imagine Jimmie in his white Sheboygan Indians uniform smashing home run after home run well over the brick outfield wall. By now, Don and Jimmie were sitting silently next to me, probably imagining, or remembering rather, the same thing. Jimmie, embarrassingly, wiped a small tear from his eye. I couldn't blame him. I understood.

We walked through the grandstand, then, taking one last look, left the park. We'd hardly said a word the whole time we were there. We didn't need to.

"Ok, reminiscing's over, now let's start living." Don was right; Jimmie Foxx didn't stay down for long. This time we walked over the not so infamous Superior Avenue viaduct, the one still standing in my time, I knew where we were headed. Led by Jimmie, our pace quickened as we approached the house on Huron Avenue. It was now early afternoon, and the temperature hadn't risen much. It was maybe forty degrees, unseasonably cool for early May. It didn't matter. My cousin and I stayed on the sidewalk while Jimmie went to the front door.

249

"I sure hope she's home," Don whispered.

She was home. The front door flew open as quickly as my young aunt's arms flew around Jimmie's neck. Several kisses later, we heard Jimmie tell her to grab a jacket, that they were going to take a walk. Only a few moments later, Jimmie brought my aunt over for introductions.

"Joan, these are my friends Dan Parker and Craig Mand. Joan Jackson."

We said our hellos, but Joan barely noticed us, understandably only having eyes for her, hopefully, returned-for-good lover. I had gotten this strange, chilling feeling while shaking her hand, a hand, and a person I had known only in her golden years. I can't even imagine what Don was going through.

250

A few more kisses, and we were off walking east on Huron Avenue. I knew where we were going. They had saved the best for last. We walked past the original Horace Mann School, a two room schoolhouse that Don once told me he had attended for a year when he was five. We passed gas stations and stores, again, none of which had survived the century.

Joan and Jimmie were chattering away in front of us, while Don and I were mostly silent behind them. Occasionally Don would point something out, but I'm sure his mind was somewhere else.

Kresge's was basically a bigger Jetzer's with a lunch counter. The counter was to the right, and as we entered, I immediately gazed in that direction, hoping to identify Mary before the inevitable emotional reunion. There was only one girl behind the counter, a striking blonde whose medium length hair was tied up into a short pony tail. She had a sad, business-like expression on her truly lovely face as she stared down at some receipts laying on the counter. It was difficult to assess the figure under the drab, white waitress uniform, but I could make an educated guess. In short, she was a very attractive girl. Marci, part one.

We were all standing near the entrance waiting for a response. Don, Jimmie, and Joan were smiling. I was expectant, waiting for the happy reunion. Mary glanced up at us for a moment, then looked back down, then quickly back up again. She let out a quick shriek, then came running around the counter and literally launched herself into my cousin's open arms.

"You came back, you came back," she kept sobbing between kisses. "I know you said you would, but..."

"I'm back, " Don said soothingly. "And I'm here to stay."

"Really?"

"Really."

While Mary wiped away a few tears, Don introduced us. Mary and Joan were best friends, of course, and were hugging happily next to me. Again, Mary hardly gave me a glance when introduced, but I didn't care and understood. Seeing Don and Jimmie happy was more than worth the trip.

"I'm off in about ten minutes. I've been taking extra hours, just waiting for you," Mary smiled at Don, explaining her still being at Kresge's so late in the afternoon.

We sat at the nearly vacant counter and ordered four Cokes. Mary continued to laugh-cry her way through the rest of her shift, then ordered a Coke for herself and joined us at the counter. The couples talked happily. I listened. As usual with young couples in

251

love, nothing of any importance was discussed. Possibly that would come later when each pair was alone. But, I doubted it. My suspicion was that neither Joan nor Mary would ever learn of their partner's secret.

The Cokes consumed, we started walking north on 8th Street, Don and Mary in front, Jimmie and Joan behind them, and me trailing the pack. I didn't mind. The whole Sheboygan, 1954 environment was still exciting, in a slow-paced sort of way.

At Fountain Park, we stopped. Mary had said she wanted to go home to change clothes before going out for the evening.

"Why don't you go with Mary," Don suggested to Joan. "Craig has to leave, and we want to talk a bit before he leaves."

"You're not going to run out on us again, are you?" Mary teased.

"Never again, promise."

Mary and Joan claimed it was good to meet me and walked happily off. I hadn't said ten words to them but knew instinctively that I would miss them.

"Sorry we put you on the back burner for awhile there, but I'm sure you'd understand," Don said once the girls had gone.

"I do, no problem."

"So, what are your impressions of our new, or should I say old home."

"This is so cool. I mean, it's the same city, yet it's so different. The cars, the buildings, the people, everything."

"Could you see yourself living here?" Jimmie asked, seriously.

"I think it would be way too big an adjustment for me. You two have lived through this era before, it's all new to me."

"Good point," Don observed. "Well, after today you'll certainly have an awful lot of cool stuff you won't be able to tell anyone about. But you will have one helluva book to write, won't you?" Don laughed.

"I sure will." I paused a minute then another question. "So, what will you two do now."

"We have plenty of money to live on for awhile. I'm sure I can get a job playing piano at the Foeste, temporarily."

"And I'm going to try to hook on with a major league team. The Braves would be nice and close, and they're going to be really good for awhile. I'd love to play in Wrigley Field for the Cubs. They're going to need a lot of help, plus that ballpark could actually make me look good."

252

We all laughed at that. "I think you could make any Park look good."

"It would be a mutually agreeable relationship."

My time here was running short. There was so much I wanted to say, still so many questions I wanted to ask. But there was one question I had to ask.

"Am I ever going to see you again?"

The guys looked at each other, obviously uncertain how to answer. "We've talked about that, and we're not sure how to answer that question. A lot is going to depend on you."

"On me?"

"Yup. This trip is a trial run for you, you know. Our traveling days are over. Yours are just beginning. It may take awhile, but you'll be doing what we've been doing. It may take some time, but it's going to happen. The reasons for it, I don't know. In short, considering all that time line mumbo jumbo we've been talking about, our paths certainly may cross again. Plus, there's always a chance that when you get back, we just might be there waiting for you."

Don smiled. Jimmie smiled. Finally, I smiled. We shook hands. There was nothing else left to do.

"Oh, by the way," Don said, "check your dining room table. We left a little going away present for you."

"Present?" I mumbled, barely getting out the words. My head ached. I got dizzy. I was gone.

PART XII

1

I was shaking. I was back home sitting on my patio, but I was shaking. It wasn't a dream, I knew that. All that had happened really did happen. I had visited with my young cousin Don, I had pitched to the great Jimmie Foxx. I had experienced the sights, sounds and people of Sheboygan, 1954. I stopped shaking. Then I remembered about about the present on my dining room table. I grabbed a Diet Coke out of the fridge on the way to the dining room. Positioned in the center of the table was a large, black briefcase. I sat down at the table, pulled the briefcase in front of me, and stared. What could be in the case? It wouldn't be money, I didn't need any money. Momentos? Pictures?

The case was unlocked, so I snapped it open and lifted the cover. I smiled. It was typical of Don and Jimmie. For me, I was like a kid at Christmas. The case loaded with goodies.

The first thing I picked was what looked like the complete set of 1954 Topps baseball cards. Brand new, still in the box. Aaron's rookie card would be in there. The set is probably worth thousands.

I set the cards aside, then picked up two autographed baseballs. One was autographed by Jimmie alone. The second had Jimmie's as well as those of Babe Ruth, Lou Gehrig, Ty Cobb, Rogers Hornsby, Al Simmons, Mickey Cochran, and Lefty Grove. Again, the balls and signatures looked new, like the autographs had been gotten yesterday.

There were two formal looking documents in the case. The first was a stock certificate in my name for one thousand shares of IBM stock, purchase date April 20, 1954. How they managed this, I can't imagine.

The second document had two keys taped to it. It was the deed to the house on Huron Avenue, once again, made out in my name. I just shook my head in disbelief; how did they pull all of this off?

Last, but not least, was a set of keys, car keys. I knew what they were for. Without needing to look, I could envision the 1950 Studebaker standing in my driveway.

At the bottom of the case was an envelope with my name on it. I opened the envelope and read the note inside.

Hi Craig. Hope you enjoy our farewell gifts. The cards are the complete set. There should be some good ones in there. The multi signed ball has autographs we picked up along the way. We didn't report everything we've done. We bought the stock at less than $6.00 a share. It now sells for about $175.00 per share. We know you really don't need the money. Consider it a wedding present. As far as the house is concerned, well, we just wanted to keep it in the family. Maybe you can spend some of that money we helped you make on a few upgrades. Finally, we bought the Studebaker with you in mind. We had some fun with it for a couple weeks, but it was going to be yours from the beginning.

So, that's it, a few momentos from your buddies. Take good care of yourself and the family. Be prepared to take a few more "trips" sometime, though we both feel that it may be a ways off yet. Still, when it happens, be on the look-out for two former travelers. We'll be watching for you.

Don and Jimmie

I placed the items back into the briefcase and closed the lid. Every item in the case was now precious to me, treasures I would hand down to my children and grandchildren. I have no idea how I'll explain to them how I got the items, but I'll worry about that later.

"You want to go out Fido?" My dog had been sitting next to me the whole time, watching me closely. Fido perked up at my question, so we headed out the front door. Fido immediately ran up to the shiny red Studebaker parked in the driveway. "Later, Fido. We'll take a drive later." Fido got the gist of my message and quickly ran over to the nearest tree. I walked around the Studebaker, marveling at the classic beauty of it. I lovingly ran my hand over the doors and hood. This beauty was all mine. I couldn't wait to take Marci for a ride in this classic.

Marci. Did she even still exist? In the midst of all this time line mumbo jumbo as Don called it, was she somehow erased? I was almost afraid to find out. Instead, I called Fido, and went around the house, to the back yard. While Fido patrolled the yard, I sat down on the patio, suddenly exhausted. My cousin had taken me through quite a run. We'd gone from a scary test visit in 1933 to a permanent residency in 1954, with a whole lot of stops in between, some, obviously, I don't even know about. And now, I feel as though I'd made every single stop with them. But now it was over.

Or was it? They said I'd be making more "trips" eventually. When would that be? Would I even want to go? Go where? When? Why?

Questions. Always questions . Where were Don and Jimmie now? And Mary and Joan? Had they gotten married? Did Jimmie, as Jerry Wolff, go on to play in the Majors and have a successful career?   Shouldn't I have a memory of him if he had?   Maybe I wouldn't remember him at the moment.   I'll have to check the "Baseball Encyclopedia " to see if he's listed. I'll also have to check my new property to see if anyone's living there. I'll also have to check if my Aunt Joan is still around or is she in another time line? Or am I?

But not today. As much as I want to know the answers to these, and many other questions, it's not going to happen today.   It was getting late, and I was beat, mentally more than physically. Tomorrow. I'd start my inquiries tomorrow.

I looked out onto the back yard. The grass needed cutting. Another job for tomorrow. Fido was rolling around in the grass, something he liked to do when it got too long. Suddenly he stopped rolling, got up and started barking and jumping around.

"Hi there Fido, how're you doin'? It was Marci's familiar greeting to my dog. I got up and walked over to her. Question number one answered. "And you too, how are you doing?

"Fine, now," I said with more relief in my voice than intended. I gave her a heart-felt hug, then led her over to the patio.

"I take it you went back in time with your friends," Marci asked, not so certainly.

"Yes, I did," I replied evenly. "I was there from early in the morning until late afternoon."

"You were really there, in 1954?" She sounded convinced and astounded at the same time.

I nodded, feeling more tired than ever. The relief I felt at having her here added to the fatigue.

"That's incredible! You have to tell me all about it!"

"I will, ok? I promise. But not today. I'm exhausted, in every way possible."

"Alright, I understand." And she did. "But you're going to have one helluva book to write."

Don had said the same thing. One helluva book, huh? A book with more questions than answers. A book with paradoxes galore. A book with no beginning and no ending. It should be some book alright.

256

"Don't you think?"
I just smiled.

Stealing Yesterday

PART XIII

1

As it tends to do, Time marched on. I bought myself one of those big, heavy , fire-proof safes. I carefully placed my momentos from the guys inside and locked the door. There was no way I was going to let any harm or damage come to these priceless treasures .

I had told Marci all about my "trip" and showed her my presents . She was amazed yet level-headed throughout everything , asking incisive and pertinent questions at the appropriate times. I was glad she was there for me. To go through everything I had just gone through without having somebody to share it with would have seemed rather hollow somehow .

My search for possible revelations as a consequence of all that had happened resulted in, well, no revelations at all. My aunt Joan was still living in this time line, though her health has been deteriorating rapidly. I've been to see her a couple times, though the visits have been sorrowfully depressing . She walks with a walker now and not very well either . Her memory isn't good, and she's lost some weight . I was saddened immensely when I remembered the bright, happy, alive nineteen year old girl I had just met. I made a mental note to visit her often, no matter how depressed it made me feel . Maybe I could bring out a few memories that could help me answer a few of the many questions that still needed answering. But, I couldn't help wondering about that young girl of a few days ago. Was she still alive in that other time line? Did she look like this Joan, or was she still nineteen ? I really wanted to know. Or did I?

My second non revelation concerned Jimmie. Checking the "Baseball Encyclopedia," I found the stats for Jimmie Foxx had not changed one bit. It was as I expected. Also as expected, there was no record of a Jerry Wolff anywhere. There wouldn't be, of course, if he had moved on to a different time line. Still, for some reason, I felt a pang of disappointment.

The third non revelation was my new, very old, house. The house was vacant and appeared to have been vacant for quite some time, except for Don and Jimmie's brief stay. When I told the fellas that I liked the house I meant it. But it needed work. Not being a handyman, I was not about to do everything that needed to be done

258

myself. Who was I kidding? I had money. I wasn't going to do any of it.

I had the basement (dungeon) cleaned up and made presentable. Though the heating system was fairly new, I had central air installed. The woodwork was still a nice dark brown, but I had all the walls and ceilings repaired where needed and painted. I had all new bathroom fixtures installed, and a new sink installed in the kitchen. I had all the carpet removed and new carpet installed. I had new vinyl flooring installed in the bathroom and kitchen. I had new window coverings hung. And I replaced the modest, well-used furniture with new modern furniture. I won't say how much all this cost me. But I didn't care. I have the money, and I figure this is as good a way to spend it as any. When all the improvements were complete, I stood in the center of the living room and looked around. I liked it. I think my ancestors would be proud.

Throughout all this, I continued to write and send new chapters to my publisher. Of course, I really didn't have to do much writing since most of what I submitted were Don's words verbatim. Still, I did enough twisting and turning with the story to make me believe I was creating something original, which I guess I was, in a way. I screened everything past Marci who offered an occasional improvement or revision. By doing this, I figured I was killing two birds with one stone. I got some critical feed-back from a different set of eyes, plus it got Marci up to speed with all that had happened. She appreciated my taking her totally into my confidence, something that seemed like a no-brainer considering all that she already knew. Our collaboration was successful as my publisher loved the new material. He kept pestering me for more, and quickly. For him it was like one of those old movie serials where you couldn't wait for the next episode. "How much more is left?," he wanted to know after receiving each new submission. I just kept telling him there was quite a bit more. How the heck did I know how much was left? This thing could go on forever. Still, I'll have to end it soon so he can get the new book into publication, and I can make more money. Any material that's left, I'll just plug into yet another book.

Anyway, like I said, time marched on. Several months have passed, and it is Spring once again. Not too surprisingly, I suppose, Marci and I got engaged this past Christmas. Though we'd only known each other only a few months, the attraction, and more important, the trust between us overwhelmed the brevity of our relationship. Actually, I think once I decided to trust her about Don's and Jimmie's secret, our engagement was inevitable. Our parents were delighted and though no date has been set, everyone is busy brainstorming ideas for everything that will be happening. I've stayed out of it mostly, leaving most of that to the girls.

Actually, despite all that's happened, what with the Studebaker, and the momentos, and the investigations, and the house, and the engagement, what I really was doing was waiting. Waiting for the inevitable. Waiting for what I knew would happen. Every time I got a little bit of a headache, I thought, "This is it." I would be going on my first solo "trip." I knew deep down that the headaches meant nothing, that they were just that, headaches. That special headache would be different. A little more intense, maybe. Anyway, it would have a different feel to it, followed by the dizziness, of course. Naturally, I tried what I would call "trip by association." Several times I drove over to Fountain Park to sit on one of the benches. And waited. And waited. And then, I went home. I really didn't think I needed to be there, but I figured it was worth a try.

Anyway, being Spring, it was time for baseball. Spring training began, and I figured that was a good omen. But nothing happened. The fellas had told me to be patient, and, for the most part, I think I have been. I had finally found a place to end my book, and my publisher was ecstatic. A sure-fire hit he proclaimed. I was looking forward to the income but not the accompanying promotional tours. Oh well, I wasn't doing much anyway. Where was I going? Certainly not on any "trips" it appeared. Besides, Marci was excited about it's upcoming publication which would be in early June. She was eager to have the finished product in her hands, the final results of something she had helped create.

Until she actually had that creation in her hands, Marci and crew were busy planning our up-coming wedding. We have finally set a date for early August, and the girls were excitedly planning every detail, right down to the last flower petal. Personally, I was happy to relinquish these duties as I was busy with other things. Like waiting.

I waited all through Spring training. I fantasized on where I would be going. Would it be as far back as a hundred years ago to watch the great Buster Braun pitch for the old Sheboygan Chairmakers? Or would it be to the early forties to assess the performance of the tragic Roman "Chipper "Wantuck? The "Chipper "was a big time prospect, both as a hitter and as a pitcher who lost his life in New Guinea in World War II. He was one of Sheboygan's all-time favorite players. Or maybe it would be back to the 1930's to watch "Unser Choe" Joe Hauser swat a few over the North Side

Athletic Park's short right field wall. Wherever I would be going, it was sure to be somewhere in this city's past. No spatial traveling yet for this rookie. Unfortunately, no temporal traveling either as Spring came and went without even so much as a twitch. I continued to wait. Something was going to happen, I could feel it. Or maybe not. I wasn't sure. But then, on Opening Day..

I've never been to an Opening Day baseball game, and I wasn't about to start this year. The Brewers were opening their season at home versus their division rival and nemesis, the St. Louis Cardinals, and while I was interested in the Brewers and their season, I had no desire to join the madness that makes up Opening Day. I would probably catch some of the game on tv later. But, I had a few things to do before then

It was a very nice day for early April, so I decided to take Fido for a nice, long walk. He liked his walks and after way too many quick ones, it was finally time for a good one. After the walk, I did a little Spring raking. I had a pretty big back yard, but I didn't rake the whole thing, just an area under my tree. The rest didn't need it, I told myself fairly convincingly.

I hung the rake in the garage and walked into the house for a Diet Coke. Fido conned me out of a biscuit, then, I settled heavily into my recliner. And then I was gone.

I didn't leave right away, of course. The usual headache and dizziness preceded it, but it didn't seem to last as long as the first time. Maybe it did. Anyway, I looked around to try to get my bearings. I didn't doubt I was still in Sheboygan, and I guessed that I wasn't far from the old ballpark. To my left, a street went as fat as I could see. To my right, maybe half a block away, stood a medium sizes building. Underneath where I stood was a train track. Behind me, cars were moving and people were walking to some place away from me. The ballpark. I could see part of it in the distance. It must be game day. I was standing on the long-gone Michigan Avenue viaduct, my cousin's first indication, way back when, that something unusual had happened. And now it's my turn. I patted the bridge's rail a couple times to confirm it's reality. I looked around. This was great! The Sheboygan of ...? When? I had to find out. It was game day, and I was going to find who was playing and when it was. I figured this must be a significant game or time or I wouldn't be here. It was time to move.

It was a seasonally cool day, and as I walked toward the park, I took stock of my attire. From bottom to top I was wearing black Oxford shoes, gray slacks, a medium blue shirt with a light Spring jacket over that. I was hat-less, unlike many of the other males who ere headed to the park. They were donning lids of every style imaginable. Except one. I didn't see one single baseball cap in the bunch, but I liked it. Judging by the cars I saw and the fan's apparel, I guessed that it was some time in the forties, either early or late, as there were no games played during the war years.

Along with dozens of others, I paid my admission and walked into the park and immediately saw what my cousin had so glowingly described so many times. The outfield grass was green. (mostly) and looked fairly lush. The infield dirt was , well, dirt, weed less dirt, groomed and ready for play. The asymmetrical outfield wall was composed of new red brick and looked great. No ivy yet, something, according to my cousin, wasn't planted until 1948 or 1949, I can't remember. That would place the time at either 1946 or 1947. I suddenly got excited sensing, no knowing, that it was 1946, and that I was about to witness the great Jimmie Foxx in action. There wouldn't be any reason to visit 1947, so that had to be it.

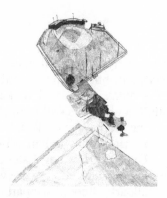

The grandstand was filling up rapidly, so I found a seat behind home plate, slightly toward the third base side, about six rows up. The seat itself was typically uncomfortable, but at least it had a back and arms.

People. People everywhere. People sitting in the stands. People walking in the aisles. People entering the park and looking for seats. Excited people. It was Opening Day, Jimmie was here; I saw him as he walked over to the third base line for the player introductions. Happy people. Another Winter was history. It was Spring, time for baseball. Time to check out the Sheboygan Indian's newest phenom, Jimmie Foxx, alias Jerry Wolff. It had been a long time. Except for a few exhibition games, there had been no baseball played in Sheboygan since 1942. Three empty years. But now it's back. This Winter hadn't lasted three months, but three years. A dreary, barren, sorrowful void that could never be recaptured. But now that's over. The boys were back. Most of them, anyway.

I stood up and looked over toward the Indian's third base dugout. Sure enough, Don was seated in his usual fourth row seat, just as he said. As I sat back down, I noticed a short, bald-headed man walking quickly towards where Don was seated. Winde Wangemann, the former Sheboygan Chairmaker infielder and current bartender at the Joseph A, Murray tavern. I watched as he climbed the four steps and sat down at Don's right. I felt as though I was watching a movie a friend had told me about and was seeing it for myself. To say I was in awe would be a huge understatement.

Eventually, the game began, and it went according to script. Indians starter Buddy Krier retired the visiting Wausau Lumberjacks easily in the top of the first inning. As Don related, the Indians quickly loaded the bases in the bottom of the first, which brought my friend and former uncle, Jerry Wolff to bat. He strode slowly to the batter's box and settled in to his stance, not even bothering to look for a sign from the third base coach. The Sheboygan fans were yelling and screaming and cheering and clapping, desperately hoping for a base hit, or even a long ball. Chills shot through my body; I was the only one in the park who knew what would happen next.

I leaned forward in my seat, studying my erstwhile uncle. He watched as the first slow curve veered just a bit wide. It was a tough pitch to take, but Jerry wasn't even tempted. The scene repeated itself with the second pitch. The next pitch would be a fastball, and Jerry, and I, were ready. I leaned ever more forward in my seat and muttered audibly, "watch this."

The pitch came in belt high. Jerry whipped the bat through the hitting zone with his usual lightening-like efficiency. The ball exploded off his bat like a missile soaring high into space. It soared over the light pole in left center field, well over the wall, landing, well, somewhere. I never did see it land. And neither did anyone else. The crowd noise was near-deafening. Between the yelling and screaming could be exclamations of awe and astonishment.

After trying to follow the flight of the ball, I watched Jerry nonchalantly circle the bases. Jimmie Foxx was used to circling bases. He had done it hundreds and hundreds of times in another life. As Jerry was heading toward the dugout, I saw him look and give a smile to my cousin Don, who, in turn, just shrugged his shoulders.

As usual, Don was right when he said the rest of the game, or games, since this was a doubleheader, was anti-climactic. The Indians won both games, Jerry going six for eight with another home run in the second game, and everyone went home happy. Except me. I didn't have a home to go to just yet. I had to wait to be taken. If the amount of money in my wallet had a direct correlation to the length of time I would be here, I knew that I would not be here long. Since I had some time to kill, I started to wander the city.

Without any conscious effort, I toured familiar haunts from Don's writings. I walked over to Jefferson School and Horace Mann schools just to say hello. I walked up and down Michigan Avenue smiling at the quaint, long-gone shops that lined each of that great street. Up to now, I had never given Michigan Avenue much thought one way or another. But this was a great street, and my memory of it will carry over to my own time, whenever it is I make it back.

I strolled west on Michigan Avenue to 14th Street, then turned left to Hermann's Grocery Store. I just had to see this.

The place definitely had an aura, an atmosphere, a feeling. I don't know if all small-time grocery stores of the past felt like this, but this one certainly put you into a different world.

A somewhat tall, slender man was behind the three-sided counter. The older lady he had been helping thanked the man and walked past me and out the door. Unlike Don's and Jimmie's first "trip" back in time, I knew that I could be seen and heard since I had talked to several people at the game.

"Anything I can help you with? The man's voice was quiet and hesitant, pleasant enoug but hardly the voice of a practiced orator, which, of course, he didn't need to be. I had been looking around the tiny store. It hadn't taken long to categorize the inventory: dairy items, bread and a candy case to the left, canned goods, cereal, and a freezer to the right, meat mostly straight ahead. I knew what I wanted.

"Yes, please. I would like some of the candy over there."

The man walked to behind the candy case, opened the sliding back door, and loaded up a bag of all the penny candy that looked interesting. I then guided the man to the ice cream freezer where I was expected to decide between all of two flavors for an ice cream cone. Today's flavors were chocolate and vanilla. After serious consideration, I selected the vanilla.

The bill came to twenty seven cents. I dug into my pocket for two quarters and told the man to keep the change, which he gratefully did. He thanked me and I thanked him and I walked out the door with my bag of candy and my five cent ice cream cone. I wanted to strike up a conversation with him, but I couldn't think of anything to say, still, John Hermann did look a lot like a beard-less Abraham Lincoln.

Clutching my bag of candy and licking my ice cream cone, I walked north on 14th Street. I noticed that 14th Street ended at Superior Avenue. To keep going north, you had to turn right, go one block to 13th Street, then turn left. I don't know when they extended 14th Street through to hook up with Calumet Drive, but this set-up sure was inconvenient.

It was beginning to get dark, yet I sensed I needn't worry about finding a place for the night. I wasn't going to be here that much longer.

I had finished my ice cream cone by the time I turned left at Huron Avenue. I just had to look at my house circa 1946. It didn't look like much. No vinyl siding covered the exterior, just some old brownish shingles which I noticed were quite popular at this time.

266

The wooden-framed windows looked like they needed replacing, the same for the front porch. And yet, it didn't look much worse than many of the houses I had seen. I was being constantly reminded that it was 1946.

But not for long. As quickly as I had arrived, that's how quickly I departed. A mild pain shot through my head triggering a dizziness that had me hold on to one of the birch trees in front of the house. And then I was back, sitting in my recliner in the family room, just as if nothing had happened.

I was sitting on the back patio sipping a Diet Coke when Fido announced his customary welcome to Marci.

"Hi Bud," Marci giggled while trying to pet a hopping Fido. "How was Opening Day?" This was to me, not the dog. "I heard they won."

"Oh, good," I replied, totally forgetting about Major League's Opening Day.

"Didn't you watch it? You said you were going to."

"Well, I did watch it, in a way." I was still coming down from my "trip" and was in sort of a semi-stupor.

"In a way, huh. What way?"

"Um, I didn't see any of the Brewers game, but I did see all of the Indians opener. Both games."

It took just a bit for Marci to catch on. "Oh Craig, you didn't? You went back? Where did you go? I mean when did you go? That sounds pretty silly, doesn't it? I mean 'when did you go'?"

"1946. A doubleheader against Wausau. I saw Jimmie's long home run that Don wrote about. The one that just went into orbit."

"And you were there."

I nodded and proceeded to tell her the whole story of my "trip." I was actually able to relate it in a fairly coherent manner, particularly considering the nature of the story. Marci, in turn, listened quietly, yet intently, seemingly hanging on every word, right up to the finish. I had earlier followed my cousin's lead and written down everything I could remember from my "trip." I actually think I spoke my "trip" better than I wrote it.

We were silent for quite some time, Marci processing all I had said. Finally it was Marci who broke the silence.

"Did you ever think about talking to Don and Jimmie while you were there?

"I thought about it, of course, but I just knew that it wasn't the thing to do. You know, since all this has started, I feel that I have a much greater awareness of what's going on. A much greater perception of things. I know what he means now. I just seem to "know" what the right thing to do is. It's kinda like that time I just knew that there was a package between my front doors, remember? It's a wonderful feeling, but a little scary too, you know?

I had quickly come down from my afternoon high and was actually a little down, or introspective maybe. Where was all this headed? Does it really matter? Was this just for entertainment purposes only? I didn't think so. Again, I "sensed" more was to come.

"I know." Marci gave me her wan, sympathetic, understanding smile. "Let's go inside, it's getting a little chilly out here." My sweet, darling fiancée took my hand, and we walked into the house, Fido following close behind.

PART XIV

1

Spring silently slid into Summer, a Summer to remember, as it turned out. The wedding plans continued non-stop, the girls, and everyone else including me I must admit, getting more excited with each passing day.   I pondered my Spring "trip" fairly often, occasionally adding something to my notes.   I don't like using the word "surreal " because I think it's way over-used, but that's the best word to describe it, maybe because while it all happened, it really didn't, since there is no record of any of it actually happening.   I know, because I checked. But I did experience it. "Surreal."

Interrupting our wedding plans and yet tied on to so much that had happened lately were the deaths of my Aunt Joan and Marci's grandmother Mary, only three days apart. The passings not only cast a pall over our plans, particularly since both ladies were so looking forward to the wedding, but affected Marci and me in a special way, one no one else could possibly be aware of.

"Do you still think your aunt and my grandma are still living in that other time line?"

It was the evening of the second funeral, my aunt's, and Marci and I were sitting on my patio trying to relax after attending two family funerals in three days.   We had not talked much about the implications of that other time line, but the events of the past week had stirred up the mysteries that had settled in my brain.   Did that time line match up pretty closely to ours? Were the people the same, the events the same, the world the same? And most importantly, how were Dan and Jerry and Mary and Joan?

"I wish I knew," I answered Marci. "I wish I knew," I repeated sadly. I didn't know. So much I didn't know, and probably never would. But there was one thing I did know. Something was going to happen, and I wasn't talking about our wedding. Something BIG was going to happen. And it was going to happen soon.

Bratwurst Day. Sheboygan's annual tribute to the sausage that made the city famous. Or visa versa. Exactly one week before the wedding. Except for two family deaths, it had been a good Summer. The planning had gone well, and the excitement was growing. My second book had been published, and, as predicted, was a huge hit. I did a few of those promotional tours, and the money began pouring in. I was currently negotiating for the movie rights. More money. More involvement in the production. I would insist on it. I liked that part of it. It made me feel I was a part of Don and Jimmie's experience and life, which, of course, I was. I decided to be a little tougher with the rights. Supposedly, the original cast was already on board. I wouldn't even consider selling the rights and getting involved without them. Another hit was almost assured. More fame, more money. A sweet, loving, beautiful, happy wife. What more could a young guy want?

Bratwurst Day. Marci and I had no plans to join the throngs of people in their mass celebrations. Our parents were coming over later for our own personal, private brat fry. One final chance to talk about the wedding, and maybe think of something that had been overlooked, which certainly has to be impossible. One final chance to hold a mini celebration of the great celebration to come.

Bratwurst Day. 8:00am. I was antsy. On edge. Off kilter. Out of whack. Whatever you want to call it. And it had nothing to do with the wedding. All of that was for next week. But this week, things weren't quite right. I busied myself with a few mundane tasks. I took Fido for a nice walk. I got a few things ready for the brat fry. I did some minor cleaning. I swept the patio. I shot a few baskets in the driveway. I sat down on a patio chair and contemplated.

Bratwurst Day. 9:45am. I was still antsy. But I now knew what I had to do. I loaded Fido into the Studebaker and drove off.

I finally settled down. It was all quite clear now. Why had it taken so long to figure it out? Was I losing my touch, or was I still so new at this that I was still learning? That was probably it. Even so, I felt I should have caught on sooner.

I needed time to compose myself and think, so we drove around for awhile. We drove past a few of the usual haunts, or former haunts, I should say: the old ballpark, Jefferson School, the Hotel Foeste, Kresge's. Maybe a few more, I really wasn't paying that much attention at times. After delaying as long a I felt I could, we finally arrived at our destination.

I let a happy Fido out of the car, and we walked the few steps to the oh-so-familiar front door. Normally, I would have unlocked the door and walked in, but this wasn't normally. I rang the recently installed doorbell and waited.

A few moments later, the front door opened.

A thin, bald-headed old man wielding a cane stood before us.

"Fido!" the old man exclaimed, rapidly petting my suddenly ecstatic dog. "And you brought Craig with you. How considerate." The old man chuckled and proceeded to give me as manly a hug as he was capable of.

"Morning, Cousin Don. It's so good to see you again." I had been considering how I would greet him, but this was the best I could do.

"Come in, come in. This is your house, after all. We've been expecting you."

"Fido!" Another exclamation, this one coming from a stout old man sitting in a rocking chair at the far end of the living room. "And you brought Craig too."

"I used that line already," Don laughingly chastised my former Uncle Jimmie.

"I know, but it was so good, I thought I'd use it again." Both men roared with laughter. Fido was jumping around in circles. I just smiled and shook my head.

Jimmie got up from his rocking chair and walked over to give me a not so gentle hug. Then he shook my hand with a firmness that had lost little over time.

"It's so good to see you again. Sit down. Sit down. We love what you've done with the house, by the way."

"Thanks. I figured you'd left it to me to keep in the family, so I decided I had to do something with it."

Jimmie retreated to his rocker, Don was seated on the couch, I sat down in a simple, modestly upholstered chair, while Fido was camped next to Jimmie, contentedly receiving the gentle ear scratching Jimmie was offering.

Though decades older than the last time I had seen them, I would have recognized each man anywhere. As usual, they were dressed in contemporary style. Don was wearing olive green cargo shorts and a gray t-shirt that said "Who Cares!" On the front. Jimmie had on a pair of black shorts and another impossibly loud Hawaiian shirt. And, of course, a cigar, an incredibly thin, long panatela. Where does he get those things?

I was about to inquire into their lives in the other time line, to finally get a few answers, but Don beat me to it.

"So, Craig, how have things been going since we last saw you? We know a few things, of course, but fill us in on the rest."

"You know a few things? Like what?" I can't say I was surprised at this. They always seemed to be at least two steps ahead of me.

"Oh, right. Of course. Silly of me. Well, let's see. Obviously we know what you've done with this house. Very impressive, I must say. You got your second book published, and it's a huge hit. No surprise considering who wrote most of it." Don chuckled at this while Jimmie smiled and blew a few smoke rings. "You and Marci are getting married next week. We're very happy for both of you. Um, I think that's about it."

"That's about it alright. How do you know all this stuff? You can't have been here very long."

"We arrived yesterday."

"Yesterday. You learned all this in one day."

Don just shrugged his shoulders and smiled. Jimmie's smoke rings kept wafting toward the ceiling.

"Don't bother telling me. You two are amazing. You'd think I'd know better by now, but you're always ahead of me."

"We've had a lot more practice, kid," Jimmie smiled.

"And speaking of practice, have you had any "trips" since we've been gone."

"You mean there's something you don't know?" I kidded.

" There is still so much we don't know, and never will," Don replied seriously. "But I take it, you've been somewhere, or some time."

I proceeded to relate the story of my "trip" back to Sheboygan, 1946 and all that I had done there. The guys listened intently, not interrupting one time.

"It was probably wise that you didn't attempt to communicate with us. I don't know what the consequences might have been, but I doubt that they would have been beneficial to anyone. I find it interesting that your first solo would have been there and then."

Don continued to ponder the possible implications. Jimmie finally looked serious and was probably doing the same. Fido had layed down next to Jimmie and was sleeping contentedly. It was my turn. Time to get a few answers.

"You seem to know all about what I've been doing these past few months, but I don't know anything about your lives for the last fifty years, or so. You have so much to tell me, so many questions you have to answer."

"Ok," Don replied. "Any place in particular you'd care to start?"

"Well, besides knowing how you and Joan, and Mary lived, and learning about that other time line, let's take first things first, like what are you two doing here?"

"Oh, that's an easy one. We've come here to die."

274

3

I looked at Don, then at Jimmie, then back to Don. Neither was smiling. Nor was I. I hadn't expected this answer, though I didn't know of any other answer I could have expected, if that makes any sense. We sat in silence for quite some time. Jimmie started puffing on his cigar. Don sat back on the couch and slowly crossed his left leg over his right. Fido stretched out on his side and continued to sleep. I stared straight ahead feeling like a dope. And probably looking like one too.

"Don't look so dopey kid. We're not ready to kick off yet."

After some tension relieving laughter, I asked for an explanation.

"I suppose we should start from the beginning," Don began. "But I'll try to keep it brief. There's so much to tell you, but that's for another day."

I nodded in agreement, eagerly anticipating just the highlights.

"Let's see. Shortly after you left us, we married the girls. Jerry and Joan got married one Saturday, and two Saturdays later, Mary and I followed suit. Even though the baseball season was well underway, Jerry managed to get a try-out with the lowly Chicago Cubs. Of course he made the team and spent fifteen seasons with them, playing everything from catcher, to third base, to pitcher, to mostly first base."

"I had a pretty good career with the Cubs. I hit .321 for my career with 515 home runs, numbers similar to what I put up here. We had a couple pretty good teams, but we never made it to the World Series. Joan and I liked Chicago, but after I retired we decided to move back to Sheboygan. We had spent our Winters here, but we decided to make it permanent. Joan work as a secretary for a couple different companies while I got into sales for a few different ones as well. Fortunately, I didn't have to travel very much or very far, so I didn't mind it. I just did it for kicks really. I'd made plenty of money playing ball, and we'd invested wisely so the money was just gravy. After about twenty years, we both retired and just took it easy mostly.

It's the most I had ever heard Jimmie say. He would usually take a back seat to Don who did most of the talking. It was good to hear him contribute so much in a simple, straightforward way. I looked at him and nodded.

"And that's probably as much as you'll get out of me, kiddo, ever." With that, Jimmie smiled and went back to puffing on his slowly shrinking panatela.

"As for Mary and I," Don began, "we stayed in Sheboygan for a few years while Mary got a degree as a licensed practical nurse. I did fairly well playing piano at the Foeste and private parties. I got to be somewhat famous, and several bands were after me to play piano and keyboards for them. So, I ended up joining a few, and Mary and I did a lot of traveling. We played all over the country as well as several foreign countries as well. I got a reputation as one of the great rock band keyboard players. Mary was always able to find a little work, no matter where we might be living at the time, so we were never short of money. With all the traveling we did, life on the road finally got to us, so I just hung up the band scene, and we moved back to Sheboygan about the same time that Jerry and Joan did. Maybe a little later. And that's about the skeleton outline of our lives in the other time line."

I paused for a moment to take it all in. It was good to hear that their lives had been successful and happy. But there were still so many questions; the fleshing out of their lives, the mechanics of time line shifting, the disappearance of Don in this time line, etc. etc. etc. I hardly knew where to start.

"Did you ever play with any famous rock bands, at least ones I would recognize? It was a superficial comeback considering the meatier questions that needed answering, but I was curious.

Don smiled. "Well, like I said, I played in a couple bands, mostly in the Midwest. They wouldn't be anyone you've heard of. I had received a reputation as being quite good, when someone, and I don't know who to this day, sent a demo tape to Mick Jagger. The Rolling Stones were just getting started and were struggling to get noticed. They decided that what they needed was a good keyboardist. The guys listened to the tape, liked what they heard, and arranged to meet with me. And the rest, as they say, is history, at least in that time line."

"You were keyboardist for The Rolling Stones?," I asked, quite astoundedly.

Don nodded. "Stayed with them for twenty two years, until the group finally stopped playing. Mary and I toured the world with them, and made a bundle of money. I helped Mick and Keith write our songs, of course, which helped us to become big stars. And yes, I know, in this time line, the Stones never had a keyboardist. Things match up reasonably well between the two time lines, but not perfectly. Anyway, once the group broke up, Mary and I came back to Sheboygan to live a significantly quieter life. Needless to say, I was a huge local celebrity."

I was so stunned, I hardly knew how to respond. Then I caught on.

"You really had me there for awhile," I smiled. "I may not be the sharpest knife in the drawer, but I do catch on eventually."

Don wasn't smiling. Jimmie crushed out his cigar and cleared his throat.

"He wasn't kidding, big guy. It's all true, every word of it."

Cousin Don shrugged his shoulders. "When we have more time, I'll fill in a few of the blanks. I have some great stories to tell."

"Same here, kiddo," Jimmie chimed in.

I sat there in amazement. Before me sat Cousin Don, a member of The Rolling Stones for over two decades, and my friend Jimmie, a Hall of Fame baseball player. I couldn't wait to hear some of the stories they had to tell.

"I'm sure you want to hear more, but for now, Jimmie and I are going to get some lunch. Care to come along?"

"Lunch! Geez! I'm supposed to be frying brats right now. Our folks are coming over for a pre-wedding fry out, and I'm here talking to you." The guys gave me a pair of mischievous grins.

"I'm sure they'd understand, if you could tell them what you were doing."

"Look, why don't you come along? I could easily pass you off in some way."

Don took a quick glance at Jimmie. "I don't think so. We need time to prepare our stories."

"Oh, right. But you have to come to the wedding next week. Marci would insist. You could blend right in there."

"We'll give that some thought."

"Great!"

I got up to leave, and Fido finally stirred. The guys also rose, and we walked to the front door.

"One more thing. How were you two able to cross back over to this time line after all those years in the other one?"

Don just shrugged his shoulders. " Special privileges. Listen, Craig. Jerry and I gave up trying to unravel the paradoxes of all this long ago. We're passing the baton on to you Cousin Craig. It will be up to you to continue our legacies, if that's the right way to put it. You're still young, and you'll probably learn a lot about all that had happened, will happen, and can happen. To a degree, I envy you.

277

There is so much yet for you to discover. We wish you the best, cousin."

"Did you have any children in the other time line?," I asked suddenly.

"Mary and I had a daughter. We named her Marci."

"And Joan and I had a son. We named him Craig."

There was silence for what seemed like the longest time. This was all too much for me, at least for now. We were standing on the front porch, three men and a dog, not knowing what to do next. Finally, I gave each man a hug. I thought of all the things they had gone through; the people they've known, the places they've seen, the paradoxes they've tried to understand. Three wan smiles graced the faces of three melancholy beings.

"Please, you absolutely must be at our wedding," I finally got out. "And after our honeymoon, we'll sit down and talk for hours."

"Don't wait too long for that, cousin. I don't remember things like I used to, you know."

AFTERWARD

This is hardly an original work. Not being an original thinker, I have been influenced by some of the finest, most original writers of fiction. Traces of Patrick Tilley, Ken Grimwood, Robert Cormier, Daryl Brock, Rod Serling, and the incomparable Walter Braden "Jack" Finney are scattered throughout the story.

I would like to thank the Mead Public Library and the "Sheboygan Press" for the information I needed to piece together the Sheboygan of various years. I would also like to thank my mother Joyce, Ray and Melba Stampfl, Shirley Snider, Mel Malzahn, Kathy Castellan, Greg Manz, Becky Dreier, Jason Fischer, Cindy Kneevers McNamra and probably a whole lot of other people I can't think of at the moment.

I would like to thank Derrek Winslow Eager for his drawings that brought some life to this seemingly endless saga.

I would particularly like to thank my cousins Kathy and Darrell Eager for all their assistance in helping to put this thing all together. Without their assistance, this work would not have been possible.

Finally, I would like to thank Jimmie Foxx. I feel I got to him pretty well through all of this. I couldn't have done it without him.

I had many doubts and reservations all through the writing of this. But I enjoyed the trials and tribulations of my two co-stars, I felt I was with them every step of the way. I'll miss them, and hope they will be happy in their new environment. Who knows, maybe I'll bump into them again someday.

Once again, this project is dedicated to my bird Finney, and my dog Rudy, both of whom died during it's writing.

Credits:
Cover and back image © Darrell Eager Photography 2019.
Illustrations © Derrek Winslow Eager 2019.

About the Author

Ron Nytes is a 1972 graduate of The University of Wisconsin-Steven Point and is an aspiring author. Besides baseball, he is a history buff and is assembling an impressive library of U.S. history books. He is co-founder of the Sheboygan Baseball Project, an on-going journey of research and discovery. Ron is a lifelong resident of Sheboygan, Wisconsin. He can be reached at rnutes@me.com.

Made in USA - Kendallville, IN
1039234_9781696932189
12.23.2019 0826